D1242832

GREAT BRITISH SHORT STORIES

WISHING YOU
THE VERY
BEST IN LIFE

DR. RATNESH & FAMILY
Bollineni Hill Side

GREAT BRITISH SHORT STORIES

Selected by the Editors of
The Reader's Digest

With an introduction by J. B. Priestley

VOLUME TWO

The Reader's Digest Association
London, Sydney, Cape Town

FIRST EDITION 1974
REPRINTED 1995

Published by
THE READER'S DIGEST ASSOCIATION LIMITED
Berkeley Square House, Berkeley Square, London W1X 6AB

(For further information see pages 374-5.)

ISBN 0-276-42200-7 (Volume 2)
ISBN 0-276-42201-5 (2-volume pack)

Printed and bound by William Clowes Ltd., Great Britain

Contents

RICHARD HUGHES

1900–1976

He began writing early, and published verse while still a student at Oxford. A somewhat tousled figure in "literary" London between the wars, his first novels (notably *A High Wind in Jamaica*, an unconventional and unsentimental novel about children captured by pirates), brought him fame. An idiosyncratic writer, who was a slow and meticulous worker, his short stories are miniatures of startling originality.

The Ghost

HE KILLED me quite easily by crashing my head on the cobbles. *Bang!* Lord, what a fool I was! All my hate went out with that first bang: a fool to have kicked up that fuss just because I had found him with another woman. And now he was doing this to me—*bang!* That was the second one, and with it *everything* went out.

My sleek young soul must have glistened somewhat in the moonlight: for I saw him look up from the body in a fixed sort of way. That gave me an idea: I would haunt him. All my life I had been scared of ghosts: now I was one myself, I would get a bit of my own back. *He* never was: he said there weren't such things as ghosts. Oh, weren't there! I'd soon teach him. John stood up, still staring in front of him: I could see him plainly: gradually all my hate came back. I thrust my face close up against his: but he didn't seem to see it, he just stared. Then he began to walk forward, as if to walk through me: and I was afeard. Silly, for me—a spirit—to be afeard of his solid flesh: but there you are, fear doesn't act as you would expect, ever: and I gave back before him, then slipped aside to let him pass. Almost he was lost in the street-shadows before I recovered myself and followed him.

And yet I don't think he could have given me the slip: there was still something between us that drew me to him—willy-nilly, you might say, I followed him up to High Street, and down Lily Lane.

Lily Lane was all shadows: but yet I could still see him as clear as if it was daylight. Then my courage came back to me: I quickened my pace till I was ahead of him—turned round, flapping my hands and making a moaning sort of noise like the ghosts did I'd read of. He began to smile a little, in a sort of satisfied way: but yet he didn't seem properly to see me. Could it be that his hard disbelief in ghosts made him so that he *couldn't* see me? "*Hoo!*" I whistled through my small teeth. "*Hoo! Murderer! Murderer!*"—Someone flung up a top window. "Who's that?" she called. "What's the matter?"—So other people could hear, at any rate. But I kept silent: I wouldn't give him away—not yet. And all the time he walked straight forward, smiling to himself. He never had any conscience, I said to myself: here he is with new murder on his mind, smiling as easy as if it was nothing. But there was a sort of hard look about him, *all* the same.

It was odd, my being a ghost so suddenly, when ten minutes ago I was a living woman: and now, walking on air, with the wind clear and wet between my shoulder-blades. Ha-ha! I gave a regular shriek and a screech of laughter, it all felt so funny . . . surely John must have heard *that*: but no, he just turned the corner into Pole Street.

All along Pole Street the plane-trees were shedding their leaves: and then I knew what I would do. I made those dead leaves rise up on their thin edges, as if the wind was doing it. All along Pole Street they followed him, pattering on the roadway with their five dry fingers. But John just stirred among them with his feet, and went on: and I followed him: for as I said, there was still some tie between us that drew me.

Once only he turned and seemed to see me: there was a sort of recognition in his face: but no fear, only triumph. "You're glad you've killed me," thought I, "but I'll make you sorry!"

And then all at once the fit left me. A nice sort of Christian, I, scarcely fifteen minutes dead and still thinking of revenge, instead of preparing to meet my Lord! Some sort of voice in me seemed to say: "Leave him, Millie, leave him alone *before it is too late*!" Too late? Surely I could leave him when I wanted to? Ghosts haunt as they like, don't they? I'd make just one more attempt at terrifying him: then I'd give it up and think about going to heaven.

He stopped, and turned, and faced me full.

I pointed at him with both my hands.

"John!" I cried. "John! It's all very well for you to stand there, and smile, and stare with your great fish-eyes and think you've won: but you haven't! I'll do you. I'll *finish* you! I'll——"

I stopped, and laughed a little. Windows shot up. "Who's that? What's the row?"—and so on. They had all heard: but he only turned and walked on.

"Leave him, Millie, before it is too late," the voice said.

So that's what the voice meant: leave him before I betrayed his secret, and had the crime of revenge on my soul. Very well, I would:

I'd leave him. I'd go straight to heaven before any accident happened. So I stretched up my two arms, and tried to float into the air: but at once some force seized me like a great gust, and I was swept away after him down the street. There was something stirring in me that still bound me to him.

Strange, that I should be so real to all those people that they thought me still a living woman: but he—who had most reason to fear me, why, it seemed doubtful whether he even saw me. And where was he going to, right up the desolate long length of Pole Street?—He turned into Rope Street. I saw a blue lamp: that was the police station.

"Oh, Lord," I thought, "I've done it! Oh, Lord, he's going to give himself up!"

"You drove him to it," the voice said. "You fool, did you think he didn't see you? What did you expect? Did you think he'd shriek, and gibber with fear at you? Did you think your John was a coward?—Now his death is on your head!"

"I didn't do it, I didn't!" I cried. "I never wished him any harm, never, not *really*! I wouldn't hurt him, not for anything, I wouldn't. Oh, John, don't stare like that. There's still time . . . time!"

And all this while he stood in the door, looking at me, while the policemen came out and stood round him in a ring. He couldn't escape now.

"Oh, John," I sobbed, "forgive me! I didn't mean to do it! It was jealousy, John, what did it . . . because I loved you."

Still the police took no notice of him.

"That's her," said one of them in a husky voice. "Done it with a hammer, she done it . . . brained him. But, Lord, isn't her face ghastly? Haunted, like."

"Look at her 'ead, poor girl. Looks as if she tried to do herself in with the 'ammer, after."

Then the sergeant stepped forward.

"Anything you say will be taken down as evidence against you."

"John!" I cried softly, and held out my arms—for at last his face had softened.

"Holy Mary!" said one policeman, crossing himself. "She's seeing him!"

"They'll not hang her," another whispered. "Did you notice her condition, poor girl?"

ALDOUS HUXLEY

1894–1963

Never overshadowed by the other brilliant literary and scientific members of the Huxley family, he fought chronic near-blindness to become himself a writer of international fame. His novels and short stories are the work of an intensely civilized man, a visionary blessed with both wit and compassionate intelligence.

Young Archimedes

IT WAS THE VIEW which finally made us take the place. True, the house had its disadvantages. It was a long way out of town and had no telephone. The rent was unduly high, the drainage system poor. On windy nights, when the ill-fitting panes were rattling so furiously in the window-frames that you could fancy yourself in an hotel omnibus, the electric light, for some mysterious reason, used invariably to go out and leave you in the noisy dark. There was a splendid bathroom; but the electric pump, which was supposed to send up water from the rain-water tanks in the terrace, did not work. Punctually every autumn the drinking well ran dry. And our landlady was a liar and a cheat.

But these are the little disadvantages of every hired house, all over the world. For Italy they were not really at all serious. I have seen plenty of houses which had them all and a hundred others, without possessing the compensating advantages of ours—the southward facing garden and terrace for the winter and spring, the large cool rooms against the midsummer heat, the hilltop air and freedom from mosquitoes, and finally the view.

And what a view it was! Or rather, what a succession of views. For it was different every day; and without stirring from the house one had the impression of an incessant change of scene: all the delights of travel without its fatigues. There were autumn days when all the valleys were filled with mist and the crests of the Apennines rose darkly out of a flat white lake. There were days when the mist invaded even our hilltop and we were enveloped in a soft vapour in which the mist-coloured olive trees, that sloped away below our windows towards the valley, disappeared as though into their own spiritual essence; and the only firm and definite things in the small, dim world within which we found ourselves confined were the two tall black cypresses growing on a little projecting terrace a hundred feet down the hill. Black, sharp, and solid, they stood there, twin pillars of Hercules at the extremity of the known universe; and beyond them there was only pale cloud and round them only the cloudy olive trees.

These were the wintry days; but there were days of spring and autumn, days unchangingly cloudless, or—more lovely still—made various by the huge floating shapes of vapour that, snowy above the far-away snow-capped mountains, gradually unfolded, against the pale bright blue, enormous heroic gestures. And in the height of the sky the bellying draperies, the swans, the aerial marbles, hewed and left unfinished by gods grown tired of creation almost before they had begun, drifted sleeping along the wind, changing form as they moved. And the sun would come and go behind them; and now the town in the valley would fade and almost vanish in the shadow, and now, like an immense fretted jewel between the hills, it would glow as though by its own light. And looking across the nearer tributary valley that wound from below our crest down towards the Arno, looking over the low dark shoulder of hill on whose extreme promontory stood the towered church of San Miniato, one saw the huge dome airily hanging on its ribs of masonry, the square campanile, the sharp spire of Santa Croce, and the canopied tower of the Signoria, rising above the intricate maze of houses, distinct and brilliant, like small treasures carved out of precious stones. For a moment only, and then their light would fade away once more, and the travelling beam would pick out, among the indigo hills beyond, a single golden crest.

There were days when the air was wet with passed or with approaching rain, and all the distances seemed miraculously near and clear. The olive trees detached themselves one from another on the distant slopes; the far-away villages were lovely and pathetic like the most exquisite small toys. There were days in summer-time, days of impending thunder when, bright and sunlit against huge bellying masses of black and purple, the hills and the white houses shone as it were precariously, in a dying splendour, on the brink of some fearful calamity.

How the hills changed and varied! Every day and every hour of the day, almost, they were different. There would be moments when, looking across the plain of Florence, one would see only a dark blue silhouette against the sky. The scene had no depth; there was only a hanging curtain painted flatly with the symbols of mountains. And then, suddenly almost, with the passing of a cloud, or when the sun had declined to a certain level in the sky, the flat scene transformed itself; and where there had been only a painted curtain, now there were ranges behind ranges of hills, graduated tone after tone from brown, or grey, or a green gold to far-away blue. Shapes that a moment before had been fused together indiscriminately into a single mass, now came apart into their constituents. Fiesole, which had seemed only a spur of Monte Morello, now revealed itself as the jutting headland of another system of hills, divided from the nearest bastions of its greater neighbour by a deep and shadowy valley.

At noon, during the heats of summer, the landscape became dim, powdery, vague, and almost colourless under the midday sun; the hills disappeared into the trembling fringes of the sky. But as the afternoon wore on the landscape emerged again, it dropped its anonymity, it climbed back out of nothingness into form and life. And its life, as the sun sank and slowly sank through the long afternoon, grew richer, grew more intense with every moment. The level light, with its attendant long, dark shadows, laid bare, so to speak, the anatomy of the land; the hills—each western escarpment shining, and each slope averted from the sunlight profoundly shadowed—became massive, jutty, and solid. Little folds and dimples in the seemingly even ground revealed themselves. Eastward from our hilltop, across the plain of the Ema, a great bluff cast its ever-increasing shadow; in the surrounding brightness of the valley a whole town lay eclipsed within it. And as the sun expired on the horizon, the further hills flushed in its warm light, till their illumined flanks were the colour of tawny roses; but the valleys were already filled with the blue mist of evening. And it mounted, mounted; the fire went out of the western windows of the populous slopes; only the crests were still alight, and at last they too were all extinct. The mountains faded and fused together again into a flat painting of mountains against the pale evening sky. In a little while it was night; and if the moon were full, a ghost of the dead scene still haunted the horizons.

Changeful in its beauty, this wide landscape always preserved a quality of humanness and domestication which made it, to my mind at any rate, the best of all landscapes to live with. Day by day one travelled through its different beauties; but the journey, like our ancestors' Grand Tour, was always a journey through civilization. For all its mountains, its steep slopes and deep valleys, the Tuscan scene is dominated by its inhabitants. They have cultivated every rood of ground that can be cultivated; their houses are thickly scattered even over the hills, and the valleys are populous. Solitary on the hilltop, one is not alone in a wilderness. Man's traces are across the country, and already—one feels it with satisfaction as one looks out across it—for centuries, for thousands of years, it has been his, submissive, tamed, and humanized. The wide, black moorlands, the sands, the forests of innumerable trees—these are places for occasional visitation, healthful to the spirit which submits itself to them for not too long. But fiendish influences as well as divine haunt these total solitudes. The vegetative life of plants and things is alien and hostile to the human. Men cannot live at ease except where they have mastered their surroundings and where their accumulated lives outnumber and outweigh the vegetative lives about them. Stripped of its dark woods, planted, terraced, and tilled almost to the mountains' tops, the Tuscan landscape is humanized and safe. Sometimes upon those who live in the midst of it there comes a longing for some place that is solitary, inhuman, lifeless, or peopled only with alien life. But the longing is soon satisfied, and one is glad to return to the civilized and submissive scene.

I found that house on the hilltop the ideal dwelling-place. For there, safe in the midst of a humanized landscape, one was yet alone; one could be as solitary as one liked. Neighbours whom one never sees at close quarters are the ideal and perfect neighbours.

Our nearest neighbours, in terms of physical proximity, lived very near. We had two sets of them, as a matter of fact, almost in the same house with us. One was the peasant family, who lived in a long, low building, part dwelling-house, part stables, storerooms and cowsheds, adjoining the villa. Our other neighbours—intermittent neighbours, however, for they only ventured out of town every now and then, during the most flawless weather—were the owners of the villa, who had reserved for themselves the smaller wing of the huge L-shaped house—a mere dozen rooms or so—leaving the remaining eighteen or twenty to us.

They were a curious couple, our proprietors. An old husband, grey, listless, tottering, seventy at least; and a signora of about forty, short, very plump, with tiny fat hands and feet and a pair of very large, very dark black eyes, which she used with all the skill of a born comedian. Her vitality, if you could have harnessed it and made it do some useful work, would have supplied a whole town with electric light. The physicists talk of deriving energy from the atom; they would be more profitably employed nearer home—in discovering some way of tapping those enormous stores of vital energy which accumulate in unemployed women of sanguine temperament and which, in the present imperfect state of social and scientific organization, vent themselves in ways that are generally so deplorable: in interfering with other people's affairs, in working up emotional scenes, in thinking about love and making it, and in bothering men till they cannot get on with their work.

Signora Bondi got rid of her superfluous energy, among other ways, by 'doing in' her tenants. The old gentleman, who was a retired merchant with a reputation for the most perfect rectitude, was allowed to have no dealings with us. When we came to see the house, it was the wife who showed us round. It was she who, with a lavish display of charm, with irresistible rollings of the eyes, expatiated on the merits of the place, sang the praises of the electric pump, glorified the bathroom (considering which, she insisted, the rent was remarkably moderate), and when we suggested calling in a surveyor to look over the house, earnestly begged us, as though our well-being were her only consideration, not to waste our money unnecessarily in doing anything so superfluous. "After all," she said, "we are honest people. I wouldn't dream of letting you the house except in perfect condition. Have confidence." And she looked at me with an appealing, pained expression in her magnificent eyes, as though begging me not to insult her by my coarse suspiciousness. And leaving us no time to pursue the subject of surveyors any further, she began assuring us that our little boy was the most beautiful angel she had ever seen. By the time our interview with Signora Bondi was at an end, we had definitely decided to take the house.

"Charming woman," I said, as we left the house. But I think that Elizabeth was not quite so certain of it as I.

Then the pump episode began.

On the evening of our arrival in the house we switched on the electricity. The pump made a very professional whirring noise; but no water came out of the taps in the bathroom. We looked at one another doubtfully.

"Charming woman?" Elizabeth raised her eyebrows.

We asked for interviews; but somehow the old gentleman could never see us, and the Signora was invariably out or indisposed. We left notes; they were never answered. In the end, we found that the only method of communicating with our landlords, who were living in the same house with us, was to go down into Florence and send a registered express letter to them. For this they had to sign two separate receipts and even, if we chose to pay forty centimes more, a third incriminating document, which was then returned to us. There could be no pretending, as there always was with ordinary letters or notes, that the communication had never been received. We began at last to get answers to our complaints. The Signora, who wrote all the letters, started by telling us that, naturally, the pump didn't work, as the cisterns were empty, owing to the long drought. I had to walk three miles to the post office in order to register my letter reminding her that there had been a violent thunderstorm only last Wednesday, and that the tanks were consequently more than half full. The answer came back: bath water had not been guaranteed in the contract; and if I wanted it, why hadn't I had the pump looked at before I took the house? Another walk into town to ask the Signora next door whether she remembered her adjurations to us to have confidence in her, and to inform her that the existence in a house of a bathroom was in itself an implicit guarantee of bath water. The reply to that was that the Signora couldn't continue to have communications with people who wrote so rudely to her. After that I put the matter into the hands of a lawyer. Two months later the pump was actually replaced. But we had to serve a writ on the lady before she gave in. And the costs were considerable.

One day, towards the end of the episode, I met the old gentleman in the road, taking his big maremman dog for a walk—or being taken, rather, for a walk by the dog. For where the dog pulled the old gentleman had perforce to follow. And when it stopped to smell, or scratch the ground, or leave against a gatepost its visiting-card or an offensive challenge, patiently, at his end of the leash, the old man had to wait. I passed him standing at the side of the road, a few hundred yards below our house. The dog was sniffing at the roots of one of the twin cypresses which grew one on either side of the entry to a farm; I heard the beast growling indignantly to itself, as though it scented an intolerable insult. Old Signor Bondi, leashed to his dog, was waiting. The knees inside the tubular grey trousers were slightly bent. Leaning on his cane, he stood gazing mournfully and vacantly at the view. The whites of his old eyes were discoloured, like ancient billiard balls. In the grey, deeply wrinkled face, his nose was dyspeptically red. His white moustache, ragged and yellowing at the fringes, drooped in a melancholy curve. In his black tie he wore a very large diamond; perhaps that was what Signora Bondi had found so attractive about him.

I took off my hat as I approached. The old man stared at me absently, and it was only when I was already almost past him that he recollected who I was.

"Wait," he called after me, "wait!" And he hastened down the road in pursuit. Taken utterly by surprise and at a disadvantage—for it was engaged in retorting to the affront imprinted on the cypress roots—the dog permitted itself to be jerked after him. Too much astonished to be anything but obedient, it followed its master. "Wait!"

I waited.

"My dear sir," said the old gentleman, catching me by the lapel of my coat and blowing most disagreeably in my face, "I want to apologize." He looked around him, as though afraid that even here he might be overheard. "I want to apologize," he went on, "about that wretched pump business. I assure you that, if it had been only my affair, I'd have put the thing right as soon as you asked. You were quite right: a bathroom is an implicit guarantee of bath water. I saw from the first that we should have no chance if it came to court. And besides, I think one ought to treat one's tenants as handsomely as one can afford to. But my wife"—he lowered his voice—"the fact is that she likes this sort of thing, even when she knows that she's in the wrong and must lose. And besides, she hoped, I dare say, that you'd get tired of asking and have the job done yourself. I told her from the first that we ought to give in; but she wouldn't listen. You see, she enjoys it. Still, now she sees that it must be done. In the course of the next two or three days you'll be having your bath water. But I thought I'd just like to tell you how . . ." But the Maremmano, which had recovered by this time from its surprise of a moment since, suddenly bounded, growling, up the road. The old gentleman tried to hold the beast, strained at the leash, tottered unsteadily, then gave way and allowed himself to be dragged off. ". . . how sorry I am," he went on, as he receded from me, "that this little misunderstanding . . ." But it was no use. "Good-bye." He smiled politely, made a little deprecating gesture, as though he had suddenly remembered a pressing engagement, and had no time to explain what it was. "Good-bye." He took off his hat and abandoned himself completely to the dog.

A week later the water really did begin to flow, and the day after our first bath Signora Bondi, dressed in dove-grey satin and wearing all her pearls, came to call.

"Is it peace now?" she asked, with a charming frankness, as she shook hands.

We assured her that, so far as we were concerned, it certainly was.

"But why *did* you write me such dreadfully rude letters?" she said, turning on me a reproachful glance that ought to have moved the most ruthless malefactor to contrition. "And then that writ. How *could* you? To a lady . . ."

I mumbled something about the pump and our wanting baths.

"But how could you expect me to listen to you while you were in that mood? Why didn't you set about it differently—politely, charmingly?" She smiled at me and dropped her fluttering eyelids.

I thought it best to change the conversation. It is disagreeable, when one is in the right, to be made to appear in the wrong.

A few weeks later we had a letter—duly registered and by express messenger—in which the Signora asked us whether we proposed to renew our lease (which was only for six months), and notifying us that, if we did, the rent would be raised 25 per cent., in consideration of the improvements which had been carried out. We thought ourselves lucky, at the end of much bargaining, to get the lease renewed for a whole year with an increase in the rent of only 15 per cent.

It was chiefly for the sake of the view that we put up with these intolerable extortions. But we had found other reasons, after a few days' residence, for liking the house. Of these the most cogent was that, in the peasant's youngest child, we had discovered what seemed the perfect playfellow for our own small boy. Between little Guido—for that was his name—and the youngest of his brothers and sisters there was a gap of six or seven years. His two elder brothers worked with their father in the fields; since the time of the mother's death, two or three years before we knew them, the eldest sister had ruled the house, and the younger, who had just left school, helped her and in between-whiles kept an eye on Guido, who by this time, however, needed very little looking after; for he was between six and seven years old and as precocious, self-assured, and responsible as the children of the poor, left as they are to themselves almost from the time they can walk, generally are.

Though fully two and a half years older than little Robin—and at that age thirty months are crammed with half a lifetime's experience—Guido took no undue advantage of his superior intelligence and strength. I have never seen a child more patient, tolerant, and untyrannical. He never laughed at Robin for his clumsy efforts to imitate his own prodigious feats; he did not tease or bully, but helped his small companion when he was in difficulties and explained when he could not understand. In return, Robin adored him, regarded him as the model and perfect Big Boy, and slavishly imitated him in every way he could.

These attempts of Robin's to imitate his companion were often exceedingly ludicrous. For by an obscure psychological law, words and actions in themselves quite serious become comic as soon as they are copied; and the more accurately, if the imitation is a deliberate parody, the funnier—for an overloaded imitation of some one we know does not make us laugh so much as one that is almost indistinguishably like the original. The bad imitation is only ludicrous when it is a piece of sincere and earnest flattery which does not quite come off. Robin's imitations were mostly of this kind. His heroic and unsuccessful attempts to perform the feats of strength and skill, which Guido could do with ease, were exquisitely comic. And his careful, long-drawn imitations of Guido's habits and mannerisms were no less amusing. Most ludicrous of all, because most earnestly undertaken and most incongruous in the imitator, were Robin's impersonations of Guido in the pensive mood. Guido was a thoughtful child, given to brooding and sudden abstractions. One would find him sitting in a corner by himself, chin in hand, elbow on knee, plunged, to all appearances, in the profoundest meditation. And sometimes, even in the midst of his play, he would suddenly break off, to stand, his hands behind his back, frowning and staring at the ground. When this happened, Robin became overawed and a little disquieted. In a puzzled silence he looked at his companion. "Guido," he would say softly, "Guido." But Guido was generally too much preoccupied to answer; and Robin, not venturing to insist, would creep near him, and throwing himself as nearly as possible into Guido's attitude—standing Napoleonically, his hands clasped behind him, or sitting in the posture of Michelangelo's Lorenzo the Magnificent—would try to meditate too. Every few seconds he would turn his bright blue eyes towards the elder child to see whether he was doing it quite right. But at the end of a minute he began to grow impatient; meditation wasn't his strong point. "Guido," he called again and, louder, "Guido!" And he would take him by the hand and try to pull him away. Sometimes Guido roused himself from his reverie and went back to the interrupted game. Sometimes he paid no attention. Melancholy, perplexed, Robin had to take himself off to play by himself. And Guido would go on sitting or standing there, quite still; and his eyes, if one looked into them, were beautiful in their grave and pensive calm.

They were large eyes, set far apart and, what was strange in a dark-haired Italian child, of a luminous pale blue-grey colour. They were not always grave and calm, as in these pensive moments. When he was playing, when he talked or laughed, they lit up; and the surface of those clear, pale lakes of thought seemed, as it were, to be shaken into brilliant sun-flashing ripples. Above those eyes was a beautiful forehead, high and steep and domed in a curve that was like the subtle curve of a rose petal. The nose was straight, the chin small and rather pointed, the mouth drooped a little sadly at the corners.

I have a snapshot of the two children sitting together on the parapet of the terrace. Guido sits almost facing the camera, but looking a little to one side and downwards; his hands are crossed in his lap and his expression, his attitude are thoughtful, grave, and meditative. It is Guido in one of those moods of abstraction into which he would pass even at the height of laughter and play—quite suddenly and completely, as though he had all at once taken it into his head to go away and had left the silent and beautiful body behind, like an empty house, to wait for his return. And by his side sits little Robin, turning to look up at him, his face half averted from the camera, but the curve of his cheek showing that he is laughing; one little raised hand is caught at the top of a gesture, the other clutches at Guido's sleeve, as though he were urging him to come away and play. And the legs dangling from the parapet have been seen by the blinking instrument in the midst of an impatient wriggle; he is on the point of slipping down and running off to play hide-and-seek in the garden. All the essential characteristics of both the children are in that little snapshot.

"If Robin were not Robin," Elizabeth used to say, "I could almost wish he were Guido."

And even at that time, when I took no particular interest in the child, I agreed with her. Guido seemed to me one of the most charming little boys I had ever seen.

We were not alone in admiring him. Signora Bondi when, in those cordial intervals between our quarrels, she came to call, was constantly speaking of him. "Such a beautiful, beautiful child!" she would exclaim with enthusiasm. "It's really a waste that he should belong to peasants who can't afford to dress him properly. If he were mine, I should put him into black velvet; or little white knickers and a white knitted silk jersey with a red line at the collar and cuffs; or perhaps a white sailor suit would be pretty. And in winter a little fur coat, with a squirrel skin cap, and possibly Russian boots . . ." Her imagination was running away with her. "And I'd let his hair grow, like a page's, and have it just curled up a little at the tips. And a straight fringe across his forehead. Every one would turn round and stare after us if I took him out with me in Via Tornabuoni."

What you want, I should have liked to tell her, is not a child; it's a clockwork doll or a performing monkey. But I did not say so—partly because I could not think of the Italian for a clockwork doll and partly because I did not want to risk having the rent raised another 15 per cent.

"Ah, if only I had a little boy like that!" She sighed and modestly dropped her eyelids. "I adore children. I sometimes think of adopting one—that is, if my husband would allow it."

I thought of the poor old gentleman being dragged along at the heels of his big white dog and inwardly smiled.

"But I don't know if he would," the Signora was continuing, "I don't know if he would." She was silent for a moment, as though considering a new idea.

A few days later, when we were sitting in the garden after luncheon, drinking our coffee, Guido's father, instead of passing with a nod and the usual cheerful good-day, halted in front of us and began to talk. He was a fine handsome man, not very tall, but well proportioned, quick and elastic in his movements, and full of life. He had a thin brown face, featured like a Roman's and lit by a pair of the most intelligent-looking grey eyes I ever saw. They exhibited almost too much intelligence when, as not infrequently happened, he was trying, with an assumption of perfect frankness and a childlike innocence, to take one in or get something out of one. Delighting in itself, the intelligence shone there mischievously. The face might be ingenuous, impassive, almost imbecile in its expression; but the eyes on these occasions gave him completely away. One knew, when they glittered like that, that one would have to be careful.

To-day, however, there was no dangerous light in them. He wanted nothing out of us, nothing of any value—only advice, which is a commodity, he knew, that most people are only too happy to part with. But he wanted advice on what was, for us, rather a delicate subject: on Signora Bondi. Carlo had often complained to us about her. The old man is good, he told us, very good and kind indeed. Which meant, I dare say, among other things, that he could easily be swindled. But his wife . . . Well, the woman was a beast. And he would tell us stories of her insatiable rapacity: she was always claiming more than the half of the produce which, by the laws of the metayage system, was the proprietor's due. He complained of her suspiciousness: she was for ever accusing him of sharp practices, of downright stealing—him, he struck his breast, the soul of honesty. He complained of her short-sighted avarice: she wouldn't spend enough on manure, wouldn't buy him another cow, wouldn't have electric light installed in the stables. And we had sympathized, but cautiously, without expressing too strong an opinion on the subject. The Italians are wonderfully non-committal in their speech; they will give nothing away to an interested person until they are quite certain that it is right and necessary and, above all, safe to do so. We had lived long enough among them to imitate their caution. What we said to Carlo would be sure sooner or later, to get back to Signora Bondi. There was nothing to be gained by unnecessarily embittering our relations with the lady—only another 15 per cent., very likely, to be lost.

To-day he wasn't so much complaining as feeling perplexed. The Signora had sent for him, it seemed, and asked him how he would like it if she were to make an offer—it was all very hypothetical in the cautious Italian style—to adopt little Guido. Carlo's first instinct had been to say that he wouldn't like it at all. But an answer like that would have been too coarsely committal. He had preferred to say that he would think about it. And now he was asking for our advice.

Do what you think best, was what in effect we replied. But we gave it distantly but distinctly to be understood that we didn't think that Signora Bondi would make a very good foster-mother for the child. And Carlo was inclined to agree. Besides, he was very fond of the boy.

"But the thing is," he concluded rather gloomily, "that if she has really set her heart on getting hold of the child, there's nothing she won't do to get him—nothing."

He too, I could see, would have liked the physicists to start on unemployed childless women of sanguine temperament before they tried to tackle the atom. Still, I reflected, as I watched him striding away along the terrace, singing powerfully from a brazen gullet as he went, there was force there, there was life enough in those elastic limbs, behind those bright grey eyes, to put up a good fight even against the accumulated vital energies of Signora Bondi.

It was a few days after this that my gramophone and two or three boxes of records arrived from England. They were a great comfort to us on the hilltop, providing as they did the only thing in which that spiritually fertile solitude—otherwise a perfect Swiss Family Robinson's island—was lacking: music. There is not much music to be heard nowadays in Florence. The times when Dr. Burney could tour through Italy, listening to an unending succession of new operas, symphonies, quartets, cantatas, are gone. Gone are the days when a learned musician, inferior only to the Reverend Father Martini of Bologna, could admire what the peasants sang and the strolling players thrummed and scraped on their instruments. I have travelled for weeks through the peninsula and hardly heard a note that was not 'Salome' or the Fascists' song. Rich in nothing else that makes life agreeable or even supportable, the northern metropolises are rich in music. That is perhaps the only inducement that a reasonable man can find for living there. The other attractions—organized gaiety, people, miscellaneous conversation, the social pleasures—what are those, after all, but an expense of spirit that buys nothing in return? And then the cold, the darkness, the mouldering dirt, the damp and squalor . . . No, where there is no necessity that retains, music can be the only inducement. And that, thanks to the ingenious Edison, can now be taken about in a box and unpacked in whatever solitude one chooses to visit. One can live at Benin, or Nuneaton, or Tozeur in the Sahara, and still hear Mozart quartets, and selections from the Well-Tempered Clavichord, and the Fifth Symphony, and the Brahms clarinet quintet, and motets by Palestrina.

Carlo, who had gone down to the station with his mule and cart to fetch the packing-case, was vastly interested in the machine. "One will hear some music again," he said, as he watched me unpacking the gramophone and the discs. "It is difficult to do much oneself."

Still, I reflected, he managed to do a good deal. On warm nights we used to hear him, where he sat at the door of his house, playing his guitar and softly singing; the eldest boy shrilled out the melody on the mandoline, and sometimes the whole family would join in, and the darkness would be filled with their passionate, throaty singing. Piedigrotta songs they mostly sang; and the voices drooped slurringly from note to note, lazily climbed or jerked themselves with sudden sobbing emphases from one tone to another. At a distance and under the stars the effect was not unpleasing.

"Before the war," he went on, "in normal times" (and Carlo had a hope, even a belief, that the normal times were coming back and that life would soon be as cheap and easy as it had been in the days before the flood), "I used to go and listen to the operas at the Politeama. Ah, they were magnificent. But it costs five lire now to get in."

"Too much," I agreed.

"Have you got *Trovatore*?" he asked.

I shook my head.

"*Rigoletto?*"

"I'm afraid not."

"*Bohème? Fanciulla del West? Pagliacci?*"

I had to go on disappointing him.

"Not even *Norma*? Or the *Barbiere*?"

I put on Battistini in 'La ci darem' out of *Don Giovanni*. He agreed that the singing was good; but I could see that he didn't much like the music. Why not? He found it difficult to explain.

"It's not like *Pagliacci*," he said at last.

"Not palpitating?" I suggested, using a word with which I was sure he would be familiar; for it occurs in every Italian political speech and patriotic leading article.

"Not palpitating," he agreed.

And I reflected that it is precisely by the difference between *Pagliacci* and *Don Giovanni*, between the palpitating and the non-palpitating, that modern musical taste is separated from the old. The corruption of the best, I thought, is the worst. Beethoven taught music to palpitate with his intellectual and spiritual passion. It has gone on palpitating ever since, but with the passion of inferior men. Indirectly, I thought, Beethoven is responsible for *Parsifal*, *Pagliacci*, and the *Poem of Fire*; still more indirectly for *Samson and Delilah* and 'Ivy, cling to me'. Mozart's melodies may be brilliant, memorable, infectious; but they don't palpitate, don't catch you between wind and water, don't send the listener off into erotic ecstasies.

Carlo and his elder children found my gramophone, I am afraid, rather a disappointment. They were too polite, however, to say so openly; they merely ceased, after the first day or two, to take any interest in the machine and the music it played. They preferred the guitar and their own singing.

Guido, on the other hand, was immensely interested. And he liked, not the cheerful dance tunes, to whose sharp rhythms our little Robin loved to go stamping round and round the room, pretending that he was a whole regiment of soldiers, but the genuine stuff. The first record he heard, I remember, was that of the slow movement of Bach's Concerto in D Minor for two violins. That was the disc I put on the turntable as soon as Carlo had left me. It seemed to me, so to speak, the most musical piece of music with which I could refresh my long-parched mind—the coolest and clearest of all draughts. The movement had just got under way and was beginning to unfold its pure and melancholy beauties in accordance with the laws of the most exacting intellectual logic, when the two children, Guido in front and little Robin breathlessly following, came clattering into the room from the loggia.

Guido came to a halt in front of the gramophone and stood there, motionless, listening. His pale blue-grey eyes opened themselves wide; making a little nervous gesture that I had often noticed in him before, he plucked at his lower lip with his thumb and forefinger. He must have taken a deep breath; for I noticed that, after listening for a few seconds, he sharply expired and drew in a fresh gulp of air. For an instant he looked at me—a questioning, astonished, rapturous look—gave a little laugh that ended in a kind of nervous shudder, and turned back towards the source of the incredible sounds. Slavishly imitating his elder comrade, Robin had also taken up his stand in front of the gramophone, and in exactly the same position, glancing at Guido from time to time to make sure that he was doing everything, down to plucking at his lip, in the correct way. But after a minute or so he became bored.

"Soldiers," he said, turning to me; "I want soldiers. Like in London." He remembered the rag-time and the jolly marches round and round the room.

I put my fingers to my lips. "Afterwards," I whispered.

Robin managed to remain silent and still for perhaps another twenty seconds. Then he seized Guido by the arm, shouting, "Vieni, Guido! Soldiers. Soldati. Vieni giuocare soldati."

It was then, for the first time, that I saw Guido impatient. "Vai!" he whispered angrily, slapped at Robin's clutching hand and pushed him roughly away. And he leaned a little closer to the instrument, as though to make up by yet intenser listening for what the interruption had caused him to miss.

Robin looked at him, astonished. Such a thing had never happened before. Then he burst out crying and came to me for consolation.

When the quarrel was made up—and Guido was sincerely repentant, was as nice as he knew how to be when the music had stopped and his mind was free to think of Robin once more—I asked him how he liked the music. He said he thought it was beautiful. But *bello* in Italian is too vague a word, too easily and frequently uttered, to mean very much.

"What did you like best?" I insisted. For he had seemed to enjoy it so much that I was curious to find out what had really impressed him.

He was silent for a moment, pensively frowning. "Well," he said at last, "I liked the bit that went like this." And he hummed a long phrase.

"And then there's the other thing singing at the same time—but what are those things," he interrupted himself, "that sing like that?"

"They're called violins," I said.

"Violins." He nodded. "Well, the other violin goes like this." He hummed again. "Why can't one sing both at once? And what is in that box? What makes it make that noise?" The child poured out his questions.

I answered him as best I could, showing him the little spirals on the disc, the needle, the diaphragm. I told him to remember how the string of the guitar trembled when one plucked it; sound is a shaking in the air, I told him, and I tried to explain how those shakings get printed on the black disc. Guido listened to me very gravely, nodding from time to time. I had the impression that he understood perfectly well everything I was saying.

By this time, however, poor Robin was so dreadfully bored that in pity for him I had to send the two children out into the garden to play. Guido went obediently; but I could see that he would have preferred to stay indoors and listen to more music. A little while later, when I looked out, he was hiding in the dark recesses of the big bay tree, roaring like a lion, and Robin, laughing, but a little nervously, as though he were afraid that the horrible noise might possibly turn out, after all, to be the roaring of a real lion, was beating the bush with a stick, and shouting, "Come out, come out! I want to shoot you."

After lunch, when Robin had gone upstairs for his afternoon sleep, he re-appeared. "May I listen to the music now?" he asked. And for an hour he sat there in front of the instrument, his head cocked slightly on one side, listening while I put on one disc after another.

Thenceforward he came every afternoon. Very soon he knew all my library of records, had his preferences and dislikes, and could ask for what he wanted by humming the principal theme.

"I don't like that one," he said of Strauss's 'Till Eulen Spiegel'. "It's like what we sing in our house. Not really like, you know. But somehow rather like, all the same. You understand?" He looked at us perplexedly and appealingly, as though begging us to understand what he meant and so save him from going on explaining. We nodded. Guido went on. "And then," he said, "the end doesn't seem to come properly out of the beginning. It's not like the one you played the first time." He hummed a bar or two from the slow movement of Bach's D Minor Concerto.

"It isn't," I suggested, "like saying: All little boys like playing. Guido is a little boy. Therefore Guido likes playing."

He frowned. "Yes, perhaps that's it," he said at last. "The one you played first is more like that. But, you know," he added, with an excessive regard for truth, "I don't like playing as much as Robin does."

Wagner was among his dislikes; so was Debussy. When I played the record of one of Debussy's Arabesques, he said, "Why does he say the same thing over and over again? He ought to say something new, or go on, or make the thing grow. Can't he think of anything different?" But he was less censorious about the 'Après-Midi d'un Faune'. "The things have beautiful voices," he said.

Mozart overwhelmed him with delight. The duet from *Don Giovanni*, which his father had found insufficiently palpitating, enchanted Guido. But he preferred the quartets and the orchestral pieces.

"I like music," he said, "better than singing."

Most people, I reflected, like singing better than music; are more interested in the executant than in what he executes, and find the impersonal orchestra less moving than the soloist. The touch of the pianist is the human touch, and the soprano's high C is the personal note. It is for the sake of this touch, that note, that audiences fill the concert halls.

Guido, however, preferred music. True, he liked 'La ci darem'; he liked 'Deh vieni alla finestra'; he thought 'Che soave zefiretto' so lovely that almost all our concerts had to begin with it. But he preferred the other things. The *Figaro* overture was one of his favourites. There is a passage not far from the beginning of the piece, where the first violins suddenly go rocketing up into the heights of loveliness; as the music approached that point, I used always to see a smile developing and gradually brightening on Guido's face, and when, punctually, the thing happened, he clapped his hands and laughed aloud with pleasure.

On the other side of the same disc, it happened, was recorded Beethoven's *Egmont* overture. He liked that almost better than *Figaro*.

"It has more voices," he explained. And I was delighted by the acuteness of the criticism; for it is precisely in the richness of its orchestration that *Egmont* goes beyond *Figaro*.

But what stirred him almost more than anything was the *Coriolan* overture. The third movement of the Fifth Symphony, the second movement of the Seventh, the slow movement of the Emperor Concerto —all these things ran it pretty close. But none excited him so much as *Coriolan*. One day he made me play it three or four times in succession; then he put it away.

"I don't think I want to hear that any more," he said.

"Why not?"

"It's too . . . too . . ." he hesitated, "too big," he said at last. "I don't really understand it. Play me the one that goes like this." He hummed the phrase from the D Minor Concerto.

"Do you like that one better?" I asked.

He shook his head. "No, it's not that exactly. But it's easier."

"Easier?" It seemed to me rather a queer word to apply to Bach.

"I understand it better."

One afternoon, while we were in the middle of our concert, Signora Bondi was ushered in. She began at once to be overwhelmingly affectionate towards the child; kissed him, patted his head, paid him the most outrageous compliments on his appearance. Guido edged away from her.

"And do you like music?" she asked.

The child nodded.

"I think he has a gift," I said. "At any rate, he has a wonderful ear and a power of listening and criticizing such as I've never met with in a child of that age. We're thinking of hiring a piano for him to learn on."

A moment later I was cursing myself for my undue frankness in praising the boy. For Signora Bondi began immediately to protest that, if she could have the upbringing of the child, she would give him the best masters, bring out his talent, make an accomplished maestro of him—and, on the way, an infant prodigy. And at that moment, I am sure, she saw herself sitting maternally, in pearls and black satin, in the lee of the huge Steinway, while an angelic Guido, dressed like little Lord Fauntleroy, rattled out Liszt and Chopin, to the loud delight of a thronged auditorium. She saw the bouquets and all the elaborate floral tributes, heard the clapping and the few well-chosen words with which the veteran maestri, touched almost to tears, would hail the coming of the little genius. It became more than ever important for her to acquire the child.

"You've sent her away fairly ravening," said Elizabeth, when Signora Bondi had gone. "Better tell her next time that you made a mistake, and that the boy's got no musical talent whatever."

In due course, the piano arrived. After giving him the minimum of preliminary instruction, I let Guido loose on it. He began by picking out for himself the melodies he had heard, reconstructing the harmonies in which they were embedded. After a few lessons, he understood the rudiments of musical notation and could read a simple passage at sight, albeit very slowly. The whole process of reading was still strange to him; he had picked up his letters somehow, but nobody had yet taught him to read whole words and sentences.

I took occasion, next time I saw Signora Bondi, to assure her that Guido had disappointed me. There was nothing in his musical talent, really. She professed to be very sorry to hear it; but I could see that she didn't for a moment believe me. Probably she thought that we were after the child too, and wanted to bag the infant prodigy for ourselves, before she could get in her claim, thus depriving her of what she regarded almost as her feudal right. For, after all, weren't they her peasants? If any one was to profit by adopting the child it ought to be herself.

Tactfully, diplomatically, she renewed her negotiations with Carlo. The boy, she put it to him, had genius. It was the foreign gentleman who had told her so, and he was the sort of man, clearly, who knew about such things. If Carlo would let her adopt the child, she'd have him trained. He'd become a great maestro and get engagements in the Argentine and the United States, in Paris and London. He'd earn millions and millions. Think of Caruso, for example. Part of the millions, she explained, would of course come to Carlo. But before they began to roll in, those millions, the boy would have to be trained. But training was very expensive. In his own interest, as well as in that of his son, he ought to let her take charge of the child. Carlo said he would think it over, and again applied to us for advice. We suggested that it would be best in any case to wait a little and see what progress the boy made.

He made, in spite of my assertions to Signora Bondi, excellent progress. Every afternoon, while Robin was asleep, he came for his concert and his lesson. He was getting along famously with his reading; his small fingers were acquiring strength and agility. But what to me was more interesting was that he had begun to make up little pieces on his own account. A few of them I took down as he played them and I have them still. Most of them, strangely enough, as I thought then, are canons. He had a passion for canons. When I explained to him the principles of the form he was enchanted. "It is beautiful," he said, with admiration. "Beautiful, beautiful. And so easy!"

Again the word surprised me. The canon is not, after all, so conspicuously simple. Thenceforward he spent most of his time at the piano in working out little canons for his own amusement. They were often remarkably ingenious. But in the invention of other kinds of music he did not show himself so fertile as I had hoped. He composed and harmonized one or two solemn little airs like hymn tunes, with a few sprightlier pieces in the spirit of the military march. They were extraordinary, of course, as being the inventions of a child. But a great many children can do extraordinary things; we are all geniuses up to the age of ten. But I had hoped that Guido was a child who was going to be a genius at forty; in which case what was extraordinary for an ordinary child was not extraordinary enough for him. "He's hardly a Mozart," we agreed, as we played his little pieces over. I felt, it must be confessed, almost aggrieved. Anything less than a Mozart, it seemed to me, was hardly worth thinking about.

He was not a Mozart. No. But he was somebody, as I was to find out, quite as extraordinary. It was one morning in the early summer that I made the discovery. I was sitting in the warm shade of our westward-facing balcony, working. Guido and Robin were playing in the little enclosed garden below. Absorbed in my work, it was only, I suppose, after the silence had prolonged itself a considerable time that I became aware that the children were making remarkably little noise. There was no shouting, no running about; only a quiet talking. Knowing by experience that when children are quiet it generally means that they are absorbed in some delicious mischief, I got up from my chair and looked over the balustrade to see what they were doing. I expected to catch them dabbling in water, making a bonfire, covering themselves with tar. But what I actually saw was Guido, with a burnt stick in his hand, demonstrating on the smooth paving-stones of the path, that the square on the hypotenuse of a right-angled triangle is equal to the sum of the squares on the other two sides.

Kneeling on the floor, he was drawing with the point of his blackened stick on the flagstones. And Robin, kneeling imitatively beside him, was growing, I could see, rather impatient with this very slow game.

"Guido," he said. But Guido paid no attention. Pensively frowning, he went on with his diagram. "Guido!" The younger child bent down and then craned round his neck so as to look up into Guido's face. "Why don't you draw a train?"

"Afterwards," said Guido. "But I just want to show you this first. It's *so* beautiful," he added cajolingly.

"But I want a train," Robin persisted.

"In a moment. Do just wait a moment." The tone was almost imploring. Robin armed himself with renewed patience. A minute later Guido had finished both his diagrams.

"There!" he said triumphantly, and straightened himself up to look at them. "Now I'll explain."

And he proceeded to prove the theorem of Pythagoras—not in Euclid's way, but by the simpler and more satisfying method which was, in all probability, employed by Pythagoras himself. He had drawn a square and dissected it, by a pair of crossed perpendiculars, into two squares and two equal rectangles. The equal rectangles he divided up by their diagonals into four equal right-angled triangles. The two squares are then seen to be the squares on the two sides of any one of these triangles other than the hypotenuse. So much for the first diagram. In the next he took the four right-angled triangles into which the rectangles had been divided and re-arranged them round the original square so that their right angles filled the corners of the square, the hypotenuses looked inwards, and the greater and less sides of the triangles were in continuation along the sides of the square (which are each equal to the sum of these sides). In this way the original square is redissected into four right-angled triangles and the square on the hypotenuse. The four triangles are equal to the two rectangles of the original dissection. Therefore the square on the hypotenuse is equal to the sum of the two squares—the squares on the other two sides—into which, with the rectangles, the original square was first dissected.

In very untechnical language, but clearly and with a relentless logic, Guido expounded his proof. Robin listened, with an expression on his bright, freckled face of perfect incomprehension.

"Treno," he repeated from time to time. "Treno. Make a train."

"In a moment," Guido implored. "Wait a moment. But do just look at this. *Do*." He coaxed and cajoled. "It's so beautiful. It's so easy."

So easy . . . The theorem of Pythagoras seemed to explain for me Guido's musical predilections. It was not an infant Mozart we had been cherishing; it was a little Archimedes with, like most of his kind, an incidental musical twist.

"Treno, treno!" shouted Robin, growing more and more restless as the exposition went on. And when Guido insisted on going on with his proof, he lost his temper. "Cattivo Guido," he shouted, and began to hit out at him with his fists.

"All right," said Guido resignedly. "I'll make a train." And with his stick of charcoal he began to scribble on the stones.

I looked on for a moment in silence. It was not a very good train. Guido might be able to invent for himself and prove the theorem of Pythagoras; but he was not much of a draughtsman.

"Guido!" I called. The two children turned and looked up. "Who taught you to draw those squares?" It was conceivable, of course, that somebody might have taught him.

"Nobody." He shook his head. Then, rather anxiously, as though he were afraid there might be something wrong about drawing squares, he went on to apologize and explain. "You see," he said, "it seemed to me so beautiful. Because those squares"—he pointed at the two small squares in the first figure—"are just as big as this one." And, indicating the square on the hypotenuse in the second diagram, he looked up at me with a deprecating smile.

I nodded. "Yes, it's very beautiful," I said—"it's very beautiful indeed."

An expression of delighted relief appeared on his face; he laughed with pleasure. "You see, it's like this," he went on, eager to initiate me into the glorious secret he had discovered. "You cut these two long squares"—he meant the rectangles—"into two slices. And then there are four slices, all just the same, because, because—oh, I ought to have said that before—because these long squares are the same, because those lines, you see . . ."

"But I want a train," protested Robin.

Leaning on the rail of the balcony, I watched the children below. I thought of the extraordinary thing I had just seen and of what it meant.

I thought of the vast differences between human beings. We classify men by the colour of their eyes and hair, the shape of their skulls. Would it not be more sensible to divide them up into intellectual species? There would be even wider gulfs between the extreme mental types than between a Bushman and a Scandinavian. This child, I thought, when he grows up, will be to me, intellectually, what a man is to a dog. And there are other men and women who are, perhaps, almost as dogs to me.

Perhaps the men of genius are the only true men. In all the history of the race there have been only a few thousand real men. And the rest of us—what are we? Teachable animals. Without the help of the real men, we should have found out almost nothing at all. Almost all the ideas with which we are familiar could never have occurred to minds like ours. Plant the seeds there and they will grow; but our minds could never spontaneously have generated them.

There have been whole nations of dogs, I thought; whole epochs in which no Man was born. From the dull Egyptians the Greeks took crude experience and rules of thumb and made sciences. More than a thousand years passed before Archimedes had a comparable successor. There has been only one Buddha, one Jesus, only one Bach that we know of, one Michelangelo.

Is it by a mere chance, I wondered, that a Man is born from time to time? What causes a whole constellation of them to come contemporaneously into being and from out of a single people? Taine thought that Leonardo, Michelangelo, and Raphael were born when they were because the time was ripe for great painters and the Italian scene congenial. In the mouth of a rationalizing nineteenth-century Frenchman the doctrine is strangely mystical; it may be none the less true for that. But what of those born out of time? Blake, for example. What of those?

This child, I thought, has had the fortune to be born at a time when he will be able to make good use of his capacities. He will find the most elaborate analytical methods lying ready to his hand; he will have a prodigious experience behind him. Suppose him born while Stone Henge was building; he might have spent a lifetime discovering the rudiments, guessing darkly where now he might have had a chance of proving. Born at the time of the Norman Conquest, he would have had to wrestle with all the preliminary difficulties created by an inadequate symbolism; it would have taken him long years, for example, to learn the art of dividing MMMCCCCLXXXVIII by MCMXIX. In five years, nowadays, he will learn what it took generations of Men to discover.

And I thought of the fate of all the Men born so hopelessly out of time that they could achieve little or nothing of value. Beethoven born in Greece, I thought, would have had to be content to play thin melodies on the flute or lyre; in those intellectual surroundings it would hardly have been possible for him to imagine the nature of harmony.

From drawing trains, the children in the garden below had gone on to playing trains. They were trotting round and round; with blown round cheeks and pouting mouth, like the cherubic symbol of a wind, Robin puff-puffed, and Guido, holding the skirt of his smock, shuffled behind him, tooting. They ran forward, backed, stopped at imaginary stations, shunted, roared over bridges, crashed through tunnels, met with occasional collisions and derailments. The young Archimedes seemed to be just as happy as the little tow-headed barbarian. A few minutes ago he had been busy with the theorem of Pythagoras. Now, tooting indefatigably along imaginary rails, he was perfectly content to shuffle backwards and forwards among the flower-beds, between the pillars of the loggia, in and out of the dark tunnels of the laurel tree. The fact that one is going to be Archimedes does not prevent one from being an ordinary cheerful child meanwhile. I thought of this strange talent distinct and separate from the rest of the mind, independent, almost, of experience. The typical child-prodigies are musical and mathematical; the other talents ripen slowly under the influence of emotional experience and growth. Till he was thirty Balzac gave proof of nothing but ineptitude; but at four the young Mozart was already a musician, and some of Pascal's most brilliant work was done before he was out of his teens.

In the weeks that followed, I alternated the daily piano lessons with lessons in mathematics. Hints rather than lessons they were; for I only made suggestions, indicated methods, and left the child himself to work out the ideas in detail. Thus I introduced him to algebra by showing him another proof of the theorem of Pythagoras. In this proof one drops a perpendicular from the right angle on to the hypotenuse, and arguing from the fact that the two triangles thus created are similar to one another and to the original triangle, and that the proportions which their corresponding sides bear to one another are therefore equal, one can show in algebraical form that c^2+d^2 (the squares on the other two sides) are equal to a^2+b^2 (the squares on the two segments of the hypotenuse) $+2ab$; which last, it is easy to show geometrically, is equal to $(a+b)^2$, or the square on the hypotenuse. Guido was as much enchanted by the rudiments of algebra as he would have been if I had given him an engine worked by steam, with a methylated spirit lamp to heat the boiler; more enchanted, perhaps—for the engine would have got broken, and, remaining always itself, would in any case have lost its charm, while the rudiments of algebra continued to grow and blossom in his mind with an unfailing luxuriance. Every day he made the discovery of something which seemed to him exquisitely beautiful; the new toy was inexhaustible in its potentialities.

In the intervals of applying algebra to the second book of Euclid, we experimented with circles; we stuck bamboos into the parched earth, measured their shadows at different hours of the day, and drew exciting conclusions from our observations. Sometimes, for fun, we cut and folded sheets of paper so as to make cubes and pyramids. One afternoon Guido arrived carrying carefully between his small and rather grubby hands a flimsy dodecahedron.

"È tanto bello!" he said, as he showed us his paper crystal; and when I asked him how he had managed to make it, he merely smiled and said it had been so easy. I looked at Elizabeth and laughed. But it would have been more symbolically to the point, I felt, if I had gone down on all fours, wagged the spiritual outgrowth of my os coccyx, and barked my astonished admiration.

It was an uncommonly hot summer. By the beginning of July our little Robin, unaccustomed to these high temperatures, began to look pale and tired; he was listless, had lost his appetite and energy. The doctor advised mountain air. We decided to spend the next ten or twelve weeks in Switzerland. My parting gift to Guido was the first six books of Euclid in Italian. He turned over the pages, looking ecstatically at the figures. "If only I knew how to read properly," he said. "I'm so stupid. But now I shall really try to learn."

From our hotel near Grindelwald we sent the child, in Robin's name, various post cards of cows, Alp-horns, Swiss chalets, edelweiss, and the like. We received no answers to these cards; but then we did not expect answers. Guido could not write, and there was no reason why his father or his sisters should take the trouble to write for him. No news, we took it, was good news. And then one day, early in September, there arrived at the hotel a strange letter The manager had it stuck up on the glass-fronted notice-board in the hall, so that all the guests might see it, and whoever conscientiously thought that it belonged to him might claim it. Passing the board on the way into lunch, Elizabeth stopped to look at it.

"But it must be from Guido," she said.

I came and looked at the envelope over her shoulder. It was unstamped and black with postmarks. Traced out in pencil, the big uncertain capital letters sprawled across its face. In the first line was written: AL

BABBO DI ROBIN, and there followed a travestied version of the name of the hotel and the place. Round the address bewildered postal officials had scrawled suggested emendations. The letter had wandered for a fortnight at least, back and forth across the face of Europe.

"Al Babbo di Robin. To Robin's father." I laughed. "Pretty smart of the postmen to have got it here at all." I went to the manager's office, set forth the justice of my claim to the letter and, having paid the fifty-centime surcharge for the missing stamp, had the case unlocked and the letter given me. We went in to lunch.

"The writing's magnificent," we agreed, laughing, as we examined the address at close quarters. "Thanks to Euclid," I added. "That's what comes of pandering to the ruling passion."

But when I opened the envelope and looked at its contents I no longer laughed. The letter was brief and almost telegraphical in style. "SONO DALLA PADRONA," it ran, "NON MI PIACE HA RUBATO IL MIO LIBRO NON VOGLIO SUONARE PIU VOGLIO TORNARE A CASA VENGA SUBITO GUIDO."

"What is it?"

I handed Elizabeth the letter. "That blasted woman's got hold of him," I said.

BUSTS OF MEN in Homburg hats, angels bathed in marble tears extinguishing torches, statues of little girls, cherubs, veiled figures, allegories and ruthless realisms—the strangest and most diverse idols beckoned and gesticulated as we passed. Printed indelibly on tin and embedded in the living rock, the brown photographs looked out, under glass, from the humbler crosses, headstones, and broken pillars. Dead ladies in the cubistic geometrical fashions of thirty years ago—two cones of black satin meeting point to point at the waist, and the arms: a sphere to the elbow, a polished cylinder below—smiled mournfully out of their marble frames; the smiling faces, the white hands, were the only recognizably human things that emerged from the solid geometry of their clothes. Men with black moustaches, men with white beards, young clean-shaven men, stared or averted their gaze to show a Roman profile. Children in their stiff best opened wide their eyes, smiled hopefully in anticipation of the little bird that was to issue from the camera's muzzle, smiled sceptically in the knowledge that it wouldn't, smiled laboriously and obediently because they had been told to. In spiky Gothic cottages of marble the richer dead privately reposed; through grilled doors one caught a glimpse of pale Inconsolables weeping, of distraught Geniuses guarding the secret of the tomb. The less prosperous sections of the majority slept in communities, close-crowded but elegantly housed under smooth continuous marble floors, whose every flagstone was the mouth of a separate grave.

These continental cemeteries, I thought, as Carlo and I made our way among the dead, are more frightful than ours, because these people pay more attention to their dead than we do. That primordial cult of corpses, that tender solicitude for their material well-being, which led the ancients to house their dead in stone, while they themselves lived between wattles and under thatch, still lingers here; persists, I thought, more vigorously than with us. There are a hundred gesticulating statues here for every one in an English graveyard. There are more family vaults, more 'luxuriously appointed' (as they say of liners and hotels) than one would find at home. And embedded in every tombstone there are photographs to remind the powdered bones within what form they will have to resume on the Day of Judgment; beside each are little hanging lamps to burn optimistically on All Souls' Day. To the Man who built the Pyramids they are nearer, I thought, than we.

"If I had known," Carlo kept repeating, "if only I had known." His voice came to me through my reflections as though from a distance. "At the time he didn't mind at all. How should I have known that he would take it so much to heart afterwards? And she deceived me, she lied to me."

I assured him yet once more that it wasn't his fault. Though, of course, it was, in part. It was mine too, in part; I ought to have thought of the possibility and somehow guarded against it. And he shouldn't have let the child go, even temporarily and on trial, even though the woman was bringing pressure to bear on him. And the pressure had been considerable. They had worked on the same holding for more than a hundred years, the men of Carlo's family; and now she had made the old man threaten to turn him out. It would be a dreadful thing to leave the place; and besides, another place wasn't so easy to find. It was made quite plain, however, that he could stay if he let her have the child. Only for a little to begin with; just to see how he got on. There would be no compulsion whatever on him to stay if he didn't like it. And it would be all to Guido's advantage; and to his father's, too, in the end. All that the Englishman had said about his not being such a good musician as he had thought at first was obviously untrue—mere jealousy and little-mindedness: the man wanted to take credit for Guido himself, that was all. And the boy, it was obvious, would learn nothing from him. What he needed was a real good professional master.

All the energy that, if the physicists had known their business, would have been driving dynamos, went into this campaign. It began the moment we were out of the house, intensively. She would have more chance of success, the Signora doubtless thought, if we weren't there. And besides, it was essential to take the opportunity when it offered itself and get hold of the child before we could make our bid—for it was obvious to her that we wanted Guido just as much as she did.

Day after day she renewed the assault. At the end of a week she sent her husband to complain about the state of the vines: they were in a shocking condition; he had decided, or very nearly decided, to give Carlo notice. Meekly, shamefacedly, in obedience to higher orders, the old gentleman uttered his threats. Next day Signora Bondi returned to the attack. The padrone, she declared, had been in a towering passion; but she'd do her best, her very best, to mollify him. And after a significant pause she went on to talk about Guido.

In the end Carlo gave in. The woman was too persistent and she held too many trump cards. The child could go and stay with her for a month or two on trial. After that, if he really expressed a desire to remain with her, she could formally adopt him.

At the idea of going for a holiday to the seaside—and it was to the seaside, Signora Bondi told him, that they were going—Guido was pleased and excited. He had heard a lot about the sea from Robin. "Tanta acqua!" It had sounded almost too good to be true. And now he was actually to go and see this marvel. It was very cheerfully that he parted from his family.

But after the holiday by the sea was over, and Signora Bondi had brought him back to her town house in Florence, he began to be homesick. The Signora, it was true, treated him exceedingly kindly, bought him new clothes, took him out to tea in the Via Tornabuoni and filled him up with cakes, iced strawberryade, whipped cream, and chocolates. But she made him practise the piano more than he liked, and what was worse, she took away his Euclid, on the score that he wasted too much time with it. And when he said that he wanted to go home, she put him off with promises and excuses and downright lies. She told him that she couldn't take him at once, but that next week, if he were good and worked hard at his piano meanwhile, next week . . . And when the time came she told him that his father didn't want him back. And she redoubled her petting, gave him expensive presents, and stuffed him with yet unhealthier foods. To no purpose. Guido didn't like his new life, didn't want to practise scales, pined for his book, and longed to be back with his brothers and sisters. Signora Bondi, meanwhile, continued to hope that time and chocolates would eventually make the child hers; and to keep his family at a distance, she wrote to Carlo every few days letters which still purported to come from the seaside (she took the trouble to send them to a friend, who posted them back again to Florence), and in which she painted the most charming picture of Guido's happiness.

It was then that Guido wrote his letter to me. Abandoned, as he supposed, by his family—for that they shouldn't take the trouble to come to see him when they were so near was only to be explained on the hypothesis that they really had given him up—he must have looked to me as his last and only hope. And the letter, with its fantastic address, had been nearly a fortnight on its way. A fortnight—it must have seemed hundreds of years; and as the centuries succeeded one another, gradually, no doubt, the poor child became convinced that I too had abandoned him. There was no hope left.

"Here we are," said Carlo.

I looked up and found myself confronted by an enormous monument. In a kind of grotto hollowed in the flanks of a monolith of grey sandstone, Sacred Love, in bronze, was embracing a funerary urn. And in bronze letters riveted into the stone was a long legend to the effect that the inconsolable Ernesto Bondi had raised this monument to the memory of his beloved wife, Annunziata, as a token of his undying love for one whom, snatched from him by a premature death, he hoped very soon to join beneath this stone. The first Signora Bondi had died in 1912. I thought of the old man leashed to his white dog; he must always, I reflected, have been a most uxorious husband.

"They buried him here."

We stood there for a long time in silence. I felt the tears coming into my eyes as I thought of the poor child lying there underground. I thought of those luminous grave eyes, and the curve of that beautiful forehead, the droop of the melancholy mouth, of the expression of delight which illumined his face when he learned of some new idea that pleased him, when he heard a piece of music that he liked. And this beautiful small being was dead; and the spirit that inhabited this form, the amazing spirit, that too had been destroyed almost before it had begun to exist. And the unhappiness that must have preceded the final act, the child's despair, the conviction of his utter abandonment—those were terrible to think of, terrible.

"I think we had better come away now," I said at last, and touched Carlo on the arm. He was standing there like a blind man, his eyes shut, his face slightly lifted towards the light; from between his closed eyelids the tears welled out, hung for a moment, and trickled down his cheeks. His lips trembled and I could see that he was making an effort to keep them still. "Come away," I repeated.

The face which had been still in its sorrow, was suddenly convulsed; he opened his eyes, and through the tears they were bright with a violent anger. "I shall kill her," he said, "I shall kill her. When I think of him throwing himself out, falling through the air . . ." With his two hands he made a violent gesture, bringing them down from over his head and arresting them with a sudden jerk when they were on a level with his breast. "And then crash," He shuddered. "She's as much responsible as though she had pushed him down herself. I shall kill her." He clenched his teeth.

To be angry is easier than to be sad, less painful. It is comforting to think of revenge. "Don't talk like that," I said. "It's no good. It's stupid. And what would be the point?" He had had those fits before, when grief became too painful and he had tried to escape from it. Anger had been the easiest way of escape. I had had, before this, to persuade him back into the harder path of grief. "It's stupid to talk like that," I repeated, and I led him away through the ghastly labyrinth of tombs, where death seemed more terrible even than it is.

By the time we had left the cemetery, and were walking down from San Miniato towards the Piazzale Michelangelo below, he had become calmer. His anger had subsided again into the sorrow from which it had derived all its strength and its bitterness. In the Piazzale we halted for a moment to look down at the city in the valley below us. It was a day of floating clouds—great shapes, white, golden, and grey; and between them patches of a thin, transparent blue. Its lantern level, almost, with our eyes, the dome of the cathedral revealed itself in all its grandiose lightness, its vastness and aerial strength. On the innumerable brown and rosy roofs of the city the afternoon sunlight lay softly, sumptuously, and the towers were as though varnished and enamelled with an old gold. I thought of all the Men who had lived here and left the visible traces of their spirit and conceived extraordinary things. I thought of the dead child.

W. W. JACOBS

1863–1943

Famous during his lifetime as a writer of humorous and romantic stories about life at sea or in the English village of "Claybury", today he is best remembered for a rather different kind of tale. When just for once he put aside his jokes and turned to the icily macabre, he wrote this story, one of the weirdest ghost stories of all time.

The Monkey's Paw

WITHOUT, the night was cold and wet, but in the small parlour of Laburnum Villa the blinds were drawn and the fire burned brightly. Father and son were at chess, the former, who possessed ideas about the game involving radical changes, putting his king into such sharp and unnecessary perils that it even provoked comment from the white-haired old lady knitting placidly by the fire.

"Hark at the wind," said Mr. White, who, having seen a fatal mistake after it was too late, was amiably desirous of preventing his son from seeing it.

"I'm listening," said the latter, grimly surveying the board as he stretched out his hand. "Check."

"I should hardly think that he'd come tonight," said his father, with his hand poised over the board.

"Mate," replied the son.

"That's the worst of living so far out," bawled Mr. White, with sudden and unlooked-for violence; "of all the beastly, slushy, out-of-the-way places to live in, this is the worst. Pathway's a bog, and the road's a torrent. I don't know what people are thinking about. I suppose because only two houses in the road are let, they think it doesn't matter."

"Never mind, dear," said his wife, soothingly; "perhaps you'll win the next one."

Mr. White looked up sharply, just in time to intercept a knowing glance between mother and son. The words died away on his lips, and he hid a guilty grin in his thin grey beard.

"There he is," said Herbert White, as the gate banged to loudly and heavy footsteps came toward the door.

The old man rose with hospitable haste, and opening the door, was heard condoling with the new arrival. The new arrival also condoled with himself, so that Mrs. White said, "Tut, tut!" and coughed gently as her husband entered the room, followed by a tall, burly man, beady of eye and rubicund of visage.

"Sergeant-Major Morris," he said, introducing him.

The sergeant-major shook hands, and taking the proffered seat by the fire, watched contentedly while his host got out whisky and tumblers and stood a small copper kettle on the fire.

At the third glass his eyes got brighter, and he began to talk, the little family circle regarding with eager interest this visitor from distant parts, as he squared his shoulders in the chair and spoke of wild scenes and doughty deeds; of wars and plagues and strange peoples.

"Twenty-one years of it," said Mr. White, nodding at his wife and son. "When he went away he was a slip of a youth in the warehouse. Now look at him."

"He don't look to have taken much harm," said Mrs. White, politely.

"I'd like to go to India myself," said the old man, "just to look round a bit, you know."

"Better where you are," said the sergeant-major, shaking his head. He put down the empty glass, and sighing softly, shook it again.

"I should like to see those old temples and fakirs and jugglers," said the old man. "What was that you started telling me the other day about a monkey's paw or something, Morris?"

"Nothing," said the soldier, hastily. "Leastways nothing worth hearing."

"Monkey's paw?" said Mrs. White, curiously.

"Well, it's just a bit of what you might call magic, perhaps," said the sergeant-major, offhandedly.

His three listeners leaned forward eagerly. The visitor absent-mindedly put his empty glass to his lips and then set it down again. His host filled it for him.

"To look at," said the sergeant-major, fumbling in his pocket, "it's just an ordinary little paw, dried to a mummy."

He took something out of his pocket and proffered it. Mrs. White drew back with a grimace, but her son, taking it, examined it curiously.

"And what is there special about it?" inquired Mr. White as he took it from his son, and having examined it, placed it upon the table.

"It had a spell put on it by an old fakir," said the sergeant-major, "a very holy man. He wanted to show that fate ruled people's lives, and that those who interfered with it did so to their sorrow. He put a spell on it so that three separate men could each have three wishes from it."

His manner was so impressive that his hearers were conscious that their light laughter jarred somewhat.

"Well, why don't you have three, sir?" said Herbert White, cleverly.

The soldier regarded him in the way that middle age is wont to regard presumptuous youth. "I have," he said, quietly, and his blotchy face whitened.

"And did you really have the three wishes granted?" asked Mrs. White.

"I did," said the sergeant-major, and his glass tapped against his strong teeth.

"And has anybody else wished?" persisted the old lady.

"The first man had his three wishes. Yes," was the reply; "I don't know what the first two were, but the third was for death. That's how I got the paw."

His tones were so grave that a hush fell upon the group.

"If you've had your three wishes, it's no good to you now, then, Morris," said the old man at last. "What do you keep it for?"

The soldier shook his head. "Fancy, I suppose," he said, slowly. "I did have some idea of selling it, but I don't think I will. It has caused enough mischief already. Besides, people won't buy. They think it's a fairy tale; some of them, and those who do think anything of it want to try it first and pay me afterward."

"If you could have another three wishes," said the old man, eyeing him keenly, "would you have them?"

"I don't know," said the other. "I don't know."

He took the paw, and dangling it between his forefinger and thumb, suddenly threw it upon the fire. White, with a slight cry, stooped down and snatched it off.

"Better let it burn," said the soldier, solemnly.

"If you don't want it, Morris," said the other, "give it to me."

"I won't," said his friend, doggedly. "I threw it on the fire. If you keep it, don't blame me for what happens. Pitch it on the fire again like a sensible man."

The other shook his head and examined his new possession closely. "How do you do it?" he inquired.

"Hold it up in your right hand and wish aloud," said the sergeant-major, "but I warn you of the consequences."

"Sounds like the *Arabian Nights*," said Mrs. White, as she rose and began to set the supper. "Don't you think you might wish for four pairs of hands for me?"

Her husband drew the talisman from his pocket, and then all three burst into laughter as the sergeant-major, with a look of alarm on his face, caught him by the arm.

"If you must wish," he said gruffly, "wish for something sensible."

Mr. White dropped it back in his pocket, and placing chairs, motioned his friend to the table.

In the business of supper the talisman was partly forgotten, and afterward the three sat listening in an enthralled fashion to a second instalment of the soldier's adventures in India.

"If the tale about the monkey's paw is not more truthful than those he has been telling us," said Herbert, as the door closed behind their guest, just in time for him to catch the last train, "we shan't make much out of it."

"Did you give him anything for it, father?" inquired Mrs. White, regarding her husband closely.

"A trifle," said he, colouring slightly. "He didn't want it, but I made him take it. And he pressed me again to throw it away."

"Likely," said Herbert, with pretended horror. "Why, we're going to be rich, and famous and happy. Wish to be an emperor, father, to begin with, then you can't be hen-pecked."

He darted round the table, pursued by the maligned Mrs. White armed with an antimacassar.

Mr. White took the paw from his pocket and eyed it dubiously. "I don't know what to wish for, and that's a fact," he said, slowly. "It seems to me I've got all I want."

"If you only cleared the house, you'd be quite happy, wouldn't you?" said Herbert, with his hand on his shoulder. "Well, wish for two hundred pounds, then; that'll just do it."

His father, smiling shamefacedly at his own credulity, held up the talisman, as his son, with a solemn face, somewhat marred by a wink at his mother, sat down at the piano and struck a few impressive chords.

"I wish for two hundred pounds," said the old man distinctly.

A fine crash from the piano greeted the words, interrupted by a shuddering cry from the old man. His wife and son ran toward him.

"It moved," he cried, with a glance of disgust at the object as it lay on the floor. "As I wished, it twisted in my hand like a snake."

"Well, I don't see the money," said his son as he picked it up and placed it on the table, "and I bet I never shall."

"It must have been your fancy, father," said his wife, regarding him anxiously.

He shook his head. "Never mind, though; there's no harm done, but it gave me a shock all the same."

They sat down by the fire again while the two men finished their pipes. Outside, the wind was higher than ever, and the old man started nervously at the sound of a door banging upstairs. A silence unusual and depressing settled upon all three, which lasted until the old couple rose to retire for the night.

"I expect you'll find the cash tied up in a big bag in the middle of your bed," said Herbert, as he bade them good night, "and something horrible squatting up on top of the wardrobe watching you as you pocket your ill-gotten gains."

He sat alone in the darkness, gazing at the dying fire, and seeing faces in it. The last face was so horrible and so simian that he gazed at it in amazement. It got so vivid that, with a little uneasy laugh, he felt on the table for a glass containing a little water to throw over it. His hand grasped the monkey's paw, and with a little shiver he wiped his hand on his coat and went up to bed.

II

IN THE BRIGHTNESS of the wintry sun next morning as it streamed over the breakfast table he laughed at his fears. There was an air of prosaic wholesomeness about the room which it had lacked on the previous night, and the dirty, shrivelled little paw was pitched on the sideboard with a carelessness which betokened no great belief in its virtues.

"I suppose all old soldiers are the same," said Mrs. White. "The idea of our listening to such nonsense! How could wishes be granted in these days? And if they could, how could two hundred pounds hurt you, father?"

"Might drop on his head from the sky," said the frivolous Herbert.

"Morris said the things happened so naturally," said his father, "that you might if you so wished attribute it to coincidence."

"Well, don't break into the money before I come back," said Herbert as he rose from the table. "I'm afraid it'll turn you into a mean, avaricious man, and we shall have to disown you."

His mother laughed, and following him to the door, watched him down the road; and returning to the breakfast table, was very happy at the expense of her husband's credulity.

All of which did not prevent her from scurrying to the door at the postman's knock, nor prevent her from referring somewhat shortly to retired sergeant-majors of bibulous habits when she found that the post brought a tailor's bill.

"Herbert will have some more of his funny remarks, I expect, when he comes home," she said, as they sat at dinner.

"I dare say," said Mr. White, pouring himself out some beer; "but for all that, the thing moved in my hand; that I'll swear to."

"You thought it did," said the old lady soothingly.

"I say it did," replied the other. "There was no thought about it; I had just—What's the matter?"

His wife made no reply. She was watching the mysterious movements of a man outside, who, peering in an undecided fashion at the house, appeared to be trying to make up his mind to enter. In mental connexion with the two hundred pounds, she noticed that the stranger was well dressed, and wore a silk hat of glossy newness. Three times he paused at the gate, and then walked on again. The fourth time he stood with his hand upon it, and then with sudden resolution flung it open and walked up the path. Mrs. White at the same moment placed her hands behind her, and hurriedly unfastening the strings of her apron, put that useful article of apparel beneath the cushion of her chair.

She brought the stranger, who seemed ill at ease, into the room. He gazed at her furtively, and listened in a preoccupied fashion as the old lady apologized for the appearance of the room, and her husband's coat, a garment which he usually reserved for the garden. She then waited as patiently as her sex would permit, for him to broach his business, but he was at first strangely silent.

"I—was asked to call," he said at last, and stooped and picked a piece of cotton from his trousers. "I come from Maw and Meggins."

The old lady started. "Is anything the matter?" she asked, breathlessly. "Has anything happened to Herbert? What is it? What is it?"

Her husband interposed. "There, there, mother," he said, hastily. "Sit down, and don't jump to conclusions. You've not brought bad news, I'm sure, sir"; and he eyed the other wistfully.

"I'm sorry—" began the visitor.

"Is he hurt?" demanded the mother, wildly.

The visitor bowed in assent. "Badly hurt," he said, quietly, "but he is not in any pain."

"Oh, thank God!" said the old woman, clasping her hands. "Thank God for that! Thank—"

She broke off suddenly as the sinister meaning of the assurance dawned upon her and she saw the awful confirmation of her fears in the other's averted face. She caught her breath, and turning to her slower-witted husband, laid her trembling old hand upon his. There was a long silence.

"He was caught in the machinery," said the visitor at length in a low voice.

"Caught in the machinery," repeated Mr. White, in a dazed fashion, "yes."

He sat staring blankly out at the window, and taking his wife's hand between his own, pressed it as he had been wont to do in their old courting-days nearly forty years before.

"He was the only one left to us," he said, turning gently to the visitor. "It is hard."

The other coughed, and rising, walked slowly to the window. "The firm wished me to convey their sincere sympathy with you in your great loss," he said, without looking round. "I beg that you will understand I am only their servant and merely obeying orders."

There was no reply; the old woman's face was white, her eyes staring, and her breath inaudible; on the husband's face was a look such as his friend the sergeant might have carried into his first action.

"I was to say that Maw and Meggins disclaim all responsibility," continued the other. "They admit no liability at all, but in consideration of your son's services, they wish to present you with a certain sum as compensation."

Mr. White dropped his wife's hand, and rising to his feet, gazed with a look of horror at his visitor. His dry lips shaped the words, "How much?"

"Two hundred pounds," was the answer.

Unconscious of his wife's shriek, the old man smiled faintly, put out his hands like a sightless man, and dropped, a senseless heap, to the floor.

III

IN THE HUGE new cemetery, some two miles distant, the old people buried their dead, and came back to a house steeped in shadow and silence. It was all over so quickly that at first they could hardly realize it, and remained in a state of expectation as though of something else to happen—something else which was to lighten this load, too heavy for old hearts to bear.

But the days passed, and expectation gave place to resignation—the hopeless resignation of the old, sometimes miscalled apathy. Sometimes they hardly exchanged a word, for now they had nothing to talk about, and their days were long to weariness.

It was about a week after that the old man, waking suddenly in the night, stretched out his hand and found himself alone. The room was in darkness, and the sound of subdued weeping came from the window. He raised himself in bed and listened.

"Come back," he said, tenderly. "You will be cold."

"It is colder for my son," said the old woman, and wept afresh.

The sound of her sobs died away on his ears. The bed was warm, and his eyes heavy with sleep.

He dozed fitfully, and then slept until a sudden wild cry from his wife awoke him with a start.

"*The paw!*" she cried wildly. "The monkey's paw!"

He started up in alarm. "Where? Where is it? What's the matter?"

She came stumbling across the room toward him. "I want it," she said, quietly. "You've not destroyed it?"

"It's in the parlour, on the bracket," he replied, marvelling. "Why?"

She cried and laughed together, and bending over, kissed his cheek.

"I only just thought of it," she said, hysterically. "Why didn't I think of it before? Why didn't *you* think of it?"

"Think of what?" he questioned.

"The other two wishes," she replied, rapidly. "We've only had one."

"Was not that enough?" he demanded, fiercely.

"No," she cried triumphantly; "we'll have one more. Go down and get it quickly, and wish our boy alive again."

The man sat up in bed and flung the bedclothes from his quaking limbs.

"Good God, you are mad!" he cried, aghast.

"Get it," she panted; "get it quickly, and wish—Oh, my boy, my boy!"

Her husband struck a match and lit the candle. "Get back to bed," he said, unsteadily. "You don't know what you are saying."

"We had the first wish granted," said the old woman, feverishly; "why not the second?"

"A coincidence," stammered the old man.

"Go and get it and wish," cried his wife, quivering with excitement.

The old man turned and regarded her, and his voice shook. "He has been dead ten days, and besides he—I would not tell you else, but—I could only recognize him by his clothing. If he was too terrible for you to see then, how now?"

"Bring him back?" cried the old woman, and dragged him toward the door. "Do you think I fear the child I have nursed?"

He went down in the darkness, and felt his way to the parlour, and then to the mantelpiece. The talisman was in its place, and a horrible fear that the unspoken wish might bring his mutilated son before him ere he could escape from the room seized upon him, and he caught his breath as he found that he had lost the direction of the door. His brow cold with sweat, he felt his way round the table, and groped along the wall until he found himself in the small passage with the unwholesome thing in his hand.

Even his wife's face seemed changed as he entered the room. It was white and expectant, and to his fears seemed to have an unnatural look upon it. He was afraid of her.

"*Wish!*" she cried, in a strong voice.

"It is foolish and wicked," he faltered.

"*Wish!*" repeated his wife.

He raised his hand. "I wish my son alive again."

The talisman fell to the floor, and he regarded it fearfully. Then he sank trembling into a chair as the old woman, with burning eyes, walked to the window and raised the blind.

He sat until he was chilled with the cold, glancing occasionally at the figure of the old woman peering through the window. The candle-end, which had burned below the rim of the china candlestick, was throwing pulsating shadows on the ceiling and walls, until, with a flicker larger than the rest, it expired. The old man, with an unspeakable sense of relief at the failure of the talisman, crept back to his bed, and in a minute or two afterward the old woman came silently and apathetically beside him.

Neither spoke, but lay silently listening to the ticking of the clock. A stair creaked, and a squeaky mouse scurried noisily through the wall. The darkness was oppressive, and after lying for some time screwing up his courage, he took the box of matches, and striking one, went downstairs for a candle.

At the foot of the stairs the match went out, and he paused to strike another; and at the same moment a knock, so quiet and stealthy as to be scarcely audible, sounded on the front door.

The matches fell from his hand and spilled in the passage. He stood motionless, his breath suspended until the knock was repeated. Then he turned and fled swiftly back to his room, and closed the door behind him. A third knock sounded through the house.

"*What's that?*" cried the old woman, starting up.

"A rat," said the old man in shaking tones—"a rat. It passed me on the stairs."

His wife sat up in bed listening. A loud knock resounded through the house.

"It's Herbert!" she screamed. "It's Herbert!"

She ran to the door, but her husband was before her, and catching her by the arm, held her tightly.

"What are you going to do?" he whispered hoarsely.

"It's my boy; it's Herbert!" she cried, struggling mechanically. "I forgot it was two miles away. What are you holding me for? Let go. I must open the door.

"For God's sake don't let it in," cried the old man, trembling.

"You're afraid of your own son," she cried, struggling. "Let me go. I'm coming, Herbert; I'm coming."

There was another knock, and another. The old woman with a sudden wrench broke free and ran from the room. Her husband followed to the landing, and called after her appealingly as she hurried downstairs. He heard the chain rattle back and the bottom bolt drawn slowly and stiffly from the socket. Then the old woman's voice, strained and panting.

"The bolt," she cried, loudly. "Come down. I can't reach it."

But her husband was on his knees groping wildly on the floor in search of the paw. If he could only find it before the thing outside got in. A perfect fusillade of knocks reverberated through the house, and he heard the scraping of a chair as his wife put it down in the passage against the door. He heard the creaking of the bolt as it came slowly back, and at the same moment he found the monkey's paw, and frantically breathed his third and last wish.

The knocking ceased suddenly, although the echoes of it were still in the house. He heard the chair drawn back, and the door opened. A cold wind rushed up the staircase, and a long loud wail of disappointment and misery from his wife gave him courage to run down to her side, and then to the gate beyond. The street lamp flickering opposite shone on a quiet and deserted road.

M.R. JAMES

1862–1936

He was a scholar, author of Bible commentaries, compiler of learned library catalogues, Provost of Eton, lecturer, and a collector of rare antiquities. He was also a collector of ghost stories—stories of inexplicable happenings which he told with a scholar's typical attention to detail, giving them a disturbing air of incontestable reality.

The Mezzotint

SOME TIME AGO I believe I had the pleasure of telling you the story of an adventure which happened to a friend of mine by the name of Dennistoun, during his pursuit of objects of art for the museum at Cambridge.

He did not publish his experiences very widely upon his return to England; but they could not fail to become known to a good many of his friends, and among others to the gentleman who at that time presided over an art museum at another University. It was to be expected that the story should make a considerable impression on the mind of a man whose vocation lay in lines similar to Dennistoun's, and that he should be eager to catch at any explanation of the matter which tended to make it seem improbable that he should ever be called upon to deal with so agitating an emergency. It was, indeed, somewhat consoling to him to reflect that he was not expected to acquire ancient MSS. for his institution; that was the business of the Shelburnian Library. The authorities of that might, if they pleased, ransack obscure corners of the Continent for such matters. He was glad to be obliged at the moment to confine his attention to enlarging the already unsurpassed collection of English topographical drawings and engravings possessed by his museum. Yet, as it turned out, even a department so homely and familiar as this may have its dark corners, and to one of these Mr. Williams was unexpectedly introduced.

Those who have taken even the most limited interest in the acquisition of topographical pictures are aware that there is one London dealer whose aid is indispensable to their researches. Mr. J. W. Britnell publishes at short intervals very admirable catalogues of a large and constantly changing stock of engravings, plans, and old sketches of mansions, churches, and towns in England and Wales. These catalogues were, of course, the ABC of his subject to Mr. Williams: but as his museum already contained an enormous accumulation of topographical pictures, he was a regular, rather than a copious, buyer; and he rather looked to Mr. Britnell to fill up gaps in the rank and file of his collection than to supply him with rarities.

Now, in February of last year there appeared upon Mr. Williams's desk at the museum a catalogue from Mr. Britnell's emporium, and accompanying it was a typewritten communication from the dealer himself. This latter ran as follows:

DEAR SIR,

We beg to call your attention to No. 978 in our accompanying catalogue, which we shall be glad to send on approval.

Yours faithfully,

J. W. BRITNELL.

To turn to No. 978 in the accompanying catalogue was with Mr. Williams (as he observed to himself) the work of a moment, and in the place indicated he found the following entry:

"978.—*Unknown*. Interesting mezzotint: View of a manor-house, early part of the century. 15 by 10 inches; black frame. £2 2*s*."

It was not specially exciting, and the price seemed high. However, as Mr. Britnell, who knew his business and his customer, seemed to set store by it, Mr. Williams wrote a postcard asking for the article to be sent on approval, along with some other engravings and sketches which appeared in the same catalogue. And so he passed without much excitement of anticipation to the ordinary labours of the day.

A parcel of any kind always arrives a day later than you expect it, and that of Mr. Britnell proved, as I believe the right phrase goes, no exception to the rule. It was delivered at the museum by the afternoon post of Saturday, after Mr. Williams had left his work, and it was accordingly brought round to his rooms in college by the attendant, in order that he might not have to wait over Sunday before looking through it and returning such of the contents as he did not propose to keep. And here he found it when he came in to tea, with a friend.

The only item with which I am concerned was the rather large, black-framed mezzotint of which I have already quoted the short description given in Mr. Britnell's catalogue. Some more details of it will have to be given, though I cannot hope to put before you the look of the picture as clearly as it is present to my own eye. Very nearly the exact duplicate of it may be seen in a good many old inn parlours, or in the passages of undisturbed country mansions at the present moment. It was a rather indifferent mezzotint, and an indifferent mezzotint is, perhaps, the worst form of engraving known. It presented a full-face view of a not very large manor-house of the last century, with three rows of plain sashed windows with rusticated masonry about them, a parapet with balls or vases at the angles, and a small portico in the centre. On either side were trees, and in front a considerable expanse of lawn. The legend 'A.W.F. sculpsit' was engraved on the narrow margin; and there was no further inscription. The whole thing gave the impression that it was the work of an amateur. What in the world Mr. Britnell could mean by affixing the price of £2 2*s.* to such an object was more than Mr. Williams could imagine. He turned it over with a good deal of contempt; upon the back was a paper label, the left-hand half of which had been torn off. All that remained were the ends of two lines of writing: the first had the letters *—ngley Hall*; the second, *—ssex*.

It would, perhaps, be just worth while to identify the place represented, which he could easily do with the help of a gazetteer, and then he would send it back to Mr. Britnell, with some remarks reflecting upon the judgment of that gentleman.

He lighted the candles, for it was now dark, made the tea, and supplied the friend with whom he had been playing golf (for I believe the authorities of the University I write of indulge in that pursuit by way of relaxation); and tea was taken to the accompaniment of a discussion which golfing persons can imagine for themselves, but which the conscientious writer has no right to inflict upon any non-golfing persons.

The conclusion arrived at was that certain strokes might have been better, and that in certain emergencies neither player had experienced that amount of luck which a human being has a right to expect. It was now that the friend—let us call him Professor Binks—took up the framed engraving, and said:

"What's this place, Williams?"

"Just what I am going to try to find out," said Williams, going to the shelf for a gazetteer. "Look at the back. Somethingley Hall, either in Sussex or Essex. Half the name's gone, you see. You don't happen to know it, I suppose?"

"It's from that man Britnell, I suppose, isn't it?" said Binks. "Is it for the museum?"

"Well, I think I should buy it if the price was five shillings," said Williams; "but for some unearthly reason he wants two guineas for it. I can't conceive why. It's a wretched engraving, and there aren't even any figures to give it life."

"It's not worth two guineas, I should think," said Binks; "but I don't think it's so badly done. The moonlight seems rather good to me; and I should have thought there *were* figures, or at least a figure, just on the edge in front."

"Let's look," said Williams. "Well, it's true the light is rather cleverly given. Where's your figure? Oh yes! Just the head, in the very front of the picture."

And indeed there was—hardly more than a black blot on the extreme edge of the engraving—the head of a man or woman, a good deal muffled up, the back turned to the spectator, and looking towards the house. Williams had not noticed it before.

"Still," he said, "though it's a cleverer thing than I thought, I can't spend two guineas of museum money on a picture of a place I don't know."

Professor Binks had his work to do, and soon went; and very nearly up to Hall time Williams was engaged in a vain attempt to identify the subject of his picture. "If the vowel before the *ng* had only been left, it would have been easy enough," he thought; "but as it is, the name may be anything from Guestingley to Langley, and there are many more names ending like this than I thought; and this rotten book has no index of terminations."

Hall in Mr. Williams's college was at seven. It need not be dwelt upon; the less so as he met there colleagues who had been playing golf during the afternoon, and words with which we have no concern were freely bandied across the table—merely golfing words, I would hasten to explain.

I suppose an hour or more to have been spent in what is called common-room after dinner. Later in the evening some few retired to Williams's rooms, and I have little doubt that whist was played and tobacco smoked. During a lull in these operations Williams picked up the mezzotint from the table without looking at it, and handed it to a person mildly interested in art, telling him where it had come from, and the other particulars which we already know.

The gentleman took it carelessly, looked at it, then said, in a tone of some interest:

"It's really a very good piece of work, Williams; it has quite a feeling of the romantic period. The light is admirably managed, it seems to me, and the figure, though it's rather too grotesque, is somehow very impressive."

"Yes, isn't it?" said Williams, who was just then busy giving whisky-and-soda to others of the company, and was unable to come across the room to look at the view again.

It was by this time rather late in the evening, and the visitors were on the move. After they went Williams was obliged to write a letter or two and clear up some odd bits of work. At last, some time past midnight, he was disposed to turn in, and he put out his lamp after lighting his bedroom candle. The picture lay face upwards on the table where the last man who looked at it had put it, and it caught his eye as he turned the lamp down. What he saw made him very nearly drop the candle on the floor, and he declares now that if he had been left in the dark at that moment he would have had a fit. But, as that did not happen, he was able to put down the light on the table and take a good look at the picture. It was indubitable—rankly impossible, no doubt, but absolutely certain. In the middle of the lawn in front of the unknown house there was a figure where no figure had been at five o'clock that afternoon. It was crawling on all-fours towards the house, and it was muffled in a strange black garment with a white cross on the back.

I do not know what is the ideal course to pursue in a situation of this kind. I can only tell you what Mr. Williams did. He took the picture by one corner and carried it across the passage to a second set of rooms which he possessed. There he locked it up in a drawer, sported the doors of both sets of rooms, and retired to bed; but first he wrote out and signed an account of the extraordinary change which the picture had undergone since it had come into his possession.

Sleep visited him rather late; but it was consoling to reflect that the behaviour of the picture did not depend upon his own unsupported testimony. Evidently the man who had looked at it the night before had seen something of the same kind as he had, otherwise he might have been tempted to think that something gravely wrong was happening either to his eyes or his mind. This possibility being fortunately precluded, two matters awaited him on the morrow. He must take stock of the picture very carefully, and call in a witness for the purpose, and he must make a determined effort to ascertain what house it was that was represented. He would therefore ask his neighbour Nisbet to breakfast with him, and he would subsequently spend a morning over the gazetteer.

Nisbet was disengaged, and arrived about 9.30. His host was not quite dressed, I am sorry to say, even at this late hour. During breakfast nothing was said about the mezzotint by Williams, save that he had a picture on which he wished for Nisbet's opinion. But those who are familiar with University life can picture for themselves the wide and delightful range of subjects over which the conversation of two Fellows of Canterbury College is likely to extend during a Sunday morning breakfast. Hardly a topic was left unchallenged, from golf to lawn-tennis. Yet I am bound to say that Williams was rather distraught; for his interest naturally centred in that very strange picture which was now reposing, face downwards, in the drawer in the room opposite.

The morning pipe was at last lighted, and the moment had arrived for which he looked. With very considerable—almost tremulous—excitement, he ran across, unlocked the drawer, and, extracting the picture—still face downwards—ran back, and put it into Nisbet's hands.

"Now," he said, "Nisbet, I want you to tell me exactly what you see in that picture. Describe it, if you don't mind, rather minutely. I'll tell you why afterwards."

"Well," said Nisbet, "I have here a view of a country-house—English, I presume—by moonlight."

"Moonlight? You're sure of that?"

"Certainly. The moon appears to be on the wane, if you wish for details, and there are clouds in the sky."

"All right. Go on. I'll swear," added Williams in an aside, "there was no moon when I saw it first."

"Well, there's not much more to be said," Nisbet continued. "The house has one—two—three rows of windows, five in each row, except at the bottom, where there's a porch instead of the middle one, and——"

"But what about figures?" said Williams, with marked interest.

"There aren't any," said Nisbet; "but——"

"What! No figure on the grass in front?"

"Not a thing."

"You'll swear to that?"

"Certainly I will. But there's just one other thing."

"What?"

"Why, one of the windows on the ground-floor—left of the door—is open."

"Is it really? My goodness! he must have got in," said Williams, with great excitement; and he hurried to the back of the sofa on which Nisbet was sitting, and, catching the picture from him, verified the matter for himself.

It was quite true. There was no figure, and there was the open window. Williams, after a moment of speechless surprise, went to the writing-table and scribbled for a short time. Then he brought two papers to Nisbet, and asked him first to sign one—it was his own description of the picture, which you have just heard—and then to read the other which was Williams's statement written the night before.

"What can it all mean?" said Nisbet.

"Exactly," said Williams. "Well, one thing I must do—or three things, now I think of it. I must find out from Garwood"—this was his last night's visitor—"what he saw, and then I must get the thing photographed before it goes further, and then I must find out what the place is."

"I can do the photographing myself," said Nisbet, "and I will. But, you know, it looks very much as if we were assisting at the working out of a tragedy somewhere. The question is, has it happened already, or is it going to come off? You must find out what the place is. Yes," he said, looking at the picture again, "I expect you're right: he has got in. And if I don't mistake there'll be the devil to pay in one of the rooms upstairs."

"I'll tell you what," said Williams: "I'll take the picture across to old Green" (this was the senior Fellow of the College, who had been Bursar for many years). "It's quite likely he'll know it. We have property in Essex and Sussex, and he must have been over the two counties a lot in his time."

"Quite likely he will," said Nisbet; "but just let me take my photograph first. But look here, I rather think Green isn't up to-day. He wasn't in Hall last night, and I think I heard him say he was going down for the Sunday."

"That's true, too," said Williams; "I know he's gone to Brighton. Well, if you'll photograph it now, I'll go across to Garwood and get his statement, and you keep an eye on it while I'm gone. I'm beginning to think two guineas is not a very exorbitant price for it now."

In a short time he had returned, and brought Mr. Garwood with him. Garwood's statement was to the effect that the figure, when he had seen it, was clear of the edge of the picture, but had not got far across the lawn. He remembered a white mark on the back of its drapery, but could not have been sure it was a cross. A document to this effect was then drawn up and signed, and Nisbet proceeded to photograph the picture. "Now what do you mean to do?" he said. "Are you going to sit and watch it all day?"

"Well, no, I think not," said Williams. "I rather imagine we're meant to see the whole thing. You see, between the time I saw it last night and this morning there was time for lots of things to happen, but the creature only got into the house. It could easily have got through its business in the time and gone to its own place again; but the fact of the window being open, I think, must mean that it's in there now. So I feel quite easy about leaving it. And, besides, I have a kind of idea that it wouldn't change much, if at all, in the daytime. We might go out for a walk this afternoon, and come in to tea, or whenever it gets dark. I shall leave it out on the table here, and sport the door. My skip can get in, but no one else."

The three agreed that this would be a good plan; and, further, that if they spent the afternoon together they would be less likely to talk about the business to other people; for any rumour of such a transaction as was going on would bring the whole of the Phasmatological Society about their ears.

We may give them a respite until five o'clock.

At or near that hour the three were entering Williams's staircase. They were at first slightly annoyed to see that the door of his rooms was unsported; but in a moment it was remembered that on Sunday the skips came for orders an hour or so earlier than on week-days. However, a surprise was awaiting them. The first thing they saw was the picture leaning up against a pile of books on the table, as it had been left, and the next thing was Williams's skip, seated on a chair opposite, gazing at it with undisguised horror. How was this? Mr. Filcher (the name is not my own invention) was a servant of considerable standing, and set the standard of etiquette to all his own college and to several neighbouring ones, and nothing could be more alien to his practice than to be found sitting on his master's chair, or appearing to take any particular notice of his master's furniture or pictures. Indeed, he seemed to feel this himself. He started violently when the three men came into the room, and got up with a marked effort. Then he said:

"I ask your pardon, sir, for taking such a freedom as to set down."

"Not at all, Robert," interposed Mr. Williams. "I was meaning to ask you some time what you thought of that picture."

"Well, sir, of course I don't set up my opinion again yours, but it ain't the pictur I should 'ang where my little girl could see it, sir."

"Wouldn't you, Robert? Why not?"

"No, sir. Why, the pore child, I recollect once she see a Door Bible, with pictures not 'alf what that is, and we 'ad to set up with her three or four nights afterwards, if you'll believe me; and if she was to ketch a sight of this skelinton here, or whatever it is, carrying off the pore baby, she would be in a taking. You know 'ow it is with children; 'ow nervish they git with a little thing and all. But what I should say, it don't seem a right pictur to be laying about, sir, not where anyone that's liable to be startled could come on it. Should you be wanting anything this evening, sir? Thank you, sir."

With these words the excellent man went to continue the round of his masters, and you may be sure the gentlemen whom he left lost no time in gathering round the engraving. There was the house, as before, under the waning moon and the drifting clouds. The window that had been open was shut, and the figure was once more on the lawn: but not this time crawling cautiously on hands and knees. Now it was erect and stepping swiftly, with long strides, towards the front of the picture. The moon was behind it, and the black drapery hung down over its face so that only hints of that could be seen, and what was visible made the spectators profoundly thankful that they could see no more than a white dome-like forehead and a few straggling hairs. The head was bent down, and the arms were tightly clasped over an object which could be dimly seen and identified as a child, whether dead or living it was not possible to say. The legs of the appearance alone could be plainly discerned, and they were horribly thin.

From five to seven the three companions sat and watched the picture by turns. But it never changed. They agreed at last that it would be safe to leave it, and that they would return after Hall and await further developments.

When they assembled again, at the earliest possible moment, the engraving was there, but the figure was gone, and the house was quiet under the moonbeams. There was nothing for it but to spend the evening over gazetteers and guide-books. Williams was the lucky one at last, and perhaps he deserved it. At 11.30 p.m. he read from Murray's *Guide to Essex* the following lines:

"16½ miles, *Anningley*. The church has been an interesting building of Norman date, but was extensively classicized in the last century. It contains the tombs of the family of Francis, whose mansion, Anningley Hall, a solid Queen Anne house, stands immediately beyond the churchyard in a park of about 80 acres. The family is now extinct, the last heir having disappeared mysteriously in infancy in the year 1802. The father, Mr. Arthur Francis, was locally known as a talented amateur engraver in mezzotint. After his son's disappearance he lived in complete retirement at the Hall, and was found dead in his studio on the third anniversary of the disaster, having just completed an engraving of the house, impressions of which are of considerable rarity."

This looked like business, and, indeed, Mr. Green on his return at once identified the house as Anningley Hall.

"Is there any kind of explanation of the figure, Green?" was the question which Williams naturally asked.

"I don't know, I'm sure, Williams. What used to be said in the place when I first knew it, which was before I came up here, was just this: old Francis was always very much down on these poaching fellows, and whenever he got a chance he used to get a man whom he suspected of it turned off the estate, and by degrees he got rid of them all but one. Squires could do a lot of things then that they daren't think of now. Well, this man that was left was what you find pretty often in that country—the last remains of a very old family. I believe they were Lords of the Manor at one time. I recollect just the same thing in my own parish."

"What, like the man in *Tess of the D'Urbervilles?*" Williams put in.

"Yes, I dare say; it's not a book I could ever read myself. But this fellow could show a row of tombs in the church there that belonged to his ancestors, and all that went to sour him a bit; but Francis, they said, could never get at him—he always kept just on the right side of the law—until one night the keepers found him at it in a wood right at the end of the estate. I could show you the place now; it marches with some land that used to belong to an uncle of mine. And you can imagine there was a row; and this man Gawdy (that was the name, to be sure—Gawdy; I thought I should get it—Gawdy), he was unlucky enough, poor chap! to shoot a keeper. Well, that was what Francis wanted, and grand juries—you know what they would have been then—and poor Gawdy was strung up in double-quick time; and I've been shown the place he was buried in, on the north side of the church—you know the way in that part of the world: anyone that's been hanged or made away with themselves, they bury them that side. And the idea was that some friend of Gawdy's—not a relation, because he had none, poor devil! he was the last of his line: kind of *spes ultima gentis*—must have planned to get hold of Francis's boy and put an end to *his* line, too. I don't know—it's rather an out-of-the-way thing for an Essex poacher to think of—but, you know, I should say now it looks more as if old Gawdy had managed the job himself. Booh! I hate to think of it! have some whisky, Williams!"

The facts were communicated by Williams to Dennistoun, and by him to a mixed company, of which I was one, and the Sadducean Professor of Ophiology another. I am sorry to say that the latter, when asked what he thought of it, only remarked: "Oh, those Bridgeford people will say anything"—a sentiment which met with the reception it deserved.

I have only to add that the picture is now in the Ashleian Museum; that it has been treated with a view to discovering whether sympathetic ink has been used in it, but without effect; that Mr. Britnell knew nothing of it save that he was sure it was uncommon; and that, though carefully watched, it has never been known to change again.

JAMES JOYCE

1882–1941

He was one of a large family described by his father as "sixteen or seventeen children". Intimations of the startlingly original talent that was to produce *Ulysses* and *Finnegans Wake* were first discernible in his short stories, in which he portrayed the people of his hometown with wit, sympathy and powerful realism.

The Boarding House

MRS. MOONEY was a butcher's daughter. She was a woman who was quite able to keep things to herself: a determined woman. She had married her father's foreman, and opened a butcher's shop near Spring Gardens. But as soon as his father-in-law was dead Mr. Mooney began to go to the devil. He drank, plundered the till, ran headlong into debt. It was no use making him take the pledge: he was sure to break out again a few days after. By fighting his wife in the presence of customers and by buying bad meat he ruined his business. One night he went for his wife with the cleaver, and she had to sleep in a neighbour's house.

After that they lived apart. She went to the priest and got a separation from him, with care of the children. She would give him neither money nor food nor house-room; and so he was obliged to enlist himself as a sheriff's man.

He was a shabby stooped little drunkard with a white face and a white moustache and white eyebrows, pencilled above his little eyes, which were pink-veined and raw; and all day long he sat in the bailiff's room, waiting to be put on a job. Mrs. Mooney, who had taken what remained of her money out of the butcher business and set up a boarding house in Hardwicke Street, was a big imposing woman. Her house had a floating population made up of tourists from Liverpool and the Isle of Man and, occasionally, *artistes* from the music halls. Its resident population was made up of clerks from the city. She governed the house cunningly and firmly, knew when to give credit, when to be stern and when to let things pass. All the resident young men spoke of her as *The Madam*.

Mrs. Mooney's young men paid fifteen shillings a week for board and lodgings (beer or stout at dinner excluded). They shared in common tastes and occupations and for this reason they were very chummy with one another. They discussed with one another the chances of favourites and outsiders. Jack Mooney, the Madam's son, who was clerk to a commission agent in Fleet Street, had the reputation of being a hard case. He was fond of using soldiers' obscenities: usually he came home in the small hours. When he met his friends he had always a good one to tell them, and he was always sure to be on to a good thing—that is to say, a likely horse or a likely *artiste*. He was also handy with the mits and sang comic songs. On Sunday nights there would often be a reunion in Mrs. Mooney's front drawing-room. The music-hall *artistes* would oblige; and Sheridan played waltzes and polkas and vamped accompaniments. Polly Mooney, the Madam's daughter, would also sing. She sang:

I'm a . . . naughty girl
You needn't sham:
You know I am.

Polly was a slim girl of nineteen; she had light soft hair and a small full mouth. Her eyes, which were grey with a shade of green through them, had a habit of glancing upwards when she spoke with anyone, which made her look like a little perverse madonna. Mrs. Mooney had first sent her daughter to be a typist in a corn-factor's office, but as a disreputable sheriff's man used to come every other day to the office, asking to be allowed to say a word to his daughter, she had taken her daughter home again and set her to do housework. As Polly was very lively, the intention was to give her the run of the young men. Besides, young men like to feel that there is a young woman not very far away. Polly, of course, flirted with the young men, but Mrs. Mooney, who was a shrewd judge, knew that the young men were only passing the time away: none of them meant business. Things went on so for a long time, and Mrs. Mooney began to think of sending Polly back to typewriting, when she noticed that something was going on between Polly and one of the young men. She watched the pair and kept her own counsel.

Polly knew that she was being watched, but still her mother's persistent silence could not be misunderstood. There had been no open complicity between mother and daughter, no open understanding, but though people in the house began to talk of the affair, still Mrs. Mooney did not intervene. Polly began to grow a little strange in her manner, and the young man was evidently perturbed. At last, when she judged it to be the right moment, Mrs. Mooney intervened. She dealt with moral problems as a cleaver deals with meat: and in this case she had made up her mind.

It was a bright Sunday morning of early summer, promising heat, but with a fresh breeze blowing. All the windows of the boarding house were open and the lace curtains ballooned gently towards the street beneath the raised sashes. The belfry of George's Church sent out constant peals, and worshippers, singly or in groups, traversed the little circus before the church, revealing their purpose by their self-contained demeanour no less than by the little volumes in their gloved hands. Breakfast was over in the boarding house, and the table of the breakfast-room was covered with plates on which lay yellow streaks of eggs with morsels of bacon-fat and bacon-rind. Mrs. Mooney sat in the straw arm-chair and watched the servant Mary remove the breakfast things. She made Mary collect the crusts and pieces of broken bread to help to make Tuesday's bread-pudding. When the table was cleared, the broken bread collected, the sugar and butter safe under lock and key, she began to reconstruct the interview which she had had the night before with Polly. Things were as she had suspected: she had been frank in her questions and Polly had been frank in her answers. Both had been somewhat awkward, of course. She had been made awkward by her not wishing to receive the news in too cavalier a fashion or to seem to have connived, and Polly had been made awkward not merely because allusions of that kind always made her awkward, but also because she did not wish it to be thought that in her wise innocence she had divined the intention behind her mother's tolerance.

Mrs. Mooney glanced instinctively at the little gilt clock on the mantelpiece as soon as she had become aware through her reverie that the bells of George's Church had stopped ringing. It was seventeen minutes past eleven: she would have lots of time to have the matter out with Mr. Doran and then catch short twelve at Marlborough Street. She was sure she would win. To begin with, she had all the weight of social opinion on her side: she was an outraged mother. She had allowed him to live beneath her roof, assuming that he was a man of honour, and he had simply abused her hospitality. He was thirty-four or thirty-five years of age, so that youth could not be pleaded as his excuse; nor could ignorance be his excuse, since he was a man who had seen something of the world. He had simply taken advantage of Polly's youth and inexperience: that was evident. The question was: What reparation would he make?

There must be reparation made in such a case. It is all very well for the man: he can go his ways as if nothing had happened, having had his moment of pleasure, but the girl has to bear the brunt. Some mothers would be content to patch up such an affair for a sum of money: she had known cases of it. But she would not do so. For her only one reparation could make up for the loss of her daughter's honour: marriage.

She counted all her cards again before sending Mary up to Mr. Doran's room to say that she wished to speak with him. She felt sure she would win. He was a serious young man, not rakish or loud-voiced like the others. If it had been Mr. Sheridan or Mr. Meade or Bantam Lyons, her task would have been much harder. She did not think he would face publicity. All the lodgers in the house knew something of the affair; details had been invented by some. Besides, he had been employed for thirteen years in a great Catholic wine-merchant's office, and publicity would mean for him, perhaps, the loss of his job. Whereas if he agreed all might be well. She knew he had a good screw for one thing, and she suspected he had a bit of stuff put by.

Nearly the half-hour! She stood up and surveyed herself in the pier-glass. The decisive expression of her great florid face satisfied her, and she thought of some mothers she knew who could not get their daughters off their hands.

Mr. Doran was very anxious indeed this Sunday morning. He had made two attempts to shave, but his hand had been so unsteady that he had been obliged to desist. Three days' reddish beard fringed his jaws, and every two or three minutes a mist gathered on his glasses so that he had to take them off and polish them with his pocket-handkerchief. The recollection of his confession of the night before was a cause of acute pain to him; the priest had drawn out every ridiculous detail of the affair, and in the end had so magnified his sin that he was almost thankful at being afforded a loophole of reparation. The harm was done. What could he do now but marry her or run away? He could not brazen it out. The affair would be sure to be talked of, and his employer would be certain to hear of it. Dublin is such a small city: everyone knows everyone else's business. He felt his heart leap warmly in his throat as he heard in his excited imagination old Mr. Leonard calling out in his rasping voice: "Send Mr. Doran here, please."

All his long years of service gone for nothing! All his industry and diligence thrown away! As a young man he had sown his wild oats, of course; he had boasted of his free-thinking and denied the existence of God to his companions in public-houses. But that was all passed and done with . . . nearly. He still bought a copy of *Reynolds Newspaper* every week, but he attended to his religious duties, and for nine-tenths of the year lived a regular life. He had money enough to settle down on; it was not that. But the family would look down on her. First of all there was her disreputable father, and then her mother's boarding house was beginning to get a certain fame. He had a notion that he was being had. He could imagine his friends talking of the affair and laughing. She *was* a little vulgar; sometimes she said "I seen" and "If I had've known". But what would grammar matter if he really loved her? He could not make up his mind whether to like her or despise her for what she had done. Of course he had done it too. His instinct urged him to remain free, not to marry. Once you are married you are done for, it said.

While he was sitting helplessly on the side of the bed in shirt and trousers, she tapped lightly at his door and entered. She told him all, that she had made a clean breast of it to her mother and that her mother would speak with him that morning. She cried and threw her arms round his neck, saying:

"O Bob! Bob! What am I to do? What am I to do at all?"

She would put an end to herself, she said.

He comforted her feebly, telling her not to cry, that it would be all right, never fear. He felt against his shirt the agitation of her bosom.

It was not altogether his fault that it had happened. He remembered well, with the curious patient memory of the celibate, the first casual caresses her dress, her breath, her fingers had given him. Then late one night as he was undressing for bed she had tapped at his door, timidly. She wanted to relight her candle at his, for hers had been blown out by a gust. It was her bath night. She wore a loose open combing-jacket of printed flannel. Her white instep shone in the opening of her furry slippers and the blood glowed warmly behind her perfumed skin. From her hands and wrists too as she lit and steadied her candle a faint perfume arose.

On nights when he came in very late it was she who warmed up his dinner. He scarcely knew what he was eating, feeling her beside him alone, at night, in the sleeping house. And her thoughtfulness! If the night was anyway cold or wet or windy there was sure to be a little tumbler of punch ready for him. Perhaps they could be happy together . . .

They used to go upstairs together on tiptoe, each with a candle, and on the third landing exchange reluctant good nights. They used to kiss. He remembered well her eyes, the touch of her hand and his delirium . . .

But delirium passes. He echoed her phrase, applying it to himself: "*What am I to do?*" The instinct of the celibate warned him to hold back. But the sin was there; even his sense of honour told him that reparation must be made for such a sin.

While he was sitting with her on the side of the bed Mary came to the door and said that the missus wanted to see him in the parlour. He stood up to put on his coat and waistcoat, more helpless than ever. When he was dressed he went over to her to comfort her. It would be all right, never fear. He left her crying on the bed and moaning softly: *"O my God!"*

Going down the stairs his glasses became so dimmed with moisture that he had to take them off and polish them. He longed to ascend through the roof and fly away to another country where he would never hear again of his trouble, and yet a force pushed him downstairs step by step. The implacable faces of his employer and of the Madam stared upon his discomfiture. On the last flight of stairs he passed Jack Mooney, who was coming up from the pantry nursing two bottles of *Bass*. They saluted coldly; and the lover's eyes rested for a second or two on a thick bulldog face and a pair of thick short arms. When he reached the foot of the staircase he glanced up and saw Jack regarding him from the door of the return-room.

Suddenly he remembered the night when one of the music-hall *artistes*, a little blond Londoner, had made a rather free allusion to Polly. The reunion had been almost broken up on account of Jack's violence. Everyone tried to quiet him. The music-hall *artiste*, a little paler than usual, kept smiling and saying that there was no harm meant; but Jack kept shouting at him that if any fellow tried that sort of a game on with his sister he'd bloody well put his teeth down his throat: so he would.

POLLY SAT FOR a little time on the side of the bed, crying. Then she dried her eyes and went over to the looking-glass. She dipped the end of the towel in the water-jug and refreshed her eyes with the cool water. She looked at herself in profile and readjusted a hairpin above her ear. Then she went back to the bed again and sat at the foot. She regarded the pillows for a long time, and the sight of them awakened in her mind secret, amiable memories. She rested the nape of her neck against the cool iron bedrail and fell into a reverie. There was no longer any perturbation visible on her face.

She waited on patiently, almost cheerfully, without alarm, her memories gradually giving place to hopes and visions of the future. Her hopes and visions were so intricate that she no longer saw the white pillows on which her gaze was fixed, or remembered that she was waiting for anything.

At last she heard her mother calling. She started to her feet and ran to the banisters.

"Polly! Polly!"

"Yes, mamma?"

"Come down, dear. Mr. Doran wants to speak to you."

Then she remembered what she had been waiting for.

FRANCIS KING

b. 1923

He was educated in England but most of his adult life has been spent abroad. As a penetrating observer and chronicler, he has been likened to Somerset Maugham. Undoubtedly his best work captures the predicament of people on foreign ground: whether that ground be actually abroad or merely in a situation foreign to their previous experience.

The Love Game

HE WAS WEARING gym-shoes, dyed orange from the tennis court, with an ungainly knot where one of the laces had snapped. The hair, thick on his bare muscular legs and arms, was almost exactly the same colour as the shoes. He had unbuttoned his shirt and the same hair, moist with sweat—he had been sitting for a long time in the sun in that corner of the garden—covered his chest like a pelt. The khaki shorts were rucked up tight over the bulging crotch; they were stained with oil from the car, at which he had been tinkering earlier that Sunday. He was squinting down at one of the colour supplements, his lower lip drawn in under teeth that were so large, white and regular that when Anna had first met him, she a nurse and he a medical student, she had asked him, jokingly, if they were false. His nose had been broken, not in a rugger-match as everyone assumed, but in a bicycle accident as a schoolboy.

A year ago, seeing him sit out in the sun in that physically arrogant posture, legs thrust out before him, she would probably have gone over to him to run a hand through his thinning hair, down his cheek and on to his chest.

But now she merely said, standing several yards away: "Oughtn't you to change?"

"Change? Why?" Bill spoke in a husky voice that always suggested he was recovering from a cold.

"Twenty to one. He'll be here at any moment."

"So what?"

"You can't greet him like that. In those filthy shorts and gym-shoes."

"I don't see why not. This is Sunday, after all."

"He's sure to be in a suit."

"I've no doubt. But I'm certainly not going to get into one, not on your nelly."

She frowned, as she tugged a dead head off one of the rose-bushes beside her and then gave an "Ow!" as a thorn ripped the ball of her thumb.

"Now what have you done?"

"Scratched myself on this bloody rose."

He threw down the newspaper and got to his feet. "Let's see."

"There's nothing *to* see."

She sucked the thumb, looking fragile and childish in her blue gingham frock, with her long, straight blond hair tied at the nape of her neck with a length of darker blue ribbon.

"It's a bore, his coming."

"He kept saying how much he wanted to see the house. And he might be useful to you."

"I doubt it. He's not exactly generous to his subordinates. Leaves us to get on with most of his N.H.S. work but no, not exactly generous. Well, it stands to reason." He flung himself back into the canvas chair. "No one cares to hear the sound of the younger generation knocking at the door."

"He hasn't much to fear. Not yet."

"My dear girl, he's slipping. Everyone knows that. Slowly slipping. Ever since his wife died and he had the coronary and his boy got into trouble." He enumerated these misfortunes with quiet malice. "If he was wise, he'd retire. He must have salted away a fortune."

"Retire!" Anna had now thrown herself on to a blanket on the grass beside him, from time to time still sucking at the thumb although it had long since ceased to bleed. "Why on earth should he retire? He's got years and years ahead of him?"

"Years and years?"

"Well, at least ten years. He's only sixty-two."

"I suppose he wants to hang on until he gets a knighthood. Some hope."

"It's on the cards."

"Well, I daresay all these foreign jaunts of his might bear some fruit." He raised a hand and scratched lazily under an armpit. "Corneal transplants. Cataracts. Not all that impressive over here these days. But in the African bush . . ."

"He's late."

Bill looked at his watch. "Perhaps he's lost the way. Or forgotten."

Anna laughed. "You'd like him to forget."

"Well, it *would* be a more peaceful Sunday without him. Wouldn't it? Not that I've really got anything against him. We hit it off all right. Being patronized never really worries me." He began to move his left shoulder up and down, frowning as he did so.

"What's the matter? Shoulder painful?"

"Hm. Must have pulled it when I tried to swallow-dive." Now he was massaging the shoulder with one of the hands that often seemed to apprehensive patients to be too large and clumsy for a surgeon. "Has he brought up the Ethiopian jaunt again?"

"Not since last week. He told me to think about it."

"Well, you're bloody well not going."

"It's a change," Anna said coolly. "What other chance would I ever get to visit Ethiopia?"

"There are lots of theatre sisters from whom he can choose. Why doesn't he take that Connors bag? She's as tough as any man."

"He loathes her."

"And how the hell am I supposed to make out while you're gadding around?"

"Only five weeks. And mother says that she'll come and look after you. You were away for almost as long on your rugby tour . . . Well, let's think about it."

She got to her feet and walked slowly behind his chair. Leaning over him, she put her cheek against his, feeling its moisture and its roughness. The smell of healthy sweat, which once used to fill her with excitement when he returned from the cricket field or rugby field, now repelled her. Why did he always have to sweat so much? It was not as though he had been *doing* anything, just sitting in the sun.

"When you're a famous consultant, then *you* can take me as one of your team."

"That'll be the day."

She knew that he knew that he would never now become a famous consultant; and that knowledge, though it had lain secret and unspoken between them for many months, suddenly pierced her with desolation. She caught him tightly against her: "You'll make it," she said. "Of course you'll make it. Think of all the people who *do* make it."

Beyond the rose-bushes and the straggling hedge of privet they heard the engine of a car.

"That must be his lordship's Bentley."

"I WISH TO GOD that he'd drop that bedside manner with us."

Lunch was over and Maurice was in the hall, enquiring over the telephone about one of his private patients, the wife of a Cabinet Minister, whose cataract he had removed the day before.

"You wouldn't catch him ringing up the hospital about a simple cataract patient in a public ward."

"He has the reputation of being very good with his N.H.S. people. Always addresses them by their names for one thing."

"That's just a trick. It *means* nothing. How naïve can you be!"

Anna frowned as she poured out the coffee. She had forgotten to buy any beans and wondered if Maurice would guess that she had had to resort to Nescafé.

The lunch had gone off well; or was it simply that the 'bedside manner' of which Bill complained had persuaded her it had? Their guest had been enthusiastic about the *lasagne*—"I've seldom eaten better in Italy"—and had had a large second helping of the *coq au vin* even though he confessed that he had recently resolved "to get rid of this awful paunch." Of the paunch Anna could see no sign. Erect and slim, he was so far from being overweight that he had that slightly wrinkled, dried-out appearance of the middle-aged when they become too stringent about their diet. He had talked amusingly but without malice, telling stories of famous colleagues or famous patients, or of his experiences in the Western Desert during the war.

More than once Bill had either said something that Anna knew to be deliberately snide, or had used a tone of faintly insolent self-depreciation when referring to himself, to Anna or to anything that concerned them. When, for example, Maurice had talked of a motoring holiday he was planning in Turkey, Bill had said: "That's a very *in* kind of trip. I'm afraid that we members of the Hoi Polloi are going to have to content ourselves with a package deal to Malta." Later, when Maurice had spoken in flattering terms about a new assistant matron, Bill had countered: "Well, of course, she puts herself out for a celebrity like yourself. But I can assure you she's much less accommodating with the rank and file. No, she certainly wouldn't do anything more than the minimum required of her for yours truly." Maurice was a subtle and perceptive man and the feelings of envy and animosity behind such comments could not have escaped him; but evidently he had decided to ignore them. It was almost as though, Anna thought, he was trying to *woo* Bill, now adroitly praising him by implication, now asking for his advice and now sympathizing with him for the lack of promotion that should have long since come his way.

Maurice returned. "Well, she seems all right. Complaining about the food but otherwise all right. I restrained myself from telling Robinson to pass on to her all the details of the splendid meal we'd just eaten. That would have been needlessly cruel. Thank you, my dear."

As he took the coffee-cup from her, she marvelled, as she had often marvelled, at the beauty of his hands. They were waxen in their whiteness and malleability and the nails must have been meticulously buffed to give them that pinkish glow. "Would you mind if I took off my jacket?"

"Of course not. With Bill in those filthy shorts, we could hardly object."

"I'm sure that Maurice would agree that these days it's not at all the thing to be *endimanché*. Suits for Sunday went out with church-going."

Maurice smiled as he removed his lavender-grey jacket and then adjusted his cuffs, fingering the heavy gold cuff-links as though to assure himself they were still there. He said nothing.

"Have you had any successes at the sales recently?" Anna asked. More than once they had run into each other at local auctions.

"Well, let me see . . . Yes . . ."

He began to tell her about the acquisition of a small Bonington drawing, unidentified in the catalogue, at a country house near Lewes, while Bill sank deeper and deeper into his chair and thrust his bare legs farther and farther out into the centre of the drawing-room. Anna was afraid that he was about to fall asleep.

"Collecting has become my chief recreation. That and music."

"Bill used to play the drums in a jazz-group when he was a student. Did you know that?"

"Hardly Maurice's kind of music, darling. In fact, I doubt if he'd regard it as music at all." Bill followed this comment with an enormous yawn, rubbing his hands up and down his cheeks.

"On the contrary. I'm a great jazz enthusiast. When you visit me—as I hope you will soon—I'll show you my collection."

Bill straightened himself in the chair, frowning down at his grubby plimsolls: "Is it true that you do this wonderful needlework?"

"I don't know about its being *wonderful*. Yes, I find it soothing to the nerves."

"I shouldn't have thought *your* nerves needed much soothing."

"You'd be surprised. Yes, I first took it up when I was convalescing in the war. Everyone thought it rather a joke—as I expect they do now. My wife's idea. Still, it was better than sitting round doing nothing, like a lot of my fellow patients."

"I'd like to see some of it," Anna said.

"If you're a very good girl and do your stuff properly in Ethiopia I might honour you with a gift." He smiled again: "That's a threat, not a promise."

Bill was about to say something, then checked himself. Instead he asked: "Would you like to take a look at the garden?" This was a ploy he often used to get rid of a guest who had overstayed his welcome.

"Why not?"

Bill and Anna tended the garden between them, with some help from the old man, a retired railwayman, who lived in a cottage at the end of their lane. The previous owner of the house had laid out and planted the flower-beds; Bill and Anna merely weeded them. The old man cut the grass.

"Ah—that must be a Vivien Leigh over there. I know it's vulgar to have a taste for hybrids—my wife wouldn't hear of them—but I must say I love that kind of bloom. Now what would that be?" He raised a rose between forefinger and middle-finger, stooping to inspect it. Neither Anna nor Bill had any idea. "No scent, unfortunately. But a marvellous shade of red." It was evidently going to be a long tour and Anna knew that Bill must already be wishing that he had never proposed it.

"Good heavens! You have a tennis court. Several tennis courts."

"Not ours, I'm afraid. They belong to the College—you know, the College of Education," Anna explained. "But they let us use them. They feel they have to, because we allowed them to cut down some of the trees that grew along that fence."

"They blocked the light," Bill took up. "Do you play tennis?"

"I used to play. It's the only game at which I've ever been any use. In fact—I once played at Wimbledon."

"Really?"

"Don't sound so astonished, young lady. Of course it was a long, long time ago. When there was much more finesse and far less power to the game. Yes, I took a set off Bunny Austin. But you're far too young even to know who Bunny Austin was. Both of you play?"

"Bill won't play with me. He says I'm too awful. Bill's rather good. As you might expect."

"Oh, darling, it's never really been my game. You know that."

"You beat the captain of the college tennis team."

"Yes, that was rather funny."

Bill began to describe how, watching two people from the college playing a game on the other side of the fence, he had not been able to resist calling out to one of them to tell him that he was repeatedly slicing the ball too high on his backhand. "Perhaps you'd like a game?" the young man had replied sarcastically. "Since you seem to know so much." "Right," said Bill, who ever since his schooldays had made a practice of issuing and taking up such challenges. "Why not? Ten shillings to the winner."

"Of course you won," said Maurice at the end of the story.
"Of course," said Anna.
Suddenly Bill turned to Maurice: "How about a game?" he said.
"A game?"
"Yes."
"Now?"
"Why not?"
"Maurice is hardly dressed for a game of tennis," Anna put in.
"I can lend him some togs."
"You're not exactly the same build."
"With shorts and an open-necked shirt that doesn't really matter," Bill persisted. He turned again to Maurice: "How about it?"
Calmly the older man deliberated, his hands deep in the pockets of his jacket as he surveyed the garden from one end to another. "Only one set," he said at last. "But I don't think I'll be able to put up much of a show after that huge meal."
"What shall we have on the game? Ten shillings? A pound? A fiver?"
"Whatever you say."
"Then let's make it a fiver. We might as well play for high stakes—or at least what paupers like ourselves consider to be high stakes. Done?"
"Done."
Anna was worried. As they returned to the house, Bill striding purposefully ahead of them, she ventured to Maurice:
"Is it really wise?"
"Is what really wise?"
"Well, playing Bill."
"Why not?"
"After your coronary, I mean."
He laughed. "Bill has obviously not been keeping you abreast with the latest pronouncements in that field. Exercise is essential—or so the experts all now tell me. No, I never think about my heart now. I play a round of golf most weeks, I even dig in the garden. And I'm a great walker."
While the two men were changing upstairs, Anna began to clear first the drawing-room and then the dining-room, the sweat beginning to bead her upper lip and her forehead from the exertion of carrying trays back and forth from room to room.
"Not too bad a fit!" Maurice appeared, with Bill behind him. "A bit baggy in the seat. But the shoes are exactly my size. Couldn't be better. They might be my own."
Your own certainly wouldn't be so dirty, Anna thought. The unwashed white shorts no doubt still had clinging to them that animal odour that exuded from Bill even an hour or two after he had had a bath

or shower; she wondered how Maurice, who smelled of nothing but expensive toilet soap, could bear to wear them.

Bill's eagerness now at the prospect of the match contrasted startlingly with the air of increasing boredom that had enveloped him after the lunch.

He made a number of practice shots as the three of them strolled through the garden and then lashed out at the long grass on the bank up which they had to climb in order to reach the courts.

"I hope that racket will be all right for you?" Anna said. She had noticed that Bill had, typically, appropriated the better of the two.

"Oh, yes. Fine. I'm not fussy about these things." He smiled at her, his pale grey eyes resting on her face. "It's not often one sees women with parasols these days."

"That's because of these awful freckles of mine."

"They're not awful. They're rather fetching."

No one else was playing on the courts; usually the students came out later on Sunday afternoons, when they had digested their mid-morning drinks and two o'clock lunches. Anna seated herself on a bench, careful to avoid the places where it was spattered with bird-droppings.

"Shall we have a knock-up first?"

"Fine."

Bill's body contorted itself into a knot and then unwound to propel the ball into the net with a loud thud.

"My goodness! What a service! I'd no idea what I was letting myself in for."

It was impossible to tell if Maurice were being ironic or not. As he spoke, he was adjusting the straps on either side of the baggy, stained shorts.

Even during the knock-up Bill played with the teeth-gritting, frowning ferocity that he brought to every game, however trivial its outcome. Maurice moved lazily about the court, his returns gentle and his concentration such that from time to time he would address some remark to Anna, usually with no relevance to the game in hand or even to tennis. Bill hated people not to take a game as seriously as himself—once he had refused to continue a rubber of friendly bridge when Anna had confessed that she had made a preposterous bid "just for the hell of it"—and Anna therefore guessed that Maurice's nonchalance must already be riling him.

"Shall we begin?"

"Whenever you like," Maurice called back. He looked over to Anna: "You must remind me to tell you about the new Osborne play. I went over to Brighton last night to catch it."

Bill won the first three games without any trouble. His play was forceful but ugly, with a number of smashes that landed in the net, but a number more that Maurice evidently regarded as irretrievable, since he made no move to retrieve them. For much of the time, Bill's face had on it that curious grimace, as of someone in acute pain, that Anna had long since got used to seeing whenever he was making a physical effort. Curiously, exactly the same expression appeared at the climax of their love-making. But she also noticed that, as he stooped to pick up a ball, he would often give a fleeting, private smile to himself. Already his shirt was sticking to his muscular back and there were dark patches under each arm-pit.

From time to time Maurice would call out "Good shot!" or "Well played!" but to such praise Bill made neither response nor reciprocation.

It was only during the fourth game that Anna realised that Maurice was not going to be trounced as she had at first supposed. He ran little and for that reason many of Bill's returns were winners, when with a more energetic opponent they would not have been. But his anticipation was adroit—even before Bill's racket had met the ball, Maurice seemed already to be ambling gently in the direction of where it would land—and no less adroit was his mixing of lobs and shots so sharply angled that Bill was always either racing back to the base-line or careering from one side of the court to the other.

Once, such was the fury with which he propelled himself in pursuit of the ball that he crashed into the wire netting that divided the courts from the garden. "Hurt yourself?" Maurice enquired, again fiddling with a strap at the side of his shorts.

"Hell, no," said Bill, who had in fact grazed a hand.

The score crept up in Maurice's favour, even though he would still often throw away a point by leaving a ball that with a minimum of running he could certainly have saved. Game after game went to him, until the score was three-all. Then the older man was in the lead and the score was four-three. Anna who, until that moment, had wanted Maurice to win, suddenly felt a pang of pity for Bill. To Maurice to win or lose was a matter of indifference, she was certain; but to Bill to lose any game was to lose yet another trick in the game of life. Often, after he had played on the losing side in a rugby match, he would sit brooding in front of the television set, refusing to eat, much less to go out that evening. As he now hurtled about the court, she could guess at his increasing fury and desperation.

In the next game, after the advantage had gone to Maurice, the older man managed to put the ball away neatly into the corner of the court farthest from Bill.

"Out!" his opponent called at once.

Anna, who was seated only a yard or two away, was certain that the ball had been in; and she was no less certain that Bill knew that it had been in.

"Out?" Maurice queried mildly.

"By about two inches. Wasn't it, Anna?"

"I don't know. I was dreaming, I'm afraid."

"Deuce," Maurice said.

Bill managed to win that game. His face was shiny and flushed, his close-cropped hair was glued to his forehead and from time to time he had to pull away the shirt that was now sticking to his torso as though it were tailored from plastic.

Maurice, whose service it was, took the lead in the next game. When he stooped to pick up a ball near Anna, she noticed that he had gone white round the mouth and nose; but otherwise he looked as unruffled as when he had first walked out on to the court.

"Out, I think," Bill said at forty-thirty against him.

"Was it? I couldn't see too well. Deuce then."

Again, Anna knew that Bill had cheated.

With a skilfully sliced service and then with a lob to the base-line after the briefest of rallies, Maurice won the next two points. Five-four.

It was in that last game that a sudden change came over Maurice. It was as though he were saying to Bill: "So far I've been toying with you, this is how one really plays" and the demonstration filled Anna with a surging conflict of emotions: admiration for the way in which this man, thirty years older than her husband and the survivor of a coronary attack that by all accounts had all but killed him, raced about the court, putting home one shot after another with devastating accuracy; bewilderment as to why he should have kept this mastery in reserve until this moment; and pity for her husband, who was now like a bull, enraged and groggy, at the moment when the toreador is finally positioning him for the kill. Point succeeded point, culminating in a gloriously angled half-volley, which Bill just failed to reach with a choked cry of "Damn!"

His chest heaving and a hand pushing his hair away from his eyes, Bill ran to the net.

"Terrific," he said. "A love game. The fiver's yours."

Years of training in 'sportsmanship' at public school and university made his expressions of pleasure in his opponent's victory sound almost authentic; but Anna knew what must, underneath, be the bitterness of his humiliation.

"That was a good game. But you must forget all about the fiver."

"Good God, no. If I'd won, I'd certainly not have forgotten about it."

"We must have a return match some time. When you come over to my place. I'm afraid that in singles a set is about as much as I can manage. I do better at doubles." He drew a handkerchief, with his monogram on it, out of the shorts and dabbed first at his forehead and then at his cheek. "Yes, I enjoyed that," he said. Then, turning to Anna: "I hope you weren't too bored, young lady?"

"On the contrary. It was tremendously exciting."

Bill had gone ahead of them, first slashing again at the long grass, and then, when he had entered the garden, hitting his racket hard against one thigh.

"Bill's quite some opponent."

"Your game's in a totally different class."

"Oh, I've played for so many years that I've picked up some tricks. That's all." He held the gate open for her, smiling gently as she went through. "I'll tell you what's the secret when you reach my age. Throw away the unimportant points, don't worry about them. But when a vital point is at stake, then do everything you can to win it."

"It's as simple as that?"

"Yes, as simple as that."

"I DON'T KNOW what's the matter with my knee. It seems to be stiffening." The two men had changed and had baths; Maurice was back in his silk shirt and lavender-grey suit, but Bill was wearing slippers and a dressing-gown over vests and pants. Anna had prepared them each a Pimm's.

"I have this cartilage trouble," he explained. "They don't seem able to make up their minds as to whether I should have an operation or not. I want to avoid it if possible."

Anna had noticed—as she was sure that Bill, who lacked self-knowledge, had never noticed—that this cartilage trouble, like his stiff shoulder, always seemed to afflict him after some game that had been not won but lost.

"You're really a tremendous all-round athlete, aren't you?" Maurice said.

Bill shrugged. "Well, I play a lot of games, if that's what you mean."

"Didn't you get a blue for rugger?"

"For rugger *and* cricket. And a half-blue for fives. But never, I regret to say, a blue for tennis."

They chattered on desultorily until Maurice looked at his watch and said that it was time that he was going.

"No, don't bother to come out to the car with me, not with that leg of yours. Please!"

Bill had got to his feet and had made his way, with an exaggerated limp, to the front-door. "I think I'll put an elastic bandage on it. That sometimes helps."

"I'll walk with you to the car," Anna said.

Anna and Maurice crossed the lawn in silence. Then, at the gate, Maurice turned to her: "Well, this has been a most enjoyable visit. Most enjoyable. And the game of tennis was great fun. I only hope Bill's knee will be all right."

"Oh, yes. It often plays him up. But never for very long."

"It's marvellous, the way he *hurls* himself into every activity. I envy him that. I wish I had his energy."

"So do I. Heavens! He's forgotten to pay you the fiver."

"Oh, that doesn't matter."

"But of course it does. I'll go and fetch it."

"You'll do nothing of the kind. Bill can buy me a drink some time instead. You can remind him." He climbed into the Bentley, started the engine and then lowered the power-operated window between them.

"Thought any more about the Ethiopian jaunt?"

She nodded.

"And what have you decided?"

"Oh, I'm coming, of course."

She said it as though the decision, reached on an impulse while the glass had whirred slowly down between them, was something that had been established irrevocably from the first moment they had met.

RUDYARD KIPLING

1865–1936

Ten years before his death, the Kipling Society was formed "to do honour to, and to extend the influence of, the most patriotic, virile, and imaginative of writers, who upholds the ideals of the English speaking world". Today, with many of those ideals outdated, his best works—especially his animal stories—retain a unique, timeless charm.

The Maltese Cat

THEY HAD GOOD reason to be proud, and better reason to be afraid, all twelve of them; for, though they had fought their way, game by game, up the teams entered for the polo tournament, they were meeting the Archangels that afternoon in the final match; and the Archangels' men were playing with half-a-dozen ponies apiece. As the game was divided into six quarters of eight minutes each, that meant a fresh pony after every halt. The Skidars' team, even supposing there were no accidents, could only supply one pony for every other change; and two to one is heavy odds. Again, as Shiraz, the grey Syrian, pointed out, they were meeting the pink and pick of the polo ponies of Upper India; ponies that had cost from a thousand rupees each, while they themselves were a cheap lot gathered, often from country carts, by their masters who belonged to a poor but honest native infantry regiment.

"Money means pace and weight," said Shiraz, rubbing his black silk nose dolefully along his neat-fitting boot, "and by the maxims of the game as I know it——"

"Ah, but we aren't playing the maxims," said the Maltese Cat. "We're playing the game, and we've the great advantage of knowing the game. Just think a stride, Shiraz. We've pulled up from bottom to second place in two weeks against all those fellows on the ground here;

and that's because we play with our heads as well as with our feet."

"It makes me feel undersized and unhappy all the same," said Kittiwynk, a mouse-coloured mare with a red browband and the cleanest pair of legs that ever an aged pony owned. "They've twice our size, these others."

Kittiwynk looked at the gathering and sighed. The hard, dusty Umballa polo-ground was lined with thousands of soldiers, black and white, not counting hundreds and hundreds of carriages, and drags, and dog-carts, and ladies with brilliant-coloured parasols, and officers in uniform and out of it, and crowds of natives behind them; and orderlies on camels who had halted to watch the game, instead of carrying letters up and down the station, and native horse-dealers running about on thin-eared Biluchi mares, looking for a chance to sell a few first-class polo ponies. Then there were the ponies of thirty teams that had entered for the Upper India Free-for-All Cup—nearly every pony of worth and dignity from Mhow to Peshawar, from Allahabad to Multan; prize ponies, Arabs, Syrian, Barb, country bred, Deccanee, Waziri, and Kabul ponies of every colour and shape and temper that you could imagine. Some of them were in mat-roofed stables close to the polo-ground, but most were under saddle while their masters, who had been defeated in the earlier games, trotted in and out and told each other exactly how the game should be played.

It was a glorious sight, and the come-and-go of the little quick hoofs, and the incessant salutations of ponies that had met before on other polo-grounds or racecourses, were enough to drive a four-footed thing wild.

But the Skidars' team were careful not to know their neighbours, though half the ponies on the ground were anxious to scrape acquaintance with the little fellows that had come from the North, and, so far, had swept the board. "Let's see," said a soft, golden-coloured Arab, who had been playing very badly the day before, to the Maltese Cat, "didn't we meet in Abdul Rahman's stable in Bombay four seasons ago? I won the Paikpattan Cup next season, you may remember."

"Not me," said the Maltese Cat politely. "I was at Malta then, pulling a vegetable cart. I don't race. I play the game."

"O-oh!" said the Arab, cocking his tail and swaggering off.

"Keep yourselves to yourselves," said the Maltese Cat to his companions. "We don't want to rub noses with all those goose-rumped half-breeds of Upper India. When we've won this cup they'll give their shoes to know us."

"*We* shan't win the cup," said Shiraz. "How do you feel?"

"Stale as last night's feed when a musk-rat has run over it," said Polaris, a rather heavy-shouldered grey, and the rest of the team agreed with him.

"The sooner you forget that the better," said the Maltese Cat cheerfully. "They've finished tiffin in the big tent. We shall be wanted now. If your saddles are not comfy, kick. If your bits aren't easy, rear, and let the *saises* know whether your boots are tight."

Each pony had his *sais*, his groom, who lived and ate and slept with the pony, and had betted a great deal more than he could afford on the result of the game. There was no chance of anything going wrong, and, to make sure, each *sais* was shampooing the legs of his pony to the last minute. Behind the *saises* sat as many of the Skidars' regiment as had leave to attend the match—about half the native officers, and a hundred or two dark, black-bearded men with the regimental pipers nervously fingering the big beribboned bagpipes. The Skidars were what they call a Pioneer regiment; and the bagpipes made the national music of half the men. The native officers held bundles of polo-sticks, long cane-handled mallets, and as the grand-stand filled after lunch they arranged themselves by ones and twos at different points round the ground, so that if a stick were broken the player would not have far to ride for a new one. An impatient British cavalry band struck up 'If you want to know the time, ask a p'leeceman!' and the two umpires in light dust-coats danced out on two little excited ponies. The four players of the Archangels' team followed, and the sight of their beautiful mounts made Shiraz groan again.

"Wait till we know," said the Maltese Cat. "Two of 'em are playing in blinkers, and that means they can't see to get out of the way of their own side, or they *may* shy at the umpires' ponies. They've *all* got white web reins that are sure to stretch or slip!"

"And," said Kittiwynk, dancing to take the stiffness out of her, "they carry their whips in their hands instead of on their wrists. Hah!"

"True enough. No man can manage his stick and his reins, and his whip that way," said the Maltese Cat. "I've fallen over every square yard of the Malta ground, and *I* ought to know." He quivered his little flea-bitten withers just to show how satisfied he felt; but his heart was not so light. Ever since he had drifted into India on a troopship, taken, with an old rifle, as part payment for a racing debt, the Maltese Cat had played and preached polo to the Skidars' team on the Skidars' stony polo-ground. Now a polo pony is like a poet. If he is born with a love for the game he can be made. The Maltese Cat knew that bamboos grew solely in order that polo-balls might be turned from their roots, that grain was given to ponies to keep them in hard condition, and that ponies were shod to prevent them slipping on a turn. But, besides all these things, he knew every trick and device of the finest game of the world, and for two seasons he had been teaching the others all he knew or guessed.

"Remember," he said for the hundredth time as the riders came up, "we *must* play together, and you *must* play with your heads. Whatever happens, follow the ball. Who goes out first?"

Kittiwynk, Shiraz, Polaris, and a short high little bay fellow with tremendous hocks and no withers worth speaking of (he was called Corks) were being girthed up, and the soldiers in the background stared with all their eyes. "I want you men to keep quiet," said Lutyens, the captain of the team, "and especially *not* to blow your pipes."

"Not if we win, Captain Sahib?" asked a piper.

"If we win, you can do what you please," said Lutyens, with a smile, as he slipped the loop of his stick over his wrist, and wheeled to canter to his place. The Archangels' ponies were a little bit above themselves on account of the many-coloured crowd so close to the ground. Their riders were excellent players, but they were a team of crack players instead of a crack team; and that made all the difference in the world. They honestly meant to play together, but it is very hard for four men, each the best of the team he is picked from, to remember that in polo no brilliancy of hitting or riding makes up for playing alone. Their captain shouted his orders to them by name, and it is a curious thing that if you call his name aloud in public after an Englishman you make him hot and fretty. Lutyens said nothing to his men because it had all been said before. He pulled up Shiraz, for he was playing 'back', to guard the goal. Powell on Polaris was half-back, and Macnamara and Hughes on Corks and Kittiwynk were forwards. The tough bamboo-root ball was put into the middle of the ground one hundred and fifty yards from the ends, and Hughes crossed sticks, heads-up, with the captain of the Archangels, who saw fit to play forward, and that is a place from which you cannot easily control the team. The little click as the cane-shafts met was heard all over the ground, and then Hughes made some sort of quick wrist-stroke that just dribbled the ball a few yards. Kittiwynk knew that stroke of old, and followed as a cat follows a mouse. While the captain of the Archangels was wrenching his pony round Hughes struck with all his strength, and next instant Kittiwynk was away, Corks followed close behind her, their little feet pattering like rain-drops on glass.

"Pull out to the left," said Kittiwynk between her teeth, "it's coming our way, Corks!"

The back and half-back of the Archangels were tearing down on her just as she was within reach of the ball. Hughes leaned forward with a loose rein, and cut it away to the left almost under Kittiwynk's feet, and it hopped and skipped off to Corks, who saw that, if he were not quick, it would run beyond the boundaries. That long bouncing drive gave the Archangels time to wheel and send three men across the ground to head off Corks. Kittwynk stayed where she was, for she knew the game.

Corks was on the ball half a fraction of a second before the others came up, and Macnamara, with a backhanded stroke, sent it back across the ground to Hughes, who saw the way clear to the Archangels' goal, and smacked the ball in before any one quite knew what had happened.

"That's luck," said Corks, as they changed ends. "A goal in three minutes for three hits and no riding to speak of."

"Don't know," said Polaris. "We've made 'em angry too soon. Shouldn't wonder if they try to rush us off our feet next time."

"Keep the ball hanging then," said Shiraz. "That wears out every pony that isn't used to it."

Next time there was no easy galloping across the ground. All the Archangels closed up as one man, but there they stayed, for Corks, Kittiwynk, and Polaris were somewhere on the top of the ball, marking time among the rattling sticks, while Shiraz circled about outside, waiting for a chance.

"*We* can do this all day," said Polaris, ramming his quarters into the side of another pony. "Where do you think you're shoving to?"

"I'll—I'll be driven in an *ekka* if I know," was the gasping reply, "and I'd give a week's feed to get my blinkers off. I can't see anything."

"The dust is rather bad. Whew! That was one for my off hock. Where's the ball, Corks?"

"Under my tail. At least a man's looking for it there. This is beautiful. They can't use their sticks, and it's driving 'em wild. Give old blinkers a push and he'll go over!"

"Here, don't touch me! I can't see. I'll—I'll back out, I think," said the pony in blinkers, who knew that if you can't see all round your head you cannot prop yourself against a shock.

Corks was watching the ball where it lay in the dust close to his near fore with Macnamara's shortened stick tap-tapping it from time to time. Kittiwynk was edging her way out of the scrimmage, whisking her stump of a tail with nervous excitement.

"Ho! They've got it," she snorted. "Let me out!" and she galloped like a rifle-bullet just behind a tall lanky pony of the Archangels, whose rider was swinging up his stick for a stroke.

"Not to-day, thank you," said Hughes, as the blow slid off his raised stick, and Kittiwynk laid her shoulder to the tall pony's quarters, and shoved him aside just as Lutyens on Shiraz sent the ball where it had come from, and the tall pony went skating and slipping away to the left. Kittiwynk, seeing that Polaris had joined Corks in the chase for the ball up the ground, dropped into Polaris's place, and then time was called.

The Skidars' ponies wasted no time in kicking or fuming. They knew each minute's rest meant so much gain, and trotted off to the rails and their *saises*, who began to scrape and blanket and rub them at once.

"Whew!" said Corks, stiffening up to get all the tickle out of the big vulcanite scraper. "If we were playing pony for pony we'd bend those Archangels double in half an hour. But they'll bring out fresh ones and fresh ones, and fresh ones after that—you see."

"Who cares?" said Polaris. "We've drawn first blood. Is my hock swelling?"

"Looks puffy," said Corks. "You must have had rather a wipe. Don't let it stiffen. You'll be wanted again in half an hour."

"What's the game like?" said the Maltese Cat.

"Ground's like your shoe, except where they've put too much water on it," said Kittiwynk. "Then it's slippery. Don't play in the centre. There's a bog there. I don't know how their next four are going to behave, but we kept the ball hanging and made 'em lather for nothing. Who goes out? Two Arabs and a couple of countrybreds! That's bad. What a comfort it is to wash your mouth out!"

Kitty was talking with a neck of a leather-covered soda-water bottle between her teeth and trying to look over her withers at the same time. This gave her a very coquettish air.

"What's bad?" said Grey Dawn, giving to the girth and admiring his well-set shoulders.

"You Arabs can't gallop fast enough to keep yourselves warm—that's what Kitty means," said Polaris, limping to show that his hock needed attention. "Are you playing 'back', Grey Dawn?"

"Looks like it," said Grey Dawn, as Lutyens swung himself up. Powell mounted the Rabbit, a plain bay countrybred much like Corks, but with mulish ears. Macnamara took Faiz Ullah, a handy short-backed little red Arab with a long tail, and Hughes mounted Benami, an old and sullen brown beast, who stood over in front more than a polo pony should.

"Benami looks like business," said Shiraz. "How's your temper, Ben?" The old campaigner hobbled off without answering, and the Maltese Cat looked at the new Archangel ponies prancing about on the ground. They were four beautiful blacks, and they saddled big enough and strong enough to eat the Skidars' team and gallop away with the meal inside them.

"Blinkers again," said the Maltese Cat. "Good enough!"

"They're chargers—cavalry chargers!" said Kittiwynk indignantly. "*They'll* never see thirteen-three again."

"They've all been fairly measured and they've all got their certificates," said the Maltese Cat, "or they wouldn't be here. We must take things as they come along, and keep our eyes on the ball."

The game began, but this time the Skidars were penned to their own end of the ground, and the watching ponies did not approve of that.

"Faiz Ullah is shirking, as usual," said Polaris, with a scornful grunt.

"Faiz Ullah is eating whip," said Corks. They could hear the leather-thonged polo quirt lacing the little fellow's well-rounded barrel. Then the Rabbit's shrill neigh came across the ground. "I can't do all the work," he cried.

"Play the game, don't talk," the Maltese Cat whickered; and all the ponies wriggled with excitement, and the soldiers and the grooms gripped the railings and shouted. A black pony with blinkers had singled out old Benami, and was interfering with him in every possible way. They could see Benami shaking his head up and down and flapping his underlip.

"There'll be a fall in a minute," said Polaris. "Benami is getting stuffy." The game flickered up and down between goal-post and goal-post, and the black ponies were getting more confident as they felt they had the legs of the others. The ball was hit out of a little scrimmage, and Benami and the Rabbit followed it; Faiz Ullah only too glad to be quiet for an instant.

The blinkered black pony came up like a hawk, with two of his own side behind him, and Benami's eye glittered as he raced. The question was which pony should make way for the other; each rider was perfectly willing to risk a fall in a good cause. The black who had been driven nearly crazy by his blinkers trusted to his weight and his temper; but Benami knew how to apply his weight and how to keep his temper. They met, and there was a cloud of dust. The black was lying on his side with all the breath knocked out of his body. The Rabbit was a hundred yards up the ground with the ball, and Benami was sitting down. He had slid nearly ten yards, but he had had his revenge, and sat cracking his nostrils till the black pony rose. "That's what you get for interfering. Do you want any more?" said Benami, and he plunged into the game. Nothing was done because Faiz Ullah would not gallop, though Macnamara beat him whenever he could spare a second. The fall of the black pony had impressed his companions tremendously, and so the Archangels could not profit by Faiz Ullah's bad behaviour.

But as the Maltese Cat said, when time was called and the four came back blowing and dripping, Faiz Ullah ought to have been kicked all round Umballa. If he did not behave better next time, the Maltese Cat promised to pull out his Arab tail by the root and eat it.

There was no time to talk, for the third four were ordered out.

The third quarter of a game is generally the hottest, for each side thinks that the others must be pumped; and most of the winning play in a game is made about that time.

Lutyens took over the Maltese Cat with a pat and a hug, for Lutyens valued him more than anything else in the world. Powell had Shikast, a little grey rat with no pedigree and no manners outside polo; Macnamara mounted Bamboo, the largest of the team, and Hughes took Who's Who, *alias* The Animal. He was supposed to have Australian blood in his veins, but he looked like a clothes-horse, and you could whack him on the legs with an iron crowbar without hurting him.

They went out to meet the very flower of the Archangels' team, and when Who's Who saw their elegantly booted legs and their beautiful satiny skins he grinned a grin through his light, well-worn bridle.

"My word!" said Who's Who. "We must give 'em a little football. Those gentlemen need a rubbing down."

"No biting," said the Maltese Cat warningly, for once or twice in his career Who's Who had been known to forget himself in that way.

"Who said anything about biting? I'm not playing tiddly-winks. I'm playing the game."

The Archangels came down like a wolf on the fold, for they were tired of football and they wanted polo. They got it more and more. Just after the game began, Lutyens hit a ball that was coming towards him rapidly, and it rose in the air, as a ball sometimes will, with the whirr of a frightened partridge. Shikast heard, but could not see it for the minute, though he looked everywhere and up into the air as the Maltese Cat had taught him. When he saw it ahead and overhead, he went forward with Powell as fast as he could put foot to ground. It was then that Powell, a quiet and level-headed man as a rule, became inspired and played a stroke that sometimes comes off successfully on a quiet afternoon of long practice. He took his stick in both hands, and standing up in his stirrups, swiped at the ball in the air, Munipore fashion. There was one second of paralysed astonishment, and then all four sides of the ground went up in a yell of applause and delight as the ball flew true (you could see the amazed Archangels ducking in their saddles to get out of the line of flight, and looking at it with open mouths), and the regimental pipes of the Skidars squealed from the railings as long as the piper had breath.

Shikast heard the stroke; but he heard the head of the stick fly off at the same time. Nine hundred and ninety-nine ponies out of a thousand would have gone tearing on after the ball with a useless player pulling at their heads, but Powell knew him, and he knew Powell; and the instant he felt Powell's right leg shift a trifle on the saddle-flap he headed to the boundary, where a native officer was frantically waving a new stick. Before the shouts had ended Powell was armed again.

Once before in his life the Maltese Cat had heard that very same stroke played off his own back, and had profited by the confusion it made. This time he acted on experience, and leaving Bamboo to guard the goal in case of accidents, came through the others like a flash, head and tail low, Lutyens standing up to ease him—swept on and on before the other side knew what was the matter, and nearly pitched on his head between the Archangels' goal-posts as Lutyens tipped the ball in after a straight scurry of a hundred and fifty yards. If there was one thing more than another upon which the Maltese Cat prided himself it was on this quick, streaking kind of run half across the ground. He did not believe in taking balls round the field unless you were clearly overmatched. After this they gave the Archangels five minutes' football, and an expensive fast pony hates football because it rumples his temper.

Who's Who showed himself even better than Polaris in this game. He did not permit any wriggling away, but bored joyfully into the scrimmage as if he had his nose in a feed-box, and were looking for something nice. Little Shikast jumped on the ball the minute it got clear, and every time an Archangel pony followed it he found Shikast standing over it asking what was the matter.

"If we can live through this quarter," said the Maltese Cat, "I shan't care. Don't take it out of yourselves. Let them do the lathering."

So the ponies, as their riders explained afterwards, 'shut up'. The Archangels kept them tied fast in front of their goal, but it cost the Archangels' ponies all that was left of their tempers; and ponies began to kick, and men began to repeat compliments, and they chopped at the legs of Who's Who, and he set his teeth and stayed where he was, and the dust stood up like a tree over the scrimmage till that hot quarter ended.

They found the ponies very excited and confident when they went to their *saises*; and the Maltese Cat had to warn them that the worst of the game was coming. "Now *we* are all going in for the second time," said he, "and *they* are trotting out fresh ponies. You'll think you can gallop, but you'll find you can't; and then you'll be sorry."

"But two goals to nothing is a halter-long lead," said Kittiwynk prancing.

"How long does it take to get a goal?" the Maltese Cat answered. "For pity's sake, don't run away with the notion that the game is half-won just because we happen to be in luck now. They'll ride you into the grand-stand if they can; you must *not* give 'em a chance. Follow the ball."

"Football, as usual?" said Polaris. "My hock's half as big as a nose-bag."

"Don't let them have a look at the ball if you can help it. Now leave me alone. I must get all the rest I can before the last quarter."

He hung down his head and let all his muscles go slack; Shikast, Bamboo, and Who's Who copying his example.

"Better not watch the game," he said. "We aren't playing, and we shall only take it out of ourselves if we grow anxious. Look at the ground and pretend it's fly-time."

They did their best, but it was hard advice to follow. The hoofs were drumming and the sticks were rattling all up and down the ground, and yells of applause from the English troops told that the Archangels were pressing the Skidars hard. The native soldiers behind the ponies groaned and grunted, and said things in undertones, and presently they heard a long-drawn shout and a clatter of hurrahs!

"One to the Archangels," said Shikast, without raising his head. "Time's nearly up. Oh, my sire and dam!"

"Faiz Ullah," said the Maltese Cat, "if you don't play to the last nail in your shoes this time, I'll kick you on the ground before all the other ponies."

"I'll do my best when my time comes," said the little Arab sturdily.

The *saises* looked at each other gravely as they rubbed their ponies' legs. This was the first time when long purses began to tell, and everybody knew it. Kittiwynk and the others came back with the sweat dripping over their hoofs and their tails telling sad stories.

"They're better than we are," said Shiraz. "I knew how it would be."

"Shut your big head," said the Maltese Cat; "we've one goal to the good yet."

"Yes, but it's two Arabs and two countrybreds to play now," said Corks. "Faiz Ullah, remember!" He spoke in a biting voice.

As Lutyens mounted Grey Dawn he looked at his men, and they did not look pretty. They were covered with dust and sweat in streaks. Their yellow boots were almost black, their wrists were red and lumpy, and their eyes seemed two inches deep in their heads, but the expression in the eyes was satisfactory. "Did you take anything at tiffin?" said Lutyens, and the team shook their heads. They were too dry to talk.

"All right. The Archangels did. They are worse pumped than we are."

"They've got the better ponies," said Powell. "I shan't be sorry when this business is over."

That fifth quarter was a sad one in every way. Faiz Ullah played like a little red demon; and the Rabbit seemed to be everywhere at once, and Benami rode straight at anything and everything that came in his way, while the umpires on their ponies wheeled like gulls outside the shifting game. But the Archangels had the better mounts—they had kept their racers till late in the game—and never allowed the Skidars to play football. They hit the ball up and down the width of the ground till Benami and the rest were outpaced. Then they went forward and time and again Lutyens and Grey Dawn were just, and only just, able to send the ball away with a long splitting back-hander. Grey Dawn forgot that he was an Arab; and turned from grey to blue as he galloped. Indeed, he forgot too well, for he did not keep his eyes on the ground as an Arab should, but stuck out his nose and scuttled for the dear honour of the game. They had watered the ground once or twice between the quarters, and a careless waterman had emptied the last of his skinful all in one place near the Skidars' goal. It was close to the end of play, and for the tenth time Grey Dawn was bolting after a ball when his near hind foot slipped on the greasy mud and he rolled over and over, pitching Lutyens just clear of the goal-post; and the triumphant Archangels made their goal. Then time was called—two goals all; but Lutyens had to be helped up, and Grey Dawn rose with his near hind leg strained somewhere.

"What's the damage?" said Powell, his arm round Lutyens.

"Collar-bone, of course," said Lutyens between his teeth. It was the third time he had broken it in two years, and it hurt him.

Powell and the others whistled. "Game's up," said Hughes.

"Hold on. We've five good minutes yet, and it isn't my right hand," said Lutyens. "We'll stick it out."

"I say," said the captain of the Archangels, trotting up. "Are you hurt, Lutyens? We'll wait if you care to put in a substitute. I wish—I mean—the fact is, you fellows deserve this game if any team does. Wish we could give you a man or some of our ponies—or something."

"You're awfully good, but we'll play it to a finish, I think."

The captain of the Archangels stared for a little. "That's not half bad," he said, and went back to his own side, while Lutyens borrowed a scarf from one of his native officers and made a sling of it. Then an Archangel galloped up with a big bath-sponge and advised Lutyens to put it under his armpit to ease his shoulder, and between them they tied up his left arm scientifically, and one of the native officers leaped forward with four long glasses that fizzed and bubbled.

The team looked at Lutyens piteously, and he nodded. It was the last quarter, and nothing would matter after that. They drank out the dark golden drink, and wiped their moustaches, and things looked more hopeful. The Maltese Cat had put his nose into the front of Lutyens's shirt, and was trying to say how sorry he was.

"He knows," said Lutyens, proudly. "The beggar knows. I've played him without a bridle before now—for fun."

"It's no fun now," said Powell. "But we haven't a decent substitute."

"No," said Lutyens. "It's the last quarter, and we've got to make our goal and win. I'll trust the Cat."

"If you fall this time you'll suffer a little," said Macnamara.

"I'll trust the Cat," said Lutyens.

"You hear that?" said the Maltese Cat proudly to the others. "It's worth while playing polo for ten years to have that said of you. Now then, my sons, come along. We'll kick up a little bit, just to show the Archangels *this* team haven't suffered." And, sure enough, as they went on to the ground the Maltese Cat, after satisfying himself that Lutyens was home in the saddle, kicked out three or four times, and Lutyens laughed. The reins were caught up anyhow in the tips of his strapped hand, and he never pretended to rely on them. He knew the Cat would answer to the least pressure of the leg, and by way of showing off—for his shoulder hurt him very much—he bent the little fellow in a close figure-of-eight in and out between the goal-posts. There was a roar from the native officers and men, who dearly loved a piece of *dugabashi* (horse-trick work), as they called it, and the pipes very quietly and scornfully droned out the first bars of a common bazaar-tune called 'Freshly Fresh and Newly New', just as a warning to the other regiments that the Skidars were fit. All the natives laughed.

"And now," said the Cat, as they took their places, "remember that this is the last quarter, and follow the ball!"

"Don't need to be told," said Who's Who.

"Let me go on. All those people on all four sides will begin to crowd in—just as they did at Malta. You'll hear people calling out, and moving forward and being pushed back, and that is going to make the Archangel ponies very unhappy. But if a ball is struck to the boundary, you go after it, and let the people get out of your way. I went over the pole of a four-in-hand once, and picked a game out of the dust by it. Back me up when I run, and follow the ball."

There was a sort of an all-round sound of sympathy and wonder as the last quarter opened, and then there began exactly what the Maltese Cat had foreseen. People crowded in close to the boundaries, and the Archangels' ponies kept looking sideways at the narrowing space. If you know how a man feels to be cramped at tennis—not because he wants to run out of the court, but because he likes to know that he can at a pinch—you will guess how ponies must feel when they are playing in a box of human beings.

"I'll bend some of those men if I can get away," said Who's Who, as he rocketed behind the ball; and Bamboo nodded without speaking. They were playing the last ounce in them, and the Maltese Cat had left the goal undefended to join them. Lutyens gave him every order that he could to bring him back, but this was the first time in his career that the little wise grey had ever played polo on his own responsibility, and he was going to make the most of it.

"What are you doing here?" said Hughes, as the Cat crossed in front of him and rode off an Archangel.

"The Cat's in charge—mind the goal!" shouted Lutyens, and bowing forward hit the ball full, and followed on, forcing the Archangels towards their own goal.

"No football," said the Cat. "Keep the ball by the boundaries and cramp 'em. Play open order and drive 'em to the boundaries."

Across and across the ground in big diagonals flew the ball, and whenever it came to a flying rush and a stroke close to the boundaries the Archangel ponies moved stiffly. They did not care to go headlong at a wall of men and carriages, though if the ground had been open they could have turned on a sixpence.

"Wriggle her up the sides," said the Cat. "Keep her close to the crowd. They hate the carriages. Shikast, keep her up this side."

Shikast with Powell lay left and right behind the uneasy scuffle of an open scrimmage, and every time the ball was hit away Shikast galloped on it at such an angle that Powell was forced to hit it towards the boundary; and when the crowd had been driven away from that side, Lutyens would send the ball over to the other, and Shikast would slide desperately after it till his friends came down to help. It was billiards, and no football, this time—billiards in a corner pocket; and the cues were not well chalked.

"If they get us out in the middle of the ground they'll walk away from us. Dribble her along the sides," cried the Cat.

So they dribbled all along the boundary, where a pony could not come on their right-hand side; and the Archangels were furious, and the umpires had to neglect the game to shout at the people to get back, and several blundering mounted policemen tried to restore order, all close to the scrimmage, and the nerves of the Archangels' ponies stretched and broke like cobwebs.

Five or six times an Archangel hit the ball up into the middle of the ground, and each time the watchful Shikast gave Powell his chance to send it back, and after each return, when the dust had settled, men could see that the Skidars had gained a few yards.

Every now and again there were shouts of "'Side! Off side!" from the spectators; but the teams were too busy to care, and the umpires had all they could do to keep their maddened ponies clear of the scuffle.

At last Lutyens missed a short easy stroke, and the Skidars had to fly back helter-skelter to protect their own goal, Shikast leading. Powell stopped the ball with a back-hander when it was not fifty yards from the goal-posts, and Shikast spun round with a wrench that nearly hoisted Powell out of his saddle.

"Now's our last chance," said the Cat, wheeling like a cockchafer on a pin. "We've got to ride it out. Come along."

Lutyens felt the little chap take a deep breath, and, as it were, crouch under his rider. The ball was hopping towards the right-hand boundary, an Archangel riding for it with both spurs and a whip; but neither spur nor whip would make his pony stretch himself as he neared the crowd. The Maltese Cat glided under his very nose, picking up his hind legs sharp, for there was not a foot to spare between his quarters and the other pony's bit. It was as neat an exhibition as fancy figure-skating. Lutyens hit with all the strength he had left, but the stick slipped a little in his hand, and the ball flew off to the left instead of keeping close to the boundary. Who's Who was far across the ground, thinking hard as he galloped. He repeated, stride for stride, the Cat's manœuvres with another Archangel pony, nipping the ball away from under his bridle, and clearing his opponent by half a fraction of an inch, for Who's Who was clumsy behind. Then he drove away towards the right as the Maltese Cat came up from the left; and Bamboo held a middle course exactly between them. The three were making a sort of Government-broad-arrow-shaped attack; and there was only the Archangels' back to guard the goal; but immediately behind them were three Archangels racing all they knew, and mixed up with them was Powell, sending Shikast along on what he felt was their last hope. It takes a very good man to stand up to the rush of seven crazy ponies in the last quarter of a cup game, when men are riding with their necks for sale, and the ponies are delirious. The Archangels' back missed his stroke, and pulled aside just in time to let the rush go by. Bamboo and Who's Who shortened stride to give the Maltese Cat room, and Lutyens got the goal with a clean, smooth, smacking stroke that was heard all over the field. But there was no stopping the ponies. They poured through the goal-posts in one mixed mob, winners and losers together, for the pace had been terrific. The Maltese Cat knew by experience what would happen, and, to save Lutyens, turned to the right with one last effort that strained a back-sinew beyond hope of repair. As he did so he heard the right-hand goal-post crack as a pony cannoned into it—crack, splinter, and fall like a mast. It had been sawed three parts through in case of accidents, but it upset the pony nevertheless, and he blundered into another, who blundered into the left-hand post, and then there was confusion and dust and wood. Bamboo was lying on the ground, seeing stars; an Archangel pony rolled beside him, breathless and angry; Shikast had sat down dog-fashion to avoid falling over the others, and was sliding along on his little bobtail in a cloud of dust; and Powell was sitting on the ground, hammering with his stick and trying to cheer. All the others were shouting at the top of what was left of their voices, and the men who had been spilt were shouting too. As soon as the people saw no one was hurt, ten thousand natives and English shouted, and clapped and yelled, and before any one could stop them the pipers of the Skidars broke on to the ground, with all the native officers and men behind them, and marched up and down, playing a wild northern tune called 'Zakhme Bagan', and through the insolent blaring of the pipes and the high-pitched native yells you could hear the Archangels' band hammering, 'For they are all jolly good fellows', and then reproachfully to the losing team, 'Ooh, Kafoozalum! Kafoozalum! Kafoozalum!'

Besides all these things and many more, there was a Commander-in-Chief, and an Inspector-General of Cavalry, and the principal veterinary officer in all India, standing on the top of a regimental coach, yelling like school-boys; and brigadiers and colonels and commissioners, and hundreds of pretty ladies joined the chorus. But the Maltese Cat stood with his head down, wondering how many legs were left to him; and Lutyens watched the men and ponies pick themselves out of the wreck of the two goal-posts, and he patted the Cat very tenderly.

"I say," said the captain of the Archangels, spitting a pebble out of his mouth, "will you take three thousand for that pony—as he stands?"

"No, thank you. I've an idea he's saved my life," said Lutyens, getting off and lying down at full length. Both teams were on the ground too, waving their boots in the air, and coughing and drawing deep breaths, as the *saises* ran up to take away the ponies, and an officious water-carrier sprinkled the players with dirty water till they sat up.

"My Aunt!" said Powell, rubbing his back and looking at the stumps of the goal-posts, "that was a game!" They played it over again, every stroke of it, that night at the big dinner, when the Free-for-All Cup was filled and passed down the table, and emptied and filled again, and everybody made most eloquent speeches. About two in the morning, when there might have been some singing, a wise little, plain little, grey little head looked in through the open door.

"Hurrah! Bring him in," said the Archangels; and his *sais*, who was very happy indeed, patted the Maltese Cat on the flank, and he limped in to the blaze of light and the glittering uniforms, looking for Lutyens. He was used to messes, and men's bedrooms, and places where ponies are not usually encouraged, and in his youth had jumped on and off a mess-table for a bet. So he behaved himself very politely, and ate bread dipped in salt, and was petted all round the table, moving gingerly; and they drank his health, because he had done more to win the Cup than any man or horse on the ground.

That was glory and honour enough for the rest of his days, and the Maltese Cat did not complain much when his veterinary surgeon said that he would be no good for polo any more. When Lutyens married, his wife did not allow him to play, so he was forced to be an umpire; and his pony on these occasions was a flea-bitten grey with a neat polo-tail, lame all round, but desperately quick on his feet, and, as everybody knew, Past Pluperfect Prestissimo Player of the Game.

D. H. LAWRENCE

1885–1930

He was a quirkish man, with a quirkish imagination—
the author of *Lady Chatterley's Lover*, but also of many less
controversial (and better) works: poems, novels, short stories,
all lit with the particular fire of his sharp and sometimes
sinister vision. "Evil, what is evil?" he said.
"There is only one evil, to deny life."

The Rocking-Horse Winner

THERE WAS A woman who was beautiful, who started with all the advantages, yet she had no luck. She married for love, and the love turned to dust. She had bonny children, yet she felt they had been thrust upon her, and she could not love them. They looked at her coldly, as if they were finding fault with her. And hurriedly she felt she must cover up some fault in herself. Yet what it was that she must cover up she never knew. Nevertheless, when her children were present, she always felt the centre of her heart go hard. This troubled her, and in her manner she was all the more gentle and anxious for her children, as if she loved them very much. Only she herself knew that at the centre of her heart was a hard little place that could not feel love, no, not for anybody. Everybody else said of her: "She is such a good mother. She adores her children." Only she herself, and her children themselves, knew it was not so. They read it in each other's eyes.

There were a boy and two little girls. They lived in a pleasant house, with a garden, and they had discreet servants and felt themselves superior to anyone in the neighbourhood.

Although they lived in style, they felt always an anxiety in the house. There was never enough money. The mother had a small income, and the father had a small income, but not nearly enough for the social position which they had to keep up. The father went in to town to some office. But though he had good prospects, these prospects never materialized. There was always the grinding sense of the shortage of money, though the style was always kept up.

At last the mother said, "I will see if *I* can't make something." But she did not know where to begin. She racked her brains, and tried this thing and the other, but could not find anything successful. The failure made deep lines come into her face. Her children were growing up, they would have to go to school. There must be more money, there must be more money. The father, who was always very handsome and expensive in his tastes, seemed as if he never *would* be able to do anything worth doing. And the mother, who had a great belief in herself, did not succeed any better, and her tastes were just as expensive.

And so the house came to be haunted by the unspoken phrase: *There must be more money! There must be more money!* The children could hear it all the time, though nobody said it aloud. They heard it at Christmas, when the expensive and splendid toys filled the nursery. Behind the shining modern rocking-horse, behind the smart doll's-house, a voice would start whispering: "There *must* be more money! There *must* be more money!" And the children would stop playing, to listen for a moment. They would look into each other's eyes, to see if they had all heard. And each one saw in the eyes of the other two that they too had heard. "There *must* be more money! There *must* be more money!"

It came whispering from the springs of the still-swaying rocking-horse, and even the horse, bending his wooden, champing head, heard it. The big doll, sitting so pink and smirking in her new pram, could hear it quite plainly, and seemed to be smirking all the more self-consciously because of it. The foolish puppy, too, that took the place of the teddy-bear, he was looking so extraordinarily foolish for no other reason but that he heard the secret whisper all over the house: "There *must* be more money."

Yet nobody ever said it aloud. The whisper was everywhere, and therefore no one spoke it. Just as no one ever says: "We are breathing!" in spite of the fact that breath is coming and going all the time.

"Mother!" said the boy Paul one day. "Why don't we keep a car of our own? Why do we always use uncle's, or else a taxi?"

"Because we're the poor members of the family," said the mother.

"But why *are* we, Mother?"

"Well—I suppose," she said slowly and bitterly, "it's because your father has no luck."

The boy was silent for some time.

"Is luck money, Mother?" he asked rather timidly.

"No, Paul! Not quite. It's what causes you to have money."

"Oh!" said Paul vaguely. "I thought when Uncle Oscar said *filthy lucker* it meant money."

"*Filthy lucre* does mean money," said the mother. "But it's lucre, not luck."

"Oh!" said the boy. "Then what *is* luck, Mother?"

"It's what causes you to have money. If you're lucky you have money. That's why it's better to be born lucky than rich. If you're rich, you may lose your money. But if you're lucky, you will always get more money."

"Oh! Will you? And is Father not lucky?"

"Very unlucky, I should say," she said bitterly.

The boy watched her with unsure eyes.

"Why?" he asked.

"I don't know. Nobody ever knows why one person is lucky and another unlucky."

"Don't they? Nobody at all? Does *nobody* know?"

"Perhaps God! But He never tells."

"He ought to, then. And aren't you lucky, either, Mother?"

"I can't be, if I married an unlucky husband."

"But by yourself, aren't you?"

"I used to think I was, before I married. Now I think I am very unlucky indeed."

"Why?"

"Well—never mind! Perhaps I'm not really," she said.

The child looked at her, to see if she meant it. But he saw, by the lines of her mouth, that she was only trying to hide something from him.

"Well, anyhow," he said stoutly, "I'm a lucky person."

"Why?" said his mother, with a sudden laugh.

He stared at her. He didn't even know why he had said it.

"God told me," he asserted, brazening it out.

"I hope He did, dear!" she said, again with a laugh, but rather bitter.

"He did, Mother!"

"Excellent!" said the mother, using one of her husband's exclamations.

The boy saw she did not believe him; or, rather, that she paid no attention to his assertion. This angered him somewhere, and made him want to compel her attention.

He went off by himself, vaguely, in a childish way, seeking for the clue to 'luck'. Absorbed, taking no heed of other people, he went about with a sort of stealth, seeking inwardly for luck. He wanted luck, he wanted it, he wanted it. When the two girls were playing dolls, in the nursery, he would sit on his big rocking-horse, charging madly into space, with a frenzy that made the little girls peer at him uneasily. Wildly the horse careered, the waving dark hair of the boy tossed, his eyes had a strange glare in them. The little girls dared not speak to him.

When he had ridden to the end of his mad little journey, he climbed down and stood in front of his rocking-horse, staring fixedly into its lowered face. Its red mouth was slightly open, its big eye was wide and glassy-bright.

"Now!" he would silently command the snorting steed. "Now take me to where there is luck! Now take me!"

And he would slash the horse on the neck with the little whip he had asked Uncle Oscar for. He *knew* the horse could take him to where there was luck, if only he forced it. So he would mount again, and start on his furious ride, hoping at last to get there. He knew he could get there.

"You'll break your horse, Paul!" said the nurse.

"He's always riding like that! I wish he'd leave off!" said his elder sister, Joan.

But he only glared down on them in silence. Nurse gave him up. She could make nothing of him. Anyhow, he was growing beyond her.

One day his mother and his Uncle Oscar came in when he was on one of his furious rides. He did not speak to them.

"Hallo, you young jockey! Riding a winner?" said his uncle.

"Aren't you growing too big for a rocking-horse? You're not a very little boy any longer, you know," said his mother.

But Paul only gave a blue glare from his big, rather close-set eyes. He would speak to nobody when he was in full tilt. His mother watched him with an anxious expression on her face.

At last he suddenly stopped forcing his horse into the mechanical gallop, and slid down.

"Well, I got there!" he announced fiercely, his blue eyes still flaring, and his sturdy long legs straddling apart.

"Where did you get to?" asked his mother.

"Where I wanted to go to," he flared back at her.

"That's right, son!" said Uncle Oscar. "Don't you stop till you get there. What's the horse's name?"

"He doesn't have a name," said the boy.

"Gets on without all right?" asked the uncle.

"Well, he has different names. He was called Sansovino last week."

"Sansovino, eh? Won the Ascot. How did you know his name?"

"He always talks about horse-races with Bassett," said Joan.

The uncle was delighted to find that his small nephew was posted with all the racing news. Bassett, the young gardener who had been wounded in the left foot in the war, and had got his present job through Oscar Cresswell, whose batman he had been, was a perfect blade of the Turf. He lived in the racing events, and the small boy lived with him.

Oscar Cresswell got it all from Bassett.

"Master Paul comes and asks me, so I can't do more than tell him, sir," said Bassett, his face terribly serious, as if he were speaking of religious matters.

"And does he ever put anything on a horse he fancies?"

"Well—I don't want to give him away—he's a young sport, a fine sport, sir. Would you mind asking him himself? He sort of takes a pleasure in it, and perhaps he'd feel I was giving him away, sir, if you don't mind." Bassett was serious as a church.

The uncle went back to his nephew and took him off for a ride in the car.

"Say, Paul, old man, do you ever put anything on a horse?" the uncle asked.

The boy watched the handsome man closely.

"Why, do you think I oughtn't to?" he parried.

"Not a bit of it! I thought perhaps you might give me a tip for the Lincoln."

The car sped on into the country, going down to Uncle Oscar's place in Hampshire.

"Honour bright?" said the nephew.

"Honour bright, son!" said the uncle.

"Well, then, Daffodil."

"Daffodil! I doubt it, sonny. What about Mirza?"

"I only know the winner," said the boy. "That's Daffodil!"

"Daffodil, eh?"

There was a pause. Daffodil was an obscure horse, comparatively.

"Uncle!"

"Yes, son?"

"You won't let it go any further, will you? I promised Bassett."

"Bassett be damned, old man! What's he got to do with it?"

"We're partners! We've been partners from the first! Uncle, he lent me my first five shillings, which I lost. I promised him, honour bright, it was only between me and him: only you gave me that ten-shilling note I started winning with, so I thought you were lucky. You won't let it go any further, will you?"

The boy gazed at his uncle from those big, hot blue eyes, set rather close together. The uncle stirred and laughed uneasily.

"Right you are, son! I'll keep your tip private. Daffodil, eh! How much are you putting on him?"

"All except twenty pounds," said the boy. "I keep that in reserve."

The uncle thought it a good joke.

"You keep twenty pounds in reserve, do you, you young romancer? What are you betting, then?"

"I'm betting three hundred," said the boy gravely. "But it's between you and me, Uncle Oscar! Honour bright?"

The uncle burst into a roar of laughter.

"It's between you and me all right, you young Nat Gould," he said, laughing. "But where's your three hundred?"

"Bassett keeps it for me. We're partners."

"You are, are you? And what is Bassett putting on Daffodil?"

"He won't go quite as high as I do, I expect. Perhaps he'll go a hundred and fifty."

"What, pennies?" laughed the uncle.

"Pounds," said the child, with a surprised look at his uncle. "Bassett keeps a bigger reserve than I do."

Between wonder and amusement, Uncle Oscar was silent. He pursued the matter no further, but he determined to take his nephew with him to the Lincoln races.

"Now, son," he said, "I'm putting twenty on Mirza, and I'll put five for you on any horse you fancy. What's your pick?"

"Daffodil, uncle!"

"No, not the fiver on Daffodil!"

"I should if it was my own fiver," said the child.

"Good! Good! Right you are! A fiver for me and a fiver for you on Daffodil."

The child had never been to a race-meeting before, and his eyes were blue fire. He pursed his mouth tight and watched. A Frenchman just in front had put his money on Lancelot. Wild with excitement, he flayed his arms up and down, yelling "*Lancelot! Lancelot!*" in his French accent.

Daffodil came in first, Lancelot second, Mirza third. The child, flushed and with eyes blazing, was curiously serene. His uncle brought him five five-pound notes: four to one.

"What am I to do with these?" he cried, waving them before the boy's eyes.

"I suppose we'll talk to Bassett," said the boy. "I expect I have fifteen hundred now: and twenty in reserve: and this twenty."

His uncle studied him for some moments.

"Look here, son!" he said. "You're not serious about Bassett and that fifteen hundred, are you?"

"Yes, I am. But it's between you and me, Uncle! Honour bright?"

"Honour bright, all right, son; but I must talk to Bassett."

"If you'd like to be a partner, Uncle, with Bassett and me, we could all be partners. Only you'd have to promise, honour bright, Uncle, not to let it go beyond us three. Bassett and I are lucky, and you must be lucky, because it was your ten shillings I started winning with . . ."

Uncle Oscar took both Bassett and Paul into Richmond Park for an afternoon, and there they talked.

"It's like this, you see, sir," Bassett said. "Master Paul would get me talking about racing events, spinning yarns, you know, sir. And he was always keen on knowing if I'd made or if I'd lost. It's about a year since, now, that I put five shillings on Blush of Dawn for him: and we lost. Then the luck turned, with that ten shillings he had from you: that we put on Singhalese. And since that time, it's been pretty steady, all things considering. What do you say, Master Paul?"

"We're all right when we're *sure*," said Paul. "It's when we're not quite sure that we go down."

"Oh, but we're careful then," said Bassett.

"But when are you *sure*?" smiled Uncle Oscar.

"It's Master Paul, sir," said Bassett, in a secret, religious voice. "It's as if he had it from heaven. Like Daffodil now, for the Lincoln. That was as sure as eggs."

"Did you put anything on Daffodil?" asked Oscar Cresswell.

"Yes, sir. I made my bit."

"And my nephew?"

Bassett was obstinately silent, looking at Paul.

"I made twelve hundred, didn't I, Bassett? I told Uncle I was putting three hundred on Daffodil."

"That's right," said Bassett, nodding.

"But where's the money?" asked the uncle.

"I keep it safe locked up, sir. Master Paul, he can have it any minute he likes to ask for it."

"What, fifteen hundred pounds?"

"And twenty! And *forty*, that is, with the twenty he made on the course."

"It's amazing!" said the uncle.

"If Master Paul offers you to be partners, sir, I would, if I were you: if you'll excuse me," said Bassett.

Oscar Cresswell thought about it.

"I'll see the money," he said.

They drove home again, and sure enough Bassett came round to the garden-house with fifteen hundred pounds in notes. The twenty pounds reserve was left with Joe Glee, in the Turf Commission deposit.

"You see, it's all right, Uncle, when I'm *sure*! Then we go strong, for all we're worth. Don't we, Bassett?"

"We do that, Master Paul."

"And when are you sure?" said the uncle, laughing.

"Oh, well, sometimes I'm *absolutely* sure, like about Daffodil," said the boy; "and sometimes I have an idea; and sometimes I haven't even an idea, have I, Bassett? Then we're careful, because we mostly go down."

"You do, do you? And when you're sure, like about Daffodil, what makes you sure, sonny?"

"Oh, well, I don't know," said the boy uneasily. "I'm sure, you know, Uncle; that's all."

"It's as if he had it from heaven, sir," Bassett reiterated.

"I should say so!" said the uncle.

But he became a partner. And when the Leger was coming on, Paul was 'sure' about Lively Spark, which was a quite inconsiderable horse. The boy insisted on putting a thousand on the horse, Bassett went for five hundred, and Oscar Cresswell two hundred. Lively Spark came in first, and the betting had been ten to one against him. Paul had made ten thousand.

"You see," he said, "I was absolutely sure of him."

Even Oscar Cresswell had cleared two thousand.

"Look here, son," he said, "this sort of thing makes me nervous."

"It needn't, Uncle! Perhaps I shan't be sure again for a long time."

"But what are you going to do with your money?" asked the uncle.

"Of course," said the boy, "I started it for Mother. She said she had no luck, because Father is unlucky, so I thought if *I* was lucky, it might stop whispering."

"What might stop whispering?"

"Our house! I *hate* our house for whispering."

"What does it whisper?"

"Why—why," the boy fidgeted, "why, I don't know! But it's always short of money, you know, Uncle."

"I know it, son, I know it."

"You know people send Mother writs, don't you, Uncle?"

"I'm afraid I do," said the uncle.

"And then the house whispers like people laughing at you behind your back. It's awful, that is! I thought if I was lucky——"

"You might stop it," added the uncle.

The boy watched him with big blue eyes that had an uncanny cold fire in them, and he said never a word.

"Well, then," said the uncle, "what are we doing?"

"I shouldn't like Mother to know I was lucky," said the boy.

"Why not, son?"

"She'd stop me."

"I don't think she would."

"Oh"—and the boy writhed in an odd way—"I *don't* want her to know, Uncle."

"All right, son! We'll manage it without her knowing."

They managed it very easily. Paul, at the other's suggestion, handed over five thousand pounds to his uncle, who deposited it with the family lawyer, who was then to inform Paul's mother that a relative had put five thousand pounds into his hands, which sum was to be paid out a thousand pounds at a time, on the mother's birthday for the next five years.

"So she'll have a birthday present of a thousand pounds for five successive years," said Uncle Oscar. "I hope it won't make it all the harder for her later."

Paul's mother had her birthday in November. The house had been 'whispering' worse than ever lately, and, even in spite of his luck, Paul could not bear up against it. He was very anxious to see the effect of the birthday letter, telling his mother about the thousand pounds.

When there were no visitors, Paul now took his meals with his parents, as he was beyond the nursery control. His mother went into town nearly every day. She had discovered that she had an odd knack of sketching furs and dress materials so she worked secretly in the studio of a friend who was the chief 'artist' for the leading drapers. She drew the figures of ladies in furs and ladies in silk and sequins for the newspaper advertisements. This young woman artist earned several thousand pounds a year, but Paul's mother only made several hundreds, and she was again dissatisfied. She so wanted to be first in something, and she did not succeed, even in making sketches for draper advertisements.

She was down to breakfast on the morning of her birthday. Paul watched her face as she read her letters. He knew the lawyer's letter. As his mother read it, her face hardened and became more expressionless. Then a cold, determined look came on her mouth. She hid the letter under the pile of others, and said not a word about it.

"Didn't you have anything nice in the post for your birthday, Mother?" said Paul.

"Quite moderately nice," she said, her voice cold and absent.

She went away to town without saying more.

But in the afternoon Uncle Oscar appeared. He said Paul's mother had had a long interview with the lawyer, asking if the whole five thousand could not be advanced at once, as she was in debt.

"What do you think, Uncle?" said the boy.

"I leave it to you, son."

"Oh, let her have it, then! We can get some more with the other," said the boy.

"A bird in the hand is worth two in the bush, laddie!" said Uncle Oscar.

"But I'm sure to *know* for the Grand National; or the Lincolnshire; or else the Derby. I'm sure to know for *one* of them," said Paul.

So Uncle Oscar signed the agreement, and Paul's mother touched the whole five thousand. Then something very curious happened. The voices in the house suddenly went mad, like a chorus of frogs on a spring evening. There were certain new furnishings, and Paul had a tutor. He was *really* going to Eton, his father's school, in the following autumn. There were flowers in the winter, and a blossoming of the luxury Paul's mother had been used to. And yet the voices in the house, behind the sprays of mimosa and almond-blossom, and from under the piles of iridescent cushions, simply trilled and screamed in a sort of ecstasy: "There *must* be more money! Oh-h-h! There *must* be more money! Oh, now, now-w, now-w-w—there *must* be more money! More than ever! More than ever!"

It frightened Paul terribly. He studied away at his Latin and Greek with his tutors. But his intense hours were spent with Bassett. The Grand National had gone by; he had not 'known', and had lost a hundred pounds. Summer was at hand. He was in agony for the Lincoln. But even for the Lincoln he didn't 'know', and he lost fifty pounds. He became wild-eyed and strange, as if something were going to explode in him.

"Let it alone, son! Don't you bother about it!" urged Uncle Oscar. But it was as if the boy couldn't really hear what his uncle was saying.

"I've got to know for the Derby! I've *got* to know for the Derby!" the child reiterated, his big blue eyes blazing with a sort of madness.

His mother noticed how overwrought he was.

"You'd better go to the seaside. Wouldn't you like to go now to the seaside, instead of waiting? I think you'd better," she said, looking down at him anxiously, her heart curiously heavy because of him.

But the child lifted his uncanny blue eyes.

"I couldn't possibly go before the Derby, Mother!" he said. "I couldn't possibly!"

"Why not?" she said, her voice becoming heavy when she was opposed. "Why not? You can still go from the seaside to see the Derby with your Uncle Oscar, if that's what you wish. No need for you to wait here. Besides, I think you care too much about these races. It's a bad sign. My family has been a gambling family, and you won't know till you grow up how much damage it has done. But it has done damage. I shall have to send Bassett away, and ask Uncle Oscar not to talk racing to you, unless you promise to be reasonable about it: go away to the seaside and forget it. You're all nerves!"

"I'll do what you like, Mother, so long as you don't send me away till after the Derby," the boy said.

"Send you away from where? Just from this house?"

"Yes," he said, gazing at her.

"Why, you curious child, what makes you care about this house so much, suddenly? I never knew you loved it!"

He gazed at her without speaking. He had a secret within a secret, something he had not divulged, even to Bassett or to his Uncle Oscar.

But his mother, after standing undecided and a little bit sullen for some moments, said:

"Very well, then! Don't go to the seaside till after the Derby, if you don't wish it. But promise me you won't let your nerves go to pieces! Promise you won't think so much about horse-racing and *events*, as you call them!"

"Oh no!" said the boy casually. "I won't think much about them, Mother. You needn't worry. I wouldn't worry, Mother, if I were you."

"If you were me and I were you," said his mother, "I wonder what we *should* do!"

"But you know you needn't worry, Mother, don't you?" the boy repeated.

"I should be awfully glad to know it," she said wearily.

"Oh, well, you *can*, you know. I mean you *ought* to know you needn't worry!" he insisted.

"Ought I? Then I'll see about it," she said.

Paul's secret of secrets was his wooden horse, that which had no name. Since he was emancipated from a nurse and a nursery-governess, he had had his rocking-horse removed to his own bedroom at the top of the house.

"Surely you're too big for a rocking-horse!" his mother had remonstrated.

"Well, you see, Mother, till I can have a *real* horse, I like to have *some* sort of animal about," had been his quaint answer.

"Do you feel he keeps you company?" she laughed.

"Oh yes! He's very good, he always keeps me company, when I'm there," said Paul.

So the horse, rather shabby, stood in an arrested prance in the boy's bedroom.

The Derby was drawing near, and the boy grew more and more tense. He hardly heard what was spoken to him, he was very frail, and his eyes were really uncanny. His mother had sudden strange seizures of uneasiness about him. Sometimes, for half an hour, she would feel a sudden anxiety about him that was almost anguish. She wanted to rush to him at once and know he was safe.

Two nights before the Derby, she was at a big party in town, when one of her rushes of anxiety about her boy, her first-born, gripped her heart till she could hardly speak. She fought with the feeling, might and main, for she believed in common sense. But it was too strong.

She had to leave the dance and go downstairs to telephone to the country. The children's nursery-governess was terribly surprised and startled at being rung up in the night.

"Are the children all right, Miss Wilmot?"

"Oh yes, they are quite all right."

"Master Paul? Is he all right?"

"He went to bed as right as a trivet. Shall I run up and look at him?"

"No!" said Paul's mother reluctantly. "No! Don't trouble. It's all right. Don't sit up. We shall be home fairly soon." She did not want her son's privacy intruded upon.

"Very good," said the governess.

It was about one o'clock when Paul's mother and father drove up to their house. All was still. Paul's mother went to her room and slipped off her white fur cloak. She had told her maid not to wait up for her. She heard her husband downstairs, mixing a whisky-and-soda.

And then, because of the strange anxiety at her heart, she stole upstairs to her son's room. Noiselessly she went along the upper corridor. Was there a faint noise? What was it?

She stood, with arrested muscles, outside his door, listening. There was a strange, heavy, and yet not loud noise. Her heart stood still. It was a soundless noise, yet rushing and powerful. Something huge, in violent, hushed motion. What was it? What in God's name was it? She ought to know. She felt that she *knew* the noise. She knew what it was.

Yet she could not place it. She couldn't say what it was. And on and on it went, like a madness.

Softly, frozen with anxiety and fear, she turned the door-handle.

The room was dark. Yet in the space near the window she heard and saw something plunging to and fro. She gazed in fear and amazement.

Then suddenly she switched on the light, and saw her son, in his green pyjamas, madly surging on his rocking-horse. The blaze of light suddenly lit him up, as he urged the wooden horse, and lit her up, as she stood, blonde, in her dress of pale green and crystal, in the doorway.

"Paul!" she cried. "Whatever are you doing?"

"It's Malabar!" he screamed in a powerful, strange voice. "It's Malabar!" His eyes blazed at her for one strange and senseless second, as he ceased urging his wooden horse. Then he fell with a crash to the ground, and she, all her tormented motherhood flooding upon her, rushed to gather him up.

But he was unconscious, and unconscious he remained, with some brain-fever. He talked and tossed, and his mother sat stonily by his side.

"Malabar! It's Malabar! Bassett, Bassett, I *know*; it's Malabar!"

So the child cried, trying to get up and urge the rocking-horse that gave him his inspiration.

"What does he mean by Malabar?" asked the heart-frozen mother.

"I don't know," said the father stonily.

"What does he mean by Malabar?" she asked her brother Oscar.

"It's one of the horses running for the Derby," was the answer.

And, in spite of himself, Oscar Cresswell spoke to Bassett, and himself put a thousand on Malabar: at fourteen to one.

The third day of the illness was critical: they were watching for a change. The boy, with his rather long curly hair, was tossing ceaselessly on the pillow. He neither slept nor regained consciousness, and his eyes were like blue stones. His mother sat, feeling her heart had gone, turned actually into a stone.

In the evening, Oscar Cresswell did not come, but Bassett sent a message, saying could he come up for one moment, just one moment? Paul's mother was very angry at the intrusion, but on second thoughts she agreed. The boy was the same. Perhaps Bassett might bring him to consciousness.

The gardener, a shortish fellow with a little brown moustache and sharp little brown eyes, tiptoed into the room, touched his imaginary cap to Paul's mother, and stole to the bedside, staring with glittering, smallish eyes at the tossing, dying child.

"Master Paul!" he whispered. "Master Paul! Malabar came in first all right, a clean win. I did as you told me. You've made over seventy thousand pounds, you have; you've got over eighty thousand. Malabar came in all right, Master Paul."

"Malabar! Malabar! Did I say Malabar, Mother? Did I say Malabar? Do you think I'm lucky, Mother? I knew Malabar, didn't I? Over eighty thousand pounds! I call that lucky, don't you, Mother? Over eighty thousand pounds! I knew, didn't I know I knew? Malabar came in all right. If I ride my horse till I'm sure, then I tell you, Bassett, you can go as high as you like. Did you go for all you were worth, Bassett?"

"I went a thousand on it, Master Paul."

"I never told you, Mother, that if I can ride my horse, and *get there*, then I'm absolutely sure—oh, absolutely! Mother, did I ever tell you? I *am* lucky!"

"No, you never did," said the mother.

But the boy died in the night.

And even as he lay dead, his mother heard her brother's voice saying to her: "My God, Hester, you're eighty-odd thousand to the good, and a poor devil of a son to the bad. But, poor devil, poor devil, he's best gone out of a life where he rides his rocking-horse to find a winner."

DORIS LESSING

b. 1919

Like the child in this story, she grew up on a farm in Rhodesia, the daughter of British emigrants. She moved to England in 1949. A strong sympathy for the dispossessed, at least partially derived from her African experience, is felt in all her work, and her many novels and short stories have been acclaimed the world over.

The Old Chief Mshlanga

THEY WERE GOOD, the years of ranging the bush over her father's farm which, like every white farm, was largely unused, broken only occasionally by small patches of cultivation. In between, nothing but trees, the long sparse grass, thorn and cactus and gully, grass and outcrop and thorn. And a jutting piece of rock which had been thrust up from the warm soil of Africa unimaginable eras of time ago, washed into hollows and whorls by sun and wind that had travelled so many thousands of miles of space and bush, would hold the weight of a small girl whose eyes were sightless for anything but a pale willowed river, a pale gleaming castle—a small girl singing: "Out flew the web and floated wide, the mirror cracked from side to side . . ."

Pushing her way through the green aisles of the mealie stalks, the leaves arching like cathedrals veined with sunlight far overhead, with the packed red earth underfoot, a fine lace of red starred witchweed would summon up a black bent figure croaking premonitions: the Northern witch, bred of cold Northern forests, would stand before her among the mealie fields, and it was the mealie fields that faded and fled, leaving her among the gnarled roots of an oak, snow falling thick and soft and white, the woodcutter's fire glowing red welcome through crowding tree trunks.

A white child, opening its eyes curiously on a sun-suffused landscape, a gaunt and violent landscape, might be supposed to accept it as her own, to take the msasa trees and the thorn trees as familiars, to feel her blood running free and responsive to the swing of the seasons.

This child could not see a msasa tree, or the thorn, for what they were. Her books held tales of alien fairies, her rivers ran slow and peaceful, and she knew the shape of the leaves of an ash or an oak, the names of the little creatures that lived in English streams, when the words 'the veld' meant strangeness, though she could remember nothing else.

Because of this, for many years, it was the veld that seemed unreal; the sun was a foreign sun, and the wind spoke a strange language.

The black people on the farm were as remote as the trees and the rocks. They were an amorphous black mass, mingling and thinning and massing like tadpoles, faceless, who existed merely to serve, to say "Yes, Baas," take their money and go. They changed season by season, moving from one farm to the next, according to their outlandish needs, which one did not have to understand, coming from perhaps hundreds of miles North or East, passing on after a few months—where? Perhaps even as far away as the fabled gold mines of Johannesburg, where the pay was so much better than the few shillings a month and the double handful of mealie meal twice a day which they earned in that part of Africa.

The child was taught to take them for granted: the servants in the house would come running a hundred yards to pick up a book if she dropped it. She was called 'Nkosikaas'—Chieftainess, even by the black children her own age.

Later, when the farm grew too small to hold her curiosity, she carried a gun in the crook of her arm and wandered miles a day, from vlei to vlei, from *kopje* to *kopje*, accompanied by two dogs: the dogs and the gun were an armour against fear. Because of them she never felt fear.

If a native came into sight along the kaffir paths half a mile away, the dogs would flush him up a tree as if he were a bird. If he expostulated (in his uncouth language which was by itself ridiculous) that was cheek. If one was in a good mood, it could be a matter for laughter. Otherwise one passed on, hardly glancing at the angry man in the tree.

On the rare occasions when white children met together they could amuse themselves by hailing a passing native in order to make a buffoon of him; they could set the dogs on him and watch him run; they could tease a small black child as if he were a puppy—save that they would not throw stones and sticks at a dog without a sense of guilt.

Later still, certain questions presented themselves in the child's mind; and because the answers were not easy to accept, they were silenced by an even greater arrogance of manner.

It was even impossible to think of the black people who worked about the house as friends, for if she talked to one of them, her mother would come running anxiously: "Come away; you mustn't talk to natives."

It was this instilled consciousness of danger, of something unpleasant, that made it easy to laugh out loud, crudely, if a servant made a mistake in his English or if he failed to understand an order—there is a certain kind of laughter that is fear, afraid of itself.

One evening, when I was about fourteen, I was walking down the side of a mealie field that had been newly ploughed, so that the great red clods showed fresh and tumbling to the vlei beyond, like a choppy red sea; it was that hushed and listening hour, when the birds send long sad calls from tree to tree, and all the colours of earth and sky and leaf are deep and golden. I had my rifle in the curve of my arm, and the dogs were at my heels.

In front of me, perhaps a couple of hundred yards away, a group of three Africans came into sight around the side of a big ant heap. I whistled the dogs close in to my skirts and let the gun swing in my hand, and advanced, waiting for them to move aside, off the path, in respect for my passing. But they came on steadily, and the dogs looked up at me for the command to chase. I was angry. It was 'cheek' for a native not to stand off a path, the moment he caught sight of you.

In front walked an old man, stooping his weight on to a stick, his hair grizzled white, a dark red blanket slung over his shoulders like a cloak. Behind him came two young men, carrying bundles of pots, assegais, hatchets.

The group was not a usual one. They were not natives seeking work. These had an air of dignity, of quietly following their own purpose. It was the dignity that checked my tongue. I walked quietly on, talking softly to the growling dogs, till I was ten paces away. Then the old man stopped, drawing his blanket close.

"Morning, Nkosikaas," he said, using the customary greeting for any time of the day.

"Good morning," I said. "Where are you going?" My voice was a little truculent.

The old man spoke in his own language, then one of the young men stepped forward politely and said in careful English: "My Chief travels to see his brothers beyond the river."

A Chief! I thought, understanding the pride that made the old man stand before me like an equal—more than an equal, for he showed courtesy, and I showed none.

The old man spoke again, wearing dignity like an inherited garment, still standing ten paces off, flanked by his entourage, not looking at me (that would have been rude) but directing his eyes somewhere over my head at the trees.

"You are the little Nkosikaas from the farm of Baas Jordan?"

"That's right," I said.

"Perhaps your father does not remember," said the interpreter for the old man, "but there was an affair with some goats. I remember seeing you when you were . . ." The young man held his hand at knee level and smiled.

We all smiled.

"What is your name?" I asked.

"This is Chief Mshlanga," said the young man.

"I will tell my father that I met you," I said.

The old man said: "My greetings to your father, little Nkosikaas."

"Good morning," I said politely, finding the politeness difficult, from lack of use.

"Morning, little Nkosikaas," said the old man, and stood aside to let me pass.

I went by, my gun hanging awkwardly, the dogs sniffing and growling, cheated of their favourite game of chasing natives like animals.

Not long afterwards I read in an old explorer's book the phrase: "Chief Mshlanga's country". It went like this: "Our destination was Chief Mshlanga's country, to the north of the river; and it was our desire to ask his permission to prospect for gold in his territory."

The phrase 'ask his permission' was so extraordinary to a white child, brought up to consider all natives as things to use, that it revived those questions, which could not be suppressed: they fermented slowly in my mind.

On another occasion one of those old prospectors who still move over Africa looking for neglected reefs, with their hammers and tents, and pans for sifting gold from crushed rock, came to the farm and, in talking of the old days, used that phrase again: "This was the Old Chief's country," he said. "It stretched from those mountains over there way back to the river, hundreds of miles of country." That was his name for our district: "The Old Chief's Country"; he did not use our name for it—a new phrase which held no implication of usurped ownership.

As I read more books about the time when this part of Africa was opened up, not much more than fifty years before, I found Old Chief Mshlanga had been a famous man, known to all the explorers and prospectors. But then he had been young; or maybe it was his father or uncle they spoke of—I never found out.

During that year I met him several times in the part of the farm that was traversed by natives moving over the country. I learned that the path up the side of the big red field where the birds sang was the recognized highway for migrants. Perhaps I even haunted it in the hope of meeting him: being greeted by him, the exchange of courtesies, seemed to answer the questions that troubled me.

Soon I carried a gun in a different spirit; I used it for shooting food and not to give me confidence. And now the dogs learned better manners.

When I saw a native approaching, we offered and took greetings; and slowly that other landscape in my mind faded, and my feet struck directly on the African soil, and I saw the shapes of tree and hill clearly, and the black people moved back, as it were, out of my life: it was as if I stood aside to watch a slow intimate dance of landscape and men, a very old dance, whose steps I could not learn.

But I thought: this is my heritage, too; I was bred here; it is my country as well as the black man's country; and there is plenty of room for all of us, without elbowing each other off the pavements and roads.

It seemed it was only necessary to let free that respect I felt when I was talking with Old Chief Mshlanga, to let both black and white people meet gently, with tolerance for each other's differences: it seemed quite easy.

Then, one day, something new happened. Working in our house as servants were always three natives: cook, houseboy, garden boy. They used to change as the farm natives changed: staying for a few months, then moving on to a new job, or back home to their kraals. They were thought of as 'good' or 'bad' natives; which meant: how did they behave as servants? Were they lazy, efficient, obedient, or disrespectful? If the family felt good-humoured, the phrase was: "What can you expect from raw black savages?" If we were angry, we said: "These damned niggers, we would be much better off without them."

One day, a white policeman was on his rounds of the district, and he said laughingly: "Did you know you have an important man in your kitchen?"

"What!" exclaimed my mother sharply. "What do you mean?"

"A Chief's son." The policeman seemed amused. "He'll boss the tribe when the old man dies."

"He'd better not put on a Chief's son act with me," said my mother.

When the policeman left, we looked with different eyes at our cook: he was a good worker, but he drank too much at week-ends—that was how we knew him.

He was a tall youth, with very black skin, like black polished metal, his tightly-growing black hair parted white man's fashion at one side, with a metal comb from the store stuck into it; very polite, very distant, very quick to obey an order. Now that it had been pointed out, we said: "Of course, you can see. Blood always tells."

My mother became strict with him now she knew about his birth and prospects. Sometimes, when she lost her temper, she would say: "You aren't the Chief yet, you know." And he would answer her very quietly, his eyes on the ground: "Yes, Nkosikaas."

One afternoon he asked for a whole day off, instead of the customary half-day, to go home next Sunday.

"How can you go home in one day?"

"It will take me half an hour on my bicycle," he explained.

I watched the direction he took; and the next day I went off to look for this kraal; I understood he must be Chief Mshlanga's successor: there was no other kraal near enough our farm.

Beyond our boundaries on that side the country was new to me. I followed unfamiliar paths past *kopjes* that till now had been part of the jagged horizon, hazed with distance. This was Government land, which had never been cultivated by white men; at first I could not understand why it was that it appeared, in merely crossing the boundary, I had entered a completely fresh type of landscape. It was a wide green valley, where a small river sparkled, and vivid water-birds darted over the rushes. The grass was thick and soft to my calves, the trees stood tall and shapely.

I was used to our farm, whose hundreds of acres of harsh eroded soil bore trees that had been cut for the mine furnaces and had grown thin and twisted, where the cattle had dragged the grass flat, leaving innumerable criss-crossing trails that deepened each season into gullies, under the force of the rains.

This country had been left untouched, save for prospectors whose picks had struck a few sparks from the surface of the rocks as they wandered by; and for migrant natives whose passing had left, perhaps, a charred patch on the trunk of a tree where their evening fire had nestled.

It was very silent: a hot morning with pigeons cooing throatily, the midday shadows lying dense and thick with clear yellow spaces of sunlight between and in all that wide green park-like valley, not a human soul but myself.

I was listening to the quick regular tapping of a woodpecker when slowly a chill feeling seemed to grow up from the small of my back to my shoulders, in a constricting spasm like a shudder, and at the roots of my hair a tingling sensation began and ran down over the surface of my flesh, leaving me goosefleshed and cold, though I was damp with sweat. Fever? I thought; then uneasily, turned to look over my shoulder; and realized suddenly that this was fear. It was extraordinary, even humiliating. It was a new fear. For all the years I had walked by myself over this country I had never known a moment's uneasiness, in the beginning because I had been supported by a gun and the dogs, then because I had learnt an easy friendliness for the Africans I might encounter.

I had read of this feeling, how the bigness and silence of Africa, under the ancient sun, grows dense and takes shape in the mind, till even the birds seem to call menacingly, and a deadly spirit comes out of the trees and the rocks.

You move warily, as if your very passing disturbs something old and evil, something dark and big and angry that might suddenly rear and strike from behind. You look at groves of entwined trees, and picture the animals that might be lurking there; you look at the river running slowly, dropping from level to level through the vlei, spreading into pools where at night the bucks come to drink, and the crocodiles rise and drag them by their soft noses into underwater caves. Fear possessed me. I found I was turning round and round, because of that shapeless menace behind me that might reach out and take me; I kept glancing at the files of *kopjes* which, seen from a different angle, seemed to change with every step so that even known landmarks, like a big mountain that had sentinelled my world since I first became conscious of it, showed an unfamiliar sunlit valley among its foothills. I did not known where I was. I was lost. Panic seized me. I found I was spinning round and round, staring anxiously at this tree and that, peering up at the sun which appeared to have moved into an eastern slant, shedding the sad yellow light of sunset. Hours must have passed! I looked at my watch and found that this state of meaningless terror had lasted perhaps ten minutes.

The point was that it was meaningless. I was not ten miles from home: I had only to take my way back along the valley to find myself at the fence; away among the foothills of the *kopjes* gleamed the roof of a neighbour's house, and a couple of hours' walking would reach it. This was the sort of fear that contracts the flesh of a dog at night and sets him howling at the full moon. It had nothing to do with what I thought or felt; and I was more disturbed by the fact that I could become its victim than of the physical sensation itself: I walked steadily on, quietened, in a divided mind, watching my own pricking nerves and apprehensive glances from side to side with a disgusted amusement. Deliberately I set myself to think of this village I was seeking, and what I should do when I entered it—if I could find it, which was doubtful, since I was walking aimlessly and it might be anywhere in the hundreds of thousands of acres of bush that stretched about me.

With my mind on that village, I realized that a new sensation was added to the fear: loneliness. Now such a terror of isolation invaded me that I could hardly walk; and if it were not that I came over the crest of a small rise and saw a village below me, I should have turned and gone home. It was a cluster of thatched huts in a clearing among trees. There were neat patches of mealies and pumpkins and millet, and cattle grazed under some trees at a distance. Fowls scratched among the huts, dogs lay sleeping on the grass, and goats friezed a *kopje* that jutted up beyond a tributary of the river lying like an enclosing arm round the village.

As I came close I saw the huts were lovingly decorated with patterns of yellow and red and ochre mud on the walls; and the thatch was tied in place with plaits of straw.

This was not at all like our farm compound, a dirty and neglected place, a temporary home for migrants who had no roots in it.

And now I did not know what to do next. I called a small black boy, who was sitting on a lot playing a stringed gourd, quite naked except for the strings of blue beads round his neck, and said: "Tell the Chief I am here." The child stuck his thumb in his mouth and stared shyly back at me.

For minutes I shifted my feet on the edge of what seemed a deserted village, till at last the child scuttled off, and then some women came. They were draped in bright cloths, with brass glinting in their ears and on their arms. They also stared, silently; then turned to chatter among themselves.

I said again: "Can I see Chief Mshlanga?" I saw they caught the name; they did not understand what I wanted. I did not understand myself.

At last I walked through them and came past the huts and saw a clearing under a big shady tree, where a dozen old men sat cross-legged on the ground, talking. Chief Mshlanga was leaning back against the tree, holding a gourd in his hand, from which he had been drinking. When he saw me, not a muscle of his face moved, and I could see he was not pleased: perhaps he was afflicted with my own shyness, due to being unable to find the right forms of courtesy for the occasion. To meet me, on our own farm, was one thing; but I should not have come here.

What had I expected? I could not join them socially: the thing was unheard of. Bad enough that I, a white girl, should be walking the veld alone as a white man might: and in this part of the bush where only Government officials had the right to move.

Again I stood, smiling foolishly, while behind me stood the groups of brightly-clad, chattering women, their faces alert with curiosity and interest, and in front of me sat the old men, with old lined faces, their eyes guarded, aloof. It was a village of ancients and children and women. Even the two young men who kneeled beside the Chief were not those I had seen with him previously: the young men were all away working on the white men's farms and mines, and the Chief must depend on relatives who were temporarily on holiday for his attendants.

"The small white Nkosikaas is far from home," remarked the old man at last.

"Yes," I agreed, "it is far." I wanted to say: "I have come to pay you a friendly visit, Chief Mshlanga." I could not say it. I might now be feeling an urgent helpless desire to get to know these men and women as people, to be accepted by them as a friend, but the truth was I had set out in a spirit of curiosity: I had wanted to see the village that one day our cook, the reserved and obedient young man who got drunk on Sundays, would one day rule over.

"The child of Nkosi Jordan is welcome," said Chief Mshlanga.

"Thank you," I said, and could think of nothing more to say. There was a silence, while the flies rose and began to buzz around my head; and the wind shook a little in the thick green tree that spread its branches over the old men.

"Good morning," I said at last. "I have to return now to my home."

"Morning, little Nkosikaas," said Chief Mshlanga.

I walked away from the indifferent village, over the rise past the staring amber-eyed goats, down through the tall stately trees into the great rich green valley where the river meandered and the pigeons cooed tales of plenty and the woodpecker tapped softly.

The fear had gone; the loneliness had set into stiff-necked stoicism; there was now a queer hostility in the landscape, a cold, hard, sullen indomitability that walked with me, as strong as a wall, as intangible as smoke; it seemed to say to me: you walk here as a destroyer. I went slowly homewards, with an empty heart: I had learned that if one cannot call a country to heel like a dog, neither can one dismiss the past with a smile in an easy gush of feeling, saying: I could not help it, I am also a victim.

I only saw Chief Mshlanga once again.

One night my father's big red land was trampled down by small sharp hooves, and it was discovered that the culprits were goats from Chief Mshlanga's kraal. This had happened once before, years ago.

My father confiscated all the goats. Then he sent a message to the old Chief that if he wanted them he would have to pay for the damage.

He arrived at our house at the time of sunset one evening, looking very old and bent now, walking stiffly under his regally-draped blanket, leaning on a big stick. My father sat himself down in his big chair below the steps of the house; the old man squatted carefully on the ground before him, flanked by his two young men.

The palaver was long and painful, because of the bad English of the young man who interpreted, and because my father could not speak dialect, but only kitchen kaffir.

From my father's point of view, at least two hundred pounds' worth of damage had been done to the crop. He knew he could not get the money from the old man. He felt he was entitled to keep the goats. As for the old Chief, he kept repeating angrily: "Twenty goats! My people cannot lose twenty goats! We are not rich, like the Nkosi Jordan, to lose twenty goats at once."

My father did not think of himself as rich, but rather as very poor. He spoke quickly and angrily in return, saying that the damage done meant a great deal to him, and that he was entitled to the goats.

At last it grew so heated that the cook, the Chief's son, was called from the kitchen to be interpreter, and now my father spoke fluently in English, and our cook translated rapidly so that the old man could understand how very angry my father was.

The young man spoke without emotion, in a mechanical way, his eyes lowered, but showing how he felt his position by a hostile uncomfortable set of the shoulders.

It was now in the late sunset, the sky a welter of colours, the birds singing their last songs, and the cattle, lowing peacefully, moving past us towards their sheds for the night. It was the hour when Africa is most beautiful; and here was this pathetic, ugly scene, doing no one any good.

At last my father stated finally: "I'm not going to argue about it. I am keeping the goats."

The old Chief flashed back in his own language: "That means that my people will go hungry when the dry season comes."

"Go to the police, then," said my father, and looked triumphant.

There was, of course, no more to be said.

The old man sat silent, his head bent, his hands dangling helplessly over his withered knees.

Then he rose, the young men helping him, and he stood facing my father. He spoke once again, very stiffly; and turned away and went home to his village.

"What did he say?" asked my father of the young man, who laughed uncomfortably and would not meet his eyes.

"What did he say?" insisted my father.

Our cook stood straight and silent, his brows knotted together. Then he spoke: "My father says: All this land, this land you call yours, is his land, and belongs to our people."

Having made this statement, he walked off into the bush after his father, and we did not see him again.

Our next cook was a migrant from Nyasaland, with no expectations of greatness.

Next time the policeman came on his rounds he was told this story.

He remarked: "That kraal has no right to be there; it should have been moved long ago. I don't know why no one has done anything about it. I'll have a chat with the Native Commissioner next week. I'm going over for tennis on Sunday, anyway."

Some time later we heard that Chief Mshlanga and his people had been moved two hundred miles east, to a proper Native Reserve; the Government land was going to be opened up for white settlement soon.

I went to see the village again, about a year afterwards. There was nothing there. Mounds of red mud, where the huts had been, had long swathes of rotting thatch over them, veined with the red galleries of the white ants. The pumpkin vines rioted everywhere, over the bushes, up the lower branches of trees so that the great golden balls rolled underfoot and dangled overhead: it was a festival of pumpkins. The bushes were crowding up, the new grass sprang vivid green.

The settler lucky enough to be allotted the lush warm valley (if he chose to cultivate this particular section) would find, suddenly, in the middle of a mealie field, the plants were growing fifteen feet tall, the weight of the cobs dragging at the stalks, and wonder what unsuspected vein of richness he had struck.

ERIC LINKLATER

1889–1974

"I shall not claim that the comic view of life is either whole or ultimately satisfying," he wrote in his autobiography, "but it has no less validity than the tragic or romantic view, or what is known as realism." Certainly, it was his comic touch that made him famous, and his early humorous tales are among the very best he wrote.

The Crusader's Key

BERTRAN DE SALARS, lord of Caraman and Salars, a Poor Knight of Christ and of the Temple of Solomon, said to his wife Jehane, "There is in my mind no smallest doubt of your honesty, nor must you think that what I am now about to do can ever be regarded as an insult to you, as a reflection on your character, or an indication of my lessening esteem. I am afraid it will be necessary for you to take off all your clothes."

With some bitterness in her voice the Lady Jehane answered, "If you do not doubt my honesty I cannot see why you should take such precautions to keep me honest as make it seem that good behaviour is contrary to my intentions."

"You are a woman," said Bertran mildly.

"It is late in the day to reproach me with that," said Jehane. "I think you have been glad of it once or twice, and now to blame me for what was God's will and has been your pleasure is mere petulance, and not worthy of a knight who proposes to venture his body for the rescue of God's holy city from the Saracens, since God in His wisdom made Eve as well as Adam, and said no word to Adam whereby he should think it right to reproach her with the nature and condition established in her to further His purpose of comforting Adam with a helpmeet and a lover. Still less did He give man warrant, in that garden where warrant was given for so much, to load a woman with chains and put padlocks on her when he went abroad on errands of his own choosing."

"You are overwrought," said Bertran, "and so you fall into a torrent of words without perceiving to what shoal of fallacy they bear you. For it was not God but the Serpent who gave to Eve that part of her nature which, in these wicked and degenerate times, appears to dominate all the rest. Nor do I believe that even the Serpent would so have worked upon her had he properly foreseen the future. In Eden there was no other man save Adam, but now there are men walking in every field. And since it is woman's part, as you have said, to be a helpmeet and a lover, man must of his own wit—that God gave him—devise means whereby his wife shall love and help him only, and not squander her mercies on all the world.—You must take off your shift as well, my dear."

"There then!" said Lady Jehane, and passionately threw the garment from her. Her cheeks were bright red, from modesty a little and from indignation a great deal, and so hot was her blood that the March wind, blowing lustily through the tower window, chilled her not at all but merely tempered her anger.

"You are very beautiful," said Bertran.

"Keep your mind on the Sepulchre," said Lady Jehane.

"My thought is fixed on it and my heart is ever grieved for its present unhappy state," said Bertran. "I do not think you will find the chain uncomfortable, and the links are so smoothly worked that they cannot chafe you. The padlock, I admit, is somewhat heavy, but were it lightly made it could not be secure."

"My heart was light, yet my love for you lay safely in it," said Lady Jehane.

"I shall be gone three years," said Bertran, "and every month of those years the temptation of benevolence will assail you, pricking of the flesh will stir your woman's wish to give, and voices in your blood will call as dry earth calls loudly for the piercing rain . . ."

"No, no!" cried Jehane. "I am your wife, faithful to you and desirous of no other man."

"You are a woman," said Bertran, "and I shall be gone three years."

Then he put round her waist the girdle that was called the Crusader's Belt—since many knights and noblemen so guarded their wives from shame and even, they hoped, imprudent thoughts while they, far off, battled with the infidel for Christ's tomb and captured city—and when he had adjusted the chain so that it lay close to her side, and yet not so close as to cause discomfort, he fastened it with a heavy padlock, locking that with a key, and tied the key to a cord that he put about his neck.

"This I shall call your heart's key," said Bertran, "and it shall lie against the beating of my own heart."

But Jehane made no answer. She put on her clothes again with abrupt and trembling movements, and in her bearing was a muted wildness. She stood by the narrow window, high in the round grey wall of the tower, and looked at the liberty of earth beyond her. Clouds rolled or swam in open sky; the wind leapt freely through black branches flushed green at their myriad tips with buds half-opened; a hawk poised, trod empty space, and swooped; lambs leapt with ungainly joy in tilted fields—but Lady Jehane, hands pressed to waist, felt under her fingers the hard steel chain, and her body shrank within its hold, and beneath its weight her strength grew weak. She breathed harshly through open mouth, and heard only as some unmeaning noise the farewell her lord was speaking. She gave him her hand to kiss, but her hand was cold, her head averted.

"I shall not be happy till Jerusalem is girt with Christian steel as you are girt," said Bertran.

"Ah, poor city!" cried Jehane.

"Poor city indeed," said Bertran, "and that is why we must ride to its relief."

From her window Jehane looked down and saw the horsemen stiffen to obedience when her lord came out to them. At his word they mounted and rode from the courtyard. Women followed, clamorous at their horses' heels, children shrilly whooped, and those with a better understanding as noisily wept. When the Crusaders had forded the river, splashing through bright shallow water, they turned southwards and rode in file. Bertran waited by the ford till they had crossed. Then he turned to his castle and saluted Lady Jehane—though he could no longer see her, because she had turned away from her window to sit on a little stool and crouch there like an old woman, thinking nothing whatever about the perils and discomfort to which her lord was riding, but very bitterly concerned with her own misery.

The lord of Caraman and Salars sighed and shook his head in a wistful movement that consorted badly with his military appearance, with the short manly beard he wore in compliance with Templar custom, and indeed with the Templar tradition to waste no time on topics of sentiment. But though he knew Jehane to be unhappy, and though the knowledge grieved him, he comforted himself with the assurance that he had acted wisely and for the ultimate benefit of both himself and his wife. He patted his brown surcoat, with the great red cross on it, and felt beneath it her heart's key. "She is safe," he thought, and putting spurs to his horse cantered to overtake his troop.

For a week of tedious days the Lady Jehane maintained a demeanour that to her household appeared the perfection of widowed grief. She was listless, she would not eat, her cheeks were pale and her eyes were red, she was irritable when spoken to, and would burst into tears to atone for her unkindness. "Ah!" said her servants and her friends, "what desire she has for that Bertran with his Templar's beard, his heavy speech, and his concern for this matter of the Sepulchre! Who would have thought that such a man could blow love's flame so hot, and leave so desolate a hearth behind him?"

But the truth was that Jehane never gave a thought to her lord except in the way of anger against his stupidity. Under a seeming gaiety and lightness of manner she was in reality extremely virtuous, and though she delighted in the society of troubadours and others who spoke much about the art of love, she had never felt the slightest inclination to abandon herself to its illicit practice. To be loved by Bertran was rather different, of course, though even his embraces, despite the favouring circumstances of the Church's blessing, had really given her very little pleasure. And love unconsecrated was mere bestiality.

That Bertran could think of her yielding to brutish heat like a heifer in the fields or some gap-toothed peasant in a barn! That was pride-shattering, that broke her heart as though her heart had been herself in a mirror broken by a stone. And then there was the intolerable burden of the chain, ever present, printing her side with its abominable links, and by its presence fixing her mind on the lewdness it prohibited. She had no wish to think of evil, but the chain held her to thoughts of evil as surely as it bound her to continence. "It makes me a slave, it makes me an animal," she thought. It was moreover extremely uncomfortable.

And then one morning Jehane was wakened by the amorous voice of the troubadour Simon Vidal singing an alba, or morning song, to her sister Maulfry, a laughing handsome girl to whom such flattery was often paid. The alba was a passionate complaint against the intrusive sun, that drove back the friendly dark and with cruel fingers tore lovers from their lovers' arms.

> "So coldly blows the wind of dawn
> Upon a naked heart,"

sang the troubadour.

"It sounds quite sincere and convincing," thought Jehane. "Someone who knew nothing of our customs might well believe that he had really spent the night in Maulfry's arms and was singing out of uncontrollable grief at parting from her. But he has probably given several days to the composition of so charming a lyric, and was wakened by his servant just in time to get up and sing it so that the sun might rise on its last notes." Vidal sang another verse. Though shrill with pain his voice retained the loveliness of conscious art, and the melody was plucked with proficient yearning from the strings of his lute:

"I flee before the sharp-edged light
Towards another dark;
How cold becomes the world at dawn—
Cover your naked heart!"

"I wonder!" thought Jehane. "That last verse seems to have a more personal note than is usual, though of course many troubadours make their songs provocative enough, and try to give the impression that even more has happened than they are willing to tell. But nobody really believes them when they are like that, and it would be a pity indeed if people did believe them, and so forced them to speak the truth, for you can't make much poetry out of truth alone or compose a song by merely saying what actually occurred. And yet I feel rather anxious about Maulfry, for there was certainly a lot of feeling in Vidal's alba, and she is brave enough for anything. Perhaps he did spend the night in her room!"

Then—"Why," thought Lady Jehane, "now I am getting like poor Bertran, who always thinks the worst has happened or is going to happen. Were it not for this wretched chain I should never have suspected anything, but under its influence I am ready to believe in all manner of impropriety. People really do seem wickeder than I used to think them, but then formerly I was so innocent that I could rarely imagine how evil occurred, and had to take the world's lewdness on trust. Which was, perhaps, a little dull on the whole. But now I have no difficulty in picturing the vicious state into which society has fallen."

And a little later she exclaimed, "It is Bertran's fault, and he has only himself to blame! It is due solely to his action that henceforth I shall not only take pleasure in believing the worst about people, but also in behaving myself with all the impropriety of which I am capable. It is true that I am not capable of much, owing to this miserable chain, but I shall do what I can to justify Bertran's belief that it was necessary!"

Lady Jehane was now happier than she had been since her lord first announced his intention of girdling her to compulsory chastity. From that morning when she heard Vidal singing, her demeanour changed, and the castle of Caraman, that had shared her gloom, now participated in her gaiety. Under the quickening influence of spring, troubadours were rivalling the mating birds in the profusion of their melodies—while far excelling the simple lark and the untutored willow-wren in fertility of invention—and some of the most accomplished paid visits to the castle of Caraman when they heard that not only the Lady Maulfry but also the Lady Jehane was in a mood to welcome their art and themselves.

Vidal, hopelessly enslaved by the beauty and gaiety of Maulfry, had become rather one of the household than a passing guest. Under the soporific influence of a permanent interest and a settled domicile his songs had acquired a certain monotony—though that which awakened Jehane had been brilliantly individual—but now, when other minstrels sang in his hearing their delight in Jehane's fair beauty, his wit was stirred afresh and his jealous pride in Maulfry found expression in ever new and more daring felicities. This championship of dark Maulfry, vaunting her eyes in a brave conceit and her lips in the most exquisite of tunes, inspired in its turn the visiting troubadours to novelties in compliment and rare device in melody when their opportunity came to hymn the golden loveliness of Jehane. For if Maulfry was starlight on the velvet breast of night, Jehane—as one of them remarked—was dawn lifting its small clouds of white and rose from a pale gold field of barley. Maulfry, to put it shortly, was dark and slender, while Jehane was very fair and somewhat inclined to plumpness.

So timing his arrival that he could bear with him the first spray of almond-blossom, Gilles de Mercadet came one morning to the castle. When his name was announced a flutter of anticipation passed over the ladies of the castle like a breeze that comes roughly into a flower-garden, and those of the gentlemen present who were interested in poetry turned with the liveliest expectancy to see him whose fame as a troubadour outstripped even his reputation as a lover.

Gilles de Mercadet was tall and excessively handsome. His legs were long, his brow was broad and white, his hair had the sombre brilliance of a raven's wing. His chin was determined, his nose severe, and his eyes were dark and lustrous under melancholy lids. His hands were shapely and a nervous passion animated his fingers. He came into the hall with his joglar behind him—a little man, ugly and red-faced—and fell on his knees before Lady Jehane. She welcomed him gladly, and took the almond-blossom from him, and put it to her lips.

After the interchange of some courtesies Jehane said, "You have travelled far, sir, I think, for had you been living in this neighbourhood, I would have heard of it."

"I have come from Perpignan," said Gilles.

"That is far enough," said Jehane, "and I am glad you have had so long a journey, since now you will be tired of travel and content to stay here."

"Does any man who has once seen you ever go farther or fare home again?"

"My husband has gone to the Holy Land," said Jehane.

"Marriage, that gives a man rights, ever robs him of reason," said Gilles.

After a little while Maulfry asked, "Did you not find the air of Perpignan to your liking, sir?"

"The air was good enough," said Gilles, "but those who used it were less to my fancy."

"I have heard the ladies there are most beautiful," said Jehane.

"Even were they as beautiful as they esteem themselves, that would not excuse their demand for admiration," said Gilles.

"We are modest people here," said Jehane.

"Then your virtue must exceed your judgment," answered the troubadour.

On the following morning de Mercadet looked white and weary. His eyes were more profoundly dark, hooded more deeply by their melancholy lids, and his cheeks were pale with the transparent pallor of suffering. With the anxiety of a hostess and a woman's pity for the pain of a young man so handsome. Lady Jehane asked if he had not slept well.

"I was visited by something more importunate than sleep," he said. "An inspiration, a thought, a vision," he explained, seeing Jehane looked questioningly from one to another of her ladies.

"Perhaps your room was not comfortable," she suggested.

"It has a window," said Gilles. Then he took his lute from the joglar, and after striking two or three preliminary chords to arrest the general attention—which he did very easily—he sang the following lines to a tune of surpassing merit:

"I looked through my window and caught my heart with a cry
To see the late moon and the dawn sharing the sky.

"I saw the slim gold crescent of the old moon lean
Over the hill in a vapour of gull's-egg-green;

"While a span to the north another day began
As the sun's bright fingers opened an apricot fan—

"Faced with the loveliness of those lovely two,
Lady Jehane, how could I help thinking of you?"

To all but one of the many compliments evoked by this charming song de Mercadet seemed indifferent. Even to Jehane, who thanked him in words as pretty as the song, he seemed more concerned with some secret thought of his own than with the expression of hers, though that might have gratified any poet on earth with its politeness. But when Simon Vidal, his fellow troubadour, said with all the enthusiasm of his generous nature how greatly he admired the contrast between the level pacing of the verse rhythm and the urgent fire of the accompaniment, why then de Mercadet was roused, grew talkative, excited even, and played again to show how the heavy words reined back the sweet impatience of the melody. Talking still, of sirventes and tenson, of alba, serena, and planh, the two poets went off together, leaving their audience somewhat astonished and rather at a loss for further amusement.

But Jehane, sitting alone, was well pleased with de Mercadet's strange behaviour, for she thought it meant—despite his reputation for gallantry—that he was a poet enthusiastic only for his art, and so not likely to embarrass her with the attentions of a lover. For though she had resolved to fling propriety to the winds she found this to be more difficult than she had expected, and much less pleasant. Adventures even upon the outermost fringes of love's play made her strangely uncomfortable. Her daughter, a child some two or three years old, was a plain little girl with a strong resemblance to her father in her small blunt nose and square chin; and whenever a courtier became gallant Jehane would unfortunately remember the little Aélis and foolishly experience a sensation of guilt. Her belief that de Mercadet would be content to sing of love, without endeavouring to practise it, was therefore most comforting.

For some days his behaviour was all she could desire. His demeanour was that of a man ravaged by passion, his pale cheeks were apparently the emblem of a lover's pain, and his black hair suggested the ensign of a dying heart. But he appeared satisfied with the composition of several charming songs, ardent indeed, but with a kind of impersonal poetic ardour rather than a lover's heat; and in a tenson with Simon Vidal he raked the visible universe for symbols and similes with which to praise his mistress, but so contrived his flattery that it had an air of detached criticism wholly devoid of any insinuation that the flatterer might be entitled to a reward for his discernment.

So completely lulled were Jehane's suspicions that one evening, some weeks after de Mercadet's arrival at the castle, she walked with him alone in a garden by the river and watched with him the moon's image in the wrinkled water, and saw it run in silver slippers to the still obscurity of the farther bank. The air was full of summer perfumes. A nightingale sang, its voice choking with sweetness, and stopped on a broken note. Then de Mercadet turned to Jehane, and with a passion in his voice that he no longer troubled to conceal, sang softly:

"Silent sits the nightingale
To hear the passion of my cry;
Paler grows the moon so pale
To see how pale am I—
Pity me, Lady Jehane,
Pity me, else I die!"

Jehane was seriously perturbed by this sudden attack. She was immediately conscious of opposing forces that tore her soul, and between the soft importunacy of her senses—stirred by music, the scented night, and the pandering moon—and the strong restraint of her moral nature—aggravated by fear of her impetuous lover—she was in a truly pitiable state. Her heart was touched by desire but her knees were trembling in their fright before a lover. The fleering moon cried "Yes!" but a memory of her snub-nosed daughter clutched her skirts and holloa'd "No!"

With a plea for gentleness and a promise for to-morrow she won respite from de Mercadet, and returned to the castle in a greater flutter than she had known since, at the age of thirteen, her sleep was spoiled by a vision of St. Michael bearing an outrageously destructive sword. Not till she was alone in her room did she remember, with a sense of anticlimax, her protective girdle and the key that hung round the lord of Caraman's neck in Acre or Cyprus or some such distant place.

Now de Mercadet laid siege in earnest, and as the constant state of excitement in which she lived notably increased Jehane's beauty, so the troubadour's ardour was maintained not only by resistance but by the steady growth of her charm. She also acquired, without knowing it, the pricking art of the coquette, and so for a week she would be coldly virtuous, for a day she would be fond and warm, kissing even, once even clinging and on the point, so it seemed, of yielding utterly. De Mercadet's manner was variable as hers, for in the morning he often behaved with the insolence of a dictator, and in the evening as frequently threw himself at Jehane's feet in the attitude of a slave. He made a certain number of songs in her honour, but it was generally remarked that they were far inferior to his earlier compositions. He added new verses to that which bore the refrain: "Pity me, Lady Jehane, Pity me, else I die!" and those best qualified to estimate the merit of such things declared that no part of it was worthy of a troubadour of his reputation. But if de Mercadet's creative power declined, so did Jehane's critical ability, for in time she grew to think that refrain the most exquisite and moving verse she had ever heard.

It was on a day in autumn that de Mercadet drove her to her last defence, and she had to confess that she wore a chain binding her to impenetrable chastity. On other occasions when the troubadour's wooing pressed her hard she had sometimes conveniently forgotten the belt, sometimes most opportunely remembered it—but she had never mentioned it. It was her last rampart, her ultimate winning card, and now when de Mercadet had at last stormed all other opposition, and treachery in her own breast cried her to surrender, she told him, in a mood between triumph and despair, of the proscriptive chain, the inviolable lock.

For a little while de Mercadet was nonplussed. His attitude proclaimed defeat. He stood by an open window and let the wind blow coldly on his tears. Then, turning the situation upside down, he saw suddenly both comfort and hope in the steely prohibition of the Crusader's belt. He cried excitedly, "This, then, is the reason you have so long refused me! This paltry chain is the only bar to our felicity! I had thought you lacked love to meet my love, and that was why you turned from me so often and so coldly, and thinking that I came near to despair. But now I know that nothing but a few steel links have kept you from my arms . . ."

"No, no!" cried Jehane.

"Now I am assured of that I grow happy indeed. For steel can be cut, links broken, or padlocks picked. I will get keys, Jehane, a sharp biting file, and loose you from these trifling shackles within the hour."

Indignant and queenly tall, Jehane said furiously, "Do you expect me to strip and stand naked while you do your tinker-work? You are mad indeed if that is what you hope."

"Then I will find a smith," exclaimed the troubadour, "some old and shrivelled smith, and pay him well for his work, and then put out his eyes for daring to see the glory of your waist."

But Jehane grew angrier still and cried, "Am I a horse that I should be taken to the smithy, or do you think me a monster that I should scratch men blind?"

De Mercadet had some difficulty in pacifying her, but presently she grew more calm, and then he left her, saying he would think of other means to get rid of the obstructive belt, and bade her be of good cheer in expectation of success.

The following day, when chance left them alone together, he said with great eagerness, "Lady Jehane, the most difficult problems often have very simple answers. Now this is the truth, that you are the most beautiful woman I have ever seen, but you are far from being the slenderest."

"So!" said Jehane, "you call me fat now. Well, that is a change from your compliments."

Patiently de Mercadet explained that he had said nothing of the sort. He had never mentioned fatness. "Is Juno fat because her beauty is more amply drawn than Diana's?" he asked. "Has not a flowing curve, an arc, more beauty than a poor straight line? What is there to see or commend in a green stick of girlhood? But every contour of your perfect womanhood is Cupid's bow bent to kill."

"Is there any point to all this?" asked Jehane.

De Mercadet hesitated. "It might be possible," he said, "to reduce the fullness of your beauty without impairing its essential quality. And if by chance you grew more slim—if Love's bow were here and there unbent . . ."

"The chain would fall off as from a green stick of girlhood?"

De Mercadet bowed. "Will you not spare a penny or two of your beauty's opulence to buy love itself?"

"And how am I to do that?" asked Jehane.

"There are various ways. Some strenuous exercise, for example . . ."

"What," said Jehane, "shall I kick and prance, turn flesh to dew, and wipe it off? You must think of some easier way than that, good Gilles."

Again the troubadour spoke with a diffidence unusual in him. "Hermits and other ascetic people grow thin by living on a meagre diet of root and herbs."

"So you would have me starve for love's sake?" said Jehane. "But such a plan appeals to me no more than jumping does, and I shall neither run to make me lean as a hunting dog, nor starve to grow thin as an anchorite, since the sole benefit from either would be yours in possessing me."

Because the Lady Jehane was in so difficult a mood de Mercadet made no attempt to expose the fallacy in her last statement, nor indeed to recommend further the courses he had already suggested. But with an air of melancholy arrogance he begged leave to go, and left her. Nor did he leave her for the moment only, but for a space of several days. Servants saw him in the early morning, when the river mist accentuated his pallor, as he walked solitary in the gardens; and in the evening twilight one might observe him by the edge of a wood, dark against its darkness, and staring into the sky as though impatient for the coming obscurity of night. But except for these crepuscular glimpses he was rarely visible, and he spoke to no one. The reason for his strange conduct was widely canvassed and gave ground for much conversation. The friends and servants of Lady Jehane were inclined to be proud of their supposition that she had broken his heart, for they would in a sense share in her prestige if this were so.

But Jehane herself was scarcely so happy. In de Mercadet's absence she felt more drawn to him than had been usual while he sat beside her, and she thought about love, even illicit love, with a broader mind when its exponent was no longer at hand to put her tolerance to the test. Since there was now no one to speak to her of love—for all others had retired before de Mercadet's wooing—she thought she would like to be loved. She remembered the troubadour's suggestion that she might grow slimmer, and so rid herself of the belt, by attention to her diet. She considered her image in several mirrors and discovered with some reluctance that her beauty might even be enhanced by judicious decrement of its superfluity. And so for an unhappy meal or two she pushed the cream-jug away from her, tortured her appetite with lettuce and a biscuit, and when her friends proffered sweetmeats turned with a shudder in the opposite direction. This asceticism was of brief duration, however. Jehane's loss of appetite was reported in the kitchens, and her cook, a loyal and loving servant, set his mind to the confection of a pie that would restore her to health by its irresistible awakening of hunger. In this he most happily succeeded.

As ambergris will proclaim its virtue from afar, so did the pie. An odour of richness came out of it, not in a great vulgar gust, but in subtle streams and airs that took the nose with sweetness and brought moisture to the tongue. When Lady Jehane smelt this enchanting smell her thought was, "How poor and frail a thing is love compared with table joys!" The idea of starving herself for such a trifling pleasure as de Mercadet's embraces appeared, in view of this magnificent pie, so wild an absurdity, that she laughed aloud, and covered the amazement that her laughter produced by calling to her sewer, "Cut quickly, man! Must our hunger wait for your convenience?"

Thereupon her sewer invaded the pie with a great knife, and cutting a thick wedge of crumbling pastry discovered beneath it a store of larks, leverets, quails, pigeons and other small fowl. "Love!" thought Lady Jehane scornfully as she filled her mouth with this succulent variety, "what man's love is worth a lark and leveret pie?" And as she pushed her manchet of bread into the hot dark gravy she was vastly amused to think of anyone forsaking the joy of eating to take a lover or find beauty in slimness. "Green sticks of girlhood!" she muttered. "Boy," she said to her page, "bring me more pie!" And patted her plumpness with a sigh of content.

She was eating sugar plums when de Mercadet found her that afternoon. She felt a little pang of remorse when she saw how pale and handsome he was, but hardening her heart she said, "Well, good Gilles, have you found new arguments to persuade me into starvation?"

But de Mercadet said eagerly, "There will be no need of that now, I think, for I have thought of someone who may help us by simpler means."

"Do not suggest a smithy again," said Jehane.

"When I was in Perpignan I taught something of my art to young Charles de Gaucelm, in whose father's house I lived for a certain time. I taught him to make an alba, to hold his own in a tenson, and how to improve his playing on the lute. For this he was grateful, as you may well imagine, and since he was adored by all that household, all that household competed with him in gratitude and still would be willing to do much for me.—It was none of their fault that I left Perpignan.—Now there is in the house an old nurse whose wisdom in leechcraft and skill in herbs are indeed remarkable. She was born in Brittany, and she learnt her secrets there. Among her most notable cures was that of a certain dowager countess whose breath grew insufficient on account of her fatness."

"What has this to do with me?" said Jehane. "I can breathe well enough."

"The old nurse paid no attention to the countess's breath," said de Mercadet, "but she gave her a certain medicine which removed her fat."

"Oh," said Jehane.

"In three or four weeks the countess was slender as a girl, and this without inconvenience to herself."

"She was not forbidden to eat?"

"Her appetite grew better and she ate more heartily every day," said Mercadet.

Jehane took another sugar plum. "You are going to see the old woman, to buy her medicine?"

"It will be neither pleasant nor safe for me to return to Perpignan," said de Mercadet, "but I count it a small adventure when your love waits for my return. Ah, Jehane, when your belt falls, how will our sadness fall! What joy will be loosed when your chain is loosed, and rapture, not steel, may gird you!"

Jehane said little to that. She was rather thoughtful, and as usual not quite sure where her thoughts tended. But she gave de Mercadet permission to leave the castle on his errand, and before he went kissed him on the mouth. The troubadour's soul was exalted by this warm and freely-given kiss, but in truth it meant little. It simply concealed the fact that she did not know what to say to him.

It was October when de Mercadet rode with his joglar from the castle of Caraman. Christmas came, and he did not return. Winter passed, and there was no news of him. Jehane thought less about him now, though with increasing frequency she thought about his errand, and the Breton medicine appeared infinitely desirable, for the coldness of winter had sharpened her appetite and the chain, in consequence, had grown somewhat tight about her waist. She desired most fervently to be rid of it, and that without any thought of love as a sequel to freedom.

Spring was ripening into summer before de Mercadet came back to Caraman. He rode in one evening, travel-stained and weary. But though the vagaries of the weather had taken the colour out of his clothes, they had put colour in his cheeks, and he looked both strong and well-contented with what he had done. He walked with a jaunty air and spoke in a ringing tone. Jehane grew uneasy when she saw his confidence, but very soon she asked if he had the medicine with him. "And why have you been so long on your journey?" she said. "Perpignan is not so far that a man needs half a year to go there and come back."

De Mercadet laughed. "I have the medicine," he said, "and I've been to Brittany for it. I lived there in a fisherman's house, breathing the smell of fish and living on haddock and black bread, till winter passed and the roads were fit to ride on again. Would you do so much for me, Madame Jehane? No? Wait till you have heard the songs I made riding south in the rain and sun to see you, and when you hear the least of them you will be fast in love and deep in love and ready to say yes to anything I ask."

"Let me see the medicine," said Jehane.

"Hear my songs first," said Gilles. And he sang, till midnight came, the loveliest songs he had ever made, and all the ladies were ready to die for him, and the gentlemen would not let him stop, and at every door were servants, hoarsely breathing, thrusting in their heads to hear this wealth of verse and melody. But Jehane, feeling the belt tight round her waist, thought crossly that he might have given her the medicine first.

She got it on the following day. "What is it, and how is it made?" she asked.

"It is prepared from a certain kind of seaweed that grows in Brittany," said Gilles. "They burn it in pits on the shore, and from the ash it is possible to extract this medicine, though the secret is known to few. But the old nurse at Perpignan, whose own store had all been used, sent me to a sister who shares her cunning, and she gave me this flask."

"It will do me no harm?" asked Jehane.

"None," said Gilles.

Then Jehane took her first dose, and made a wry face after it, but filled her mouth with a sugar plum to take away the bitterness. In two weeks' time she was slimmer than she had been for months, and after another week the chain hung loosely down on her hips. She was greatly pleased by this, but less contented to observe de Mercadet's growing exultation, and to hear each evening a serena inspired by the pleasures which he anticipated with increasing confidence. She preferred his old mood of melancholy, and a year of continence had made her so used to it that she felt an extreme reluctance to bother herself with the untidiness of love, the heat and proximity of a lover.

The morning came when the diminished ambit of her hips was no more than an inch or two greater than the circumference of the confining belt. In great excitement she wriggled and twisted and thrust down the links. They were slow to overpass her hinder plumpness, but after some more squeezing, kneading, and pushing, they fell clear, with a rattle and chink, and lay loosely about her ankles. With a cry of delight Jehane leapt over them, threw out her arms, capered and bent and shook herself in the ecstasy of release. Truly light-hearted, she became almost light-headed with joy. She was sobered only by the obtrusive thought of her obligation to de Mercadet. She grew resentful then, to think that the perfection of her happiness should be so impaired. She sulked, she looked out of the window, frowning. She was, it happened, in the tower room where she had said good-bye to her husband. By leaning far out of the window—it was just broad enough to let her shoulders go through—she could almost see her image in the green moat beneath her. But she was not dressed for leaning out of windows, and hurriedly she withdrew her head.

There was a mirror in the room, and she saw that slimness truly suited her. She had not looked so lovely for years. She turned this way and that, and with shame for her meagre gratitude admitted what she owed to de Mercadet. He had restored her freedom and renewed her beauty. What a pity that he wanted a reward. And how deplorably his manner had changed from that attractive melancholy air. Ah, if only she desired to love! If love were not so rude and overwhelming! And yet he deserved reward, and generosity would suit her best in bestowing it.

But he must give her time. He must be content with seeing her and singing to her. He must not be roughly importunate. She would talk to him and tell him so, and promise her love for some day next year, or the year after. She herself was not impatient for embraces, so why should he be in a hurry?

Having come to this decision Jehane dressed herself, called for a page, and bade him find the troubadour and request his presence in the tower room.

She waited him calmly. But Gilles came in with exultant laughter, saw the discarded chain immediately, and bearing down her protesting hands caught her in his arms and hugged her with alarming vigour. He was in a rollicking mood and it seemed to Jehane as though he meant to claim his reward on the spot.

She was extremely irritated by his jocular manner, and repulsed him sharply. Had he wept, had he fallen to his knees, had he sought her with a melancholy hope and humble passion, it would have been easy to be kind—kind and yet firm. But that he should canvass her love with hilarity was abominable. "Let go, Gilles! Take your hands away! Stand back from me!" she cried.

"Ah, little prude," he said. "Have I not waited long enough? What hinders now?"

"Don't come near me," cried Jehane.

"Little prude!" he cried. "Bed is the place for little prudes, and the place for me. Come, sweeting, to bed, to bed!"

Jehane was horrified. Hands out to ward him off, she backed away from him, round the room and round again, and Gilles followed close, laughing loudly, calling her miser's money, wild bees' honey, and little prude. Round the room they went again, but as Jehane re-passed the window she stopped suddenly with a cry different from her protesting cries. She forgot de Mercadet, she stood motionless, and stared in a white silence at what she saw. His exuberance dulled, de Mercadet came quietly behind her and looked over her shoulder. He saw two men crossing the river at the ford, a few hundred paces from the castle gates. One wore the white surcoat of the Temple, but the red cross on it was faded to a dull and lifeless hue. They drew nearer, and rode in across the lowered drawbridge. Jehane ran to the opposite window, that looked into the courtyard. It filled with clamour as the horsemen rode in and were surrounded by twenty, thirty, forty people shouting and begging for news.

"Do you know these men?" asked Gilles.

"One is my husband's squire," she said, and spoke in a queer breathless voice. They waited uncomfortably, saying nothing, and heard him climbing the tower stairs. He came in. He was a boy in years, but older than his years, brown-faced, and with a certain grimness stamped on his youth.

"Where is he, Piers?" asked Jehane. "My lord, I mean. Your lord and mine, Piers?"

"Have courage, madame," he answered. "The Knights Templar never showed more gloriously. It was at Damietta. We were the first to attack and the last to retreat. But for us the Christian army had been destroyed."

"He is dead?"

"Yes, madame."

"Ah, God, God!" she cried, and for a little while stood blank of face while the grim young squire told his story. Then she said, "Tell me again, for I did not hear you."

When he had told the whole tale again he fumbled in a pouch, found a key tied to a cord, and gave it to Jehane. "My lord took that from his neck a little time before he died," he said, "and bade me bring it home to you."

Jehane took the key and wept, wildly at first and with great sobs. The squire left her then, being given leave, and de Mercadet stood silent. But after a while he said softly, "Love lives though many die."

Jehane looked at the key. "Go now," she said, "and leave me alone. I must be alone," she repeated, and thrust de Mercadet to the door.

"I also will say a prayer," he said.

Jehane sat for a long time, holding the key in her hand, and many thoughts came into her head, but into her heart came slowly a feeling that, she was horrified to find, seemed very like relief. Shocked by this discovery she conjured up a picture of Bertran on their wedding day, another of Bertran bleeding to death at Damietta, and contrived to squeeze out a few more tears. But they came reluctantly. Only under the shock of foreign news, the sudden wound made by the word of death, had the fountain of misery truly opened, and now its small store was shed. For though she had loved Bertran once, her love had not flourished since he tried to make it prisoner and lock it up; and so she thought of his death coolly enough when the shock of its announcement had passed. But she did not like to admit this, even to herself, and preferred to think she was truly grief-stricken and most tragically bereaved. And now came creeping a cunning thought, a sly round-the-corner thought, that here, in new widowhood, was an excuse for getting rid of de Mercadet. "How dare he talk of love at such a time as this," she thought. "Grief for poor Bertran is my only interest now, and little Aélis orphaned now!" She sniffed and sighed, and three small tears fell slowly. The key was pressed between her hands. "To send it back was a kind and noble thought," she cried, "but how lonely and insecure it makes me feel to have it." And then she thought, "It is my duty to requite that last kindness, and if I sacrifice my liberty again it will be well requited—I can be as noble as you, Bertran—and also I should feel secure again, and Gilles can fret and plead as he pleases then. But that is not why I shall do it. I shall do it to show my grief for Bertran's death, and because I am widowed now, cut off from joy.—And Gilles can think what he likes."

The next day de Mercadet came to talk with her in the room in the tower. She said, "You have served me well in your love for me, Gilles, and I had not meant to leave you unrewarded. But now this news has come that drives love from my heart, and all joy from this castle, and our love is no longer possible. Bertran's death made it impossible, and I have made it doubly impossible."

"What have you done?" he asked.

"My lord sent me a key to unlock the belt he clasped me with. As things have come about there was no need for that. And yet I have made use of the key."

"You have put on the belt again?"

"I put it on again, and pulled it tight, and locked it," said Jehane, "and now I have no more need of the key."

She went to that window that overlooked the moat, and threw it out. They heard the tiny splash it made as it struck the water.

"You did that because of the great love you had for your husband? You did it in sorrow, renouncing the joys of this world?" asked the troubadour.

"Yes," said Jehane.

De Mercadet laughed. "Little liar! Little prude!" he said. "Yes, weep if you like, for your tears mean little enough to you and nothing at all to me. Yet I do not bear you ill will. Not now. Were I as other men I might, but I am not like other men. For I am a poet. Other men would complain at spending a barren year in your service, but my year has not been barren, for I have made some good songs. It often happens that the women for whom one writes the best poetry do least to deserve it—but what does that matter? The poems are there, and will serve to praise and thank less prudent ladies, whose kindness comes so quickly there is no time to write well in their honour. Were it not for prudes like you, little prude, the generous ones would scarce get a verse at all to praise their sweet lips and lovely eyes. This most wise thought came suddenly to me in the night—for I guessed what you might be doing—and so I bear you no ill will, for you have done me no wrong. But neither do I love you, Jehane. My love was put away in the cupboard for too long, and when you cracked it I found it was like a rotten nut. There was nothing in it, Jehane. So do not eat too much, for the old woman's medicine is done and I shall not be at your service another year to ride to Brittany."

Having uttered this rude and abominable speech de Mercadet took leave of Jehane and went to his own chamber. With no sign of sorrow or distress he made speedy preparations for departure, and a little after noon rode out of the castle, singing as he went, to the scandalizing and horror of all who heard him. Nor did Jehane ever see him again, though for the rest of that year he lived in the castle of Hauterive, that was no more than forty miles away. And there he sang again the songs he had made for Jehane, and had by them great honour, and also, it is said, the favour of the Lady Saill, who dwelt there.

And one day de Mercadet was talking to a soldier on guard at the gate when a bowman, a mercenary from Italy, came and asked if he could find employment there, for he had just been thrown out of the castle of Caraman for drunkenness—though he had not been so much drunk as smitten with a sudden fever, he explained. De Mercadet asked him what news he had from Caraman.

"The Lady Jehane has been out of sorts this last week or two," said the archer. "She is a lady who likes to eat well—and who shall blame her for that?—and now whenever she takes a heavy meal she experiences, it is said, a feeling of pressure round her middle. And for that reason she is looking somewhat unhappy. Nor is that all, for she says that she suffered a loss one day while walking by the moat. And the moat has been drained and everybody is paddling in the mud seeking what she let fall there."

"And what was that?" asked de Mercadet.

"A key; a key tied to a piece of cord," said the archer.

KATHERINE MANSFIELD

1888–1923

She was born in New Zealand, and educated in England.
Her first story was published when she was only nine.
Although a long life and career were denied her by ill health,
she acquired complete mastery of the short story,
establishing a distinctive manner which enabled her delicately
to capture the subtleties of human relationships.

Marriage à la Mode

ON HIS WAY to the station William remembered with a fresh pang of disappointment that he was taking nothing down to the kiddies. Poor little chaps! It was hard lines on them. Their first words always were as they ran to greet him, "What have you got for me, daddy?" and he had nothing. He would have to buy them some sweets at the station. But that was what he had done for the past four Saturdays; their faces had fallen last time when they saw the same old boxes produced again.

And Paddy had said, "I had red ribbing on mine *bee*-fore!"

And Johnny had said, "It's always pink on mine. I hate pink."

But what was William to do? The affair wasn't so easily settled. In the old days, of course, he would have taken a taxi off to a decent toyshop and chosen them something in five minutes. But nowadays they had Russian toys, French toys, Serbian toys—toys from God knows where. It was over a year since Isabel had scrapped the old donkeys and engines and so on because they were so "dreadfully sentimental" and "so appallingly bad for the babies' sense of form".

"It's so important," the new Isabel had explained, "that they should like the right things from the very beginning. It saves so much time later on. Really, if the poor pets have to spend their infant years staring at these horrors, one can imagine them growing up and asking to be taken to the Royal Academy."

And she spoke as though a visit to the Royal Academy was certain immediate death to any one . . .

"Well, I don't know," said William slowly. "When I was their age I used to go to bed hugging an old towel with a knot in it."

The new Isabel looked at him, her eyes narrowed, her lips apart.

"*Dear* William! I'm sure you did!" She laughed in the new way.

Sweets it would have to be, however, thought William gloomily, fishing in his pocket for change for the taxi-man. And he saw the kiddies handing the boxes round—they were awfully generous little chaps—while Isabel's precious friends didn't hesitate to help themselves . . .

What about fruit? William hovered before a stall just inside the station. What about a melon each? Would they have to share that, too? Or a pineapple for Pad, and a melon for Johnny? Isabel's friends could hardly go sneaking up to the nursery at the children's meal-times. All the same, as he bought the melon William had a horrible vision of one of Isabel's young poets lapping up a slice, for some reason, behind the nursery door.

With his two very awkward parcels he strode off to his train. The platform was crowded, the train was in. Doors banged open and shut. There came such a loud hissing from the engine that people looked dazed as they scurried to and fro. William made straight for a first-class smoker, stowed away his suit-case and parcels, and taking a huge wad of papers out of his inner pocket, he flung down in the corner and began to read.

"Our client moreover is positive . . . We are inclined to reconsider . . . in the event of—" Ah, that was better. William pressed back his flattened hair and stretched his legs across the carriage floor. The familiar dull gnawing in his breast quietened down. "With regard to our decision—" He took out a blue pencil and scored a paragraph slowly.

Two men came in, stepped across him, and made for the farther corner. A young fellow swung his golf clubs into the rack and sat down opposite. The train gave a gentle lurch, they were off. William glanced up and saw the hot, bright station slipping away. A red-faced girl raced along by the carriages, there was something strained and almost desperate in the way she waved and called. "Hysterical!" thought William dully. Then a greasy, black-faced workman at the end of the platform grinned at the passing train. And William thought, "A filthy life!" and went back to his papers.

When he looked up again there were fields, and beasts standing for shelter under the dark trees. A wide river, with naked children splashing in the shallows, glided into sight and was gone again. The sky shone pale, and one bird drifted high like a dark fleck in a jewel.

"We have examined our client's correspondence files . . ." The last sentence he had read echoed in his mind. "We have examined . . ."

William hung on to that sentence, but it was no good; it snapped in the middle, and the fields, the sky, the sailing bird, the water, all said, 'Isabel'. The same thing happened every Saturday afternoon. When he was on his way to meet Isabel there began those countless imaginary meetings. She was at the station, standing just a little apart from everybody else; she was sitting in the open taxi outside; she was at the garden gate; walking across the parched grass; at the door, or just inside the hall.

And her clear, light voice said, "It's William," or "Hillo, William!" or "So William has come!" He touched her cool hand, her cool cheek.

The exquisite freshness of Isabel! When he had been a little boy, it was his delight to run into the garden after a shower of rain and shake the rose-bush over him. Isabel was that rose-bush, petal-soft, sparkling and cool. And he was still that little boy. But there was no running into the garden now, no laughing and shaking. The dull, persistent gnawing in his breast started again. He drew up his legs, tossed the papers aside, and shut his eyes.

"What is it, Isabel? What is it?" he said tenderly. They were in their bedroom in the new house. Isabel sat on a painted stool before the dressing-table that was strewn with little black and green boxes.

"What is what, William?" And she bent forward, and her fine light hair fell over her cheeks.

"Ah, you know!" He stood in the middle of the strange room and he felt a stranger. At that Isabel wheeled round quickly and faced him.

"Oh, William!" she cried imploringly, and she held up the hairbrush: "Please! Please don't be so dreadfully stuffy and—tragic. You're always saying or looking or hinting that I've changed. Just because I've got to know really congenial people, and go about more, and am frightfully keen on—on everything, you behave as though I'd—" Isabel tossed back her hair and laughed—"killed our love or something. It's so awfully absurd"—she bit her lip—"and it's so maddening, William. Even this new house and the servants you grudge me."

"Isabel!"

"Yes, yes, it's true in a way," said Isabel quickly. "You think they are another bad sign. Oh, I know you do. I feel it," she said softly, "every time you come up the stairs. But we couldn't have gone on living in that other poky little hole, William. Be practical, at least! Why, there wasn't enough room for the babies even."

No, it was true. Every morning when he came back from chambers it was to find the babies with Isabel in the back drawing-room. They were having rides on the leopard skin thrown over the sofa back, or they were playing shops with Isabel's desk for a counter, or Pad was sitting on the hearthrug rowing away for dear life with a little brass fire shovel, while

Johnny shot at pirates with the tongs. Every evening they each had a pick-a-back up the narrow stairs to their fat old Nanny.

Yes, he supposed it was a poky little house. A little white house with blue curtains and a window-box of petunias. William met their friends at the door with "Seen our petunias? Pretty terrific for London, don't you think?"

But the imbecile thing, the absolutely extraordinary thing was that he hadn't the slightest idea that Isabel wasn't as happy as he. God, what blindness! He hadn't the remotest notion in those days that she really hated that inconvenient little house, that she thought the fat Nanny was ruining the babies, that she was desperately lonely, pining for new people and new music and pictures and so on. If they hadn't gone to that studio party at Moira Morrison's—if Moira Morrison hadn't said as they were leaving, "I'm going to rescue your wife, selfish man. She's like an exquisite little Titania"—if Isabel hadn't gone with Moira to Paris—if—if . . .

The train stopped at another station. Bettingford. Good heavens! They'd be there in ten minutes. William stuffed the papers back into his pockets; the young man opposite had long since disappeared. Now the other two got out. The late afternoon sun shone on women in cotton frocks and little sunburnt, barefoot children. It blazed on a silky yellow flower with coarse leaves which sprawled over a bank of rock. The air ruffling through the window smelled of the sea. Had Isabel the same crowd with her this week-end, wondered William?

And he remembered the holidays they used to have, the four of them, with a little farm girl, Rose, to look after the babies. Isabel wore a jersey and her hair in a plait; she looked about fourteen. Lord! how his nose used to peel! And the amount they ate, and the amount they slept in that immense feather bed with their feet locked together . . . William couldn't help a grim smile as he thought of Isabel's horror if she knew the full extent of his sentimentality.

"HILLO, WILLIAM!" She was at the station after all, standing just as he had imagined, apart from the others, and—William's heart leapt—she was alone.

"Hallo, Isabel!" William stared. He thought she looked so beautiful that he had to say something, "You look very cool."

"Do I?" said Isabel. "I don't feel very cool. Come along, your horrid old train is late. The taxi's outside." She put her hand lightly on his arm as they passed the ticket collector. "We've all come to meet you," she said. "But we've left Bobby Kane at the sweet shop, to be called for."

"Oh!" said William. It was all he could say for the moment.

There in the glare waited the taxi, with Bill Hunt and Dennis Green sprawling on one side, their hats tilted over their faces, while on the other, Moira Morrison, in a bonnet like a huge strawberry, jumped up and down.

"No ice! No ice! No ice!" she shouted gaily.

And Dennis chimed in from under his hat. "*Only* to be had from the fishmonger's."

And Bill Hunt, emerging, added, "With *whole* fish in it."

"Oh, what a bore!" wailed Isabel. And she explained to William how they had been chasing round the town for ice while she waited for him. "Simply everything is running down the steep cliffs into the sea, beginning with the butter."

"We shall have to anoint ourselves with the butter," said Dennis. "May thy head, William, lack not ointment."

"Look here," said William, "how are we going to sit? I'd better get up by the driver."

"No, Bobby Kane's by the driver," said Isabel. "You're to sit between Moira and me." The taxi started. "What have you got in those mysterious parcels?"

"De-cap-it-ated heads!" said Bill Hunt, shuddering beneath his hat.

"Oh, fruit!" Isabel sounded very pleased. "Wise William! A melon and a pineapple. How too nice!"

"No, wait a bit," said William, smiling. But he really was anxious. "I brought them down for the kiddies."

"Oh, my dear!" Isabel laughed, and slipped her hand through his arm. "They'd be rolling in agonies if they were to eat them. No"—she patted his hand—"you must bring them something next time. I refuse to part with my pineapple."

"Cruel Isabel! Do let me smell it!" said Moira. She flung her arms across William appealingly. "Oh!" The strawberry bonnet fell forward: she sounded quite faint.

"A Lady in Love with a Pineapple," said Dennis, as the taxi drew up before a little shop with a striped blind. Out came Bobby Kane, his arms full of little packets.

"I do hope they'll be good. I've chosen them because of the colours. There are some round things which really look too divine. And just look at this nougat," he cried ecstatically, "just look at it! It's a perfect little ballet."

But at that moment the shopman appeared. "Oh, I forgot. They're none of them paid for," said Bobby, looking frightened. Isabel gave the shopman a note, and Bobby was radiant again. "Hallo, William! I'm sitting by the driver." And bareheaded, all in white, with his sleeves rolled up to the shoulders, he leapt into his place. "Avanti!" he cried . . .

After tea the others went off to bathe, while William stayed and made his peace with the kiddies. But Johnny and Paddy were asleep, the rose-red glow had paled, bats were flying, and still the bathers had not returned. As William wandered downstairs, the maid crossed the hall carrying a lamp. He followed her into the sitting-room. It was a long room, coloured yellow. On the wall opposite William someone had painted a young man, over life-size, with very wobbly legs, offering a wide-eyed daisy to a young woman who had one very short arm and one very long, thin one. Over the chairs and sofa there hung strips of black material, covered with big splashes like broken eggs, and everywhere one looked there seemed to be an ash-tray full of cigarette ends. William sat down in one of the arm-chairs. Nowadays, when one felt with one hand down the sides, it wasn't to come upon a sheep with three legs or a cow that had lost one horn, or a very fat dove out of the Noah's Ark. One fished up yet another little paper-covered book of smudged-looking poems . . . He thought of the wad of papers in his pocket, but he was too hungry and tired to read. The door was open; sounds came from the kitchen. The servants were talking as if they were alone in the house. Suddenly there came a loud screech of laughter and an equally loud "Sh!" They had remembered him. William got up and went through the French windows into the garden, and as he stood there in the shadow he heard the bathers coming up the sandy road; their voices rang through the quiet. "I think it's up to Moira to use her little arts and wiles." A tragic moan from Moira.

"We ought to have a gramophone for the week-ends that played 'The Maid of the Mountains'."

"Oh no! Oh no!" cried Isabel's voice. "That's not fair to William. Be nice to him, my children! He's only staying until tomorrow evening."

"Leave him to me," cried Bobby Kane. "I'm awfully good at looking after people." The gate swung open and shut. William moved on the terrace; they had seen him. "Hallo, William!" And Bobby Kane, flapping his towel, began to leap and pirouette on the parched lawn. "Pity you didn't come, William. The water was divine. And we all went to a little pub afterwards and had sloe gin." The others had reached the house. "I say, Isabel," called Bobby, "would you like me to wear my Nijinsky dress to-night?"

"No," said Isabel, "nobody's going to dress. We're all starving. William's starving, too. Come along, *mes amis*, let's begin with sardines."

"I've found the sardines," said Moira, and she ran into the hall, holding a box high in the air.

"A Lady with a Box of Sardines," said Dennis gravely.

"Well, William, and how's London?" asked Bill Hunt, drawing the cork out of a bottle of whisky.

"Oh, London's not much changed," answered William.

"Good old London," said Bobby, very hearty, spearing a sardine.

But a moment later William was forgotten. Moira Morrison began wondering what colour one's legs really were under water.

"Mine are the palest, palest mushroom colour."

Bill and Dennis ate enormously. And Isabel filled glasses, and changed plates, and found matches, smiling blissfully. At one moment she said, "I do wish, Bill, you'd paint it."

"Paint what?" said Bill loudly, stuffing his mouth with bread.

"Us," said Isabel, "round the table. It would be so fascinating in twenty years' time."

Bill screwed up his eyes and chewed. "Light's wrong," he said rudely, "far too much yellow"; and went on eating. And that seemed to charm Isabel, too.

But after supper they were all so tired they could do nothing but yawn until it was late enough to go to bed . . .

It was not until William was waiting for his taxi the next afternoon that he found himself alone with Isabel. When he brought his suit-case down into the hall, Isabel left the others and went over to him. She stooped down and picked up the suit-case. "What a weight!" she said, and she gave a little awkward laugh. "Let me carry it! To the gate."

"No, why should you?" said William. "Of course not. Give it to me."

"Oh, please do let me," said Isabel. "I want to, really." They walked together silently. William felt there was nothing to say now.

"There," said Isabel triumphantly, setting the suit-case down, and she looked anxiously along the sandy road. "I hardly seem to have seen you this time," she said breathlessly. "It's so short, isn't it? I feel you've only just come. Next time—" The taxi came into sight. "I hope they look after you properly in London. I'm so sorry the babies have been out all day, but Miss Neil had arranged it. They'll hate missing you. Poor William, going back to London." The taxi turned. "Good-bye!" She gave him a little hurried kiss; she was gone.

Fields, trees, hedges streamed by. They shook through the empty, blind-looking little town, ground up the steep pull to the station.

The train was in. William made straight for a first-class smoker, flung back into the corner, but this time he let the papers alone. He folded his arms against the dull, persistent gnawing, and began in his mind to write a letter to Isabel.

THE POST was late as usual. They sat outside the house in long chairs under coloured parasols. Only Bobby Kane lay on the turf at Isabel's feet. It was dull, stifling; the day drooped like a flag. "Do you think there will be Mondays in Heaven?" asked Bobby childishly.

And Dennis murmured, "Heaven will be one long Monday."

But Isabel couldn't help wondering what had happened to the salmon they had for supper last night. She had meant to have fish mayonnaise for lunch and now . . .

Moira was asleep. Sleeping was her latest discovery. "It's *so* wonderful. One simply shuts one's eyes, that's all. It's *so* delicious."

When the old ruddy postman came beating along the sandy road on his tricycle one felt the handlebars ought to have been oars.

Bill Hunt put down his book. "Letters," he said complacently, and they all waited. But, heartless postman—O malignant world! There was only one, a fat one for Isabel. Not even a paper.

"And mine's only from William," said Isabel mournfully.

"From William—already?"

"He's sending you back your marriage lines as a gentle reminder."

"Does everybody have marriage lines? I thought they were only for servants."

"Pages and pages! Look at her! A Lady reading a Letter," said Dennis.

My darling, precious Isabel. Pages and pages there were. As Isabel read on her feeling of astonishment changed to a stifled feeling. What on earth had induced William . . .? How extraordinary it was . . . What could have made him . . .? She felt confused, more and more excited, even frightened. It was just like William. Was it? It was absurd, of course, it must be absurd, ridiculous. "Ha, ha, ha! Oh dear!" What was she to do? Isabel flung back in her chair and laughed till she couldn't stop laughing.

"Do, do tell us," said the others. "You must tell us."

"I'm longing to," gurgled Isabel. She sat up, gathered the letter, and waved it at them. "Gather round," she said. "Listen, it's too marvellous. A love-letter!"

"A love-letter! But how divine!" *Darling, precious Isabel.* But she had hardly begun before their laughter interrupted her.

"Go on, Isabel, it's perfect."

"It's the most marvellous find."

"Oh, do go on, Isabel!"

God forbid, my darling, that I should be a drag on your happiness.

"Oh! oh! oh!"

"Sh! sh! sh!" And Isabel went on. When she reached the end they were hysterical: Bobby rolled on the turf and almost sobbed.

"You must let me have it just as it is, entire, for my new book," said Dennis firmly. "I shall give it a whole chapter."

"Oh, Isabel," moaned Moira, "that wonderful bit about holding you in his arms!"

"I always thought those letters in divorce cases were made up. But they pale before this."

"Let me hold it. Let me read it, mine own self," said Bobby Kane.

But, to their surprise, Isabel crushed the letter in her hand. She was laughing no longer. She glanced quickly at them all; she looked exhausted. "No, not just now. Not just now," she stammered.

And before they could recover she had run into the house, through the hall, up the stairs into her bedroom. Down she sat on the side of the bed. "How vile, odious, abominable, vulgar," muttered Isabel. She pressed her eyes with her knuckles and rocked to and fro. And again she saw them, but not four, more like forty, laughing, sneering, jeering, stretching out their hands while she read them William's letter. Oh, what a loathsome thing to have done. How could she have done it! *God forbid, my darling, that I should be a drag on your happiness.* William! Isabel pressed her face into the pillow. But she felt that even the grave bedroom knew her for what she was, shallow, tinkling, vain . . .

Presently from the garden below there came voices.

"Isabel, we're all going for a bathe. Do come!"

"Come, thou wife of William!"

"Call her once before you go, call once yet!"

Isabel sat up. Now was the moment, now she must decide. Would she go with them, or stay here and write to William. Which, which should it be? "I must make up my mind." Oh, but how could there be any question? Of course she would stay here and write.

"Titania!" piped Moira.

"Isa-bel?"

No, it was too difficult. "I'll—I'll go with them, and write to William later. Some other time. Later. Not now. But I shall *certainly* write," thought Isabel hurriedly.

And, laughing in the new way, she ran down the stairs.

W. SOMERSET MAUGHAM

1874–1965

"I find all people interesting. I don't like them, but I must admit they're interesting . . ." Luckily for the world Maugham communicated this interest, writing of the people he met on his ceaseless travels with understanding, and wit, and a surprising gentleness. He died at ninety-one, a millionaire, and lonely, but still interested.

The Outstation

THE NEW ASSISTANT arrived in the afternoon. When the Resident, Mr. Warburton, was told that the prahu was in sight he put on his solar topee and went down to the landing-stage. The guard, eight little Dyak soldiers, stood to attention as he passed. He noted with satisfaction that their bearing was martial, their uniforms neat and clean, and their guns shining. They were a credit to him. From the landing-stage he watched the bend of the river round which in a moment the boat would sweep. He looked very smart in his spotless ducks and white shoes. He held under his arm a gold-headed Malacca cane which had been given him by the Sultan of Perak. He awaited the newcomer with mingled feelings. There was more work in the district than one man could properly do, and during his periodical tours of the country under his charge it had been inconvenient to leave the station in the hands of a native clerk, but he had been so long the only white man there that he could not face the arrival of another without misgiving. He was accustomed to loneliness. During the war he had not seen an English face for three years; and once when he was instructed to put up an afforestation officer he was seized with panic, so that when the stranger was due to arrive, having arranged everything for his reception, he wrote a note telling him he was obliged to go up-river, and fled; he remained away till he was informed by a messenger that his guest had left.

Now the prahu appeared in the broad reach. It was manned by prisoners, Dyaks under various sentences, and a couple of warders were waiting on the landing-stage to take them back to gaol. They were sturdy fellows, used to the river, and they rowed with a powerful stroke. As the boat reached the side a man got out from under the attap awning and stepped on shore. The guard presented arms.

"Here we are at last. By God, I'm as cramped as the devil. I've brought you your mail."

He spoke with exuberant joviality. Mr. Warburton politely held out his hand.

"Mr. Cooper, I presume?"

"That's right. Were you expecting anyone else?"

The question had a facetious intent, but the Resident did not smile.

"My name is Warburton. I'll show you your quarters. They'll bring your kit along."

He preceded Cooper along the narrow pathway and they entered a compound in which stood a small bungalow.

"I've had it made as habitable as I could, but of course no one has lived in it for a good many years."

It was built on piles. It consisted of a long living-room which opened on to a broad verandah, and behind, on each side of a passage, were two bedrooms.

"This'll do me all right," said Cooper.

"I dare say you want to have a bath and a change. I shall be very much pleased if you'll dine with me to-night. Will eight o'clock suit you?"

"Any old time will do for me."

The Resident gave a polite, but slightly disconcerted smile, and withdrew. He returned to the Fort where his own residence was. The impression which Allen Cooper had given him was not very favourable, but he was a fair man, and he knew that it was unjust to form an opinion on so brief a glimpse. Cooper seemed to be about thirty. He was a tall, thin fellow, with a sallow face in which there was not a spot of colour. It was a face all in one tone. He had a large, hooked nose and blue eyes. When, entering the bungalow, he had taken off his topee and flung it to a waiting boy, Mr. Warburton noticed that his large skull, covered with short, brown hair, contrasted somewhat oddly with a weak, small chin. He was dressed in khaki shorts and a khaki shirt, but they were shabby and soiled; and his battered topee had not been cleaned for days. Mr. Warburton reflected that the young man had spent a week on a coasting steamer and had passed the last forty-eight hours lying in the bottom of a prahu.

"We'll see what he looks like when he comes in to dinner."

He went into his room, where his things were as neatly laid out as if he had an English valet, undressed, and, walking down the stairs to the bath-house, sluiced himself with cool water. The only concession he made to the climate was to wear a white dinner jacket; but otherwise, in a boiled shirt and a high collar, silk socks and patent-leather shoes, he dressed as formally as though he were dining at his club in Pall Mall. A careful host, he went into the dining-room to see that the table was properly laid. It was gay with orchids, and the silver shone brightly. The napkins were folded into elaborate shapes. Shaded candles in silver candlesticks shed a soft light. Mr. Warburton smiled his approval and returned to the sitting-room to await his guest. Presently he appeared. Cooper was wearing the khaki shorts, the khaki shirt, and the ragged jacket in which he had landed. Mr. Warburton's smile of greeting froze on his face.

"Hulloa, you're all dressed up," said Cooper. "I didn't know you were going to do that. I very nearly put on a sarong."

"It doesn't matter at all. I dare say your boys were busy."

"You needn't have bothered to dress on my account, you know."

"I didn't. I always dress for dinner."

"Even when you're alone?"

"Especially when I'm alone," replied Mr. Warburton, with a frigid stare.

He saw a twinkle of amusement in Cooper's eyes, and he flushed an angry red. Mr. Warburton was a hot-tempered man; you might have guessed that from his red face with its pugnacious features and from his red hair now growing white; his blue eyes, cold as a rule and observing, could flash with sudden wrath; but he was a man of the world and he hoped a just one. He must do his best to get on with this fellow.

"When I lived in London I moved in circles in which it would have been just as eccentric not to dress for dinner every night as not to have a bath every morning. When I came to Borneo I saw no reason to discontinue so good a habit. For three years during the war I never saw a white man. I never omitted to dress on a single occasion on which I was well enough to come into dinner. You have not been very long in this country; believe me, there is no better way to maintain the proper pride which you should have in yourself. When a white man surrenders in the slightest degree to the influences that surround him he very soon loses his self-respect, and when he loses his self-respect you may be quite sure the natives will soon cease to respect him."

"Well, if you expect me to put on a boiled shirt and a stiff collar in this heat I'm afraid you'll be disappointed."

"When you are dining in your own bungalow you will, of course, dress as you think fit, but when you do me the pleasure of dining with me, perhaps you will come to the conclusion that it is only polite to wear the costume usual in civilized society."

Two Malay boys, in sarongs and songkoks, with smart white coats and brass buttons, came in, one bearing gin pahits, and the other a tray on which were olives and anchovies. Then they went in to dinner. Mr. Warburton flattered himself that he had the best cook, a Chinese, in Borneo, and he took great trouble to have as good food as in the difficult circumstances was possible. He exercised much ingenuity in making the best of his materials.

"Would you care to look at the menu?" he said, handing it to Cooper.

It was written in French and the dishes had resounding names. They were waited on by the two boys. In opposite corners of the room two more waved immense fans, and so gave movement to the sultry air. The fare was sumptuous and the champagne excellent.

"Do you do yourself like this every day?" said Cooper.

Mr. Warburton gave the menu a careless glance.

"I have not noticed that the dinner is any different from usual," he said. "I eat very little myself, but I make a point of having a proper dinner served to me every night. It keeps the cook in practice and it's good discipline for the boys."

The conversation proceeded with effort. Mr. Warburton was elaborately courteous and, it may be, found a slightly malicious amusement in the embarrassment which he thereby occasioned in his companion. Cooper had not been more than a few months in Sembulu, and Mr. Warburton's enquiries about friends of his in Kuala Solor were soon exhausted.

"By the way," he said presently, "did you meet a lad called Hennerley? He's come out recently, I believe."

"Oh yes, he's in the police. A rotten bounder."

"I should hardly have expected him to be that. His uncle is my friend Lord Barraclough. I had a letter from Lady Barraclough only the other day asking me to look out for him."

"I heard he was related to somebody or other. I suppose that's how he got the job. He's been to Eton and Oxford and he doesn't forget to let you know it."

"You surprise me," said Mr. Warburton. "All his family have been at Eton and Oxford for a couple of hundred years. I should have expected him to take it as a matter of course."

"I thought him a damned prig."

"To what school did you go?"

"I was born in Barbados. I was educated there."

"Oh, I see."

Mr. Warburton managed to put so much offensiveness into his brief reply that Cooper flushed. For a moment he was silent.

"I've had two or three letters from Kuala Solor," continued Mr. Warburton, "and my impression was that young Hennerley was a great success. They say he's a first-rate sportsman."

"Oh, yes, he's very popular. He's just the sort of fellow they would like in K.S. I haven't got much use for the first-rate sportsman myself. What does it amount to in the long run that a man can play golf and tennis better than other people? And who cares if he can make a break of seventy-five at billiards? They attach a damned sight too much importance to that sort of thing in England."

"Do you think so? I was under the impression that the first-rate sportsman had come out of the war certainly no worse than anyone else."

"Oh, if you're going to talk of the war then I do know what I'm talking about. I was in the same regiment as Hennerley and I can tell you that the men couldn't stick him at any price."

"How do you know?"

"Because I was one of the men."

"Oh, you hadn't got a commission.

"A fat chance I had of getting a commission. I was what was called a Colonial. I hadn't been to a public school and I had no influence. I was in the ranks the whole damned time."

Cooper frowned. He seemed to have difficulty in preventing himself from breaking out into violent invective. Mr. Warburton watched him, his little blue eyes narrowed, watched him and formed his opinion. Changing the conversation, he began to speak to Cooper about the work that would be required of him, and as the clock struck ten he rose.

"Well, I won't keep you any more. I dare say you're tired by your journey."

They shook hands.

"Oh, I say, look here," said Cooper, "I wonder if you can find me a boy. The boy I had before never turned up when I was starting from K.S. He took my kit on board and all that, and then disappeared. I didn't know he wasn't there till we were out of the river."

"I'll ask my head-boy. I have no doubt he can find you someone."

"All right. Just tell him to send the boy along and if I like the look of him I'll take him."

There was a moon, so that no lantern was needed. Cooper walked across from the Fort to his bungalow.

"I wonder why on earth they've sent me a fellow like that?" reflected Mr. Warburton. "If that's the kind of man they're going to get now I don't think much of it."

He strolled down his garden. The Fort was built on the top of a little hill and the garden ran down to the river's edge; on the bank was an arbour, and hither it was his habit to come after dinner to smoke a cheroot. And often from the river that flowed below him a voice was heard, the voice of some Malay too timorous to venture into the light of day, and a complaint or an accusation was softly wafted to his ears, a piece of information was whispered to him or a useful hint, which otherwise would never have come into his official ken. He threw himself heavily into a long rattan chair. Cooper! An envious, ill-bred fellow, bumptious, self-assertive and vain. But Mr. Warburton's irritation could not withstand the silent beauty of the night. The air was scented with the sweet-smelling flowers of a tree that grew at the entrance to the arbour, and the fire-flies, sparkling dimly, flew with their slow and silvery flight. The moon made a pathway on the broad river for the light feet of Sila's bride, and on the further bank a row of palm trees was delicately silhouetted against the sky. Peace stole into the soul of Mr. Warburton.

He was a queer creature and he had had a singular career. At the age of twenty-one he had inherited a considerable fortune, a hundred thousand pounds, and when he left Oxford he threw himself into the gay life, which in those days (now Mr. Warburton was a man of four and fifty) offered itself to the young man of good family. He had his flat in Mount Street, his private hansom, and his hunting-box in Warwickshire. He went to all the places where the fashionable congregate. He was handsome, amusing, and generous. He was a figure in the society of London in the early nineties, and society then had not lost its exclusiveness nor its brilliance. The Boer War which shook it was unthought of; the Great War which destroyed it was prophesied only by the pessimists. It was no unpleasant thing to be a rich young man in those days, and Mr. Warburton's chimney-piece during the season was packed with cards for one great function after another. Mr. Warburton displayed them with complacency. For Mr. Warburton was a snob. He was not a timid snob, a little ashamed of being impressed by his betters, nor a snob who sought the intimacy of persons who had acquired celebrity in politics or notoriety in the arts, nor the snob who was dazzled by riches; he was the naked, unadulterated common snob who dearly loved a lord. He was touchy and quick-tempered, but he would much rather have been snubbed by a person of quality than flattered by a commoner. His name figured insignificantly in Burke's Peerage, and it was marvellous to watch the ingenuity he used to mention his distant relationship to the noble family he belonged to; but never a word did he say of the honest Liverpool manufacturer from whom, through his mother, a Miss Gubbins, he had come by his fortune. It was the terror of his fashionable life that at Cowes, maybe, or at Ascot, when he was with a duchess or even with a prince of the blood, one of these relatives would claim acquaintance with him.

His failing was too obvious not soon to become notorious, but its extravagence saved it from being merely despicable. The great whom he adored laughed at him, but in their hearts felt his adoration not unnatural. Poor Warburton was a dreadful snob, of course, but after all he was a good fellow. He was always ready to back a bill for an impecunious nobleman, and if you were in a tight corner you could safely count on him for a hundred pounds. He gave good dinners. He played whist badly, but never minded how much he lost if the company was select. He happened to be a gambler, an unlucky one, but he was a good loser, and it was impossible not to admire the coolness with which he lost five hundred pounds at a sitting. His passion for cards, almost as strong as his passion for titles, was the cause of his undoing. The life he led was expensive and his gambling losses were formidable. He began to plunge more heavily, first on horses, and then on the Stock Exchange. He had a certain simplicity of character, and the unscrupulous found him an ingenuous prey. I do not know if he ever realised that his smart friends laughed at him behind his back, but I think he had an obscure instinct that he could not afford to appear other than careless of his money. He got into the hands of money-lenders. At the age of thirty-four he was ruined.

He was too much imbued with the spirit of his class to hesitate in the choice of his next step. When a man in his set had run through his money, he went out to the colonies. No one heard Mr. Warburton repine. He made no complaint because a noble friend had advised a disastrous speculation, he pressed nobody to whom he had lent money to repay it, he paid his debts (if he had only known it, the despised blood of the Liverpool manufacturer came out in him there), sought help from no one, and, never having done a stroke of work in his life, looked for a means of livelihood. He remained cheerful, unconcerned and full of humour. He had no wish to make anyone with whom he happened to be uncomfortable by the recital of his misfortune. Mr. Warburton was a snob, but he was also a gentleman.

The only favour he asked of any of the great friends in whose daily company he had lived for years was a recommendation. The able man who was at that time Sultan of Sembulu took him into his service. The night before he sailed he dined for the last time at his club.

"I hear you're going away, Warburton," the old Duke of Hereford said to him.

"Yes, I'm going to Borneo."

"Good God, what are you going there for?"

"Oh, I'm broke."

"Are you? I'm sorry. Well, let us know when you come back. I hope you have a good time."

"Oh yes. Lots of shooting, you know."

The Duke nodded and passed on. A few hours later Mr. Warburton watched the coast of England recede into the mist, and he left behind everything which to him made life worth living.

Twenty years had passed since then. He kept up a busy correspondence with various great ladies and his letters were amusing and chatty. He never lost his love for titled persons and paid careful attention to the announcements in *The Times* (which reached him six weeks after publication) of their comings and goings. He perused the column which records births, deaths, and marriages, and he was always ready with his letter of congratulation or condolence. The illustrated papers told him how people looked and on his periodical visits to England, able to take up the threads as though they had never been broken, he knew all about any new person who might have appeared on the social surface. His interest in the world of fashion was as vivid as when himself had been a figure in it. It still seemed to him the only thing that mattered.

But insensibly another interest had entered into his life. The position he found himself in flattered his vanity; he was no longer the sycophant craving the smiles of the great, he was the master whose word was law. He was gratified by the guard of Dyak soldiers who presented arms as he passed. He liked to sit in judgement on his fellow men. It pleased him to compose quarrels between rival chiefs. When the head-hunters were troublesome in the old days he set out to chastise them with a thrill of pride in his own behaviour. He was too vain not to be of dauntless courage, and a pretty story was told of his coolness in adventuring single-handed into a stockaded village and demanding the surrender of a bloodthirsty pirate. He became a skilful administrator. He was strict, just and honest.

And little by little he conceived a deep love for the Malays. He interested himself in their habits and customs. He was never tired of listening to their talk. He admired their virtues, and with a smile and a shrug of the shoulders condoned their vices.

"In my day," he would say, "I have been on intimate terms with some of the greatest gentlemen in England, but I have never known finer gentlemen than some well-born Malays whom I am proud to call my friends."

He liked their courtesy and their distinguished manners, their gentleness and their sudden passions. He knew by instinct exactly how to treat them. He had a genuine tenderness for them. But he never forgot that he was an English gentleman, and he had no patience with the white men who yielded to native customs. He made no surrenders. And he did not imitate so many of the white men in taking a native woman to wife, for an intrigue of this nature, however sanctified by custom, seemed to him not only shocking but undignified. A man who had been called George by Albert Edward, Prince of Wales, could hardly be expected to have any connection with a native. And when he returned to Borneo from his visits to England it was now with something like relief. His friends, like himself, were no longer young, and there was a new generation which looked upon him as a tiresome old man. It seemed to him that the England of to-day had lost a good deal of what he had loved in the England of his youth. But Borneo remained the same. It was home to him now. He meant to remain in service as long as was possible, and the hope in his heart was that he would die before at last he was forced to retire. He had stated in his will that wherever he died he wished his body to be brought back to Sembulu, and buried among the people he loved within the sound of the softly flowing river.

But these emotions he kept hidden from the eyes of men; and no one, seeing this spruce, stout, well-set up man, with his clean-shaven strong face and his whitening hair, would have dreamed that he cherished so profound a sentiment.

He knew how the work of the station should be done, and during the next few days he kept a suspicious eye on his assistant. He saw very soon that he was painstaking and competent. The only fault he had to find with him was that he was brusque with the natives.

"The Malays are shy and very sensitive," he said to him. "I think you will find that you will get much better results if you take care always to be polite, patient and kindly.

Cooper gave a short, grating laugh.

"I was born in Barbados and I was in Africa in the war. I don't think there's much about niggers that I don't know."

"I know nothing," said Mr. Warburton acidly. "But we were not talking of them. We were talking of Malays."

"Aren't they niggers?"

"You are very ignorant," replied Mr. Warburton.

He said no more.

On the first Sunday after Cooper's arrival he asked him to dinner. He did everything ceremoniously, and though they had met on the previous day in the office and later, on the Fort verandah where they drank a gin and bitters together at six o'clock, he sent a polite note across to the bungalow by a boy. Cooper, however unwillingly, came in evening dress and Mr. Warburton, though gratified that his wish was respected, noticed with disdain that the young man's clothes were badly cut and his shirt ill-fitting. But Mr. Warburton was in a good temper that evening.

"By the way," he said to him, as he shook hands, "I've talked to my head-boy about finding you someone and he recommends his nephew. I've seen him and he seems a bright and willing lad. Would you like to see him?"

"I don't mind."

"He's waiting now."

Mr. Warburton called his boy and told him to send for his nephew. In a moment a tall, slender youth of twenty appeared. He had large dark eyes and a good profile. He was very neat in his sarong, a little white coat, and a fez, without a tassel, of plum-covered velvet. He answered to the name of Abas. Mr. Warburton looked on him with approval, and his manner insensibly softened as he spoke to him in fluent and idiomatic Malay. He was inclined to be sarcastic with white people, but with the Malays he had a happy mixture of condescension and kindliness. He stood in the place of the Sultan. He knew perfectly how to preserve his own dignity and at the same time put a native at his ease.

"Will he do?" said Mr. Warburton, turning to Cooper.

"Yes, I dare say he's no more of a scoundrel than any of the rest of them."

Mr. Warburton informed the boy that he was engaged, and dismissed him.

"You're very lucky to get a boy like that," he told Cooper. "He belongs to a very good family. They came over from Malacca nearly a hundred years ago."

"I don't much mind if the boy who cleans my shoes and brings me a drink when I want it has blue blood in his veins or not. All I ask is that he should do what I tell him and look sharp about it."

Mr. Warburton pursed his lips, but made no reply. They went in to dinner. It was excellent, and the wine was good. Its influence presently had its effect on them, and they talked not only without acrimony, but even with friendliness. Mr. Warburton liked to do himself well, and on Sunday night he made it a habit to do himself even a little better than usual. He began to think he was unfair to Cooper. Of course he was not a gentleman, but that was not his fault, and when you got to know him it might be that he would turn out a very good fellow. His faults, perhaps, were faults of manner. And he was certainly good at his work, quick, conscientious and thorough. When they reached the dessert Mr. Warburton was feeling kindly disposed towards all mankind.

"This is your first Sunday, and I'm going to give you a very special glass of port. I've only got about two dozen of it left and I keep it for special occasions."

He gave his boy instructions and presently the bottle was brought. Mr. Warburton watched the boy open it.

"I got this port from my old friend Charles Hollington. He'd had it for forty years, and I've had it for a good many. He was well known to have the best cellar in England."

"Is he a wine merchant?"

"Not exactly," smiled Mr. Warburton. "I was speaking of Lord Hollington of Castle Reagh. He's one of the richest peers in England. A very old friend of mine. I was at Eton with his brother."

This was an opportunity that Mr. Warburton could never resist, and he told a little anecdote of which the only point seemed to be that he knew an Earl. The port was certainly very good; he drank a glass and then a second. He lost all caution. He had not talked to a white man for months. He began to tell stories. He showed himself in the company of the great. Hearing him, you would have thought that at one time ministries were formed and policies decided on his suggestion whispered into the ear of a duchess or thrown over the dinner-table to be gratefully acted on by the confidential adviser of the Sovereign. The old days at Ascot, Goodwood and Cowes lived again for him. Another glass of port. There were the great house-parties in Yorkshire and in Scotland to which he went every year.

"I had a man called Foreman then, the best valet I ever had, and why do you think he gave me notice? You know in the Housekeeper's Room the ladies' maids and the gentlemen's gentlemen sit according to the precedence of their masters. He told me he was sick of going to party after party at which I was the only commoner. It meant that he always had to sit at the bottom of the table, and all the best bits were taken before a dish reached him. I told the story to the old Duke of Hereford, and he roared. 'By God, sir,' he said, 'if I were King of England, I'd make you a viscount just to give your man a chance.' 'Take him yourself, Duke,' I said. 'He's the best valet I've ever had.' 'Well, Warburton,' he said, 'if he's good enough for you he's good enough for me. Send him along'."

Then there was Monte Carlo, where Mr. Warburton and the Grand Duke Fyodor, playing in partnership, had broken the bank one evening; and there was Marienbad. At Marienbad Mr. Warburton had played baccarat with Edward VII.

"He was only Prince of Wales then, of course. I remember him saying to me, 'George, if you draw on a five you'll lose your shirt.' He was right; I don't think he ever said a truer word in his life. He was a wonderful man. I always said he was the greatest diplomatist in Europe. But I was a young fool in those days, I hadn't the sense to take his advice. If I had, if I'd never drawn on a five, I dare say I shouldn't be here to-day."

Cooper was watching him. His brown eyes, deep in their sockets, were hard and supercilious, and on his lips was a mocking smile. He had heard a good deal about Mr. Warburton in Kuala Solor, not a bad sort, and he ran his district like clockwork, they said, but by heaven, what a snob! They laughed at him good-naturedly, for it was impossible to dislike a man who was so generous and so kindly, and Cooper had already heard the story of the Prince of Wales and the game of baccarat. But Cooper listened without indulgence. From the beginning he had resented the Resident's manner. He was very sensitive, and he writhed under Mr. Warburton's polite sarcasms. Mr. Warburton had a knack of receiving a remark of which he disapproved with a devastating silence. Cooper had lived little in England and he had a peculiar dislike of the English. He resented especially the public-school boy since he always feared that he was going to patronize him. He was so much afraid of others putting on airs with him that, in order as it were to get in first, he put on such airs as to make everyone think him insufferably conceited.

"Well, at all events the war has done one good thing for us," he said at last. "It's smashed up the power of the aristocracy. The Boer War started it, and 1914 put the lid on."

"The great families of England are doomed," said Mr. Warburton with the complacent melancholy of an *émigré* who remembered the court of Louis XV. "They cannot afford any longer to live in their splendid palaces and their princely hospitality will soon be nothing but a memory."

"And a damned good job too in my opinion."

"My poor Cooper, what can you know of the glory that was Greece and the grandeur that was Rome?" Mr. Warburton made an ample gesture. His eyes for an instant grew dreamy with a vision of the past.

"Well, believe me, we're fed up with all that rot. What we want is a business government by business men. I was born in a Crown Colony, and I've lived practically all my life in the colonies. I don't give a row of pins for a lord. What's wrong with England is snobbishness. And if there's anything that gets my goat it's a snob."

A snob! Mr. Warburton's face grew purple and his eyes blazed with anger. That was a word that had pursued him all his life. The great ladies whose society he had enjoyed in his youth were not inclined to look upon his appreciation of themselves as unworthy, but even great ladies are sometimes out of temper and more than once Mr. Warburton had had the dreadful word flung in his teeth. He knew, he could not help knowing, that there were odious people who called him a snob. How unfair it was! Why, there was no vice he found so detestable as snobbishness. After all, he liked to mix with people of his own class, he was only at home in their company, and how in heaven's name could anyone say that was snobbish? Birds of a feather.

"I quite agree with you," he answered. "A snob is a man who admires or despises another because he is of a higher social rank than his own. It is the most vulgar failing of our English middle-class."

He saw a flicker of amusement in Cooper's eyes. Cooper put up his hand to hide the broad smile that rose to his lips, and so made it more noticeable. Mr. Warburton's hands trembled a little.

Probably Cooper never knew how greatly he had offended his chief. A sensitive man himself he was strangely insensitive to the feelings of others.

Their work forced them to see one another for a few minutes now and then during the day, and they met at six to have a drink on Mr. Warburton's verandah. This was an old-established custom of the country which Mr. Warburton would not for the world have broken. But they ate their meals separately, Cooper in his bungalow and Mr. Warburton at the Fort. After the office work was over they walked till dusk fell, but they walked apart. There were but few paths in this country where the jungle pressed close upon the plantations of the village, and when Mr. Warburton caught sight of his assistant passing along with his loose stride, he would make a circuit in order to avoid him. Cooper with his bad manners, his conceit in his own judgment and his intolerance had already got on his nerves; but it was not till Cooper had been on the station for a couple of months that an incident happened which turned the Resident's dislike into bitter hatred.

Mr. Warburton was obliged to go up-country on a tour of inspection, and he left the station in Cooper's charge with more confidence, since he had definitely come to the conclusion that he was a capable fellow. The only thing he did not like was that he had no indulgence. He was honest, just and painstaking, but he had no sympathy for the natives. It bitterly amused Mr. Warburton to observe that this man who looked upon himself as every man's equal should look upon so many men as his own inferiors. He was hard, he had no patience with the native mind, and he was a bully. Mr. Warburton very quickly realised that the Malays disliked and feared him. He was not altogether displeased. He would not have liked it very much if his assistant had enjoyed a popularity which might rival his own. Mr. Warburton made his elaborate preparations, set out on his expedition, and in three weeks returned. Meanwhile the mail had arrived. The first thing that struck his eyes when he entered his sitting-room was a great pile of open newspapers. Cooper had met him, and they went into the room together. Mr. Warburton turned to one of the servants who had been left behind, and sternly asked him what was the meaning of those open papers. Cooper hastened to explain.

"I wanted to read all about the Wolverhampton murder, and so I borrowed your *Times*. I brought them back again. I knew you wouldn't mind."

Mr. Warburton turned on him, white with anger.

"But I do mind. I mind very much."

"I'm sorry," said Cooper, with composure. "The fact is, I simply couldn't wait till you came back."

"I wonder you didn't open my letters as well."

Cooper, unmoved, smiled at his chief's exasperation.

"Oh, that's not quite the same thing. After all, I couldn't imagine you'd mind my looking at your newspapers. There's nothing private in them."

"I very much object to anyone reading my paper before me." He went up to the pile. There were nearly thirty numbers there. "I think it extremely impertinent of you. They're all mixed up."

"We can easily put them in order," said Cooper, joining him at the table.

"Don't touch them," cried Mr. Warburton.

"I say, it's childish to make a scene about a little thing like that."

"How dare you speak to me like that?"

"Oh, go to hell," said Cooper, and he flung out of the room.

Mr. Warburton, trembling with passion, was left contemplating his papers. His greatest pleasure in life had been destroyed by those callous, brutal hands. Most people living in out-of-the-way places when the mail comes tear open impatiently their papers and taking the last ones first glance at the latest news from home. Not so Mr. Warburton. His newsagent had instructions to write on the outside of the wrapper the date of each paper he despatched, and when the great bundle arrived Mr. Warburton looked at these dates and with his blue pencil numbered them. His headboy's orders were to place one on the table every morning in the verandah with the early cup of tea and it was Mr. Warburton's especial delight to break the wrapper as he sipped his tea, and read the morning paper. It gave him the illusion of living at home. Every Monday morning he read the Monday *Times* of six weeks back, and so went through the week. On Sunday he read the *Observer*. Like his habit of dressing for dinner it was a tie to civilization. And it was his pride that no matter how exciting the news was he had never yielded to the temptation of opening a paper before its allotted time. During the war the suspense sometimes had been intolerable, and when he read one day that a push was begun he had undergone agonies of suspense which he might have saved himself by the simple expedient of opening a later paper which lay waiting for him on a shelf. It had been the severest trial to which he had ever exposed himself, but he victoriously surmounted it. And that clumsy fool had broken open those neat tight packages because he wanted to know whether some horrid woman had murdered her odious husband.

Mr. Warburton sent for his boy and told him to bring wrappers. He folded up the papers as neatly as he could, placed a wrapper round each and numbered it. But it was a melancholy task.

"I shall never forgive him," he said. "Never."

Of course his boy had been with him on his expedition; he never travelled without him, for his boy knew exactly how he liked things, and Mr. Warburton was not the kind of jungle traveller who was prepared to dispense with his comforts; but in the interval since their arrival he had been gossiping in the servants' quarters. He had learnt that Cooper had had trouble with his boys. All but the youth Abas had left him. Abas had desired to go too, but his uncle had placed him there on the instructions of the Resident, and he was afraid to leave without his uncle's permission.

"I told him he had done well, Tuan," said the boy. "But he is unhappy. He says it is not a good house, and he wishes to know if he may go as the others have gone."

"No, he must stay. The Tuan must have servants. Have those who went been replaced?"

"No, Tuan, no one will go."

Mr. Warburton frowned. Cooper was an insolent fool, but he had an official position and must be suitably provided with servants. It was not seemly that his house should be improperly conducted.

"Where are the boys who ran away?"

"They are in the kampong, Tuan."

"Go and see them to-night, and tell them that I expect them to be back in Tuan Cooper's house at dawn to-morrow."

"They say they will not go, Tuan."

"On my order?"

The boy had been with Mr. Warburton for fifteen years, and he knew every intonation of his master's voice. He was not afraid of him, they had gone through too much together, once in the jungle the Resident had saved his life, and once, upset in some rapids, but for him the Resident would have been drowned; but he knew when the Resident must be obeyed without question. "I will go to the kampong," he said.

Mr. Warburton expected that his subordinate would take the first opportunity to apologize for his rudeness, but Cooper had the ill-bred man's inability to express regret; and when they met next morning in the office he ignored the incident. Since Mr. Warburton had been away for three weeks it was necessary for them to have a somewhat prolonged interview. At the end of it, Mr. Warburton dismissed him.

"I don't think there's anything else, thank you." Cooper turned to go, but Mr. Warburton stopped him. "I understand you've been having some trouble with your boys."

Cooper gave a harsh laugh.

"They tried to blackmail me. They had the damned cheek to run away, all except that incompetent fellow Abas—he knew when he was well off—but I just sat tight. They've all come to heel again."

"What do you mean by that?"

"This morning they were all back on their jobs, the Chinese cook and all. There they were, as cool as cucumbers; you would have thought they owned the place. I suppose they'd come to the conclusion that I wasn't such a fool as I looked."

"By no means. They came back on my express order."

Cooper flushed slightly.

"I should be obliged if you wouldn't interfere with my private concerns."

"They're not your private concerns. When your servants run away it makes you ridiculous. You are perfectly free to make a fool of yourself, but I cannot allow you to be made a fool of. It is unseemly that your house should not be properly staffed. As soon as I heard that your boys had left you, I had them told to be back in their places at dawn. That'll do."

Mr. Warburton nodded to signify that the interview was at an end. Cooper took no notice.

"Shall I tell you what I did? I called them and gave the whole bally lot the sack. I gave them ten minutes to get out of the compound."

Mr. Warburton shrugged his shoulders.

"What makes you think you can get others?"

"I've told my own clerk to see about it."

Mr. Warburton reflected for a moment.

"I think you behaved very foolishly. You will do well to remember in future that good masters make good servants."

"Is there anything else you want to teach me?"

"I should like to teach you manners, but it would be an arduous task, and I have not the time to waste. I will see that you get boys."

"Please don't put yourself to any trouble on my account. I'm quite capable of getting them for myself."

Mr. Warburton smiled acidly. He had an inkling that Cooper disliked him as much as he disliked Cooper, and he knew that nothing is more galling than to be forced to accept the favours of a man you detest.

"Allow me to tell you that you have no more chance of getting Malay or Chinese servants here now than you have of getting an English butler or a French chef. No one will come to you except on an order from me. Would you like me to give it?"

"No."

"As you please. Good-morning."

Mr. Warburton watched the development of the situation with acrid humour. Cooper's clerk was unable to persuade Malay, Dyak or Chinese to enter the house of such a master. Abas, the boy who remained faithful to him, knew how to cook only native food, and Cooper, a coarse feeder, found his gorge rise against the everlasting rice. There was no water-carrier, and in that great heat he needed several baths a day. He cursed Abas, but Abas opposed him with sullen resistance and would not do more than he chose. It was galling to know that the lad stayed with him only because the Resident insisted. This went on for a fortnight and then, one morning, he found in his house the very servants whom he had previously dismissed. He fell into a violent rage, but he had learnt a little sense, and this time, without a word, he let them stay. He swallowed his humiliation, but the impatient contempt he had felt for Mr. Warburton's idiosyncrasies changed into a sullen hatred: the Resident with this malicious stroke had made him the laughing-stock of all the natives.

The two men now held no communication with one another. They broke the time-honoured custom of sharing, notwithstanding personal dislike, a drink at six o'clock with any white man who happened to be at the station. Each lived in his own house as though the other did not exist. Now that Cooper had fallen into the work, it was necessary for them to have little to do with one another in the office. Mr. Warburton used his orderly to send any message he had to give his assistant, and his instructions he sent by formal letter. They saw one another constantly, that was inevitable, but did not exchange half a dozen words in a week. The fact that they could not avoid catching sight of one another got on their nerves. They brooded over their antagonism, and Mr. Warburton, taking his daily walk, could think of nothing but how much he detested his assistant.

And the dreadful thing was that in all probability they would remain thus, facing each other in deadly enmity, till Mr. Warburton went on leave. It might be three years. He had no reason to send in a complaint to headquarters: Cooper did his work very well, and at the time men were hard to get. True, vague complaints reached him and hints that the natives found Cooper harsh. There was certainly a feeling of dissatisfaction among them. But when Mr. Warburton looked into specific cases, all he could say was that Cooper had shown severity where mildness would not have been misplaced, and had been unfeeling when himself would have been sympathetic. He had done nothing for which he could be taken to task. But Mr. Warburton watched him. Hatred will often make a man clear-sighted, and he had a suspicion that Cooper was using the natives without consideration, yet keeping within the law, because he felt that thus he could exasperate his chief. One day perhaps he would go too far. None knew better than Mr. Warburton how irritable the incessant heat could make a man and how difficult it was to keep one's self-control after a sleepless night. He smiled softly to himself. Sooner or later Cooper would deliver himself into his hand.

When at last the opportunity came, Mr. Warburton laughed aloud. Cooper had charge of the prisoners; they made roads, built sheds, rowed when it was necessary to send the prahu up or down stream, kept the town clean and otherwise usefully employed themselves. If well-behaved they even on occasion served as house-boys. Cooper kept them hard at it. He liked to see them work. He took pleasure in devising tasks for them; and seeing quickly enough that they were being made to do useless things the prisoners worked badly. He punished them by lengthening their hours. This was contrary to the regulations, and as soon as it was brought to the attention of Mr. Warburton, without referring the matter back to his subordinate, he gave instructions that the old hours should be kept; Cooper, going out for his walk, was astounded to see the prisoners strolling back to the gaol; he had given instructions that they were not to knock off till dusk. When he asked the warder in charge why they had left off work he was told that it was the Resident's bidding.

White with rage he strode to the Fort. Mr. Warburton, in his spotless white ducks and his neat topee, with a walking-stick in his hand, followed by his dogs, was on the point of starting out on his afternoon stroll. He had watched Cooper go, and knew that he had taken the road by the river. Cooper jumped up the steps and went straight up to the Resident.

"I want to know what the hell you mean by countermanding my order that the prisoners were to work till six," he burst out, beside himself with fury.

Mr. Warburton opened his cold blue eyes very wide and assumed an expression of great surprise.

"Are you out of your mind? Are you so ignorant that you do not know that that is not the way to speak to your official superior?"

"Oh, go to hell. The prisoners are my pidgin, and you've got no right to interfere. You mind your business and I'll mind mine. I want to know what the devil you mean by making a damned fool of me. Everyone in the place will know that you've countermanded my order."

Mr. Warburton kept very cool.

"You had no power to give the order you did. I countermanded it because it was harsh and tyrannical. Believe me, I have not made half such a damned fool of you as you have made of yourself."

"You disliked me from the first moment I came here. You've done everything you could to make the place impossible for me because I wouldn't lick your boots for you. You got your knife into me because I wouldn't flatter you."

Cooper, spluttering with rage, was nearing dangerous ground, and Mr. Warburton's eyes grew on a sudden colder and more piercing.

"You are wrong. I thought you were a cad, but I was perfectly satisfied with the way you did your work."

"You snob. You damned snob. You thought me a cad because I hadn't been to Eton. Oh, they told me in K.S. what to expect. Why, don't you know that you're the laughing-stock of the whole country? I could hardly help bursting into a roar of laughter when you told your celebrated story about the Prince of Wales. My God, how they shouted at the club when they told it. By God, I'd rather be the cad I am than the snob you are."

He got Mr. Warburton on the raw.

"If you don't get out of my house this minute I shall knock you down," he cried.

The other came a little closer to him and put his face in his.

"Touch me, touch me," he said. "By God, I'd like to see you hit me. Do you want me to say it again? Snob. Snob."

Cooper was three inches taller than Mr. Warburton, a strong, muscular young man. Mr. Warburton was fat and fifty-four. His clenched fist shot out. Cooper caught him by the arm and pushed him back. "Don't be a damned fool. Remember I'm not a gentleman. I know how to use my hands."

He gave a sort of hoot, and grinning all over his pale, sharp face jumped down the verandah steps. Mr. Warburton, his heart in his anger pounding against his ribs, sank exhausted into a chair. His body tingled as though he had prickly heat. For one horrible moment he thought he was going to cry. But suddenly he was conscious that his head-boy was on the verandah and instinctively regained control of himself. The boy came forward and filled him a glass of whisky and soda. Without a word Mr. Warburton took it and drank it to the dregs.

"What do you want to say to me?" asked Mr. Warburton, trying to force a smile on to his strained lips.

"Tuan, the assistant Tuan is a bad man. Abas wishes again to leave him."

"Let him wait a little. I shall write to Kuala Solor and ask that Tuan Cooper should go elsewhere."

"Tuan Cooper is not good with the Malays."

"Leave me."

The boy silently withdrew. Mr. Warburton was left alone with his thoughts. He saw the club at Kuala Solor, the men sitting round the table in the window in their flannels, when the night had driven them in from golf and tennis, drinking whiskies and gin pahits, and laughing when they told the celebrated story of the Prince of Wales and himself at Marienbad. He was hot with shame and misery. A snob! They all thought him a snob. And he had always thought them very good fellows, he had always been gentleman enough to let it make no difference to him that they were of very second-rate position. He hated them now. But his hatred for them was nothing compared with his hatred for Cooper. And if it had come to blows Cooper could have thrashed him. Tears of mortification ran down his red, fat face. He sat there for a couple of hours smoking cigarette after cigarette, and he wished he were dead.

At last the boy came back and asked him if he would dress for dinner. Of course! He always dressed for dinner. He rose wearily from his chair and put on his stiff shirt and the high collar. He sat down at the prettily decorated table, and was waited on as usual by the two boys while two others waved their great fans. Over there in the bungalow, two hundred yards away, Cooper was eating a filthy meal clad only in a sarong and a baju. His feet were bare and while he ate he probably read a detective story. After dinner Mr. Warburton sat down to write a letter. The Sultan was away, but he wrote, privately and confidentially, to his representative. Cooper did his work very well, he said, but the fact was that he couldn't get on with him. They were getting dreadfully on each other's nerves and he would look upon it as a very great favour if Cooper could be transferred to another post.

He despatched the letter next morning by special messenger. The answer came a fortnight later with the month's mail. It was a private note, and ran as follows:

My dear Warburton,

I do not want to answer your letter officially, and so I am writing you a few lines myself. Of course if you insist I will put the matter up to the Sultan, but I think you would be much wiser to drop it. I know Cooper is a rough diamond, but he is capable, and he had a pretty thin time in the war, and I think he should be given every chance. I think you are a little too much inclined to attach importance to a man's social position. You must remember that times have changed. Of course it's a very good thing for a man to be a gentleman, but it's better that he should be competent and hard-working. I think if you'll exercise a little tolerance you'll get on very well with Cooper.

Yours very sincerely, Richard Temple.

The letter dropped from Mr. Warburton's hand. It was easy to read between the lines. Dick Temple, whom he had known for twenty years, Dick Temple who came from quite a good county family, thought him a snob, and for that reason had no patience with his request. Mr. Warburton felt on a sudden discouraged with life. The world of which he was a part had passed away and the future belonged to a meaner generation. Cooper represented it and Cooper he hated with all his heart. He stretched out his hand to fill his glass, and at the gesture his head-boy stepped forward.

"I didn't know you were there."

The boy picked up the official letter. Ah, that was why he was waiting.

"Does Tuan Cooper go, Tuan?"

"No."

"There will be a misfortune."

For a moment the words conveyed nothing to his lassitude. But only for a moment. He sat up in his chair and looked at the boy. He was all attention.

"What do you mean by that?"

"Tuan Cooper is not behaving rightly with Abas."

Mr. Warburton shrugged his shoulders. How should a man like Cooper know how to treat servants? Mr. Warburton knew the type: he would be grossly familiar with them at one moment and rude and inconsiderate the next.

"Let Abas go back to his family."

"Tuan Cooper holds back his wages so that he may not run away. He has paid him nothing for three months. I tell him to be patient. But he is angry, he will not listen to reason. If the Tuan continues to use him ill there will be a misfortune."

"You were right to tell me."

The fool! Did he know so little of the Malays as to think he could safely injure them? It would serve him damned well right if he got a kris in his back. A kris. Mr. Warburton's heart seemed on a sudden to miss a beat. He had only to let things take their course and one fine day he would be rid of Cooper. He smiled faintly as the phrase, a masterly inactivity, crossed his mind. And now his heart beat a little quicker, for he saw the man he hated lying on his face in a pathway of the jungle with a knife in his back. A fit end for the cad and the bully. Mr. Warburton sighed. It was his duty to warn him, and of course he must do it. He wrote a brief and formal note to Cooper asking him to come to the Fort at once.

In ten minutes Cooper stood before him. They had not spoken to one another since the day when Mr. Warburton had nearly struck him. He did not now ask him to sit down.

"Did you wish to see me?" asked Cooper.

He was untidy and none too clean. His face and hands were covered with little red blotches where mosquitoes had bitten him and he had scratched himself till the blood came. His long, thin face bore a sullen look.

"I understand that you are again having trouble with your servants. Abas, my head-boy's nephew, complains that you have held back his wages for three months. I consider it a most arbitrary proceeding. The lad wishes to leave you, and I certainly do not blame him. I must insist on your paying what is due to him."

"I don't choose that he should leave me. I am holding back his wages as a pledge of his good behaviour."

"You do not know the Malay character. The Malays are very sensitive to injury and ridicule. They are passionate and revengeful. It is my duty to warn you that if you drive this boy beyond a certain point you run a great risk."

Cooper gave a contemptuous chuckle.

"What do you think he'll do?"

"I think he'll kill you."

"Why should you mind?"

"Oh, I wouldn't," replied Mr. Warburton, with a faint laugh. "I should bear it with the utmost fortitude. But I feel the official obligation to give you a proper warning."

"Do you think I'm afraid of a damned nigger?"

"It's a matter of entire indifference to me."

"Well, let me tell you this, I know how to take care of myself; that boy Abas is a dirty, thieving rascal, and if he tries any monkey tricks on me, by God, I'll wring his bloody neck."

"That was all I wished to say to you," said Mr. Warburton. "Good-evening."

Mr. Warburton gave him a little nod of dismissal. Cooper flushed, did not for a moment know what to say or do, turned on his heel and stumbled out of the room. Mr. Warburton watched him go with an icy smile on his lips. He had done his duty. But what would he have thought had he known that when Cooper got back to his bungalow, so silent and cheerless, he threw himself down on his bed and in his bitter loneliness on a sudden lost all control of himself? Painful sobs tore his chest and heavy tears rolled down his thin cheeks.

After this Mr. Warburton seldom saw Cooper, and never spoke to him. He read his *Times* every morning, did his work at the office, took his exercise, dressed for dinner, dined and sat by the river smoking his cheroot. If by chance he ran across Cooper he cut him dead. Each, though never for a moment unconscious of the propinquity, acted as though the other did not exist. Time did nothing to assuage their animosity. They watched one another's actions and each knew what the other did. Though Mr. Warburton had been a keen shot in his youth, with age he had acquired a distaste for killing the wild things of the jungle, but on Sundays and holidays Cooper went out with his gun: if he got something it was a triumph over Mr. Warburton; if not, Mr. Warburton shrugged his shoulders and chuckled. These counter-jumpers trying to be sportsmen! Christmas was a bad time for both of them: they ate their dinners alone, each in his own quarters, and they got deliberately drunk. They were the only white men within two hundred miles and they lived within shouting distance of each other. At the beginning of the year Cooper went down with fever, and when Mr. Warburton caught sight of him again he was surprised to see how thin he had grown. He looked ill and worn. The solitude, so much more unnatural because it was due to no necessity, was getting on his nerves. It was getting on Mr. Warburton's too, and often he could not sleep at night. He lay awake brooding. Cooper was drinking heavily and surely the breaking point was near; but in his dealings with the natives he took care to do nothing that might expose him to his chief's rebuke. They fought a grim and silent battle with one another. It was a test of endurance. The months passed, and neither gave sign of weakening. They were like men dwelling in regions of eternal night, and their souls were oppressed with the knowledge that never would the day dawn for them. It looked as though their lives would continue for ever in this dull and hideous monotony of hatred.

And when at last the inevitable happened it came upon Mr. Warburton with all the shock of the unexpected. Cooper accused the boy Abas of stealing some of his clothes, and when the boy denied the theft took him by the scruff of the neck and kicked him down the steps of the bungalow. The boy demanded his wages and Cooper flung at his head every word of abuse he knew. If he saw him in the compound in an hour he would hand him over to the police. Next morning the boy waylaid him outside the Fort when he was walking over to his office, and again demanded his wages. Cooper struck him in the face with his clenched fist. The boy fell to the ground and got up with blood streaming from his nose.

Cooper walked on and set about his work. But he could not attend to it. The blow had calmed his irritation, and he knew that he had gone too far. He was worried. He felt ill, miserable and discouraged. In the adjoining office sat Mr. Warburton, and his impulse was to go and tell him what he had done; he made a movement in his chair, but he knew with what icy scorn he would listen to the story. He could see his patronizing smile. For a moment he had an uneasy fear of what Abas might do. Warburton had warned him all right. He sighed. What a fool he had been! But he shrugged his shoulders impatiently. He did not care; a fat lot he had to live for. It was all Warburton's fault; if he hadn't put his back up nothing like this would have happened. Warburton had made life a hell for him from the start. The snob. But they were all like that: it was because he was a Colonial. It was a damned shame that he had never got his commission in the war; he was as good as anyone else. They were a lot of dirty snobs. He was damned if he was going to knuckle under now. Of course Warburton would hear of what had happened; the old devil knew everything. He wasn't afraid. He wasn't afraid of any Malay in Borneo, and Warburton could go to blazes.

He was right in thinking that Mr. Warburton would know what had happened. His head-boy told him when he went in to tiffin.

"Where is your nephew now?"

"I do not know, Tuan. He has gone."

Mr. Warburton remained silent. After luncheon as a rule he slept a little, but to-day he found himself very wide awake. His eyes involuntarily sought the bungalow where Cooper was now resting.

The idiot! Hesitation for a little was in Mr. Warburton's mind. Did the man know in what peril he was? He supposed he ought to send for him. But each time he had tried to reason with Cooper, Cooper had insulted him. Anger, furious anger welled up suddenly in Mr. Warburton's heart, so that the veins on his temples stood out and he clenched his fists. The cad had had his warning. Now let him take what was coming to him. It was no business of his, and if anything happened it was not his fault. But perhaps they would wish in Kuala Solor that they had taken his advice and transferred Cooper to another station.

He was strangely restless that night. After dinner he walked up and down the verandah. When the boy went away to his own quarters, Mr. Warburton asked him whether anything had been seen of Abas.

"No, Tuan, I think maybe he has gone to the village of his mother's brother."

Mr. Warburton gave him a sharp glance, but the boy was looking down, and their eyes did not meet. Mr. Warburton went down to the river and sat in his arbour. But peace was denied him. The river flowed ominously silent. It was like a great serpent gliding with sluggish movement towards the sea. And the trees of the jungle over the water were heavy with a breathless menace. No bird sang. No breeze ruffled the leaves of the cassias. All around him it seemed as though something waited.

He walked across the garden to the road. He had Cooper's bungalow in full view from there. There was a light in his sitting-room, and across the road floated the sound of rag-time. Cooper was playing his gramophone. Mr. Warburton shuddered; he had never got over his instinctive dislike of that instrument. But for that he would have gone over and spoken to Cooper. He turned and went back to his own house.

He read late into the night, and at last he slept. But he did not sleep very long, he had terrible dreams, and he seemed to be awakened by a cry. Of course that was a dream too, for no cry—from the bungalow for instance—could be heard in his room. He lay awake till dawn. Then he heard hurried steps and the sound of voices, his head-boy burst suddenly into the room without his fez, and Mr. Warburton's heart stood still.

"Tuan, Tuan."

Mr. Warburton jumped out of bed.

"I'll come at once."

He put on his slippers, and in his sarong and pyjama-jacket walked across his compound and into Cooper's. Cooper was lying in bed, with his mouth open, and a kris sticking in his heart. He had been killed in his sleep. Mr. Warburton started, but not because he had not expected to see just such a sight, he started because he felt in himself a sudden glow of exultation. A great burden had been lifted from his shoulders.

Cooper was quite cold. Mr. Warburton took the kris out of the wound, it had been thrust in with such force that he had to use an effort to get it out, and looked at it. He recognized it. It was a kris that a dealer had offered him some weeks before, and which he knew Cooper had bought.

"Where is Abas?" he asked sternly.

"Abas is at the village of his mother's brother."

The sergeant of the native police was standing at the foot of the bed.

"Take two men and go to the village and arrest him."

Mr. Warburton did what was immediately necessary. With set face he gave orders. His words were short and peremptory. Then he went back to the Fort. He shaved and had his bath, dressed and went into the dining-room. By the side of his plate *The Times* in its wrapper lay waiting for him. He helped himself to some fruit. The head-boy poured out his tea while the second handed him a dish of eggs. Mr. Warburton ate with a good appetite. The head-boy waited.

"What is it?" asked Mr. Warburton.

"Tuan, Abas, my nephew, was in the house of his mother's brother all night. It can be proved. His uncle will swear that he did not leave the kampong."

Mr. Warburton turned upon him with a frown. "Tuan Cooper was killed by Abas. You know it as well as I know it. Justice must be done."

"Tuan, you would not hang him?"

Mr. Warburton hesitated an instant, and though his voice remained set and stern a change came into his eyes. It was a flicker which the Malay was quick to notice and across his own eyes flashed an answering look of understanding.

"The provocation was very great. Abas will be sentenced to a term of imprisonment." There was a pause while Mr. Warburton helped himself to marmalade. "When he has served a part of his sentence in prison I will take him into this house as a boy. You can train him in his duties. I have no doubt that in the house of Tuan Cooper he got into bad habits."

"Shall Abas give himself up, Tuan?"

"It would be wise of him."

The boy withdrew. Mr. Warburton took his *Times* and neatly slit the wrapper. He loved to unfold the heavy, rustling pages. The morning, so fresh and cool, was delicious and for a moment his eyes wandered out over the garden with a friendly glance. A great weight had been lifted from his mind. He turned to the columns in which were announced the births, deaths, and marriages. That was what he always looked at first. A name he knew caught his attention. Lady Ormskirk had had a son at last. By George, how pleased the old dowager must be! He would write her a note of congratulation by the next mail.

Abas would make a very good house-boy.

That fool Cooper!

LIAM O'FLAHERTY

1897–1984

He was born on the Aran Islands off the Galway coast, served with the Irish Guards in the First World War and afterwards roamed the globe as deck-hand, porter, and clerk. In the civil conflict of 1922 he fought for the Republicans. His novels, such as *The Informer*, speak harshly of the world's violence, but his short stories are touched with poetry.

Three Lambs

LITTLE MICHAEL rose before dawn. He tried to make as little noise as possible. He ate two slices of bread and butter and drank a cup of milk, although he hated cold milk with bread and butter in the morning. But on an occasion like this, what did it matter what a boy ate? He was going out to watch the black sheep having a lamb. His father had mentioned the night before that the black sheep was sure to lamb that morning, and of course there was a prize, three pancakes, for the first one who saw the lamb.

He lifted the latch gently and stole out. It was best not to let his brother John know he was going. He would be sure to want to come too. As he ran down the lane, his sleeves, brushing against the evergreen bushes, were wetted by the dew, and the tip of his cap was just visible above the hedge, bobbing up and down as he ran. He was in too great a hurry to open the gate and tore a little hole in the breast of his blue jersey climbing over it. But he didn't mind that. He would get another one on his thirteenth birthday.

He turned to the left from the main road, up a lane that led to the field where his father, the magistrate, kept his prize sheep. It was only a quarter of a mile, that lane, but he thought that it would never end and he kept tripping among the stones that strewed the road. It was so awkward to run on the stones wearing shoes, and it was too early in the year yet to be allowed to go barefooted. He envied Little Jimmy, the son of the farm labourer, who was allowed to go barefooted all the year round, even in the depths of winter, and who always had such wonderful cuts on his big toes, the envy of all the little boys in the village school.

He climbed over the fence leading into the fields and, clapping his hands together, said "Oh, you devil," a swear word he had learned from Little Jimmy and of which he was very proud. He took off his shoes and stockings and hid them in a hole in the fence. Then he ran jumping, his bare heels looking like round brown spots as he tossed them up behind him. The grass was wet and the ground was hard, but he persuaded himself that it was great fun.

Going through a gap into the next field, he saw a rabbit nibbling grass. He halted suddenly, his heart beating loudly. Pity he hadn't a dog. The rabbit stopped eating. He cocked up his ears. He stood on his tail, with his neck craned up and his forefeet hanging limp. Then he came down again. He thrust his ears forward. Then he lay flat with his ears buried in his back and lay still. With a great yell Little Michael darted forward imitating a dog barking and the rabbit scurried away in short sharp leaps. Only his white tail was visible in the grey light.

Little Michael went into the next field, but the sheep were nowhere to be seen. He stood on a hillock and called out "Chowin, chowin," three times. Then he heard "Mah-m-m-m" in the next field and ran on. The sheep were in the last two fields, two oblong little fields, running in a hollow between two crags, surrounded by high thick fences, the walls of an old fort. In the nearest of the two fields he found ten of the sheep, standing side by side, looking at him, with their fifteen lambs in front of them also looking at him curiously. He counted them out loud and then he saw that the black sheep was not there. He panted with excitement. Perhaps she already had a lamb in the next field. He hurried to the gap leading into the next field, walking stealthily, avoiding the spots where the grass was high, so as to make less noise. It was bad to disturb a sheep that was lambing. He peered through a hole in the fence and could see nothing. Then he crawled to the gap and peered around the corner. The black sheep was just inside standing with her forefeet on a little mound.

Her belly was swollen out until it ended on each side in a sharp point and her legs appeared to be incapable of supporting her body. She turned her head sharply and listened. Little Michael held his breath, afraid to make a noise. It was of vital importance not to disturb the sheep. Straining back to lie down he burst a button on his trousers and he knew his braces were undone. He said, "Oh, you devil," again and decided to ask his mother to let him wear a belt instead of braces, same as Little Jimmy wore. Then he crawled farther back from the gap and taking off his braces altogether made it into a belt. It hurt his hips, but he felt far better and manly.

Then he came back again to the gap and looked. The black sheep was still in the same place. She was scratching the earth with her forefeet and going around in a circle, as if she wanted to lie down but was afraid to lie down. Sometimes she ground her teeth and made an awful noise, baring her jaws and turning her head around sideways. Little Michael felt a pain in his heart in pity for her, and he wondered why the other sheep didn't come to keep her company. Then he wondered whether his mother had felt the same pain when she had Ethna the autumn before. She must have, because the doctor was there.

Suddenly the black sheep went on her knees. She stayed a few seconds on her knees and then she moaned and sank to the ground and stretched herself out with her neck on the little hillock and her hind quarters falling down the little slope. Little Michael forgot about the pain now. His heart thumped with excitement. He forgot to breathe, looking intently. "Ah," he said. The sheep stretched again and struggled to her feet and circled around once stamping and grinding her teeth. Little Michael moved up to her slowly. She looked at him anxiously, but she was too sick to move away. He broke the bladder and he saw two little feet sticking out. He seized them carefully and pulled. The sheep moaned again and pressed with all her might. The lamb dropped on the grass.

Little Michael sighed with delight and began to rub its body with his finger nails furiously. The sheep turned around and smelt it, making a funny happy noise in its throat. The lamb, its white body covered with yellow slime, began to move, and presently it tried to stand up, but it fell again and Little Michael kept rubbing it, sticking his fingers into its ears and nostrils to clear them. He was so intent on this work that he did not notice the sheep had moved away again, and it was only when the lamb was able to stand up and he wanted to give it suck, that he noticed the sheep was lying again giving birth to another lamb. "Oh, you devil," gasped Little Michael, "six pancakes."

The second lamb was white like the first but with a black spot on its right ear. Little Michael rubbed it vigorously, pausing now and again to help the first lamb to its feet as it tried to stagger about. The sheep circled around making low noises in her throat, putting her nostrils to each lamb in turn, stopping nowhere, as giddy as a young schoolgirl, while the hard pellets of earth that stuck to her belly jingled like beads when she moved. Little Michael then took the first lamb and tried to put it to suck, but it refused to take the teat, stupidly sticking its mouth into the wool. Then he put his finger in its mouth and gradually got the teat in with his other hand. Then he pressed the teat and the hot milk squirted into the lamb's mouth. The lamb shook its tail, shrugged its body, made a little drive with its head, and began to suck.

Little Michael was just going to give the second lamb suck, when the sheep moaned and moved away again. He said "chowin, chowin, poor chowin," and put the lamb to her head, but she turned away moaning and grinding her teeth and stamping. "Oh, you devil," said Little Michael, "she is going to have another lamb."

The sheep lay down again, with her foreleg stretched out in front of her and, straining her neck backwards, gave birth to a third lamb, a black lamb.

Then she rose smartly to her feet, her two sides hollow now. She shrugged herself violently and, without noticing the lambs, started to eat grass fiercely, just pausing now and again to say "mah-m-m-m".

Little Michael, in an ecstasy of delight, rubbed the black lamb until it was able to stand. Then he put all the lambs to suck, the sheep eating around her in a circle, without changing her feet, smelling a lamb now and again. "Oh, you devil," Little Michael kept saying, thinking he would be quite famous now, and talked about for a whole week. It was not every day that a sheep had three lambs.

He brought them to a sheltered spot under the fence. He wiped the birth slime from his hands with some grass. He opened his penknife and cut the dirty wool from the sheep's udder, lest the lambs might swallow some and die. Then he gave a final look at them, said, "Chowin, chowin," tenderly, and turned to go.

He was already at the gap when he stopped with a start. He raced back to the lambs and examined each of them. "Three she lambs," he gasped. "Oh, you devil, that never happened before. Maybe father will give me half-a-crown."

And as he raced homeward, he barked like a dog in his delight.

GLEN PETRIE

b. 1931

His grandfather was a land-owning M.P. who voted against three early Education Acts. Perhaps to redress the balance, Petrie, who was handsomely educated at Exeter and Oxford, taught at a state school. A distinguished biographer and novelist, he draws his characters—particularly women—with perception and warmth.

Sad About Miss Brent

MISS BRENT heard them as she was about to turn the corner of Cuthbert Mayne (each of the four wings of the Community School was named for one of the more distinguished of the Forty Martyrs).

"Hey! Sandra! You in there, then?"

The girl, whoever she was, had the cheek of the devil. She must be standing right out on the main drive calling up at the dormitory window, during working hours at that, and Reverend Mother's office not twenty yards distant.

"Hey, Sandra! We know you're up there!"

Another girl out on the drive. Miss Brent stood still. She switched her book-laden briefcase from one hand to the other. Really, she supposed, she should go round the corner and confront the delinquents. But then, she decided, it wasn't her job; it was up to the Sisters, not a member of the lay staff like herself.

"Tell yer! She ain't talkin' to us no more!" said one of the voices.

"Hey! Sandra! Ain't yer talkin' to us no more, then?" called the other.

It would be murder if one of the girls were to come round the corner and catch her eavesdropping, thought Miss Brent. On the other hand, if she were to step out on to the drive, it would be obvious, from the sudden sound of her footfall on the gravel, that she had been lurking out of sight.

There was the click of a window being unlatched.

"What do you want, for God's sake?" came a voice from the first floor.

There were at least five Sandras at the School, but Miss Brent recognized the voice immediately. This Sandra was not the same as the others: she was not feckless, she was never given to outbursts of foul-mouthed and uncontrollable temper; she was, in fact, quite extraordinarily self-possessed. Whereas, according to the Sisters, the hardest, most wanton-appearing girls who came to the School would spend night after night crying for their mothers, Sandra had always slept easily at night. Whereas the other girls, pot-smokers, prostitutes, petty but habitual pilferers, under-age groupies, or gang-followers, were all in need of care and protection, society needed to be protected from Sandra who, at the age of fourteen, had committed an offence many judges described as "worse than murder", and she coming from a good, stable, middle-class background. Moreover—and this, to Miss Brent, was most extraordinary—whereas the diet provided by the institution resulted in most of the girls becoming stodgy in appearance, and the lack of incentive to be otherwise caused their essential gracelessness to increase, Sandra's complexion remained clear, her figure graceful, her appearance poised.

"When yer goin', Sandra?"

"Mid-day. Now go away!"

"Hey! Is yer officer fetchin' yer?"

"What do you think. Honestly, Sister Francis'll catch you if you don't watch out!"

It was stiflingly hot in the garden. Miss Brent felt a prick of sweat under her slip. It trickled down the side of her stomach and lodged in the elastic of her pants. She winced.

"Hey! Sandra! Write us, will yer?"

"All right. But go away!"

"Tell us what yer gets up to outside, eh?"

"Here! Catch!" Sandra called.

"Cor, thanks!"

Miss Brent heard the girls' feet scrabbling on the gravel. Afraid that they might come round the corner, she moved at last. As she turned into the drive, she saw the two girls slouching away arm in arm, going in the opposite direction. They looked, even from behind, vaguely familiar. Sister Justinian, cool in her white habit, was watching them from the front doorstep.

"Hello, Miss Brent," came from the window above her head.

Sandra was perched comfortably on the sill.

"I'll bet you're glad to be seeing the last of me!" she said.

Now why should she say that, wondered Miss Brent. Sandra had never caused a moment's trouble in lessons—her particular brand of nastiness had always been too subtle for that. But, of course, she was glad to see the last of her—very glad indeed—and you had to give Sandra full marks for percipience.

"Of course I'm not, Sandra," she called back. "Except for your own sake. I shall miss you."

She had the most lovely dark brown hair which fell lustrous and straight on either side of her clear cheeks, and her eyes which were thus framed were a bright, penetrating brown, so penetrating, in fact, that they seemed to look right into the deeds of men. There was something frightening about her composure. She knew, thought Miss Brent, that she was glad she was leaving; to gainsay it was no more than a useless formality which gave the girl an advantage.

"Really, Miss Brent?"

Only Sandra could manage that expression of seeming-genuine pleasure.

"Of course, Sandra."

"Now, Sandra! Have you finished your packing?" Sister Justinian had come up.

"Very nearly, Sister."

"That's good."

Sandra slipped off the sill, and closed the window. Sister Justinian glanced at the retreating backs of the two girls who were vanishing round the far corner of the block.

"Ah, but they're naughty, those two. Sister Francis'll have a word to say to them, I'll be bound. Still, it's a lovely day is it not, Miss Brent? Too nice to be sitting in a classroom, I dare say."

Miss Brent wondered whether she should mention that Sandra had thrown something from her window to the two girls, but she thought better of it. Sister Justinian was the wrong person; too much of a reformatory nun as dreamed up by a Hollywood scriptwriter, all saintliness and gentle smiles.

They walked in through the lobby, and into the small Victorian cloister beyond with its large plaster Madonna at one end, simpering despite the gilt dagger thrust into its breast.

"What a hit you made with that girl!" said Sister Justinian.

"Who? Sandra?"

"She said to me: Sister, she said, I didn't know why people thought old pictures were beautiful until Miss Brent started explaining them to us; I really enjoy Miss Brent's lessons, she said."

That was Sandra's way, of course. Any other girl who stopped behind after a lesson to talk about a picture, you knew she was simply avoiding going back to work in the laundry. But Sandra had a deeper motive. By displaying apparent interest in the lesson, and then reporting how much she enjoyed the lesson and the teacher, she was subtly manœuvring herself into a position of advantage.

"She's a hard case, that girl," said Miss Brent, using exactly the same terminology as Reverend Mother used about many girls.

Sister Justinian looked at her curiously.

"Would you say that, now?" she said politely.

"Oh, yes," said Miss Brent.

"You've worked wonders with her, at any rate," said Sister Justinian.

Miss Brent left her, and went through the kitchen area to the classroom block. It was so easy for a girl like Sandra to deceive someone like Sister Justinian, she thought. As a child in an orphanage run by nuns, she remembered how the Superior would come into a classroom with half-a-dozen holy pictures and ask which girls had regularly attended May Devotions, and how it was always the girls who hadn't who leaped up from their desks, hands upstretched, and received the tinsel-embossed cards. It had made her very sad at the time, even though she had often told herself that Our Blessed Lady knew the truth of it.

The classroom block, unlike the rest of the building, was modern, with a flat, leaded roof apparently supported by walls of plate glass; a heat-trap in summer and an ice-box in winter. At the moment, it was a heat-trap, and Miss Brent took off her summer coat, which she wore because she had on a sleeveless dress and knew that the upper edges of her bra and slip were visible under her arms, and sat down at her desk. She had time for a cigarette, so she lit one, carefully knocking the ash into an unused brown envelope.

Cigarettes, she thought. Of course! How stupid not to have thought of that before! Perhaps she should have told Sister Justinian; better still, she would report it to Reverend Mother at lunch-time. Smoking was a serious offence, except for the older girls during the evening recreation hour.

She finished her own cigarette, stood it up on its filter so that it would extinguish itself without making a mess, then placed it in the envelope with the ash, sealed the envelope and threw it into the waste-paper basket. Five minutes later, the first class of the morning, some twenty girls, filed in silently and slouched to their desks. There they sat and stared in front of them, some brimming with unspoken insolence which, since they knew Miss Brent too well, they would never let spill over, some sunk into that vacant boredom which they would maintain for the next forty minutes. The nun who had escorted them from the laundry where they had been working, waited in the doorway only long enough to nod and smile sympathetically to Miss Brent.

"Please sit silently," said Miss Brent, in a sharp, effective voice.

She left the hot, shuffling room, and caught up with the nun at the head of the stairs.

"Sister Sebastian! Excuse me, Sister!"

There was a rattle of pencils and rulers on the desk-tops in the classroom. Somebody giggled furtively.

"I thought I'd just ask your advice, Sister."

Sister Sebastian was ridiculously young, she thought. Nuns are always well preserved of course, but Sister Sebastian looks a freckle-faced seventeen-year-old. Straight from school into the novitiate, of course, with no intermediate experience of the outside world and what it's like . . .

"These two girls were standing out on the drive shouting up to the dormitory window . . ."

"Ah yes," said Sister Sebastian. "They were saying goodbye to Sandra. That's what it was. A bit naughty, mind you, but Sandra's been such a popular girl, hasn't she? And so good with the younger ones when they've just arrived. I think we can call it a special occasion."

Miss Brent wondered what she would say if you suggested breaking the Ten Commandments to celebrate your birthday.

"Besides," said Sister Sebastian, "we don't want to give them a sense of grievance."

She laughed.

"They do so love having a good grievance, don't they?" she added, and went off down the stairs.

In the classroom, those girls, which was most of them, who had been leaning over whispering to each other, straightened up as soon as they saw Miss Brent.

"Stand up!" she said briskly.

They dragged themselves to their feet, clearly afraid that she was angry. She turned to the crucifix on the wall.

"In the name of the Father, and of the Son, and of the Holy Ghost," she began, emphasizing the 'ands' rather than the persons of the Trinity.

Obediently, the girls blessed themselves and, with evident relief, launched themselves into the Morning Offering.

"Linda! Maureen! Give out the drawing-boards and paper, please!"

Jackie put up her hand.

"Yes, Jacqueline?"

"Go to the toilet, Miss?"

"Why didn't you go before?"

"Sister di'n't give us a chance, Miss. Said we was late—or somefing."

"Be quick then."

"Yer, quick as I can, Miss!"

Somebody sniggered.

"Be quiet!"

Jackie and Denise always sat at the back, pallid-faced, and suety under their nylon overalls; Sandra's familiars, their dullness hanging on her quickness. Miss Brent realised whose backs she had seen as soon as Jackie drew attention to herself. She watched the girl as she slouched out, fist clenched in her overall pocket.

Six minutes elapsed before she returned, timed precisely on Miss Brent's wrist-watch.

"Go to your place, Jacqueline," she said coldly.

Suddenly, she got up, and without saying another word she went downstairs. The sound of astonished and unconcealed whispering followed her—never before had she gone downstairs leaving her class unattended. She went round the back of the ground floor to the lavatories. There, she opened the doors of each of the deserted cubicles. In the fourth, and furthest from the window, where it was most dark and insufferably close, there was a trapped and pungent smell of cigarette smoke. As her eyes became used to the gloom, she saw a small grey cylinder of ash on the floor, and grains of ash on the black plastic seat. The girls were slovenly and careless even in breaking the rules.

Whispering had resolved into raucous conversation by the time she returned to the classroom. Two of the girls looked distinctly ruffled up, and one of them was tearful. As soon as the class saw Miss Brent they lapsed into silence. She walked straight to the back row.

"Jacqueline! Denise! Stand up!"

They both gave her a 'who, me?' look as they lumbered to their feet. The whole class swivelled round to watch. Miss Brent stared at them fixedly. Jackie looked sheepishly at her desk-top, and Denise fumbled with the Woolworth's ring on her finger.

"Sister said we could," muttered Denise.

"Could what?"

"Say good-bye to Sandra an' that."

"Sandra's our friend an' that," said Jackie, swinging her hips from side to side and scraping her finger along the desk.

"I haven't the foggiest idea what you're talking about," said Miss Brent.

"When you was round the corner, an' we was talkin' ter Sandra an' all," said Denise.

She put her hand behind her back and scratched her bottom. Her nail scraped on the nylon.

"Stand still!"

Denise did so, then glanced miserably about her.

"I'm not interested in what you were doing with Sandra," said Miss Brent. "What I'm interested in is what Sandra was doing in the toilets."

The mistake opened before her like a sudden chasm ripping open at one's feet in an earth tremor. Denise grinned broadly, and there was a ripple of sniggering round the class.

"Be quiet!" shouted Miss Brent. "You don't have to tell each other what dirty little minds you've got!"

Her voice struck the plaster ceiling and glass walls and went dead. The girls were genuinely shocked. She had never lost her temper like that. She recovered.

"I meant Jacqueline," she said. "Well, Jacqueline?"

"I were bein' excused, Miss."

"And was that all?"

"Yer, Miss!"

"Empty your pockets!"

Jackie looked defiant.

"You ain't got no right . . ." she began.

"Empty your pockets," said Miss Brent, very quietly this time.

From the depths of her overall, Jackie pulled out five screwed-up paper handkerchiefs, a plastic compact, and a Miraculous Medal on a strand of green tape. She placed them on the desk.

"Now you, Denise."

"Why me, Miss?"

"Do as I say."

Denise pulled out a piece of string with a tiny plastic toy puppy on the end, a stick of lipstick in a greasy holder, and a creased picture-card of a pop-singer long faded from the charts.

"Is that all?" asked Miss Brent.

The girls nodded. They were frightened by this unexpected turn of events. Miss Brent leaned forward and thrust her fingers into the narrow top pocket of Jackie's overall. Against her hand, the girl's breast gave like a half-deflated balloon, soft, flabby, and disgusting. From the fluff and grit at the bottom, she dragged up a cigarette three-quarters smoked.

"Do you want me to look in your pocket?" she asked Denise.

Denise slid her fingers into her pocket and produced one battered cigarette.

"Thank you," said Miss Brent, with a sharp upward inflexion on the 'you'. "I'll have to tell Reverend Mother about this, of course."

The two girls slumped back into their seats. They looked animal-pathetic. Denise, fiddling with her pencil, was on the verge of tears, while the atmosphere of hostility among the other members of the class was palpable in the leaden heat of the room, far worse than anything Miss Brent could ever remember. During the twenty minutes which remained of the lesson, it was so strong that anything she said seemed totally irrelevant.

Sister Sebastian came to the door to take the girls back to the laundry. As they slouched out, Miss Brent noticed, penetrating her general sense of unease, how short they wore their overalls. The nuns were ridiculously easy-going; that was the trouble really. Not that she was narrow-minded about such things—until she came to London, she had worn mini-dresses. And then the underground. Escalators, and men sitting opposite. Eyes raped. Funny, she'd never noticed that men's eyes shone a sort of beam—like a laser—until the underground. And the sun, burning the plate glass into your head.

As the girls' footsteps pattered down the stairs and out on to the garden path, she had to sit down in the empty classroom to settle her nerves. She lit a cigarette, and found that her hand was shaking. On an impulse, she pinched the end of the cigarette, and, leaving her things on the desk, she ran down the stairs and out into the garden. Sister Sebastian and her small column of girls were just passing the entry to the kitchen yards on their way to the laundry shop in the far wing.

"Sister Sebastian!" she called, and ran down the path after her.

Sister Sebastian stopped and turned back. The girls remained in a group, keeping their distance and staring back sullenly when they saw who it was approaching them. "Sister Sebastian! Sister! I really must have a word with you about these girls!"

She caught her breath.

"The girls I told you about. Jacqueline and Denise, that's who they were."

Sister Sebastian took a slightly longer breath than usual.

"Yes, Miss Brent?"

"Jacqueline. She was smoking in the toilet during my lesson!"

"Oh? Now that is naughty."

"And I found a cigarette in Denise's pocket."

She held out her hand to show the battered cigarette and its accompanying cigarette-end. Then she saw the gleam of sweat on her palm, and closed her fist abruptly.

"They got them from Sandra. That's where they got them from!"

"That's not important, now is it? But smoking during lessons, that's very naughty. I shall report it to Sister Francis."

Miss Brent had taken no more than two or three paces back towards the classroom block when Sister Sebastian caught up with her.

"Miss Brent," she said, "I've just been thinking. Perhaps it would not be such a bad thing to forget all about it this time. Of course Jackie was very bad to do such a thing, but the girls now: they're a bit over-excited about Sandra leaving, and we don't want to excite them more. I'll have a quiet word with her myself. On the whole, she's not a troublesome girl."

Typical of the Sisters—they always made it clear that they alone knew what was best for the girls, despite the fact that few of them had ever experienced the moral rigours of the outside world. Miss Brent had learnt that the hard way, when she left her convent-orphanage for College and realised exactly how unprepared she was for mixing with her pagan colleagues.

"If you think it best, Sister," she said.

You don't argue with nuns. She returned to the classroom block, the incriminating cigarettes clutched in her hand. And the way they talked about Sandra, as if it was a positive virtue for her to be popular with the sort of girls they had to deal with! It wouldn't be a bad idea to go and warn Reverend Mother about the lax discipline imposed by Sister Sebastian and Sister Justinian, except that nuns were just the same as all closely-knit groups—they covered up for their own kind.

"Hallo, Janis!"

Mary Fisher came out of one of the downstairs classrooms.

"Had your coffee yet?" she asked.

Miss Brent had forgotten all about mid-morning break, and coffee.

"Not yet," she said. "Actually, I've been rather busy."

And there seemed to be something wrong with the way the time was passing. She felt, at least, that she had only just dismissed her first class of the morning.

"How time flies!" she said, with a slightly unsteady laugh.

She went into the little washroom adjoining the classroom, and sluiced her hands under the cold tap. It would have been nice to have washed her face in the cold water, but there wouldn't have been time to have made up afterwards, so she patted her forehead with a Kleenex. Her legs suddenly felt weak, so she leant over the basin and rested her head on her hand. She didn't look up when the door opened behind her.

"Too hot for comfort if you ask me," said Mary Fisher.

"I suppose it is," said Miss Brent, still not raising her head.

"I say, are you feeling all right?" asked Mary.

You couldn't call Mary a close friend; not if you're being honest with yourself. She had come over to the bed-sitter for coffee the other night, and she had invited Miss Brent over to her place on a number of occasions, but Miss Brent wouldn't go—Mary Fisher was married, and she didn't like to intrude.

"Yes, of course I am," she said, drawing herself erect. "Actually," she admitted, "I've had a spot of bother."

"Oh yes?" said Mary. "Which one in particular?"

Miss Brent had to smile. "Sandra," she said. "Sandra Jones."

"Oh, well, that's all right, isn't it? I mean she's leaving, if she hasn't left already."

"She's leaving at mid-day," said Miss Brent. "The trouble is, a girl like her can do an awful lot of harm in one morning."

"A girl like her?" asked Mary Fisher.

"She should never have been sent here," said Miss Brent. "Holloway's the place for her sort. She'll end up there, at any rate, and that'll be a blessing."

"Janis!" said Mary.

"All right, so you're shocked," said Miss Brent. "But do you know why she was sent here?"

"I don't. I take care never to find out," said Mary. "It's not our business."

"She's pure evil," said Miss Brent. "Pure unadulterated evil."

"She's never caused me a moment's worry," objected Mary.

"She doesn't cause trouble," said Miss Brent. "Not the way you mean."

If only her mind was clear, and she could explain what she meant—but the brightness of everything this morning was unbearable.

"I suppose it's a spiritual thing really," she said. "It's as if she gives off a sort of—well—aura of evil."

"Like B.O.?" asked Mary, and laughed.

Miss Brent ignored Mary's coarseness.

"She's been giving cigarettes to the girls," she said.

"Oh, has she?" said Mary.

"She persuaded them to smoke them in the toilets during my lesson!"

She had placed the cigarettes in the soap-holder beside the basin; the paper had separated in the damp, and the sodden tobacco was leaking out. Carefully, she picked up each wet butt and wrapped them in a Kleenex for safe-keeping.

"I'm going to show these to Reverend Mother," she explained. "It's about time somebody in this place realised . . ."

She broke off. Her voice had sounded so strident.

She placed the folded handkerchief in her bag and snapped it shut.

"Janis?" asked Mary Fisher. "Don't you think perhaps you should go home?"

"Whatever do you mean?" asked Miss Brent.

"Janis! Please let me run you home!"

"Don't be ridiculous, Mary! You'd think there was something wrong with me! I've got a lot of important things to do today, let me tell you!"

She decided to go to the parlour set aside for the lay teaching staff. Passing through the back gate of the kitchen yards, she ducked under the rows of washing-lines which sagged under the weight of dripping overalls, white cotton bras, and slips as austere as the convent pillow-cases. Beyond, was a group of some half-dozen girls swathed in plastic waterproof aprons. They were standing round a pair of trestle tables, and were supposed to be cleaning out what looked like breadbins and waste containers, but in fact, since they were effectually concealed from the gaze of authority by the lines of washing, they were jostling one another, scrapping and flicking water at one another. This they stopped as soon as they saw Miss Brent.

"Haven't you girls got any work to do?"

They regarded her with dumb insolence. Clearly they had heard what had happened in class this morning.

"Well, Shirley?" Miss Brent demanded of the most senior of the girls.

"Done all we was told to do," Shirley replied.

"Then you'd better take these things back to the kitchen and report to Sister Sebastian in the laundry!"

It was surprising, the degree of venom they could reveal in their stupid faces. They were volatile, menacing, ready for some unplanned, unconsidered act of physical violence, as they were when one of their number escaped over the wall or was removed for a spell of solitary confinement in the infirmary wing. Today it must be Sandra's departure, and the weather. Above all, the weather. Perhaps there was a good reason why God had walked in the garden in the cool of the day; sunlight and oppressive heat engendered violence, indolence, and lust—just think of Naples and Sicily, and the Mafia. "The day is hot," thought Miss Brent, "the Capulets abroad, and if we meet we shall not 'scape a brawl."

But she would escape.

"Do what I tell you," she said, and without waiting to see that her instruction was carried out, she went down the steps to the inner yard. Behind her back, one of the girls said as audibly as she dared:

"Yer! Get away, yer rotten old shit!"

There was an uncertain burst of slightly nervous sniggering at this act of defiance. It was Sandra's legacy to her, thought Miss Brent. Only yesterday she would have sworn these girls liked her. A few of them had even pretended to enjoy her lessons. But now Sandra, cool, pretty, and assured, sat in the dormitory in Cuthbert Mayne, while the poison spilled over and trickled outwards from her like black ink creeping and feeling its way to every room, every mind, in the convent. What malice was in Sandra, thought Miss Brent, that she was not prepared to allow her the little affection she could gain from these pitiful, squalid children?

She was suddenly engulfed in self-pity. She began to cry. Now that was stupid; but she couldn't help it, the tears just seemed to come, more and more of them streaming from her eyes and down her cheeks. Suppose one of the nuns, she told herself, or worse still some of the girls working in the back-kitchens, were to see her like this? She looked round for some refuge in which she could hide until this strange weakness had passed.

There was a coal shed. Once it had been one of the stables of the house, and the wooden stalls were still there. She went into the gloom, fragments of coal crunching under her feet, and hid behind one of the wooden partitions, coke piled about her ankles.

Long ago, she had hidden like this when she found she was crying uncontrollably, in a linen cupboard. One of the orphanage sisters had seen her, and led her out.

"Why, Janis! Whatever would you be doing in there, now?"

She pretended to hide the tears. Sister saw them, and knelt beside her; a gentle, freckled, unlined face, like Sister Sebastian's.

"Now that's naughty, isn't it? You shouldn't be crying any more, now should you? Your Mam and Da's with Our Blessed Lord, you know that, don't you? And your Mam would want you to be happy, wouldn't she? And your Da' would want you to be happy? And your Guardian Angel would want you to be happy? And Our Blessed Lady would want you to be happy? And Our Blessed Lord Himself? He'd want you to be happy, wouldn't He now? There! Are there not a lot of people all wanting for Janis to be happy!" You couldn't explain you were happier crying than when you weren't.

Footsteps came pattering across the yard towards the coal shed. Miss Brent shrank back into the darkness of the stall. From her new position she could see the door through the gap left by a broken slat in the partition, and standing there, silhouetted against the bright sunlight outside, was the girl Shirley. Another girl joined her, and they peered into the gloom.

"'s all right," said the second girl. "Ain't nobody in 'ere!"

"'course it's all right," said Shirley. "Ain't used 'cept winter an' all."

They advanced cautiously into the shed.

"Ain' 'alf dark in 'ere!" said the second girl. "Sort o' scarey an' 'at."

"Want a light on, then?" asked Shirley. "So's any bugger can see us?"

Miss Brent thought she was going to have a heart attack the way her heart was pounding; and the sweat was pouring down her body and her hands and forehead were soaking. She moved, and a small avalanche of coke scraped and rattled off the pile at her feet, and slid out into the open.

"Someone's 'ere!" said Shirley.

"Let's get out of it, Shirl!" said the other girl.

Shirley appeared round the end of the partition and saw Miss Brent. No words, no explanation came into Miss Brent's mind. It was Shirley who spoke.

"You're spyin' on us!" she said. "You come in 'ere to spy on us!"

Like many of the girls who had long been deprived of parental affection she was as short as an eleven-year-old for all she was nearly nineteen, but her face was as worn and embittered as if she were twice her age.

"There ain't no call for you to go spyin' on us! You ain't one er the Sisters!"

"I wasn't spying," said Miss Brent.

The other girl took Shirley's arm. She looked nervously at Miss Brent.

"'ere. Come on Shirl," she whispered.

"Please believe me," begged Miss Brent. "I wasn't spying!"

She sobbed.

"Eh, Shirl! Let's get out of it!" urged the other girl.

"I'm not spying!"

Her voice sounded weird—not her own. And then tears were pouring down again. The girls shrank back to the door. Then they turned and went off across the yard, arm in arm, and glancing nervously over their shoulders as they went.

Now they would tell their friends. They wouldn't be nervous for long; they'd soon see the funny side. The laughter would ripple through the whole School, passing up each strand of the spider's web till it reached the middle and Sandra, bloated with victory. Oh God, they were repulsive! Shabby, dirty, graceless; and all of them were experienced in sex, you could tell—the furtive way they looked—they'd all practised the most disgusting forms of sex. What had she ever done to harm them? And yet the way they looked at her in the class, out in the yard, and now Shirley and that other girl, with those dirty, sexually-knowing eyes . . .

And then she understood with an awful, inspirational clarity. Despite her utter weariness, she understood. They had no souls.

On the heels of this realization, the words of a long-forgotten hymn came into her mind:

"Christian, dost thou see them
On the holy ground,
How the troops of Midian
Prowl and prowl around?"

Oh, she saw them all right, the troops of Midian. But, she reminded herself, her part was with the Lord Jesus. Consciously she had to cling to that knowledge in order to find the courage to leave the shed, to cross the yard and through the building, in order to reach the parlour where, at least for a time, she would be safe.

The parlour was empty, and the coffee lukewarm, but she felt better and stronger for a drink even of lukewarm coffee. As she finished it, Sister Francis came in.

"Ah, Miss Brent. So there you are!"

"So here I am, Sister!" she replied quite gaily.

Sister Francis hesitated.

"Mrs. Fisher's been talking to me," she said.

"Has she now," said Miss Brent, imitating the Sister's soft Irish accent—but in the most affectionate way.

"She says that she thinks you've been overdoing things a little. She thinks it would be best if you took the rest of the day off."

"But Sister," said Miss Brent. "You're in charge of the school here, not Mary Fisher."

"I am, Miss Brent. And I think it would be no bad thing if you were to go home for the rest of the day."

"Sister," said Miss Brent. "Just because I tell Mary Fisher the truth about Sandra Jones doesn't mean that I'm ill."

"And what," asked Sister Francis gently, "is the truth about Sandra Jones?"

"That she deliberately set out to ruin my lesson this morning. That she has spent the day poisoning everybody's mind against me."

"I'm sure you're wrong, Miss Brent. To my certain knowledge, Sandra has been up in the dormitory all morning, titivating herself at what some of us might consider inordinate length in preparation for going home. I have no doubt that the girl is much too excited at the prospect to be concerned with anything, least of all a lesson she is not attending."

To be sensible, thought Miss Brent, is not enough. You must sound sensible.

"I'm afraid you're wrong, Sister," she said, very quietly, very unexcitedly. "She's probably tried to give that impression. But you don't know how much that girl hates me."

"I'm sure you're mistaken, Miss Brent. We all know how much she's enjoyed your lessons."

Miss Brent had to laugh. The naïvety of the Sisters was beyond all belief.

"She's cunning all right," she said. "They've all got animal cunning, but Sandra's got something more. She's got an intellect. She's made sure nobody will ever believe that she hates me. But she does. And with good reason. Shall I tell you why?"

"Go on, Miss Brent."

"Because I've seen through her. You learn to see through people when you've been out in the world for a bit. You learn when a man pretends to be your friend when actually he just wants to—well—touch you."

Sister Francis nodded.

"It came to me quite suddenly, Sister, though I think I'd realised it sort of subconsciously for a long time: the difference between Sandra and the other girls. Most of the girls are innocent—like animals. They've got no spiritual life. None. But Sandra has a spiritual life, only it's dark and evil. That's the difference."

She had done rather well, she thought. She had spoken lucidly; she had not raised her voice.

"Miss Brent," said Sister Francis. "I shall ask Mrs. Fisher to take you home."

"But Sister, I've so much to do . . ."

"No, Miss Brent," said Sister Francis firmly. "I insist that you let Mrs. Fisher take you home. Now you just wait here while I fetch her."

"But she'll be in class," said Miss Brent.

"That doesn't matter."

"Oh, but it does. I'd never forgive myself . . ."

"Sister Justinian can take over her class. Now you stay here. Have a smoke. Another cup of coffee."

Another cup of tepid coffee?

"And if I were you, Miss Brent, I'd go and have a talk with your doctor tonight."

"Why, Sister?"

"Because, Miss Brent, you most certainly need a rest, I do assure you. You go and talk it over with your doctor."

Miss Brent smiled. She was trying so hard to be polite to Sister Francis.

"I'll talk it over with my friends," she said. "I'll see what they think."

The postman, the milkman, the breadman, the landlord who brings the rent book round once a month?

Sister Francis closed the parlour door behind her. It was quiet and peaceful now she was alone. There was a cobweb up on the ceiling—any minute now, one end might drift to the floor to form a barrier between the door and herself. But if she ran, she would reach the door before the trap closed, and then the front door was only ten yards away, and she would be safe. Only ten yards, and she could leave all the squalor and the evil behind.

Sunlight streamed in through the pointed window. The leaves on the elm trees across the drive were vivid, almost luminous—God's wonderful creation. She sat down on the faded settee and lay back against the cushion. The cobweb quivered slightly suggesting a faint breeze. From the mantelpiece beyond the cobweb, the statue of the Sacred Heart smiled benignly down at her. As she looked at it, a miracle occurred. She experienced a quite fantastic sense of relaxation. It was as if all her limbs and nerves had been strung taut by invisible wires, and that, on an instruction from the statue, some unseen hand was slackening their tension from one end of her body to the other. As the ease crept over her, she was conscious of the sound of girls' voices coming from some remote part of the garden, clear, bell-like, and purified by the summer distance. A distinct breeze now rippled the lace curtains, bearing with it the smell of mown grass.

She took a cigarette from her bag and lit it. She had been smoking rather too much these last few days. Still, they do say that when you're relaxing a cigarette increases the pleasure. Footsteps padded up the passage outside, and there was the clatter of a pail being put down on the tiled floor. O dear Lord Jesus, she had been so hard on the girls, this morning; so hard on herself for that matter. No wonder Sister Francis thought she ought to go home, ought to see a doctor. Actually, a priest would be more to the point after the terrible things she had been thinking and saying about the girls. Lack of Charity; that was it. Complete lack of Charity leading almost to madness. Well? Lack of Charity is a kind of madness, isn't it? You become a tinkling cymbal (not sounding brass, not if you're only five foot and people tell you you're quite pretty really).

The magic word is 'restitution'. You have to make restitution. It's all right having that marvellous feeling that Jesus loves you when you're coming out of the confessional, but he won't go on loving you if you don't make some form of restitution. It was quite obvious—God makes it so easy when you're really trying, slipping the thoughts into your mind as it were. You must go and say a proper good-bye to Sandra, show her that you do feel friendly towards her. However much you dislike the idea, you must go up to the dormitory and say good-bye to her. After all, you've nothing to fear. Jesus will be with you all the time.

Miss Brent got up and went to the door. She still had this weak feeling in her legs, rather like the aftermath of 'flu. In the passage, a girl was washing the floor; very clumsily at that, splashing the water from the bucket so that it overran her kneeling pad, soaked the hem of her overall, and trickled in rivulets under Miss Brent's shoes.

"Oh dear, you do seem to be making a mess, Pauline," said Miss Brent.

"Yes, Miss," said the girl sullenly, without looking up.

Like the others, she was dwarfish and dirty, but Miss Brent's heart was filled with love.

"Let me show you how to do it properly," she said.

"Come on! Get up!" she added, when the girl hesitated.

She glanced up and down the passage to make sure that Sister Francis was not returning. "Give me the cloth," she said.

Then she got down on the kneeling pad. She did not work as efficiently as she would have liked because she was afraid that Sister Francis would come any minute and wouldn't understand. In fact, she splashed almost as much as Pauline had done, and the water drenched the front of her dress, soaking through to her knees.

"I'm afraid I seem to have left one or two patches," she laughed, handing the cloth back to the girl.

"Yes, Miss," said the girl.

Water was dribbling down Miss Brent's legs—not an unpleasant sensation in this heat.

"Anyway, there you are, kitten," she said.

A long time ago, she had been standing in a convent garden. The orphanage medical officer had passed her.

"Hullo, kitten! All by yourself, are you?" he had said to her.

He had given her a sweet. She had never forgotten that moment. Now she had the opportunity to share it with somebody else. She took her cigarettes from her bag, and handed one to the girl.

"Don't let Sister Francis catch you smoking it," she laughed.

She went up the stairs from the entrance hall, and made her way down the long passage to the dormitory wing in Cuthbert Mayne. Sunlight poured through the windows on to the polished linoleum of the passage floor. Outside, she could see the girls working in the kitchen gardens, raking the mown grass into heaps under the apple trees. With their hair bound up in scarves, their blue and yellow overalls, their beefy legs, and their wooden rakes, they looked like peasant girls from an Age of Innocence depicted in a brightly coloured medieval illuminated manuscript. She wished there was someone with whom she could share her pleasure in the scene.

The dormitory was swept, shining, and polished; the hospital beds in their two long rows were flat-topped and with precise, sharp corners. Photographs of relatives, of boy friends who might or might not be waiting, with puppet-stiff smiles, stood beside holy pictures in tinsel frames on the lockers. On the beds lay the checked cotton dresses and white ankle-socks of the girls working in the laundry and about the convent.

Sandra was at the far end, inspecting her make-up in the mirror. Miss Brent had never seen her when she was not in institution dress. Now, in a plain black mini-dress with white lace collar and cuffs, with her long hair soft, glistening and unlacquered, and her long slim stockinged legs, she was even further removed from the other girls. Somebody must have given her a bottle of scent, of reasonably good quality at that.

"Hallo, Sandra," said Miss Brent.

"Hallo, Miss," said Sandra.

You would have thought that she was quite surprised and pleased to see her. Perhaps she was.

"I—well—I was just going home, actually, so I thought I'd drop in and say good-bye."

She laughed apologetically.

"You see? It isn't true, what you said about my being glad to see the back of you."

She laughed again.

"I was only joking, Miss," said Sandra. "I mean, we've always got on well together, haven't we, Miss?"

She was so self-assured. You couldn't help remembering, however unworthy the thought, why she had been sent to the School.

"I do like your dress, Sandra."

"Do you, Miss? It is nice, isn't it? Nice change from these awful things."

She pointed to the cotton dress and overall on the bed beside her.

"Look, Sandra. I wondered if you'd like some cigarettes for the journey. I know you smoke."

Sandra giggled.

"Like a chimney, Miss, given the chance."

"Only ten, I'm afraid."

"That's all right, Miss. Mrs. Fisher gave me a packet of ten earlier on, so I'm well set up, aren't I?"

The sense of disappointment was dreadful. Then Sandra said, quite blandly,

"Could you let me have a box of matches, Miss? I've nearly run out."

"Yes, of course," said Miss Brent, and fumbled in her bag. "Here you are."

Then the desire to offer something special overwhelmed her. She was almost in tears again.

"Sandra? I want you to have this," she said.

She pulled out the tiny crucifix on its silver chain. She sniffed.

"You see? It opens. And inside—see there?—is a tiny scrap of parchment—real parchment—with the Our Father written on it. Do you see?"

"Oh yes!" said Sandra.

"It isn't worth anything really. But it is real silver. I'd very much like you to have it!"

Sandra shook her head.

"I couldn't, Miss. It's much too nice!"

"You do like it, don't you?" asked Miss Brent, anxiously.

"Oh yes! But I couldn't take it. I mean, it's yours, isn't it?"

"Please, Sandra! Here, let me put it round your neck."

Sandra shrank back.

"No, Miss! Please! I mean, I'm not a Catholic, Miss!"

"That doesn't matter, now does it!"

She reached over to try to put the chain over the girl's head, but Sandra ducked away.

"I'd rather not, Miss! Honestly!"

"Please, Sandra! Please! You must!"

Sandra tried to move away from the bed. Miss Brent took her by the shoulders.

"I'll be terribly hurt, Sandra," she said, fighting to keep her voice under control. "I'll be terribly hurt if you don't take it."

The girl tried to twist away.

"Please, Miss! Let go! You're hurting me, Miss!"

Miss Brent tried to hold her with one arm in order to force the chain over her head. The girl began to scream.

"Stop it, Miss! Stop it! Stop it!"

She writhed against her, her hair falling about her face.

"Stop it! You're hurting me! You're hurting me!"

"What is going on?"

Sister Francis was standing by the door. Sandra broke free and stood at the foot of the bed gasping for breath.

"It's Miss Brent, Sister! She . . . she!"

Tears ran through her mascara, blotching her face. Miss Brent said nothing but simply held out the little crucifix dangling by its chain from her clenched hand.

Sister Francis summed up the situation.

"Take your things, Sandra, and wait for me in my room," she said calmly.

Her suitcase was not two feet from where Miss Brent was standing. Sandra hesitated.

"Come on, Sandra," said Sister Francis.

The girl reached over and took the case. Suddenly she turned to Sister Francis.

"She was trying to kiss me!" she screamed.

Then she turned and looked at Miss Brent. There was an unmistakable triumph in her face.

"Come along, Sandra," said Sister Francis.

Suitcase in hand, Sandra clicked away down the corridor and went out. Sister Francis came over to Miss Brent. Miss Brent had to keep her lips tight closed to prevent herself from laughing.

"Now you just sit down there," said Sister Francis, "and take it easy. I won't be a moment. You just take it easy."

The laugh burst Miss Brent's lips apart. Sister Francis was trying so hard to convince her that she cared about her. The expression on her face was such a ludicrous parody of maternal sympathy, a parody she had seen so often before—on the face of the staff-nurse in hospital telling her about the death of her parents, on the faces of the Sisters in the orphanage comforting her when she had those awful dreams, on the face of her room-mate at college when another boy had dropped her without explanation or apology. But the expression on the face of Sister Francis was the best of the lot. You could tell straight away that the only thing she cared about was getting her out of the place as quietly as possible.

But really, she must stop laughing. It isn't fair. Sister Francis is only doing her best as she sees it. Remember about Charity. She must try to explain, choosing words very, very carefully.

"I hid from my Lord," she said slowly. "But he found me out, and told me to give my cloak to a beggar."

"I understand, dear," said Sister Francis.

"Do you really?" asked Miss Brent.

"Yes. Yes, of course, dear. Now you rest here. Just for a moment. I'll be back in a moment. You will stay, this time, won't you, dear?"

"Yes, Sister. If you tell me to."

"There's a good girl."

Sister Francis bustled off out of the dormitory.

Almost as soon as she was gone, Miss Brent felt herself lifted up by a huge, invisible hand. Laughter bubbled up into her throat, this time in a joyous stream of release pouring out until it filled the room. She was moving forward now, gliding effortlessly down the rows of beds, borne up by a cloud of crystalline laughter, and out into the passage. Now she was running as if on air. Before her loomed the steep descent of the stairs to the shadows of the hallway. For a moment she feared lest she should fall, like an over-proud Lucifer into the darkness, but the invisible hand bore her safely as she glided down at a terrifying yet exhilarating speed, and out of the building into the dazzling, overwhelming sunlight.

Behind her, laughter trailed like long wisps of silk in a light breeze. She could feel the soft paradisaic grass beneath her feet, and the wonderful smell of the garden all round her. Branches and leaves closed in above her head, shading her from the unendurable ecstasy of the light, and she knew that she had returned to Eden.

She plunged into a heap of mown grass, and lay there, still and at peace in the midst of the glory.

"Janis! Janis!"

The voice was insistent. She could feel dry grass pricking against her arms and thighs. Even in Eden there could be trouble; some of the Sisters got very angry if they caught you with your sleeves rolled up and if you weren't careful to keep your skirt below your knees. She wanted to go to sleep.

"Janis! Janis!"

The voice was excited, as if bringing good news. She could hear other girls chattering excitedly in the distance.

"Has Mummy come for me?" she asked. "She said she'd come and kiss me good-night when she got back. She promised."

Voices in the distance, talking seriously, grown up.

"Yes, Janis. Mummy's here. You must come along now."

Funny, I didn't know Mary Fisher knew Mummy. But it doesn't matter. Nothing matters now she's back, and I've been crying for ever so long I was so worried! How silly, not to trust Mummy!

They watched—Denise, Jackie, Maureen, Linda, and the other girls—with horrified yet pleasurable amazement, as Sister Francis and Mrs. Fisher led Miss Brent away up the path under the trees, chattering and laughing excitedly like a six-year-old as she went.

JOHN PREBBLE

b. 1915

His books on Scottish history are admired on both sides of the Atlantic. Similarly acclaimed are his action-filled stories of the American West—remarkably authentic tales for a Middlesex-born author, even though he is the great-great-nephew of a native American Indian.

The Regulator

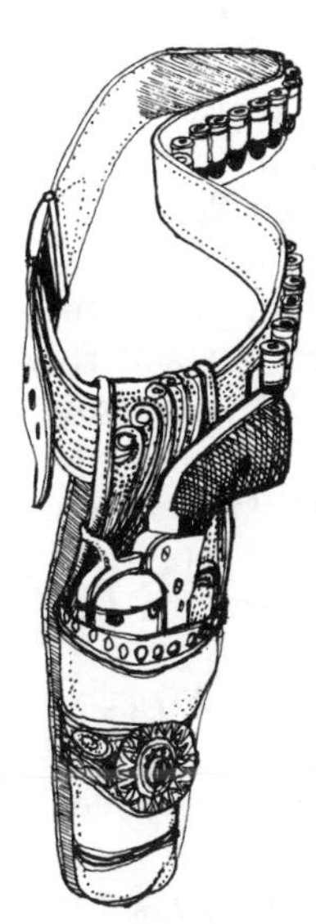

THE DRIFTERS came an hour after dawn. Walter James and his boy heard the nervous beat of hooves down by the corral, and then a man's laugh, an insanely mirthless sound that scratched unpleasantly on the morning air.

Walter put down the skilly of beans and wiped his hands slowly on his hips. He looked at the Henry rifle that hung on a peg by the door. He looked at it cautiously, moving his eyes only so that his son might not catch the glance and wonder at the reason for it. He knew that most men who recognized that laugh would expect him to take down the rifle and use it.

He looked away from the gun. He said flatly "Somebody come calling, son. You stay here."

But the boy was already bounding into the sunlight outside. Walter James looked once more at the rifle and then he went out too.

Three men sat their ponies near the sunflower patch, their bodies fallen into that hunched unconcern that comes on a man after a hard ride. When he saw them Walter took his son's shoulder in a hard grip, and he said "You stay quiet, boy. Mind what your Paw says, you stay quiet."

One of the riders was a thin, yellow man who wore a Rebel cavalry cap, although the war had been over for years. There was a fat Mexican in a striped poncho. His face was wet with sweat beneath the brim of his needle-crowned sombrero. The third rider was a half-breed with plaited hair. Behind them a riderless horse leant over a crooked fore-leg, dirty white lather on its neck and flanks.

A fourth man was inside the corral, passing his hands over Walter's blue roan. He said something, and the man in the Rebel cap laughed again.

Walter stared at the fourth man and knew that this was worse than he expected. This man was big, and he wore a hickory shirt and a cowhide vest. His black felt hat had a punched-in crown and a snakeskin band. Every movement of his powerful body was like an evil answer to a threat, and as he moved the sun shone on his hand-gun. He wore it strapped to his right thigh, and the holster had been cut away below the trigger-guard.

The Mexican looked up to the house and called "*Olé!*" He pulled his rifle from its scabbard and pumped it, resting it on his saddle-horn.

"Paw . . . ?" said Billy.

Walter pushed his hand down on the boy's shoulder and said nothing.

The man in the black hat climbed over the fence and spoke to the breed who dismounted and began to unsaddle the fourth horse. Then the others came up to the house, the big man grinning as he walked through the dust, but with his humourless eyes fixed on Walter's face. The Mexican had a handful of sunflower seeds and he pushed them into his mouth, chewing noisily. His right hand pointed the rifle straight at Walter James.

The big man stopped about four yards from the step, still grinning, a hand hooked in his belt above the gun. His lips were wet and red beneath black stubble. "You're Walt James," he said. "I know you. You know me?"

Walter kept his body still. "Everybody hereabouts knows you. You're Johnny Owens." He nodded at the rider in the Rebel cap. "He's your brother Virgil. The others I don't know, but I guess the Law wants them too."

They laughed. The Mexican spat a mouthful of seed-husks at Walter's feet. "That's right," said Johnny Owens. He jerked his left thumb at the Mexican. "This here's Cholla." He ignored the half-breed. "You think maybe you're the Law?"

Virgil Owens heeled his horse to the left, shifting in the saddle so that his gun-hand was free. In the sudden silence Walter could hear the quickened breathing of his son.

"No," he said soberly. "No, I ain't the Law. I'm just homesteading here."

"No, you ain't the Law. Sure you ain't," said Virgil, and he pointed at the apron that was still tied about Walter's waist. He looked at the Mexican. "*Olé*, Cholla," he said, "*Olé la senora!*"

The Mexican kissed his finger-tips and his belly shook with laughter.

Walter looked down at his son. Below the straw-yellow hair a dark flush coloured the boy's neck.

"You've got a gun, maybe?" said Johnny Owens.

"There's an old Henry on the wall inside."

"Go get it, Virgil."

The thin man slid from the saddle and walked into the house. Walter wondered if he would look in Mary's settle where there was a shell-belt with a Navy Colt in the holster. But Virgil came out with the rifle only, and Johnny Owens casually smashed it on the chopping-block.

"Who else you got here, James?"

"There's no one else. Just me and the boy. He's only twelve, Owens." And Walter wondered why he thought this appeal would mean anything.

Owens looked at Billy. "Where's your Maw?"

"She's dead," said Walter James quickly, and was surprised to find that it was still not easy to say after all this time. "She died a year last fall. I told you, there's just me and the boy."

Virgil Owens leant his back against the hitching-rail and said lazily. "Heard you was in the war, James."

"Seventh Michigan," said Walter.

"Georgia Volunteers," said Virgil, as if exchanging pleasantries, and then "Beats me how the Yankees won with yellow-bellies like you."

The drifters looked at Walter curiously, waiting to see the effect of this taunt. Walter felt the twist of his son's body beneath his hand and knew, without looking, that the boy's face was upturned on him.

Virgil laughed, and the Mexican spat the last of the seed-husks on Walter's boot-toe.

"We got no call to stay," said Johnny Owens, "You understand me?"

"I heard the Regulators were looking for you."

Johnny Owens grinned. "They're looking," he said. "They're homesteading, too, so we ain't worried. I'm trading my horse for that roan of yours. That's a fair trade, you say?"

"If you want it that way."

Owens nodded, still grinning. "You're an accommodating man, James." Then the grin left his face. "See what food they got inside, Virgil." The thin man went into the house again. When he returned he was carrying a bag of flour, some bacon and a sack of coffee. He was eating some of the beans that had been in the skilly. He was also carrying the Navy Colt, and Walter felt a rush of anger at the thought of Virgil Owens' hands pawing among Mary's things.

Virgil said "Lookut what the Yankee forgot, Johnny. That's downright dishonest, Johnny. Ain't it Johnny?"

Johnny Owens looked at the gun, stepped forward, measured the blow and hit Walter across the face with the back of his hand. As Walter went back with the blow, his hand released his son's shoulder. Billy squealed with anger and flung himself at Johnny Owens, his yellow head down to butt, his arms flailing. Virgil caught him by the neckband of his shirt and pulled him into the air.

"Spunky kid," said Virgil, loose-lipped in his insane laugh. "Sure he's yours, James?" He threw Billy back to Walter.

The half-breed came up with the roan, and Johnny Owens swung himself on to it. For a moment he stared down at Walter, his hand resting on his gun, and the other drifters looked at him, as if they knew what was going to happen because it had happened before. The Mexican was grinning, and Virgil chewed the side of his mouth. Then Johnny Owens shrugged, kicked his heels into the roan, and the four men rode down to the draw and away to the southwest.

Walter watched them until the dust was gone. He wiped the salt blood from his lips and looked at it where it smeared the back of his hand. "Go get some kindling, son," he said.

The boy went obediently, but with his head down and his feet dragging. He stopped at the corner of the barn and stood there, and Walter waited for him to turn, willing him to turn and look back, but Billy did not turn. Walter walked into the house and sat in the rocker with his hands between his knees. Mary's clothes had been dragged from the settle and spilled on the floor. The anger in Walter's throat choked him. He went down on his knees and gathered the clothes gently, the cotton prints and the ginghams, returning them to the settle, putting away with each a recollected memory of the woman who had once worn them. She would have found some way of explaining to the boy why his father had acted that way before the Owens. If there could be an explanation, that is, that Walter was sure was the right and true one.

He went over to the basin and threw cold water on his face, washing the blood from his mouth. Feeling came back into his lips, and with it the pain. He looked at his reflection in the splinter of mirror-glass by the towel, young-old and thin, grey in the long black hair at the temples. For a moment in his mind the reflection was replaced by the picture of a younger face, one that had stared back at him often enough five years before, self-assured and challenging beneath a Union-blue cap. It occurred to him that this was the face Billy had seen whenever he looked at his father, until this morning. And he knew that there was no explanation that could restore that picture.

He left the house and went to the barn. Billy was sitting there, staring out across the plain, and his face was dirty where he had rubbed at the tears, but he was not crying now. Even more than was usual, the colour of his hair reminded Walter of Mary.

"Billy? Billy, you all right, boy?"

When his son did not answer Walter put out a hand. Billy flinched away from it.

"All right," said Walter James, much troubled. "It's all right, Billy. You just sit there." And he went back to the house.

The sun was well past noon when the Regulators arrived. There were fifteen or twenty of them, mostly neighbours who held sections across the river, and Walter thought it strange to see them wearing guns. Old Man Prescott was leading them, sitting upright, with his long legs straight and thrust forward in wooden stirrups, and his grey hair coming out in spikes from beneath his dirty hat. He looked down from the saddle at Walter James, and bit his yellow moustache. "Get a horse and gun, Walt. We're going after the Owens boys."

"I guess you are," said Walter. "They stopped by here this morning. Took my roan and left a spent horse that's no good to itself or a man now. It ought to be shot. I'd be obliged for the loan of a gun, Mr. Prescott. The Owens took mine."

"They stopped by here," said one of the riders, "and you're still living?"

"We're both still living. Me and my boy. I'd like the loan of that gun, Mr. Prescott, before you leave."

Old Man Prescott wiped the back of his hand across his moustache, bringing the movement up sharply at the end. "Then you coming along?" he asked.

"No," said Walter, "There's just me and the boy. I'm not leaving him."

One of the Regulators laughed. "What happened to your face, Walt? Somebody hit you?"

Old Man Prescott turned in the saddle slowly and stared at the speaker. "Shut your face," he said easily. Then he looked back at Walter and said softly. "You signed the articles, Walt. We remember that."

"That was before Mary died. The boy's only got me now."

Nobody spoke. The horses moved uneasily, stirred up dust and sneezed in it.

"It won't look good, Walt," said Old Man Prescott at last. "You remember what you signed? *We the undersigned uniting ourselves in a party for the laudable purpose of arresting thieves and murderers do pledge ourselves on our sacred honour to . . .*"

"The words are in my mind, Mr. Prescott," said Walter.

"You took an oath, Walt."

"I got the boy to think of, Mr. Prescott."

The old man wiped his moustache again, and then suddenly leant down, his saddle creaking. "Give me your hand, boy." He pulled Billy up before him, and the boy straddled the horse, his hands gripping the horn and his eyes looking away from his father. His cheeks were red beneath the pale hair.

"Put the boy down, Mr. Prescott."

"You know why the Regulators was formed, Walt." Old Man Prescott spoke gently, as if it meant a lot to him to be understood. "On account of men like the Owens, and no Law being in this country to handle them."

"I know that."

"You signed, Walt, along of the rest of us. There's all of us with folks at home. If you won't leave the boy we'll take him along. You got another horse?"

"I got a pony out on graze. They didn't see it."

"You get it. We'll wait." The old man looked at Walter and there was no anger, no condemnation in his expression, just patient confidence.

For a moment Walter held that gaze, and then he turned and went into the house. When he came out he was wearing his old Army blouse, faded, except on the sleeves where the chevrons had been. He saw Billy stare at it, open his mouth, and then turn his head away. Old Man Prescott gave Walter a pistol and he went to the corral and shot the drifter's horse. When he came back, riding the pony, the gun was stuck into his waistband. He pulled up beside Old Man Prescott.

He said "It ain't right to take the boy, Mr. Prescott."

"There's no choice."

Walter stood in his stirrups, his body inclined forward. Then he settled in the saddle and his voice was harsh. "Anything happens to the boy, Mr. Prescott, and I'll hold you for it."

"You got that privilege," said Old Man Prescott easily, "But ain't nothing going to happen to him. Let's ride."

But Walter held Prescott's bridle. He spoke to his son. "Billy, you want to ride with me?" The boy shook his head, his mouth puckered.

"Let's ride," said Old Man Prescott again, and he turned his horse to the southwest, with the others curving after him.

They rode until dusk, dismounting and walking their horses for ten minutes in every hour. The Cherokee tracker, Joe Grey Shirt, rode with Old Man Prescott, bending from the saddle, or getting down now and then to touch the trail with his finger. Each time he grinned. But the trail was leading to the border, and the going was slow.

Once Old Man Prescott looked back to where Walter James rode at the tail, his feet below the belly of his pony, his back straight like a cavalryman's. Old Man Prescott pulled out and waited until Walter came up. He said "You want to ride with your Paw now, Billy?"

"No," said the boy.

Old Man Prescott said nothing more, but he looked across at Walter, chewed the side of his mouth, and then pushed his horse forward again.

They camped out that night in an arroyo thirty miles from the border. It was a dry camp because Joe Grey Shirt said that the drifters were not more than two hours ahead. Old Man Prescott grunted and said "We'll catch up tomorrow." Joe Grey Shirt went out later, on foot, and he came back after three hours, grinning more than usual. He said that the drifters were camped six or seven miles on, nearer than he had thought, but they had not unsaddled. Some of the Regulators wanted to ride on them, but Old Man Prescott looked at them with contempt. "And lose them as soon as they hear us? And there ain't no sense in risking the boy." His chuckle was sardonic. "You get to shooting in the dark and some of you'll do yourselves an injury."

The men stirred resentfully. One said "Why'd you bring the boy? We could've done this without him and his Paw."

"Walter signed the articles," said Old Man Prescott.

The boy lay that night with his head and shoulders on the old man's saddle. When he was asleep Walter covered him with a blanket, and crouched beside him, watching the still face in the moonlight. Walter sat there for an hour until at last he went over to where Old Man Prescott was sitting with his back against the crumbling bank of the arroyo, sucking a cold pipe. They were both silent for a while, and then Walter said "What I meant about holding you for it if the boy was hurt, Mr. Prescott. I'd be obliged if you forgot that."

Old Man Prescott took the pipe from his mouth and pushed it inside his shirt. He said nothing.

"What're you thinking of this, Mr. Prescott?"

"I'm thinking of them Owens boys," said the old man. "A homesteader below the rim crossed them a couple of days ago when they rode in on him, just like they rode in on you. He was a big hero that homesteader. He tried to take a gun to them. They shot up his family before they killed him."

"I had that in mind."

"I figure you did," said Old Man Prescott.

"You think it was that and nothing else?"

The Old Man moved a little in the moonlight. "No, I guess you was afraid, too. My boy was with you in the War, Walt . . ." He stopped, and at last went on slowly. "You did nothing nobody else wouldn't do."

"The homesteader didn't. The one you said."

"He's dead," said the old man in sudden anger. "And his boy, too. A boy of Billy's age I heard. He's dead, on account of his father being a hero."

"Billy won't see it that way."

"He might," said Old Man Prescott, "When he's a man and gotten himself a son."

"That's a long way off."

"It is. You want he should ride with you in the morning?"

Walter stood up. "I guess he'll ride where he's a mind to. I'm grateful to you, Mr. Prescott."

"Good-night, Walt."

The trail was broken by the river the next morning, an hour after the drifter's camp was passed, and Old Man Prescott split the Regulators into four parties to ride the banks. He took the south bank with Joe Grey Shirt and Walter and two of the others, and they rode up it to the west. Four miles on, the Cherokee moved into mid-stream where a sand-bank cleared the water and there he found some horse-droppings. He nodded.

"They're getting careless," said Old Man Prescott.

Another mile and there were hoof-marks in the mud where the drifters had come out on the south bank. The old man called the other party over and they all rode at a trot to the southwest. They were bunched up now, standing slightly in the stirrups, their faces set. Walter rode half a length behind Old Man Prescott, watching the bobbing banner of Billy's fair hair. The heat was thick and it pricked the riders beneath their shirts. Old Man Prescott had tied his bandana about Billy's nose and throat holding the boy's body to his.

The trail led southwards to the mouth of a canyon, rising up there to the rocky shale where it was lost. The Regulators came suddenly upon bodies lying, and the leading horses shied. One of the riders went back over the cantle of his saddle into the dust.

"*Get up!*" said Old Man Prescott bitterly. He looked up at the wheeling buzzard and then down at the bodies. The bodies of two men and two horses. Walter could scarcely recognize what the buzzards had left of his roan. The Mexican and the half-breed had been shot in the back and had bled to death. The blood was black in the dust.

Old Man Prescott put his hand over Billy's eyes. "Ho, Joe Grey Shirt!" he called.

The Cherokee grinned pleasantly. He pointed up the canyon and shook his head.

The old man looked approvingly at the canyon walls, the angry rocks, and the yellow candlesticks of the *cholla*. He almost smiled. "Box canyon," he said, "Men should know the country they run through."

Then he chewed his thumb, looking at the bodies and working out the story aloud. Johnny and Virgil had been riding the dead horses, he said, and broken their legs most likely in bad country like this. He had never known a bad man who thought of his horse first. So Johnny and Virgil had killed the breed and the Mexican and taken their horses. He went over the story again and again, phrasing it in different ways. Nobody contradicted him. Joe Grey Shirt nodded his head.

"We got 'em!" said Old Man Prescott. He lifted his reins above the saddle horn and moved his horse forward.

They rode until the canyon turned and then the old man lifted Billy to the ground. "Stay there, boy," he said. "You stay there. Mind what I say?"

Walter James looked at his son, the smallness of the boy there beside the old man's great horse. His face white, and his eyes looking up at Old Man Prescott, looking at nobody but Old Man Prescott, who shifted round in his saddle to say "You want to stay with the boy, Walt?" Walter shook his head, and the old man shouted, "Joe Grey Shirt!"

"Sure, Mr. Prescott, I stay."

Then something hummed violently above them, and there was the bang of a Winchester, bouncing down, wall to wall, from the rocks ahead. The Regulators fell from their horses and scrabbled down behind the boulders. Old Man Prescott caught Billy and pulled him down beside him. There was another vicious whirr, the bang of a gun, and Virgil Owens' insane laugh.

"Johnny Owens!" called the old man, "Johnny Owens! You and Virgil come on down!"

The only answer was another laugh, and Old Man Prescott turned over on his back and pulled his hat-brim down over his eyes.

From where he lay Walter studied the rockfall and the rise of it to the sky. He looked long at the south face and then he looked round at the Regulators where they were hunched behind cover, their faces turned in question to Old Man Prescott and doubt in their eyes. The old man ignored them, and the air was still in sardonic silence. A red-tongued lizard flicked out of its hole a foot from Walter's face, blinked at him nervously, and then was gone in one green-yellow movement.

Walter pulled himself to his knees, held his body as if it were an aimed projectile, and in one quick roll flung himself across to the stone where Joe Grey Shirt squatted contentedly with eyes closed. The Cherokee's expression was non-committal as he answered Walter's questions. He pointed once to the south face and chopped his hand through the air conclusively.

Walter went back to his rock and he called "Mr. Prescott!"

The old man came over in a queer, aged crouch, and Virgil's Winchester spat up the dust behind him. Old Man Prescott swore. "You figure you're too old and infirm to step over to me?" he asked bitterly.

"I don't want the boy to know."

"What? Know what?"

"What's your plan, Mr. Prescott?"

"Ain't got no plan." The old man looked reflectively at Walter's tight face. He pushed his hat back, pulled his pipe from his shirt and thrust it between his teeth "Them Owens boys can't get out. If we want them though, we got to go up."

"They'll kill some of us."

"Maybe. You know any way round that?"

Walter James told him.

"You don't have to do that Walt."

"Joe Grey Shirt says it can be done."

"If I told him to do it and meant it, then he'd say it couldn't be done."

"I'll do it."

Old Man Prescott wiped his chin with his hand. "You doing this because of the boy?"

"I'm doing it because I thought of it."

"No you ain't," said the old man, "We're waiting for sundown and then we're all going up. We'll all be heroes together."

"I'm sorry, Mr. Prescott," said Walter. He stood up suddenly and ran into the open, down the slope to where the horses had drifted. He felt the nakedness of what he was doing as if the temperature of the air had suddenly changed. He heard Virgil's high yell, and a bullet stabbed the dirt to the left of him and a little ahead. And then others. And one catching his shirt-sleeve and ripping it. He reached the horses, he gripped the saddle-horn of one, swinging himself up as the animal began to move. He heard Old Man Prescott shouting above the gunfire, and then there was nothing but the sound of the pony's hooves, and the swing and the sway of it beneath him.

When Old Man Prescott got back to the boy he saw the expression on Billy's face. "Now, look here!" he said, and he tried to control the anger within him. "Do you know why your Paw let them Owens boys whip him around?"

The boy said nothing. He put his face in the crook of his elbow.

"Boy, don't you know your own Paw?"

Billy said "Why'd you let him run away, Mr. Prescott?"

The old man bit savagely on his pipe, and snapped the stem of it between his teeth.

WALTER PULLED in the horse at the mouth of the canyon. His tongue was dry, and appeared to be swollen. It was not only the dust that gave him this sensation, there was that old feeling with which he had been familiar enough five years before. A man less familiar with it might have been ashamed. He lifted his canteen to his lips, washed his mouth and spat out the water. The sun was now two handsbreadths from the horizon and he could feel the sweat beginning to cool beneath his blouse. He passed his hand over his chin, over the rasp of stubble. For a moment the incredible foolishness of what he intended to do paralysed his mind. This, his memory told him, was the moment of decision, when a man might easily become a coward. He tried to erase his mind of all but the immediate problem.

He looked back at the canyon. It went into the rockface like an arm-thrust, crooked at the elbow. He tried to translate what he remembered of it, and what Joe Grey Shirt had told him of it, into a map's precise contours. The arm, from shoulder to elbow as it might be, ran from south to north, and the forearm from east to west. At the elbow the Regulators lay behind their cover, and somewhere on the steep south wall of the forearm were Johnny and Virgil Owens.

Yet, if Joe Grey Shirt were right, a man of courage might climb the escarpment, look down on the Owens boys and turn their advantage against them. Walter thought of it in half-remembered military terms—scout, flank, attack—but this did not seem to simplify the problem.

Darkening against the sinking sun the high rock ridge ran like the turreted wall of a fortress, and Walter remembered that the Cherokee had given it its old Spanish name *Ciudad Coronado*, the crowned city. He looked up at it and felt his imagination stir. Then he pointed his horse off the trail and rode toward the shattered rise of shale at the foot of the escarpment.

At first it was a gentle slope, and the pony's plunging feet sent the loose stones down in little sibilant falls, but it ended suddenly where the red rock-face rose perpendicularly.

Walter dismounted. He unbuttoned the old cavalry blouse, pulled it from his shoulders and hung it on the apple of his saddle-horn. He pushed the hand-gun round to the small of his back, tightening the waist-band of his levis. He tugged his hat firmly over his brow and walked up to the rock-face as a man might walk boldly up to an opponent.

The climb was deceptively easy at first, for the shallow strata, pushed out by their prehistoric cooling, formed a rough but adequate stairway, ledges of crumbling stone the width of a man's boot-sole. But as he went higher the strata became deeper, and in some places the next ledge was beyond the reach of his upstretched arms. He unstrapped a spur from his right heel, sweating fingers slipping on steel and leather. With the spur he began to cut a painful hand-hold and foot-hold. Once he grasped a scrag of brush, which some miracle of wind and germination had set to grow there, and as he grasped it he saw it slowly pull free from the thin soil that had given it life. He fell ten feet down the rock-face, spread-eagled, pressing his body against it, feeling the tearing of shirt and flesh on his chest, until his feet jarred on the ledge he had just left and held him.

Then up again, by kicking heels and jabbing spur, feeling the agonizing snap of his nails, seeing the blood oozing darkly below the dust, a furnace breathing in his lungs. He lived a year of his life on the escarpment, now climbing directly upward, now moving to the left or to the right in a ridiculous, slithering slide along the ledges, until suddenly there was nothing left of the wall to climb, and he was lying on his belly with his legs still hanging in space. He listened indifferently to the faint, ringing descent of the spur as it dropped from his fingers and fell back the way he had climbed.

He pulled himself forward until his legs were no longer hanging free, yet still he lay there, unbelieving, until the report of a Winchester jarred his brain. He lifted his head and shoulders. The gunfire came up from his right, up from the dark canyon, and before the echoes had bounced away, he heard Virgil's laugh and Old Man Prescott's answering shout of anger.

He lifted a hand to wipe the sweat from his face, and he saw the blood running down each finger from each torn nail. He was suddenly full of a wild exultation, a pride in having come this far, and he wanted to shout. But the feeling passed quickly into fear. He pulled himself forward on his belly, pretending that the drop of the rockface was no longer behind him, yet fearing it still, as if it had the power to pull him down.

Away ahead of him stretched the hog-back of the ridge, and he realised that his climb, although it had seemed perpendicular, had in fact carried him along the parallel of the canyon until he was now above the elbow. Below, to his right, the canyon was a black river, yet on his left the sun still rolled redly to the horizon.

A cat, he thought, would have trouble walking along that hog-back. He must crawl, taking the cover of each boulder and looking down always for a sign that would tell him where the Owens brothers lay hidden.

So he crawled. He crawled first to the shelter of an outcrop of hard rock where he braced his feet, forced his buttocks into a niche, and took the hand-gun from his waistband. He broke it and blew the dust from the barrel. He spilled the shells from the cylinder and then spun it. He worked the action once, twice, and then a third time. The gun was heavy and unfamiliar in his hand. There was a crack in the butt that bit the ball of his thumb. The foresight had been filed away, and he wondered if he would be able to sight it by the hammer alone. He weighed it in his hand, and he felt no sympathy between him and it. He hated it.

With his shirt-tail he cleaned the shells. There had been five when Old Man Prescott had given him the gun, but one had been used on Johnny Owens' horse. Now, because his fingers were trembling, he lost another. It bounced from the rock between his feet and went spinning down, a momentary yellow fleck before it was lost. With terrible care he held the remaining three in his mouth until he had wiped each and inserted it in the cylinder. He lowered the hammer to an empty chamber. Again and again he examined the gun to make sure that when he thumbed back the hammer it would fall on to a full chamber. At last he thrust the gun into his waist-band, butt hard against his ribs.

He crawled on, marvelling at the heat of the rock beneath his hands and thighs, his throat closing in dryness that was part thirst and part fear. He crawled, and he halted for long minutes, looking down into the dark of the canyon for a sign.

When the sign came it was sudden and ridiculously unexpected, the flare of a match that lit Virgil's cupped hands, his long nose and deep eye-sockets, the crouch of his body, the stroke of a rifle below his arm-pit. When the match died there was still a sign, the faint patch of the neckerchief which Virgil had tucked beneath the Rebel cap to keep the sun from his neck.

He was thirty, perhaps forty feet below Walter, and there was no sign of Johnny Owens. He could be below Virgil still, or between Virgil and the rim.

Walter rolled silently over the edge, and with torn hands, that had miraculously found a skill in this, lowered himself rock by rock until he lay on the flat top of a slab fifteen feet above Virgil. He took the gun from his waist and lay there with his thumb on the hammer.

Now, away from the last glow of the sun, his eyes grew accustomed to the dusk of the canyon. He saw the floor, the stipple of greasewood, the boulders where the Regulators lay, and beyond them their horses, neck-stretched to the sparse earth. Johnny Owens' voice came out of the rocks below. "Virgil, get them horses."

The voice drew Walter's eyes down to where Johnny Owens sat below Virgil, on his heels behind a rock, his hat hanging by its thong between his shoulder-blades, a white grin bisecting his black beard.

Virgil pressed his cheeks against the rifle stock. He fired once and swore, pumped the lever and fired again. Old Man Prescott's yellow horse sat down suddenly on its haunches, rolled over squealing.

"Try another, Virgil," said Johnny.

In the dusk below, Billy's tiny figure skidded out from cover and began to run toward the horses. Walter saw the muzzle of Virgil's rifle move from one of the horses and follow the crazy path of the boy. The spark of Virgil's cigarette glowed.

Walter stood up and leapt downward. The stones rolled as he hit the slope.

Virgil turned, bringing the rifle down. He opened his mouth. He shouted "*Johnny!*"

He fired the rifle once toward Walter. He worked the lever again and vaulted on to the rock, bringing the stock up to his shoulder. Walter braced his feet, lifted the handgun until barrel and arm were a line from his shoulder, and he fired. The bullet took Virgil in the throat, twisting his body as it dropped.

Walter fell behind the rock that Virgil had left, and he listened to the rolling fall of the dead man going down to the floor of the canyon. The noise lasted a long time.

Then there was silence, an unsympathetic silence out of which at last came the thudding of his heart. In the dust beside him Virgil's cigarette burnt acridly where it had fallen. Walter ground it out with fierce satisfaction.

"Owens!" he shouted, "Johnny Owens! You hear me?"

There was no reply. Then the faint scrape of a spur on stone.

"Owens, this is Walter James! You hear me?"

A single stone rattled in the darkness below.

"Owens, I'm coming down!"

A cough. Then a harsh voice. It said "Don't talk. Come down!"

Walter looked back up the cliff face. Although the sky was red above the wall of rock, below was black and formless. He had that advantage, the only advantage. He pushed himself to his knees and then to his feet, crouching on his heels, and he moved as silently as he could to the left-hand edge, forcing to his mind the one glimpse he had had of Johnny Owens, hoping the man was still in the same spot, but only half-believing he would be.

He picked up a rock with his left-hand and threw it to the right. As it fell, unseating others, he stood up and stepped out. He saw a shadow rise from the ground, the flash of gun, firing to the right where the stone had fallen, and then the shadow turned quickly to meet him.

He waited for it. The shadow became a body, a body crouched, the smear of a face and white teeth. He fired at it. He fired again as Johnny Owens shot once more, this time at a target he could see.

WHEN HE HEARD the first report of the hand-gun Old Man Prescott said "The Lord be with him."

They heard the roll of Virgil's body falling and wondered. "Lord be with him, too," said Old Man Prescott.

One of the Regulators called. "How about that, Mr. Prescott? You want we should do something?"

"Ain't nothing to do yet, son."

He bit his yellow moustache, and then they heard Walter's voice. It echoed from rock to rock. Old Man Prescott put his hand on the boy's shoulder. "Hear that, Billy? That's your Paw." He wished that he could see the boy's face in the dusk.

Then there were three more shots, but the second and third so close as to appear almost one. And silence now. One by one the Regulators stood up, staring into the darkness.

"Mr. Prescott, sir . . .?" said Billy.

"It's all right, son." He took off his hat and rubbed his eyes, staring, as they were all staring.

They heard footsteps coming down, coming down in the way a tired man will walk when he knows that there is no hurry. One of the Regulators pumped his rifle and Old Man Prescott swore at him blasphemously, asking the Almighty's pardon in the same voice.

A single spur was striking the stones prettily, and a long-legged shadow came out of the dusk. It paused for a moment and then came on. In its right hand it carried two pairs of boots, and they were the boots of Johnny and Virgil Owens. Old Man Prescott yipped and slapped his thigh with his hat. He threw it on the ground and stamped it delightedly.

Walter James did not look at the grinning Regulators. He dropped the boots in the dust, and he took the gun from his waist-band and dropped that too. Then he walked toward his son.

V. S. PRITCHETT

b. 1900

The distinguished writer, critic and broadcaster spent years in the leather trade until he discovered the great interest in his life, foreign travel. His first book described a journey in Spain. Since then, many travel books and novels and short stories have all shown his insight into the lives of ordinary people the world over.

Eleven O'Clock

FROM YEARS of habit the mare stopped a minute or two at the right houses in all the streets waiting for the milkman's voice to call, "Good day, ma'am, thank you, ma'am," in the alleys. Then she gave a slouching heave, the cans and bottles would start jingling, and, with the man following, she was off to the next stop. But when eleven o'clock came she stopped dead. She knew the house they were at now. She knew it well. An ungainly, warty and piebald creature, she loosened her shoulders, her head and neck hung to the ground, her forelegs splayed out, and she looked old, rakish and cynical.

For here was no stop of a minute or two. Down the passage strode the milkman, his lips whistling. Five minutes passed into ten, ten into twenty. Some mornings it was half an hour, three-quarters or the full hour. And when the milkman came back he was not whistling.

He was a short, ruddy man in a brown dustcoat with the firm's name on it and a hat like a police inspector's. But there is nothing like a uniform for concealing the soul. He was bald and battered under his hat and his eyebrows were thick and inky. If he took his hat off in the middle of a sentence, that sentence would become suddenly very easy and rather free; if he wiped his bald head with his handkerchief, *that* was a sign he might get freer. The first time the milkman went to the house a woman came across the kitchen towards him. The fire was murmuring in the range and a pot of coffee was standing on it. A tray of cakes had just been taken out of the oven and was standing on the table. The milkman's nostrils had small sensitive black hairs in them, and they quivered.

"Oh, I do like a nice mince-pie," said the milkman.

She was a kind woman. "The early bird catches the worm," she said. "Have one."

She was a big creature, lazy and soft in the arms and shoulders. She had several chins. The small chin shook like a cup in its saucer on the second chin that was under it, and she had freckles on her neck. She was warm and untidy with cooking, and her yellow hair was coming undone at the back. Her mouth was short and surly, but now it softened in harmony with the rest of her into an easy placid smile; the rest of her body seemed to be laughing at her fatness, and the smile broadened from her lips to her neck and so on downwards, until the milkman put his foot on the doorstep, took off his hat and wiped his bald head with pleasure. "I'm a rollin' stone, ma'am," said the milkman. "I don't mind if I do."

She turned round and walked slowly to the table and the cakes. They were small cherry cakes. When she turned, the crease in the back of her neck seemed to be a smile and even her shoes seemed to be making smiles of pleasure on the floor. "Come in," she said. "I'm Yorkshire. I'm not like the people round here. I'm neighbourly."

"I'm Yorkshire. I'm neighbourly too," said the milkman, rubbing his hands, and he stepped in. It was warm and cosy in the kitchen, warm with the smell of the cakes and the coffee, and warm with the good-natured woman.

"Take a seat," said the woman. "I'm sitting down myself. I've been on my feet all morning. I come from Leeds and this is my bake."

"I come from Hull," said the milkman. "We never say 'no' and we never say die. I've been on my feet too. What I mean to say—in my job, you can't ride because you're always stopping and you can't stop because you've got to keep moving, if you get me." The milkman sat down opposite her.

"I could tell you were from the north," said the hospitable woman. She pushed the cakes towards him. "Go on," she said. "Take one. Take two. They're a mean lot of people down here. There's nothing mean about me."

"After you, ma'am," he said.

"No," she said. "I dassn't." She laughed.

"Slimming?" said the milkman.

"Oh, ha ha," laughed the woman. "That's a good one. Look at me. I've got the spread. I don't get any exercise." She went into a new peal of laughter. "And I don't want it."

"We're as God made us," said the milkman. "All sizes."

"And all shapes," said the woman, recovering. "It wouldn't do for all of us to be thin."

"You want some heavyweights," said the man.

"They're all thin round here, and mean," said the woman.

The woman laughed until tears came into the small grey eyes which were sunk like oyster pearls between her plump fire-reddened cheeks and her almost hairless brows. She laughed and laughed, and her laughter was like her smile. She laughed not only with her mouth, but her cheeks gave a jump and her chins jumped together and her big breasts shook, and she spread her legs with laughter, too, under the table.

"Oh dear! Oh dear!" she said. "When I was a girl I was in the catering business and they starved me. One house I was in the boss used to follow me into the kitchen when I was putting away the snacks to see I didn't pinch anything. And I can tell you it was a work of art slipping a bit of cheese down the neck of me blouse to eat when I got up to bed, it was."

The milkman looked at her blouse.

The milkman widened one eye and winked with the other.

"Oh, don't!" cried the woman, going off again. "Don't! Stop it! Don't start me off."

"Don't mind me," said the woman, wiping her eyes. "I've been here seven weeks and this is the first laugh I've had. My husband's a cripple. He's a watchmaker. Tick-tock, tick-tock, tick-tock, all day long. He hangs up the watches on the wall and that's all I've heard for seven weeks! Tick-tock, tick-tock, tick-tock."

She wiped the tears from her eyes with her apron and waved an arm to the wall. There were four clocks on the kitchen wall and three on the mantelpiece, and there were watches hanging on nails. The tall brown clock with the pendulum gave a slow grating 'Tock'; the blue alarm on the mantelpiece went at a run; the big wooden clock next to it made a sweet sound like a man sucking a pipe, and the rest croaked, scratched, ticked and chattered. Carved in fretwork was a small cuckoo clock beside the door.

"Who winds them?" asked the milkman with his mouth full of cake.

"Who winds them?" said the woman. "He winds them. He comes home and spends all night winding them. Have some coffee. You ought to see what I've got inside and upstairs."

"I bet," said the milkman, gazing at her from his still wide eyes. "If there's a drop of coffee I'll have it."

"Laugh," said the woman. "You can't tell night from day in this house. They all say something different. I've been seven weeks here, but it might be seven years. It's a good thing I can laugh."

"It's slimming," he said.

"It's spreading," she said.

"Well, I like a bit of spread myself," said the milkman.

The milkman watched her go to the range. He watched her bring the coffee-pot over and bring a couple of white cups from the dresser. He got up and went to the door. "My Jenny," he said. "My mare. Whoa! Listen to her. She's kicking up the pavement."

The mare was kicking the kerb. She was standing with her forelegs on it, gazing down the alley and striking a hoof on the pavement.

"She knows I'm in here," he said, coming back. "I bet she knows I'm having a cup of coffee. I bet she's wondering what's happening. I bet she's thinking it out. Wonderful things horses are. Jealous, you know, too," he said. "If she knew you was in here, I'd never hear the last of it."

"Eating's her trouble. She's old," said the milkman. "She's terrible. I've never seen an animal eat what she does. I bet she knows there's something going on." The milkman sipped his coffee. His lips made bubbling sounds as he drank. Soon there were no sounds in the room but the ticking of the clocks and the bubbling noise of the woman's lips and the man's lips at their cups, and a click of the cups and a murmur of laughter from the woman.

Then the little fretwork clock which hung by the door gave a small sneezing buzz, a door clipped open, a tiny hammer rang and out bobbed the bird. "Cuckoo! Cuckoo!" it called, and "Clap" went the door. The milkman put down his cup with a start and gaped.

"They're all wrong," said the woman. "Sit down. Have another cake, just a little one. Have a tart? That cuckoo's never right. 'Oh, shut up,' I tell it. 'Keep quiet'."

"I used to do fretwork myself," said the milkman.

"Sit down," she pressed him. "Another cup will warm you up."

"You're warm in here," said the milkman.

"I'm warm anywhere," the woman said.

"Don't want winding up, I bet," said the milkman with a wink. He was short beside her and he took a long easy look at her. He wiped his bald head and put on his hat.

"Well," he said. "Talking of time, one thing leads to another."

She looked at him sadly, and with a lazy yawn raised her big arms above her head. "Come and see those clocks."

The milkman had his pencil in his ear, a small red stump of pencil. He took it out and, quickly, he gave her a soft poke in the waist with it and went off. "Good day, ma'am, thank you, ma'am," he called, and went off whistling.

The next day the milk-cart stopped again at the house. Behind the cart the milkman walked, humming to himself. He looked up at the house. There was the short brick wall and the iron rail on top of it. There was the green hedge coming into leaf. He took his basket, he swung open the gate and he went down the alley. There was a smell of pastry just out of the oven. For a long time while he was gone the mare stood, then she stepped on to the kerb and began knocking her hoof upon it. The sound could be heard down the deserted road. "Whoa!" shouted the milkman down the alley. The mare stretched her neck and sniffed the ground and then began pawing again. She got both forefeet on the pavement and kept stretching and shaking her smooth white neck. "Whoa!" shouted the milkman's voice. She pricked her ears. He was shouting from the front room window.

Half an hour passed. The mare had now stepped farther on to the pavement. Her neck was stretched out to its full length. She was sniffing the wall, the iron rail, and behind it the juicy green shoots of the hedge. She strained, her nostrils trembling, her soft mouth opening to seize a shoot in her old yellow teeth. She paused and made a greater effort, pulling the cart, and now her nose was over the top of the railing. Grunting, chewing, slopping, crunching sounds came from her mouth. She had bitten off her first piece. And, once on it, appetite leapt. She gave a wilder tug and now she could get at the hedge. Her teeth dragged at the hedge and crunched. She raised her neck, looked with discrimination at the shoots, then went on quietly browsing.

No sounds came from the house, no sound from the road but the chewing of the horse, the bit chinking like marbles in her slobber. Hearing him come at last, she backed on to the road. He came out very thoughtful and not whistling.

And some mornings there was the smell of cake in the alley, sometimes it was pie and sometimes it was coffee. Again a quarter of an hour passed, or maybe twenty minutes or half an hour, and often enough a full hour, and a shout of "Whoa!" came from an upstairs window. He had his coat off. "That clock's wrong," said the woman. "They're all wrong." The mare's neck was right over the railings and this was necessary because, as she chewed, the hedge got lower and lower.

"Eh, whoa there!" the milkman shouted down from the top floor of the house one morning and, looking in amazement at the torn and bitten green hedge and the mare still tearing it, he came down to the street.

"What's the idea? Come off it," he said, taking the mare by the bridle and jerking her head off the hedge.

He drew her off the pavement and went back and looked over the railings at the hedge, ruined by weeks of eating.

"Been getting your greens, haven't you?" he said. He stared at the mare and, bright under their blinkers, he saw the eyes of that cynical animal, secretive and glistening, gazing back at him.

SIR ARTHUR QUILLER-COUCH

1863–1944

His books and lectures on literature opened up new vistas
for students. His anthology, *The Oxford Book of English Verse,*
is a household work. Intensely critical and modest about
his own writing (he published his novels under the pseudonym "Q")
he could be brought to admit occasionally that he had done
"a few decent short stories".

A Town's Memory

THE RETURNED Emigrant was not one of those who sometimes creep back to Tregarrick and scan the folk wistfully and the names over the shops till they bethink themselves of stepping up the hill to take a look at the cemetery, and there find all they sought. This man stood under the archway of the Pack-horse Inn (by A. Walters), with his soft hat tilted over his nose, a cigar in his mouth, hands in his trouser-pockets, and legs a-straddle, and smoked and eyed the passers-by with a twinkle of humour.

He knew them all again, or nearly all. He had quitted Tregarrick for the Cape at the age of fifteen, under the wing of a cousin from the Mining District; had made money out there, and meant to return to make more; and was home just now on a holiday, with gold in his pocket and the merest trace of silver in his hair. He watched the people passing, and it all seemed very queer to him and amusing.

They were one and all acting and behaving just as they had used to act and behave. Some were a trifle greyer, perhaps, and others stooped a bit; but they went about their business in the old fashion, and their occupations had not changed. It was just as if he had wound up a clockwork toy before leaving England, and had returned after many years to find it still working. Here came old Dymond, the postman, with the usual midday delivery, light as ever, and the well-remembered dot-and-go-one gait. The maids who came out to take the letters were different; in one of them the Emigrant recognized a little girl who had once sat facing him in the Wesleyan day-school; but the bells that fetched them out were those on which he had sounded runaway peals in former days, and with his eyes shut he could have sworn to old Dymond's double knock. The cart that rattled its load of empty cans up the street belonged to Nicholas Retallack ('Old Nick'), the milkman, and that was Retallack beside it, returning from his morning round. The Emigrant took the cigar from his mouth and blew a lazy cloud. But for Retallack he might never have seen South Africa or known Johannesburg. Retallack had caught him surreptitiously milking the Alderney into a battered straw hat, and had threatened a summons. There had been a previous summons with a conviction, and the Mayor had hinted at the Reformatory, so the Emigrant had been packed off. And here he was, back again; and here was Retallack trudging around, the same as ever.

In the window across the road a saddler sat cutting out a strap, and reminding the Emigrant of a certain First of April when he had ventured in and inquired for half a pint of strap-oil. It might almost be the same strap, as it certainly was the same saddler.

Down at the street corner, by the clock, a couple of Town Councillors stood chatting. While the Emigrant looked there came round the corner a ruck of boys from school chivvying and shouting after an ungainly man, who turned twice and threatened them with a stick. The Town Councillors did not interfere, and the rabble passed bawling by the 'Pack-horse'. Long before it came the Emigrant had recognized the ungainly man. It was Dick Loony, the town butt. He had chivvied the imbecile a hundred times in just the same fashion, yelling "Black Cat!" after him as these young imps were yelling—though why "Black Cat" neither he nor the imps could have told. But Dicky had always resented it as he resented it now, wheeling round, shaking his stick, and sputtering maledictions. A stone or two flew harmlessly by. The Emigrant did not interfere.

As yet no one had recognized him. He had arrived the night before, and taken a room at the 'Pack-horse', nobody asking his name; had sat after supper in a corner of the smoking-room and listened to the gossip there, saying nothing.

"Who's he travellin' for?" somebody had asked of Abel Walters, the landlord. "He ain't a commercial. He hadn't got the trunks, only a kit-bag. By the soft hat he wears I should say *a* agent in advance. Likely we'll have a circus before long."

His father and mother were dead these ten years. He had sent home money to pay the funeral expenses and buy a substantial headstone.

But he had not been up to the cemetery yet. He was not a sentimental man. Still, he had expected his return to make some little stir in Tregarrick, and now a shade of disappointment began to creep over his humour.

He flung away the end of his cigar and strolled up the sunny pavement to a sweet-shop where he had once bought ha'porths of liquorice and cinnamon-rock. The legend, 'E. Hosking, Maker of Cheesecakes to Queen Victoria', still decorated the window. He entered and demanded a pound of best 'fairing', smiling at the magnificence of the order. Mrs. Hosking—her white mob-cap and apron clean as ever—offered him a macaroon for luck, and weighed out the sweets. Her hand shook more than of old.

"You don't remember me, Mrs. Hosking?"

"What is it you say? You must speak a little louder, please, I'm deaf."

"You don't remember me?"

"No, I don't," she said composedly. "I'm gone terrible blind this last year or two."

The Emigrant paid for his sweets and walked out. He had bought them with a purpose, and now bent his steps down Market Street. At the foot of the hill he paused before a row of whitewashed cottages. A green fence ran along their front, and a pebbled path; and here he found a stout, matronly woman bent over a wash-tub.

"Does Mrs. Best live here?" he asked.

The woman withdrew about a dozen pins from her mouth and answered all in one breath:

"She isn't called Best any longer; she married agen five year ago; second husbing, he died too; she doesn' live here any more."

With this she stuck the pins very deliberately, one by one, in the bosom of her print gown, and plunged her hands into the wash-tub again.

The Emigrant stood nonplussed for a moment and scratched the back of his head, tilting his soft hat still farther forward on his nose.

"She used to be very fond of me when I was a boy," he said lamely.

"Yes?" The tone seemed to ask what business that could be of hers.

"She came as nurse to my mother when I was born. I suppose that made her take a fancy to me."

"Ah, no doubt," replied the woman vaguely, and added, while she soaped a long black stocking, "she did a lot o' that, one time and another."

"She had a little girl of her own before I left Tregarrick," the Emigrant persisted, not because she appeared interested—she did not, at all—but with some vague hope of making himself appear a little less trivial. "Lizzie she called her. I suppose you don't know what has become of the old woman?"

"Well, considerin' that I'm her daughter Elizabeth"—she lengthened the name with an implied reproof—"I reckon I ought to know."

The Emigrant's hand sought and crushed the big packet of sweets well into his pocket. He flushed scarlet. At the same time he could hardly keep back a smile at his absurd mistake. To be here with lollipops for a woman of thirty and more!

"You haven't any little ones of your own?"

"No, I haven't. Why?"

"Oh, well; only a question. My name is Peter Jago—Pete, I used to be called."

"Yes?"

He took notice that she had said nothing of her mother's whereabouts; and concluded, rightly, that the old woman must be in the workhouse.

"Well, I'm sorry," he said. "I thought I might be able to do something for her."

The woman became attentive at last.

"Any small trifle you might think o' leavin' with me, sir, it should duly reach her. She've failed a lot, lately."

"Thank you; I'll think it over. Good day."

He strolled back to the 'Pack-horse' and ate his dinner. Abel Walters, coming in after with a pint of port to his order, found the Emigrant with a great packet of sugared almonds and angelica spread open beside his cheese.

"I suppose, sir," said Mr. Walters, eyeing the heap, "you've travelled a great deal in foreign parts."

TWO DAYS PASSED. The Emigrant visited the cemetery, inspected his parents' tombstone, and found about it a number of tombstones belonging to people whose faces he had not hitherto missed. But after his experiment upon Elizabeth Best he had not declared himself a second time. Indeed, his humour by this time had turned sour, and his mind was made up that, if no one recognized him spontaneously he would leave his native town as quietly as he had come—would go back without revealing himself to a soul. It would be unfair to say that he felt aggrieved; but he certainly dismissed a project, with which he had often played in South Africa, of erecting a public drinking-fountain on Mount Folly, as the citizens of Tregarrick call the slope in front of the County Assize Hall.

The third day was Sunday, and he went to church in the morning. The Vicar who preached was a stranger to him; but in the sidesman who came down the aisle afterwards with the offertory-plate he recognized one Billy Smithers, who had been a crony of his some twenty years ago; who had, in fact, helped him more than once to milk Retallack's

Alderney. He felt in his pocket and dropped a sovereign into the plate. The sidesman halted and rubbed his chin.

"Han't you made a mistake?" he asked in a stage whisper.

The Emigrant waved his hand in rather a lordly manner, and William Smithers, sidesman, proceeded down the aisle, wondering, but not suspecting.

The Vicar recited the prayer for the whole state of Christ's Church militant here on earth, and the Emigrant joined the crowd trooping out by the western door.

But in the press just outside the door two hands suddenly seized his right hand and shook it violently. He turned and faced—Dicky Loony.

"Me know, eh? Pete—Mas'r Pete!" The idiot bent over his hand and mumbled it with his wry mouth, then shook it again, peering up in his face. "Eh? Peter—Pete. Yes. All right!"

The Emigrant looked down on this poor creature at whom he had flung scores of stones, but never a kind word. And the idiot ran on:

"Dicky, eh?"—tapping his chest. "You know—Dicky. Pete—Pete, eh?"—and he made the gesture of one flinging a stone. "Often, ha, ha! *So* high." He spread his hand, palm downward, about five feet from the ground.

"Well I'm blest!" said the Emigrant softly. They stood now on the green together, a little apart from the crowd.

"*So* high, eh? Li'l boy, eh? Fling—me know!" He took the Emigrant's hand again and shook it, smiling and looking him straight in the eyes with innocent gaiety. "These boys—no good; no good now. Pete, *he* fling *so*. Li'l boy—quite li'l boy. Me know, eh? Dicky know!"

"Well," repeated the Emigrant; "I'm blest, but this is funny!"

SAKI

1870–1916

H. H. Munro, who wrote under the name of the cup-bearer in *The Rubá'iyát* by Omar Khayyám, was a humorist (often in a macabre vein) who specialized in the short story with a twist to its tail. After brief service in the Burma police, he became a journalist and writer. His brilliant career ended on the battlefields of France.

The Open Window

"MY AUNT will be down presently, Mr. Nuttel," said a very self-possessed young lady of fifteen; "in the meantime you must try and put up with me."

Framton Nuttel endeavoured to say the correct something which should duly flatter the niece of the moment without unduly discounting the aunt that was to come. Privately he doubted more than ever whether these formal visits on a succession of total strangers would do much towards helping the nerve cure which he was supposed to be undergoing.

"I know how it will be," his sister had said when he was preparing to migrate to this rural retreat; "you will bury yourself down there and not speak to a living soul, and your nerves will be worse than ever from moping. I shall just give you letters of introduction to all the people I know there. Some of them, as far as I can remember, were quite nice."

Framton wondered whether Mrs. Sappleton, the lady to whom he was presenting one of the letters of introduction, came into the nice division.

"Do you know many of the people round here?" asked the niece, when she judged that they had had sufficient silent communion.

"Hardly a soul," said Framton. "My sister was staying here, at the rectory, you know, some four years ago, and she gave me letters of introduction to some of the people here."

He made the last statement in a tone of distinct regret.

"Then you know practically nothing about my aunt?" pursued the self-possessed young lady.

"Only her name and address," admitted the caller. He was wondering whether Mrs. Sappleton was in the married or widowed state. An undefinable something about the room seemed to suggest masculine habitation.

"Her great tragedy happened just three years ago," said the child; "that would be since your sister's time."

"Her tragedy?" asked Framton; somehow in this restful country spot tragedies seemed out of place.

"You may wonder why we keep that window wide open on an October afternoon," said the niece, indicating a large French window that opened on to a lawn.

"It is quite warm for the time of the year," said Framton; "but has that window got anything to do with the tragedy?"

"Out through that window, three years ago to a day, her husband and her two young brothers went off for their day's shooting. They never came back. In crossing the moor to their favourite snipe-shooting ground they were all three engulfed in a treacherous piece of bog. It had been that dreadful wet summer, you know, and places that were safe in other years gave way suddenly without warning. Their bodies were never recovered. That was the dreadful part of it." Here the child's voice lost its self-possessed note and became falteringly human. "Poor aunt always thinks that they will come back some day, they and the little brown spaniel that was lost with them, and walk in at that window just as they used to do. That is why the window is kept open every evening till it is quite dusk. Poor dear aunt, she has often told me how they went out, her husband with his white waterproof coat over his arm, and Ronnie, her youngest brother, singing, 'Bertie, why do you bound?' as he always did to tease her, because she said it got on her nerves. Do you know, sometimes on still, quiet evenings like this, I almost get a creepy feeling that they will all walk in through that window—" She broke off with a little shudder. It was a relief to Framton when the aunt bustled into the room with a whirl of apologies for being late in making her appearance.

"I hope Vera has been amusing you?" she said.

"She has been very interesting," said Framton.

"I hope you don't mind the open window," said Mrs. Sappleton briskly; "my husband and brothers will be home directly from shooting, and they always come in this way. They've been out for snipe in the marshes today, so they'll make a fine mess over my poor carpets. So like you men-folk, isn't it?" She rattled on cheerfully about the shooting and the scarcity of birds, and the prospects for duck in the winter. To Framton it was all purely horrible. He made a desperate but only partially successful effort to turn the talk to a less ghastly topic; he was conscious that his hostess was giving him only a fragment of her attention, and her eyes were constantly straying past him to the open window and the lawn beyond. It was certainly an unfortunate coincidence that he should have paid his visit on this tragic anniversary.

"The doctors agree in ordering me complete rest, an absence of mental excitement, and avoidance of anything in the nature of violent physical exercise," announced Framton, who laboured under the tolerably wide-spread delusion that total strangers and chance acquaintances are hungry for the least detail of one's ailments and infirmities, their cause and cure. "On the matter of diet they are not so much in agreement," he continued.

"No?" said Mrs. Sappleton, in a voice which only replaced a yawn at the last moment. Then she suddenly brightened into alert attention —but not to what Framton was saying.

"Here they are at last!" she cried. "Just in time for tea, and don't they look as if they were muddy up to the eyes!"

Framton shivered slightly and turned towards the niece with a look intended to convey sympathetic comprehension. The child was staring out through the open window with dazed horror in her eyes. In a chill shock of nameless fear Framton swung round in his seat and looked in the same direction. In the deepening twilight three figures were walking across the lawn towards the window; they all carried guns under their arms, and one of them was additionally burdened with a white coat hung over his shoulders. A tired brown spaniel kept close at their heels. Noiselessly they neared the house, and then a hoarse young voice chanted out of the dusk: "I said, Bertie, why do you bound?"

Framton grabbed wildly at his stick and hat; the hall-door, the gravel-drive, and the front gate were dimly noted stages in his headlong retreat. A cyclist coming along the road had to run into the hedge to avoid imminent collision.

"Here we are, my dear," said the bearer of the white mackintosh, coming in through the window; "fairly muddy, but most of it's dry. Who was that who bolted out as we came up?"

"A most extraordinary man, a Mr. Nuttel," said Mrs. Sappleton; "could only talk about his illnesses, and dashed off without a word of good-bye or apology when you arrived. One would think he had seen a ghost."

"I expect it was the spaniel," said the niece calmly; "he told me he had a horror of dogs. He was once hunted into a cemetery somewhere on the banks of the Ganges by a pack of pariah dogs, and had to spend the night in a newly dug grave with the creatures snarling and grinning and foaming just above him. Enough to make any one lose their nerve."

Romance at short notice was her speciality.

WILLIAM SANSOM

1912–1976

Master of both the novel and the short story, he preferred the latter as he liked to examine a character within a particular episode—"seen in a picture frame" as he put it. In fact, he had always wanted to be a painter but was unable to afford the training. He developed his literary talents during the war, in spare moments at a fire station.

The Wall

IT WAS OUR third job that night.

Until this thing happened, work had been without incident. There had been shrapnel, a few enquiring bombs, and some huge fires; but these were unremarkable and have since merged without identity into the neutral maze of fire and noise and water and night, without date and without hour, with neither time nor form, that lowers mistily at the back of my mind as a picture of the air-raid season.

I suppose we were worn down and shivering. Three a.m. is a meanspirited hour. I suppose we were drenched, with the cold hose water trickling in at our collars and settling down at the tails of our shirts. Without doubt the heavy brass couplings felt moulded from metal-ice. Probably the open roar of the pumps drowned the petulant buzz of the raiders above, and certainly the ubiquitous fire-glow made an orange stage-set of the streets. Black water would have puddled the City alleys and I suppose our hands and our faces were black as the water. Black with hacking about among the burnt up rafters. These things were an every-night nonentity. They happened and they were not forgotten because they were never even remembered.

But I do remember it was our third job. And there we were—Len, Lofty, Verno and myself, playing a fifty foot jet up the face of a tall city warehouse and thinking of nothing at all. You don't think of anything after the first few hours. You just watch the white pole of water lose itself in the fire and you think of nothing. Sometimes you move the jet over to another window. Sometimes the orange dims to black—but you only ease your grip on the ice-cold nozzle and continue pouring careless gallons through the window. You know the fire will fester for hours yet.

However, that night the blank, indefinite hours of waiting were sharply interrupted—by an unusual sound. Very suddenly a long rattling crack of bursting brick and mortar perforated the moment. And then the upper half of that five-storey building heaved over towards us. It hung there, poised for a timeless second before rumbling down at us. I was thinking of nothing at all and then I was thinking of everything in the world.

In that single second my brain digested every detail of the scene. New eyes opened at the sides of my head so that, from within, I photographed a hemispherical panorama bounded by the huge length of the building in front of me and the narrow lane on either side.

Blocking us on the left was the squat trailer pump, roaring and quivering with effort. Water throbbed from its overflow valves and from leakages in the hose and couplings. A ceaseless stream spewed down its grey sides into the gutter. But nevertheless a fat iron exhaust pipe glowed red-hot in the middle of the wet engine. I had to look past Lofty's face. Lofty was staring at the controls, hands tucked into his armpits for warmth. Lofty was thinking of nothing. He had a black diamond of soot over one eye, like the White-eyed Kaffir in negative.

To the other side of me was a free run up the alley. Overhead swung a sign—'Catto and Henley'. I wondered what in hell they sold. Old stamps? The alley was quite free. A couple of lengths of dead, deflated hose wound over the darkly glistening pavement. Charred flotsam dammed up one of the gutters. A needle of water fountained from a hole in a live hose-length. Beneath a blue shelter light lay a shattered coping stone. The next shop along was a tobacconist's, windowless, with fake display cartons torn open for anybody to see. The alley was quite free.

Behind me, Len and Verno shared the weight of the hose. They heaved up against the strong backward drag of waterpressure. All I had to do was yell "Drop it"—and then run. We could risk the live hose snaking up at us. We could run to the right down the free alley—Len, Verno and me. But I never moved. I never said "Drop it" or anything else. That long second held me hypnotized, rubber boots cemented to the pavement. Ton upon ton of red-hot brick hovering in the air above us numbed all initiative. I could only think. I couldn't move.

Six yards in front stood the blazing building. A minute before I would never have distinguished it from any other drab Victorian atrocity happily on fire. Now I was immediately certain of every minute detail. The building was five storeys high. The top four storeys were fiercely alight. The rooms inside were alive with red fire. The black outside walls remained untouched. And thus, like the lighted carriages of a night express, there appeared alternating rectangles of black and red that emphasized vividly the extreme symmetry of the window spacing: each oblong window shape posed as a vermilion panel set in perfect order upon the dark face of the wall. There were ten windows to each floor, making forty windows in all. In rigid rows of ten, one row placed precisely above the other, with strong contrasts of black and red, the blazing windows stood to attention in strict formation. The oblong building, the oblong windows, the oblong spacing. Orange-red colour seemed to *bulge* from the black frame-work, assumed tactile values, like boiling jelly that expanded inside a thick black squared grill.

Three of the storeys, thirty blazing windows and their huge frame of black brick, a hundred solid tons of hard, deep Victorian wall, pivoted over towards us and hung flatly over the alley. Whether the descending wall actually paused in its fall I can never know. Probably it never did. Probably it only seemed to hang there. Probably my eyes digested its action at an early period of momentum, so that I saw it 'off true' but before it had gathered speed.

The night grew darker as the great mass hung over us. Through smoke-fogged fireglow the moonlight had hitherto penetrated to the pit of our alley through declivities in the skyline. Now some of the moonlight was being shut out as the wall hung ever further over us. The wall shaded the moonlight like an inverted awning. Now the pathway of light above had been squeezed to a thin line. That was the only silver lining I ever believed in.

It shone out—a ray of hope. But it was a declining hope, for although at this time the entire hemispherical scene appeared static, an imminence of movement could be sensed throughout—presumably because the scene was actually moving. Even the speed of the shutter which closed the photograph on my mind was powerless to exclude this motion from a deeper consciousness. The picture appeared static to the limited surface senses, the eyes and the material brain, but beyond that there was hidden movement.

The second was timeless. I had leisure to remark many things. For instance, that an iron derrick, slightly to the left, would not hit me. This derrick stuck out from the building and I could feel its sharpness and hardness as clearly as if I had run my body intimately over its contour. I had time to notice that it carried a footlong hook, a chain with three-inch rings, two girder supports and a wheel more than twice as large as my head.

A wall will fall in many ways. It may sway over to the one side or the other. It may crumble at the very beginning of its fall. It may remain intact and fall flat. This wall fell as flat as a pancake. It clung to its shape through ninety degrees to the horizontal. Then it detached itself from the pivot and slammed down on top of us.

The last resistance of bricks and mortar at the pivot point cracked off like automatic gunfire. The violent sound both deafened us and brought us to our senses. We dropped the hose and crouched. Afterwards Verno said that I knelt slowly on one knee with bowed head, like a man about to be knighted. Well, I got my knighting. There was an incredible noise —a thunderclap condensed into the space of an eardrum—and then the bricks and the mortar came tearing and burning into the flesh of my face.

Lofty, away by the pump, was killed. Len, Verno and myself they dug out. There was very little brick on top of us. We had been lucky. We had been framed by one of those symmetrical, oblong window spaces.

DOROTHY L. SAYERS

1893–1957

She was steeped early in the academic life: her father was a headmaster, and she became one of Oxford's first female graduates. (Lord Peter Wimsey, her erudite detective, was modelled on one of the more popular dons.) She wrote on religious subjects, translated Dante's *Inferno*, but was most famous for her detective stories.

Suspicion

As the atmosphere of the railway carriage thickened with tobacco smoke, Mr. Mummery became increasingly aware that his breakfast had not agreed with him.

There could have been nothing wrong with the breakfast itself. Brown bread, rich in vitamin content, as advised by the *Morning Star*'s health expert; bacon fried to a delicious crispness; eggs just nicely set; coffee made as only Mrs. Sutton knew how to make it. Mrs. Sutton had been a real find, and that was something to be thankful for. For Ethel, since her nervous breakdown in the summer, had really not been fit to wrestle with the untrained girls who had come and gone in tempestuous succession. It took very little to upset Ethel nowadays, poor child. Mr. Mummery, trying hard to ignore his growing internal discomfort, hoped he was not in for an illness. Apart from the trouble it would cause at the office, it would worry Ethel terribly, and Mr. Mummery would cheerfully have laid down his rather uninteresting little life to spare Ethel a moment's uneasiness.

He slipped a digestive tablet into his mouth—he had taken lately to carrying a few tablets about with him—and opened his paper. There did not seem to be very much news. A question had been asked in the House about government typewriters. The Prince of Wales had smilingly opened an all-British exhibition of footwear. A further split had occurred in the Liberal Party. The police were still looking for the woman who was supposed to have poisoned a family in Lincoln. Two girls had been trapped in a burning factory. A film star had obtained her fourth decree nisi.

At Paragon Station, Mr. Mummery descended and took a tram. The internal discomfort was taking the form of a definite nausea. Happily he contrived to reach his office before the worst occurred. He was seated at his desk, pale but in control of himself, when his partner came breezing in. "'Morning, Mummery," said Mr. Brookes in his loud tones, adding inevitably, "Cold enough for you?"

"Quite," replied Mr. Mummery. "Unpleasantly raw, in fact."

"Beastly, beastly," said Mr. Brookes. "Your bulbs all in?"

"Not quite all," confessed Mr. Mummery. "As a matter of fact I haven't been feeling—"

"Pity," interrupted his partner. "Great pity. Ought to get 'em in early. Mine were in last week. My little place will be a picture in the spring. For a town garden, that is. You're lucky, living in the country. Find it better than Hull, I expect, eh? Though we get plenty of fresh air up in the avenues. How's the missus?"

"Thank you, she's very much better."

"Glad to hear that, very glad. Hope we shall have her about again this winter as usual. Can't do without her in the Drama Society, you know. By Jove! I shan't forget her acting last year in *Romance*. She and young Welbeck positively brought the house down, didn't they? The Welbecks were asking after her only yesterday."

"Thank you, yes. I hope she will soon be able to take up her social activities again. But the doctor says she mustn't overdo it. No worry, he says—that's the important thing. She is to go easy and not rush about or undertake too much."

"Quite right, quite right. Worry's the devil and all. I cut out worrying years ago and look at me! Fit as a fiddle, for all I shan't see fifty again. *You're* not looking altogether the thing, by the way."

"A touch of dyspepsia," said Mr. Mummery. "Nothing much. Chill on the liver, that's what I put it down to."

"That's what it is," said Mr. Brookes, seizing his opportunity. "Is life worth living? It depends upon the liver. Ha, ha! Well now, well now—we must do a spot of work, I suppose. Where's that lease of Ferraby's?"

Mr. Mummery, who did not feel at his conversational best that morning, rather welcomed this suggestion, and for half an hour was allowed to proceed in peace with the duties of an estate agent. Presently, however, Mr. Brookes burst into speech again.

"By the way," he said abruptly, "I suppose your wife doesn't know of a good cook, does she?"

"Well, no," replied Mr. Mummery. "They aren't so easy to find nowadays. In fact, we've only just got suited ourselves. But why? Surely your old Cookie isn't leaving you?"

"Good lord, no!" Mr. Brookes laughed heartily. "It would take an earthquake to shake off old Cookie. No. It's for the Philipsons. Their girl's getting married. That's the worst of girls. I said to Philipson, 'You mind what you're doing,' I said. 'Get somebody you know something about, or you may find yourself landed with this poisoning woman —what's her name—Andrews. Don't want to be sending wreaths to your funeral yet awhile,' I said. He laughed, but it's no laughing matter and so I told him. What we pay the police for I simply don't know. Nearly a month now, and they can't seem to lay hands on the woman. All they say is, they think she's hanging about the neighbourhood and 'may seek a situation as cook'. As cook! Now I ask you!"

"You don't think she committed suicide, then?" suggested Mr. Mummery.

"Suicide my foot!" retorted Mr. Brookes coarsely. "Don't you believe it, my boy. That coat found in the river was all eyewash. *They* don't commit suicide, that sort don't."

"What sort?"

"Those arsenic maniacs. They're too damned careful of their own skins. Cunning as weasels, that's what they are. It's only to be hoped they'll manage to catch her before she tries her hand on anybody else. As I told Philipson—"

"You think Mrs. Andrews did it, then?"

"Did it? Of course she did it. It's plain as the nose on your face. Looked after her old father, and he died suddenly—left her a bit of money, too. Then she keeps house for an elderly gentleman, and *he* dies suddenly. Now there's this husband and wife—man dies and woman taken very ill, of arsenic poisoning. Cook runs away, and you ask, did she do it? I don't mind betting that when they dig up the father and the other old bird they'll find *them* bung-full of arsenic, too. Once that sort gets started, they don't stop. Grows on 'em, as you might say."

"I suppose it does," said Mr. Mummery. He picked up his paper again and studied the photograph of the missing woman. "She looks harmless enough," he remarked. "Rather a nice, motherly-looking kind of woman."

"She's got a bad mouth," pronounced Mr. Brookes. He had a theory that character showed in the mouth. "I wouldn't trust that woman an inch."

AS THE DAY went on, Mr. Mummery felt better. He was rather nervous about his lunch, choosing carefully a little boiled fish and custard pudding and being particular not to rush about immediately after the meal. To his great relief, the fish and custard remained where they were put, and he was not visited by that tiresome pain which had become almost habitual in the last fortnight. By the end of the day he became quite lighthearted. The bogey of illness and doctor's bills ceased to haunt him. He bought a bunch of bronze chrysanthemums to carry home to Ethel, and it was with a feeling of pleasant anticipation that he left the train and walked up the garden path of Mon Abri.

He was a little dashed by not finding his wife in the sitting room. Still clutching the bunch of chrysanthemums he pattered down the passage and pushed open the kitchen door.

Nobody was there but the cook. She was sitting at the table with her back to him, and started up almost guiltily as he approached.

"Lor', sir," she said, "you give me quite a start. I didn't hear the front door go."

"Where is Mrs. Mummery? Not feeling bad again, is she?"

"Well, sir, she's got a bit of a headache, poor lamb. I made her lay down and took her up a nice cup o' tea at half past four. I think she's dozing nicely now."

"Dear, dear," said Mr. Mummery.

"It was turning out the dining room done it, if you ask me," said Mrs. Sutton. "'Now, don't you overdo yourself, ma'am,' I says to her, but you know how she is, sir. She gets that restless, she can't abear to be doing nothing."

"I know," said Mr. Mummery. "It's not your fault, Mrs. Sutton. I'm sure you look after us both admirably. I'll just run up and have a peep at her. I won't disturb her if she's asleep. By the way, what are we having for dinner?"

"Well, I *had* made a nice steak-and-kidney pie," said Mrs. Sutton, in accents suggesting that she would readily turn it into a pumpkin or a coach-and-four if it was not approved of.

"Oh!" said Mr. Mummery. "Pastry? Well, I—"

"You'll find it beautiful and light," protested the cook, whisking open the oven door for Mr. Mummery to see. "And it's made with butter, sir, you having said that you found lard indigestible."

"Thank you, thank you," said Mr. Mummery. "I'm sure it will be most excellent. I haven't been feeling altogether the thing just lately, and lard does not seem to suit me nowadays."

"Well, it don't suit some people, and that's a fact," agreed Mrs. Sutton. "I shouldn't wonder if you've got a bit of a chill on the liver. I'm sure this weather is enough to upset anybody." She bustled to the table and cleared away the picture paper which she had been reading.

"Perhaps the mistress would like her dinner sent up to her?" she suggested.

Mr. Mummery said he would go and see, and tiptoed his way upstairs.

Ethel was lying snuggled under the eiderdown and looked very small and fragile in the big double bed. She stirred as he came in and smiled up at him. "Hullo, darling!" said Mr. Mummery.

"Hullo! You back? I must have been asleep. I got tired and headachy, and Mrs. Sutton packed me off upstairs."

"You've been doing too much, sweetheart," said her husband, taking her hand in his and sitting down on the edge of the bed.

"Yes—it was naughty of me. What lovely flowers, Harold. All for me?"

"All for you, Tiddleywinks," said Mr. Mummery tenderly. "Don't I deserve something for that?" Mrs. Mummery smiled, and Mr. Mummery took his reward several times over.

"That's quite enough, you sentimental old thing," said Mrs. Mummery. "Run away, now, I'm going to get up."

"Much better go to bed, my precious, and let Mrs. Sutton send your dinner up," said her husband.

Ethel protested, but he was firm with her. If she didn't take care of herself, she wouldn't be allowed to go to the Drama Society meetings. And everybody was so anxious to have her back. The Welbecks had been asking after her and saying that they really couldn't get on without her.

"Did they?" said Ethel with some animation. "It's very sweet of them to want me. Well, perhaps I'll go to bed after all. And how has my old hubby been all day?"

"Not too bad, not too bad."

"No more tummyaches?"

"Well, just a *little* tummyache. But it's quite gone now. Nothing for Tiddleywinks to worry about."

MR. MUMMERY experienced no more distressing symptoms the next day or the next. Following the advice of the newspaper expert, he took to drinking orange juice, and was delighted with the results of the treatment. On Thursday, however, he was taken so ill in the night that Ethel was alarmed and insisted on sending for the doctor. The doctor felt his pulse and looked at his tongue and appeared to take the matter lightly. An inquiry into what he had been eating elicited the fact that dinner had consisted of pigs' trotters, followed by a milk pudding, and that, before retiring, Mr. Mummery had consumed a large glass of orange juice, according to his new regime.

"There's your trouble," said Dr. Griffiths cheerfully. "Orange juice is an excellent thing, and so are trotters, but not in combination. Pig and oranges together are extraordinarily bad for the liver. I don't know why they should be, but there's no doubt that they are. Now I'll send you round a little prescription and you stick to slops for a day or two and keep off pork. And don't you worry about him, Mrs. Mummery, he's as sound as a trout. *You're* the one we've got to look after. I don't want to see those black rings under the eyes, you know. Disturbed night, of course—yes. Taking your tonic regularly? That's right. Well, don't be alarmed about your hubby. We'll soon have him out and about again."

The prophecy was fulfilled, but not immediately. Mr. Mummery, though confining his diet to baby food, bread and milk, and beef tea skilfully prepared by Mrs. Sutton and brought to his bedside by Ethel, remained very seedy all through Friday, and was only able to stagger rather shakily downstairs on Saturday afternoon. He had evidently suffered a 'thorough upset'. However, he was able to attend to a few papers which Brookes had sent down from the office for his signature, and to deal with the household books. Ethel was not a businesswoman, and Mr. Mummery always ran over the accounts with her. Having settled up with the butcher, the baker, the dairy and the coal merchant, Mr. Mummery looked up inquiringly. "Anything more, darling?"

"Well, there's Mrs. Sutton. This is the end of her month, you know."

"So it is. Well, you're quite satisfied with her, aren't you, darling?"

"Yes, rather—aren't you? She's a good cook, and a sweet, motherly old thing, too. Don't you think it was a real brainwave of mine, engaging her like that, on the spot?"

"I do, indeed," said Mr. Mummery.

"It was a perfect providence, her turning up like that, just after that wretched Janet had gone off without even giving notice. I was in absolute *despair*. It was a little bit of a gamble, of course, taking her without any references, but naturally, if she'd been looking after a widowed mother, you couldn't expect her to give references."

"N-no," said Mr. Mummery. At the time he had felt uneasy about the matter, though he had not liked to say much because, of course, they simply had to have somebody. And the experiment had justified itself so triumphantly in practice that one couldn't say much about it now. He had once rather tentatively suggested writing to the clergyman of Mrs. Sutton's parish but, as Ethel had said, the clergyman wouldn't have been able to tell them anything about cooking, and cooking, after all, was the chief point.

Mr. Mummery counted out the month's money.

"And by the way, my dear," he said, "you might just mention to Mrs. Sutton that if she *must* read the morning paper before I come down, I should be obliged if she would fold it neatly afterwards."

"What an old fussbox you are, darling," said his wife.

Mr. Mummery sighed. He could not explain that it was somehow important that the morning paper should come to him fresh and prim, like a virgin. Women did not feel these things.

On Sunday, Mr. Mummery felt very much better—quite his old self, in fact. He enjoyed the *News of the World* over breakfast in bed, reading the murders rather carefully. Mr. Mummery got quite a lot of pleasure out of murders—they gave him an agreeable thrill of vicarious adventure, for, naturally, they were matters quite remote from daily life in the outskirts of Hull. He noticed that Brookes had been perfectly right. Mrs. Andrews' father and former employer had been 'dug up' and had, indeed, proved to be 'bung-full' of arsenic.

He came downstairs for dinner—roast sirloin, with the potatoes done under the meat and Yorkshire pudding of delicious lightness, and an apple tart to follow. After three days of invalid diet, it was delightful to savour the crisp fat and underdone lean. He ate moderately, but with a sensuous enjoyment. Ethel, on the other hand, seemed a little lacking in appetite, but then, she had never been a great meat eater. She was fastidious and, besides, she was (quite unnecessarily) afraid of getting fat.

It was a fine afternoon, and at three o'clock, when he was quite certain that the roast beef was 'settling' properly, it occurred to Mr. Mummery that it would be a good thing to put the rest of those bulbs in. He slipped on his old gardening coat and wandered out to the potting shed. Here he picked up a bag of tulips and a trowel, and then, remembering that he was wearing his good trousers, decided that it would be wise to take a mat to kneel on. When had he had the mat last? He could not recollect, but he rather fancied he had put it away in the corner under the potting shelf. Stooping down, he felt about in the dark among the flowerpots. Yes, there it was, but there was a tin of something in the way. He lifted the tin carefully out. Of course, yes—the remains of the weed killer.

Mr. Mummery glanced at the pink label, printed in staring letters with the legend: ARSENICAL WEED KILLER. *POISON*, and observed, with a mild feeling of excitement, that it was the same brand of stuff that had been associated with Mrs. Andrews' latest victim. He was rather pleased about it. It gave him a sensation of being remotely but definitely in touch with important events. Then he noticed, with surprise and a little annoyance, that the stopper had been put in quite loosely.

"However'd I come to leave it like that?" he grunted. "Shouldn't wonder if all the goodness has gone off." He removed the stopper and squinted into the can, which appeared to be half full. Then he rammed the thing home again, giving it a sharp thump with the handle of the trowel for better security. After that he washed his hands carefully at the scullery tap, for he did not believe in taking risks.

He was a trifle disconcerted, when he came in after planting the tulips, to find visitors in the sitting room. He was always pleased to see Mrs. Welbeck and her son, but he would rather have had warning, so that he could have scrubbed the garden mould out of his nails more thoroughly. Not that Mrs. Welbeck appeared to notice. She was a talkative woman and paid little attention to anything but her own conversation. Much to Mr. Mummery's annoyance, she chose to prattle about the Lincoln poisoning case. A most unsuitable subject for the tea table, thought Mr. Mummery, at the best of times. His own 'upset' was vivid enough in his memory to make him queasy over the discussion of medical symptoms, and besides, this kind of talk was not good enough for Ethel. After all, the poisoner was still supposed to be in the neighbourhood. It was enough to make even a strong-nerved woman uneasy. A glance at Ethel showed him that she was looking quite white and tremulous. He must stop Mrs. Welbeck somehow, or there would be a repetition of one of the old dreadful, hysterical scenes. He broke into the conversation with violent abruptness. "Those forsythia cuttings, Mrs. Welbeck," he said. "Now is just about the time to take them. If you care to come down the garden I will get them for you."

He saw a relieved glance pass between Ethel and young Welbeck. Evidently the boy understood the situation and was chafing at his mother's tactlessness. Mrs. Welbeck, brought up all standing, gasped slightly and then veered off with obliging readiness on the new tack. She accompanied her host down the garden and chattered cheerfully about horticulture while he selected and trimmed the cuttings. She complimented Mr. Mummery on the immaculacy of his gravel paths. "I simply *cannot* keep the weeds down," she said.

Mr. Mummery mentioned the weed killer and praised its efficacy.

"That stuff!" Mrs. Welbeck stared at him. Then she shuddered. "I wouldn't have it in my place for a thousand pounds," she said, with emphasis.

Mr. Mummery smiled. "Oh, we keep it well away from the house," he said. "Even if I were a careless sort of person—"

He broke off. The recollection of the loosened stopper had come to him suddenly, and it was as though, deep down in his mind, some obscure assembling of ideas had taken place. He left it at that, and went into the kitchen to fetch a newspaper to wrap up the cuttings.

Their approach to the house had evidently been seen from the sitting-room window, for when they entered, young Welbeck was already on his feet and holding Ethel's hand in the act of saying good-bye. He manœuvred his mother out of the house with tactful promptness and Mr. Mummery returned to the kitchen to clear up the newspapers he had fished out of the drawer. To clear them up and to examine them more closely. Something had struck him about them, which he wanted to verify. He turned them over very carefully, sheet by sheet. Yes—he had been right. Every portrait of Mrs. Andrews, every paragraph and line about the Lincoln poisoning case, had been carefully cut out.

Mr. Mummery sat down by the kitchen fire. He felt as though he needed warmth. There seemed to be a curious cold lump of something at the pit of his stomach—something that he was chary of investigating.

He tried to recall the appearance of Mrs. Andrews as shown in the newspaper photographs, but he had not a good visual memory. He remembered having remarked to Brookes that it was a 'motherly' face. Then he tried counting up the time since the disappearance. Nearly a month, Brookes had said—and that was a week ago. Must be over a month now. A month. He had just paid Mrs. Sutton her month's money.

Ethel! was the thought that hammered at the door of his brain. At all costs, he must cope with this monstrous suspicion on his own. He must spare her any shock or anxiety. And he must be sure of his ground. To dismiss the only decent cook they had ever had out of sheer, unfounded panic, would be wanton cruelty to both women. If he did it at all, it would have to be done arbitrarily, preposterously—he could not suggest horrors to Ethel. However it was done, there would be trouble. Ethel would not understand and he dared not tell her.

But if by any chance there was anything in this ghastly doubt—how could he expose Ethel to the appalling danger of having the woman in the house a moment longer? He thought of the family at Lincoln—the husband dead, the wife escaped by a miracle with her life. Was not any shock, any risk, better than that?

Mr. Mummery felt suddenly very lonely and tired. His illness had taken it out of him. Those illnesses—they had begun, when? Three weeks ago he had had the first attack. Yes, but then he had always been rather subject to gastric troubles. Bilious attacks. Not so violent, perhaps, as these last, but undoubted bilious attacks.

He pulled himself together and went, rather heavily, into the sitting room. Ethel was tucked up in a corner of the chesterfield.

"Tired, darling?"

"Yes, a little."

"That woman has worn you out with talking. She oughtn't to talk so much."

"No." Her head shifted wearily in the cushions. "All about that horrible case. I don't like hearing about such things."

"Of course not. Still, when a thing like that happens in the neighbourhood, people will gossip and talk. It would be a relief if they caught the woman. One doesn't like to think—"

"I don't want to think of anything so hateful. She must be a horrible creature."

"Horrible. Brookes was saying the other day—"

"I don't want to hear what he said. I don't want to hear about it at all. I want to be quiet. I want to be quiet!"

He recognized the note of rising hysteria. "Tiddleywinks shall be quiet. Don't worry, darling. We won't talk about horrors."

No. It would not do to talk about them.

Ethel went to bed early. It was understood that on Sundays Mr. Mummery should sit up till Mrs. Sutton came in. Ethel was a little anxious about this, but he assured her that he felt quite strong enough. In body, indeed, he did; it was his mind that felt weak and confused. He had decided to make a casual remark about the mutilated newspapers —just to see what Mrs. Sutton would say.

He allowed himself the usual indulgence of a whisky and soda as he sat waiting. At a quarter to ten he heard the familiar click of the garden gate. Footsteps passed up the gravel—squeak, squeak, to the back door. Then the sound of the latch, the shutting of the door, the rattle of the bolts being shot home. Then a pause. Mrs. Sutton would be taking off her hat. The moment was coming. The step sounded in the passage. The door opened. Mrs. Sutton in her neat black dress stood on the threshold. He was aware of a reluctance to face her. Then he looked up. A plump-faced woman, her eyes obscured by thick horn-rimmed spectacles. Was there, perhaps, something hard about the mouth? Or was it just that she had lost most of her front teeth?

"Would you be requiring anything tonight, sir, before I go up?"

"No, thank you, Mrs. Sutton."

"I hope you are feeling better, sir." Her eager interest in his health seemed to him almost sinister, but the eyes, behind the thick glasses, were inscrutable.

"Quite better, thank you, Mrs. Sutton."

"Mrs. Mummery is not indisposed, is she, sir? Should I take her up a glass of hot milk or anything?"

"No, thank you, no." He spoke hurriedly, and fancied that she looked disappointed.

"Very well, sir. Good night, sir."

"Good night. Oh! by the way, Mrs. Sutton—"

"Yes, sir?"

"Oh, nothing," said Mr. Mummery, "nothing."

NEXT MORNING Mr. Mummery opened his paper eagerly. He would have been glad to learn that an arrest had been made over the weekend. But there was no news for him. The chairman of a trust company had blown out his brains, and the headlines were all occupied with tales about lost millions and ruined shareholders. Both in his own paper and in those he purchased on the way to the office, the Lincoln poisoning tragedy had been relegated to an obscure paragraph on a back page, which informed him that the police were still baffled.

The next few days were the most uncomfortable that Mr. Mummery had ever spent. He developed a habit of coming down early in the morning and prowling about the kitchen. This made Ethel nervous, but Mrs. Sutton offered no remark. She watched him tolerantly, even, he thought, with something like amusement. After all, it was ridiculous. What was the use of supervising the breakfast, when he had to be out of the house every day between half past nine and six?

At the office, Brookes rallied him on the frequency with which he rang up Ethel. Mr. Mummery paid no attention. It was reassuring to hear her voice and to know that she was safe and well.

Nothing happened, and by the following Thursday he began to think that he had been a fool. He came home late that night. Brookes had persuaded him to go with him to a little bachelor dinner for a friend who was about to get married. He left the others at eleven o'clock, however, refusing to make a night of it. The household was in bed when he got back but a note from Mrs. Sutton lay on the table, informing him that there was cocoa for him in the kitchen, ready for hotting up. He hotted it up accordingly in the little saucepan where it stood. There was just one good cupful.

He sipped it thoughtfully, standing by the kitchen stove. After the first sip, he put the cup down. Was it his fancy, or was there something queer about the taste? He sipped it again, rolling it upon his tongue. It seemed to him to have a faint tang, metallic and unpleasant. In a sudden dread he ran out to the scullery and spat the mouthful into the sink.

After this, he stood quite still for a moment or two. Then, with a curious deliberation, as though his movements had been dictated to him, he fetched an empty medicine bottle from the pantry shelf, rinsed it under the tap and tipped the contents of the cup carefully into it. He slipped the bottle into his coat pocket and moved on tiptoe to the back door. The bolts were difficult to draw without noise, but he managed it at last. Still on tiptoe, he stole across the garden to the potting shed. Stooping down, he struck a match. He knew exactly where he had left the tin of weed killer, under the shelf behind the pots at the back. Cautiously he lifted it out. The match flared up and burnt his fingers, but before he could light another his sense of touch had told him what he wanted to know. The stopper was loose again.

Panic seized Mr. Mummery, standing there in the earthy-smelling shed, in his dress suit and overcoat, holding the tin in one hand and the matchbox in the other. He wanted very badly to run and tell somebody what he had discovered.

Instead, he replaced the tin exactly where he had found it and went back to the house. As he crossed the garden again, he noticed a light in Mrs. Sutton's bedroom. This terrified him more than anything which had gone before. Was she watching him? Ethel's window was dark. If she had drunk anything deadly there would be lights everywhere, movements, calls for the doctor, just as when he himself had been attacked. Attacked—that was the right word.

Still with the same odd presence of mind and precision, he went in, washed out the utensils and made a second brew of cocoa, which he left standing in the saucepan. He crept quietly to his bedroom. Ethel's voice greeted him on the threshold.

"How late you are, Harold. Naughty old boy! Have a good time?"

"Not bad. You all right, darling?"

"Quite all right. Did Mrs. Sutton leave something hot for you? She said she would."

"Yes, but I wasn't thirsty."

Ethel laughed. "Oh! it was *that* sort of party, was it?"

Mr. Mummery did not attempt any denials. He undressed and got into bed and clutched his wife to him as though defying death and hell to take her from him. Next morning he would act. He thanked God that he was not too late.

MR. DIMTHORPE, the chemist, was a great friend of Mr. Mummery's. They had often sat together in the untidy little shop on Spring Bank and exchanged views on greenfly and clubroot. Mr. Mummery told his story frankly to Mr. Dimthorpe and handed over the bottle of cocoa. Mr. Dimthorpe congratulated him on his prudence and intelligence. "I will have it ready for you by this evening," he said, "and if it's what you think it is, then we shall have a clear case on which to take action."

Mr. Mummery thanked him, and was extremely vague and inattentive at business all day. But that hardly mattered, for Mr. Brookes, who had seen the party through to a riotous end in the small hours, was in no very observant mood. At half past four, Mr. Mummery shut up his desk decisively and announced that he was off early, he had a call to make. Mr. Dimthorpe was ready for him.

"No doubt about it," he said. "I used the Marsh test. It's a heavy dose—no wonder you tasted it. There must be four or five grains of pure arsenic in that bottle. Look, here's the test tube. You can see the mirror for yourself."

Mr. Mummery gazed at the little glass tube with its ominous purple-black stain.

"Will you ring up the police from here?" asked the chemist.

"No," said Mr. Mummery. "No—I want to get home. God knows what's happening there. And I've only just time to catch my train."

"All right," said Mr. Dimthorpe. "Leave it to me. I'll ring them up for you."

The local train was not fast enough for Mr. Mummery. Ethel—poisoned—dying—dead—Ethel—poisoned—dying—dead—the wheels drummed in his ears. He almost ran out of the station and along the road. A car was standing at his door. He saw it from the end of the street and broke into a gallop. It had happened already. The doctor was there. Fool, murderer that he was, to have left things so late.

Then, while he was still a hundred and fifty yards off, he saw the front door open. A man came out followed by Ethel herself. The visitor got into his car and was driven away. Ethel went in again. She was safe—safe! He could hardly control himself to hang up his hat and coat and go in looking reasonably calm. His wife had returned to the armchair by the fire and greeted him in some surprise. There were tea things on the table.

"Back early, aren't you?"

"Yes—business was slack. Somebody been to tea?"

"Yes, young Welbeck. About the arrangements for the Drama Society." She spoke briefly but with an undertone of excitement.

A qualm came over Mr. Mummery. Would a guest be any protection? His face must have shown his feelings, for Ethel stared at him in amazement.

"What's the matter, Harold, you look so queer?"

"Darling," said Mr. Mummery, "there's something I want to tell you about." He sat down and took her hand in his. "Something a little unpleasant, I'm afraid—"

"Oh, ma'am!" The cook was in the doorway.

"I beg your pardon, sir—I didn't know you was in. Will you be taking tea or can I clear away? And oh, ma'am, there was a young man at the fishmonger's and he's just come from Grimsby and they've caught that dreadful woman—that Mrs. Andrews. Isn't it a good thing? It's worritted me dreadful to think she was going about like that, but they've caught her. Taken a job as housekeeper she had to two elderly ladies and they found the wicked poison on her. Girl as spotted her will get a reward. I been keeping my eyes open for her, but it's at Grimsby she was all the time."

Mr. Mummery clutched at the arm of his chair. It had all been a mad mistake then. He wanted to shout or cry. He wanted to apologize to this foolish, pleasant, excited woman. All a mistake.

But there had been the cocoa. Mr. Dimthorpe. The Marsh test. Five grains of arsenic. Who, then—?

He glanced around at his wife, and in her eyes he saw something that he had never seen before . . .

BERNARD SHAW

1856–1950

"I first caught the ear of the British public on a cart in Hyde Park, to the blaring of brass bands," he once wrote. "I am a natural born mountebank." In fact, he was a Dubliner, an individualist whose wit, charm and intellect made him not only the Fabian Society's prized orator but also the greatest playwright of his day.

The Serenade

I CELEBRATED my fortieth birthday by one of the amateur theatrical performances for which my house at Beckenham is famous. The piece, written, as usual, by myself, was a fairy play in three acts; and the plot turned upon the possession of a magic horn by the hero, a young Persian prince. My works are so well known that it is unnecessary to describe the action minutely. I need only remind the reader that an important feature in the second act is the interruption of a festival by the sound of the horn, blown by the Prince in the heart of a loadstone mountain in which he has been entombed by a malignant fairy. I had engaged a cornist from the band of my regiment to blow the horn; and it was arranged that he should place himself, not upon the stage, but downstairs in the hall, so that the required effect of extreme distance should be produced.

The entertainment began pleasantly. Some natural disappointment was felt when it became known that I was not to act; but my guests excused me with perfect good humor when I pleaded my double duty as host and stage manager. The best seat in the auditorium was occupied by the beautiful Linda Fitznightingale. The next chair, which I had intended for myself, had been taken (rather coolly) by Porcharlester of the 12th, a young man of amiable disposition, and of some musical talent, which enables him to make the most of a somewhat effeminate baritone voice which he is weak enough to put forward as a tenor.

As Linda's taste for music approached fanaticism, Porcharlester's single accomplishment gave him, in her eyes, an advantage over men of more solid parts and mature age. I resolved to interrupt their conversation as soon as I was at leisure. It was some time before this occurred; for I make it a rule to see for myself that everything needed at the performances in my house is at hand in its proper place. At last Miss Waterloo, who enacted the heroine, complained that my anxiety made her nervous, and begged me to go to the front and rest myself. I complied willingly and hastened to the side of Linda. As I approached, Porcharlester rose, saying, "I am going to take a peep behind: that is, if non-performers may be admitted."

"Oh, certainly," I said, glad to be rid of him. "But pray do not meddle with anything. The slightest hitch—"

"All right," he said, interrupting me. "I know how fidgety you are. I will keep my hands in my pockets all the time."

"You should not allow him to be disrespectful to you, Colonel Green," said Linda, when he was gone. "And I feel sure he will do no end of mischief behind the scenes."

"Boys will be boys," I replied. "Porcharlester's manner is just the same to General Johnston, who is quite an old man. How are your musical studies progressing?"

"I am full of Schubert just now. Oh, Colonel Green, *do* you know Schubert's serenade?"

"Ah! a charming thing. It is something like this, I think. Diddledidum, deediddledi-dum, deedum, dee-diddledyday."

"Yes, it is a little like that. Does Mr. Porcharlester sing it?"

"He tries to sing it. But he only appears to advantage when he sings trivial music. In nothing that demands serious sentiment, depth of feeling, matured sympathy, as it were—"

"Yes, yes. I know you think Mr. Porcharlester flippant. Do you like the serenade?"

"Hm! well, the fact is—Do *you* like it?"

"I love it. I dream of it. I have lived on it for the last three days."

"I must confess that it has always struck me as being a singularly beautiful piece of music. I hope to have the pleasure of hearing justice done to it by your voice when our little play is over."

"*I* sing it! Oh, I dare not. Ah! here is Mr. Porcharlester. I will make him promise to sing it for us."

"Green," said Porcharlester with ill-bred jocosity: "I dont wish to disturb you groundlessly; but the fellow who is to play the magic horn hasnt turned up."

"Good heavens!" I exclaimed. "I ordered him for half-past seven sharp. If he fails, the play will be spoilt."

I excused myself briefly to Linda, and hurried to the hall. The horn was there, on the table. Porcharlester had resorted to an infamous trick to get rid of me. I was about to return and demand an explanation, when it occurred to me that, after all, the bandsman might have left his instrument there at the morning rehearsal and had perhaps not come. But a servant whom I called told me that the man had arrived with military punctuality at half-past seven, and had, according to my orders, been shewn into the supper room joining the hall, and left there with a glass of wine and a sandwich. Porcharlester, then, had deceived me. As the servant returned to his duties, leaving me alone and angry in the hall, my attention was curiously arrested by the gleaming brass curves of the instrument on the table. Amid the inanimate objects around me the horn seemed silent and motionless in a way apart, as though, pregnant with dreadful sound, it were consciously biding its time for utterance. I stole to the table, and cautiously touched one of the valves with my forefinger. After a moment I ventured to press it down. It clicked. At a sound in the supper room I started back guiltily. Then the prompter's bell tinkled. It was the signal for the cornist to prepare for his cue.

I awaited the appearance of the bandsman with some shame, hoping that he would not discover that I had been childishly meddling with his instrument. But he did not come. My anxiety increased; I hurried into the supper room. There, at the head of the table, sat the soldier, fast asleep. Before him were five decanters empty. I seized his shoulder and shook him violently. He grunted; made a drunken blow at me; and relapsed into insensibility.

Swearing, in my anger, to have him shot for this mutiny, I rushed back to the hall. The bell rang again. This second bell was for the horn to sound. The stage was waiting. In that extremity I saw but one way to save the piece from failure. I snatched up the instrument; put the smaller end into my mouth; and puffed vigorously through it. Waste of breath! not a sound responded. I became faint with my exertions; and the polished brass slipped through my clammy hands. The bell again urgently broke the ruinous silence. Then I grasped the horn like a vice; inflated my lungs; jammed the mouthpiece against my lips and set my teeth until it nearly cut me; and spat fiercely into it. The result was a titanic blast. My ears received a deafening shock; the lamp glasses whirred; the hats of my visitors rained from their pegs; and I pressed my bursting temples between my palms as the soldier reeled out, pale as though the last trumpet had roused him, and confronted the throng of amazed guests who appeared on the stairs.

FOR THE NEXT three months I studied the art of horn-blowing under the direction of an adept. He worried me by his lower middle class manners and his wearisome trick of repeating that the 'orn, as he called it, resembled the human voice more than any other instrument; but he was competent and conscientious; and I was persevering, in spite of some remonstrances from the neighbors. At last I ventured to ask him whether he considered me sufficiently advanced to play a solo in private for a friend.

"Well, Colonel," he said, "I tell you the truth, you havnt a born lip for it: at least, not yet. Then, you see, you blow so tremenjous. If youll believe me, sir, it dont need all the muscle you put into it: it spoils the tone. What was you thinking of playing for your friend?"

"Something that you must teach me. Schubert's serenade."

He stared at me, and shook his head. "It aint written for the hinstrument, sir." he said. "Youll never play it."

"The first time I play it through without a mistake, I will give you five guineas, besides our regular terms."

This overcame his doubts. I found the execution of the serenade, even after diligent practice, uncertain and very difficult. But I succeeded at last.

"If I was you, Colonel," said my instructor, as he pocketed the five guineas, "I'd keep that tune to myself, and play summat simpler for my friends. You can play it well enough here after half an hour's exercise; but when I'm not at your elbow youll find it wont come so steady."

I made light of this hint, the prudence of which I now fully recognize. But at that time I was bent on a long cherished project of serenading Linda. Her house, near the northern end of Park Lane, was favorably situated for the purpose; and I had already bribed a servant to admit me to the small pleasure ground that lay between the house and the roadway. Late in June, I learned that she intended to repose for an evening from the fatigues of society. This was my opportunity. At nine o'clock I placed my horn in a travelling bag, and drove to the Marble Arch, where I alighted and walked to my destination. I was arrested by the voice of Porcharlester calling, "Hallo, Colonel!" As I did not wish to be questioned, I thought it best to forestall him by asking whither he was bound.

"I am going to see Linda," he replied. "She contrived to let me know last night that she would be alone all this evening. I dont mind telling you these things, Colonel: you are a man of honor, and you know how good she is. I adore her. If I could only be certain that it is myself, and not merely my voice that she likes, I should be the happiest man in England."

"I am quite sure that it cannot be your voice," I said.

"Thank you," he exclaimed, grasping my hand: "it's very kind of you to say so; but I hardly dare flatter myself that you are right. It almost chokes me to look at her. Do you know I have never had the pluck to sing that serenade of Schubert's since she told me it was a favorite of hers?"

"Why? Does she not like your singing of it?"

"I tell you I have never ventured to sing it before her, though she is always at me for it. I am half jealous of that confounded tune. But I would do anything to please her; and I am going to surprise her with it tomorrow at Mrs. Locksly Hall's. I have been taking lessons and working like a dog to be able to sing it in really first-rate style. If you meet her, mind you dont breathe a word of this. It is to be a surprise."

"I have no doubt you will startle her," I said, exulting at the thought that he would be a day too late. I knew that it would take a finer voice than his to bear comparison with the melancholy sweetness, the sombre menace, the self-contained power with which the instrument I carried would respond to a skilful performer. We parted; and I saw him enter the house of Linda. A few minutes later, I was in the garden, looking up at them from my place in the shadow as they sat near the open window. Their conversation did not reach me: I thought he would never go. The night was a little cold: and the ground was damp. Ten o'clock struck—a quarter past—half past—I almost resolved to go home. Had not the tedium been relieved by some pieces which she played on the pianoforte, I could not have held out. At last they rose; and I was now able to distinguish their words.

"Yes," she said, "it is time for you to go." How heartily I agreed with her! "But you might have sung the serenade for me. I have played three times for you."

"I have a frightful cold," he said. "I really cannot. Goodnight."

"What nonsense! You have not the least symptom of a cold. No matter: I will never ask you again. Goodnight, Mr. Porcharlester."

"Do not be savage with me," he said. "You shall hear me sing it sooner than you think, perhaps."

"Ah! you say that very significantly. Sooner than I think! If you are preparing a surprise for me, I will forgive you. I shall see you at Mrs. Locksly Hall's tomorrow, I hope."

He assented, and hurried away, fearful, I suppose, lest he should betray his plan. When he was gone, she came to the window, and looked out at the stars. Gazing at her, I forgot my impatience: my teeth ceased to chatter. I took the horn from my travelling bag. She sighed; closed the window; and drew down a white blind. The sight of her hand alone as she did so would have inspired me to excel all my previous efforts. She seated herself so that I could see the shadow of her figure in profile.

My hour was come. Park Lane was nearly still: the traffic in Oxford Street was too distant to be distracting.

I began. At the first note I saw her start and listen. When the completed phrase revealed to her what air I was playing, she laid down her book. The mouthpiece of my instrument was like ice; and my lips were stiff and chilly, so that in spite of my utmost care I was interrupted more than once by those uncouth guggling sounds which the best cornists cannot always avoid. Nevertheless, considering that I was cold and very nervous, I succeeded fairly well. Gaining confidence as I went on, I partly atoned for the imperfection of the beginning by playing the concluding bars with commanding sonority, and even achieving a tolerable shake on the penultimate note.

An encouraging cheer from the street as I finished shewed me that a crowd was collected there, and that immediate flight was out of the question. I replaced the horn in my bag, and made ready to go when the mob should disperse. Meanwhile I gazed at the shadow on the blind. She was writing now. Could she, I think, be writing to me? She rose; and the shadow overspread the window so that I could no longer distinguish her movements. I heard a bell ring. A minute later the door of the house opened. I retreated behind an aloe tub; but on recognizing the servant whom I had bribed, I whistled softly to him. He came towards me with a letter in his hand. My heart beat strongly as I saw it.

"All right, sir," he said. "Miss Linda told me to give you this; but you are not to open it, if you please, until you get home."

"Then she knew who I was," I said eagerly.

"I suppose so, sir. When I heard her bell, I took care to answer it myself. Then she says to me, 'Youll find a gentleman somewhere in the pleasure ground. Give him this note; and beg him to go home at once. He is not to read it here.' "

"Is there any crowd outside?"

"All gone, sir. Thank you, sir. Goodnight, sir."

I ran all the way to Hamilton Place, where I got into a hansom. Ten minutes afterwards I was in my study, opening the letter with unsteady hands. It was not enclosed in an envelope, but folded in three, with a corner turned down. I opened it and read,

714, Park Lane, Friday.

Dear Mr. Porcharlester

—I stopped. Had she then given him credit for my performance? A more immediately important question was whether I had any right to read a letter not addressed to me. Curiosity and love prevailed over this scruple. The letter continued thus:

I am sorry that you have seen nothing in my fancy for Schubert's serenade except matter for ridicule. Perhaps it was an exaggerated fancy; but I would not have expressed it to you had I not believed you capable of understanding it. If it be any satisfaction to you to know that you have cured me of it thoroughly, pray believe that I shall never again hear the serenade without a strange mixture of mirth and pain. I did not know that a human throat could compass such sounds; and I little thought, when you promised that I should hear your voice sooner than I expected, that you contemplated such a performance. I have only one word more: Adieu. I shall not have the pleasure of meeting you at Mrs. Locksly Hall's tomorrow, as my engagements will not permit me to go there. For the same reason I fear I must deny myself the pleasure of receiving you again this season. I am, dear Mr. Porcharlester, yours truly,

Linda Fitznightingale.

I felt that to forward this letter to Porcharlester would only pain him uselessly. I felt also that my instructor was right, and that I have not the lip for the French horn. I have accordingly given it up.

Linda is now my wife. I sometimes ask her why she persists in cutting Porcharlester, who has pledged me his word as an officer and a gentleman that he is unconscious of having given her the slightest ground for offence. She always refuses to tell me.

G.E. M. SKUES

1858–1949

He was a family lawyer in London who also applied his acute legal mind to the matter of fishing. Indeed, he invented a new style of fly-fishing called "nymph fishing". The author of several esoteric books on his favourite hobby, such as *Minor Tactics of the Chalk Stream*, he could also communicate the sport's amusing side.

"Well I'm——!"

MR. THEODORE CASTWELL, having devoted a long, strenuous, and not unenjoyable life to hunting to their doom innumerable salmon trout and grayling in many quarters of the globe, and having gained much credit among his fellows for his many ingenious improvements in rods, flies and tackle employed for that end, in the fullness of time died and was taken to his own place.

ST. PETER looked up from a draft balance sheet at the entry of the attendant angel.

"A gentleman giving the name of Castwell. Says he is a fisherman, your Holiness, and has 'Fly-Fishers' Club, London', on his card."

"Hm-hm," says St. Peter. "Fetch me the ledger with his account."

St. Peter perused it.

"Hm-hm," said St. Peter. "Show him in."

Mr. Castwell entered cheerfully and offered a cordial right hand to St. Peter. "As a brother of the angle——" he began.

"Hm-hm," said St. Peter.

"I am sure I shall not appeal to you in vain for special consideration in connection with the quarters to be assigned to me here."

"Hm-hm," said St. Peter. "I have been looking at your account from below."

"Nothing wrong with it, I hope," said Mr. Castwell.

"Hm-hm," said St. Peter. "I have seen worse. What sort of quarters would you like?"

"Well," said Mr. Castwell. "Do you think you could manage something in the way of a country cottage of the Test Valley type, with modern conveniences and say three-quarters of a mile of one of those pleasant chalk-streams, clear as crystal, which proceed from out the throne, attached?"

"Why, yes," said St. Peter. "I think we can manage that for you. Then what about your gear? You must have left your fly rods and tackle down below. I see you prefer a light split cane of nine foot or so, with appropriate fittings. I will indent upon the Works Department for what you require, including a supply of flies. I think you will approve of our dressers' productions. Then you will want a keeper to attend you."

"Thanks awfully, your Holiness," said Mr. Castwell. "That will be first-rate. To tell you the truth, from the Revelations I read, I was inclined to fear that I might be just a teeny-weeny bit bored in heaven."

"In H—hm-hm," said St. Peter, checking himself.

IT WAS NOT LONG before Mr. Castwell found himself alongside an enchantingly beautiful clear chalk-stream, some fifteen yards wide, swarming with fine trout feeding greedily; and presently the attendant angel assigned to him had handed him the daintiest, most exquisite, light split-cane rod conceivable—perfectly balanced with reel and line—with a beautifully damped tapered cast of incredible fineness and strength—and a box of flies of such marvellous tying, as to be almost mistakable for the natural insects they were to simulate.

Mr. Castwell scooped up a natural fly from the water, matched it perfectly from the fly-box, and knelt down to cast to a riser putting up just under a tussock ten yards or so above him. The fly lit like gossamer, six inches above the last ring, floated a moment and went under in the next ring; and next moment the rod was making the curve of beauty. Presently, after an exciting battle, the keeper netted out a beauty of about two-and-a-half pounds.

"Heavens," cried Mr. Castwell. "This is something like."

"I am sure his Holiness will be pleased to hear it," said the keeper.

Mr. Castwell prepared to move up-stream to the next riser when he became aware that another trout had taken up the position of that which he had just landed, and was rising. "Just look at that," he said, dropping instantaneously to his knee and drawing off some line. A moment later an accurate fly fell just above the neb of the fish, and instantly Mr. Castwell engaged in battle with another lusty fish. All went well, and presently the landing net received its two-and-a-half pounds.

"A very pretty brace," said Mr. Castwell, preparing to move on to the next of the string of busy nebs which he had observed putting up round the bend. As he approached the tussock, however, he became aware that the place from which he had just extracted so satisfactory a brace was already occupied by another busy feeder.

"Well I'm damned!" cried Mr. Castwell. "Do you see that?"

"Yes, sir," said the keeper.

The chance of extracting three successive trout from the same spot was too attractive to be forgone, and once more Mr. Castwell knelt down and delivered a perfect cast to the spot. Instantly it was accepted and battle was joined. All held, and presently a third gleaming trout joined his brethren in the creel.

"Heavens!" exclaimed Mr. Castwell. "Was there ever anything like it?"

"No, sir," said the keeper.

"Look here," said he to the keeper. "I think I really must give this chap a miss and pass on to the next."

"Sorry! It can't be done, sir. His Holiness would not like it."

"Well, if that's really so," said Mr. Castwell, and knelt reluctantly to his task.

SEVERAL HOURS later he was still casting to the same tussock.

"How long is this confounded rise going to last?" enquired Mr. Castwell. "I suppose it will stop soon?"

"No, sir," said the keeper.

"What, isn't there a slack hour in the afternoon?"

"No afternoon, sir."

"What? Then what about the evening rise?"

"No evening, sir," said the keeper.

"Well, I shall knock off, now. I must have had about thirty brace from that corner."

"Beg pardon, sir, but his Holiness would not like that."

"What?" said Mr. Castwell. "Mayn't I even stop at night?"

"No night here, sir," said the keeper.

"Then do you mean that I have got to go on catching these damned two-and-a-half-pounders at this corner for ever and ever?"

The keeper nodded.

"Hell!" said Mr. Castwell.

"Yes," said his keeper.

E. Œ. SOMERVILLE and MARTIN ROSS

1858–1949 1865–1915

They were female cousins who lived in County Cork. This story is from their best-known work *Some Experiences of an Irish RM* (a series of humorous incidents related by a Resident Magistrate). According to Somerville, even after the death of Ross (whose real name was Violet Martin) the partnership continued by means of spiritualism.

Lisheen Races, Secondhand

IT MAY OR may not be agreeable to have attained the age of thirty-eight, but, judging from old photographs, the privilege of being nineteen has also its drawbacks. I turned over page after page of an ancient book in which were enshrined portraits of the friends of my youth, singly, in David and Jonathan couples, and in groups in which I, as it seemed to my mature and possibly jaundiced perception, always contrived to look the most immeasurable young bounder of the lot. Our faces were fat, and yet I cannot remember ever having been considered fat in my life; we indulged in low-necked shirts, in 'Jemima' ties with diagonal stripes; we wore coats that seemed three sizes too small, and trousers that were three sizes too big; we also wore small whiskers.

I stopped at last at one of the David and Jonathan memorial portraits. Yes, here was the object of my researches; this stout and earnestly romantic youth was Leigh Kelway, and that fatuous and chubby young person seated on the arm of his chair was myself. Leigh Kelway was a young man ardently believed in by a large circle of admirers, headed by himself and seconded by me, and for some time after I had left Magdalen for Sandhurst, I maintained a correspondence with him on large and abstract subjects. This phase of our friendship did not survive; I went soldiering to India, and Leigh Kelway took honours and moved suitably on into politics, as is the duty of an earnest young Radical with useful family connexions and an independent income. Since then I had at intervals seen in the papers the name of the Honourable Basil Leigh Kelway mentioned as a speaker at elections, as a writer of thoughtful articles in the reviews, but we had never met, and nothing could have been less expected by me than the letter, written from Mrs. Raverty's Hotel, Skebawn, in which he told me he was making a tour in Ireland with Lord Waterbury, to whom he was private secretary. Lord Waterbury was at present having a few days' fishing near Killarney, and he himself, not being a fisherman, was collecting statistics for his chief on various points connected with the Liquor Question in Ireland. He had heard that I was in the neighbourhood, and was kind enough to add that it would give him much pleasure to meet me again.

With a stir of the old enthusiasm I wrote begging him to be my guest for as long as it suited him, and the following afternoon he arrived at Shreelane. The stout young friend of my youth had changed considerably. His important nose and slightly prominent teeth remained, but his wavy hair had withdrawn intellectually from his temples; his eyes had acquired a statesmanlike absence of expression, and his neck had grown long and bird-like. It was his first visit to Ireland, as he lost no time in telling me, and he and his chief had already collected much valuable information on the subject to which they had dedicated the Easter recess. He further informed me that he thought of popularizing the subject in a novel, and therefore intended to, as he put it, "master the brogue" before his return.

During the next few days I did my best for Leigh Kelway. I turned him loose on Father Scanlan; I showed him Mohona, our champion village, that boasts fifteen public-houses out of twenty buildings of sorts and a railway station; I took him to hear the prosecution of a publican for selling drink on a Sunday, which gave him an opportunity of studying perjury as a fine art, and of hearing a lady, on whom police suspicion justly rested, profoundly summed up by the sergeant as "a woman who had th' appairance of having knocked at a back door".

The net result of these experiences has not yet been given to the world by Leigh Kelway. For my own part, I had at the end of three days arrived at the conclusion that his society, when combined with a notebook and a thirst for statistics, was not what I used to find it at Oxford. I therefore welcomed a suggestion from Mr. Flurry Knox that we should accompany him to some typical country races, got up by the farmers at a place called Lisheen, some twelve miles away. It was the worst road in the district, the races of the most grossly unorthodox character; in fact, it was the very place for Leigh Kelway to collect impressions of Irish life, and in any case it was a blessed opportunity of disposing of him for the day.

In my guest's attire next morning I discerned an unbending from the role of cabinet minister towards that of sportsman; the outlines of the notebook might be traced in his breast pocket, but traversing it was the strap of a pair of field-glasses, and his light grey suit was smart enough for Goodwood.

Flurry was to drive us to the races at one o'clock, and we walked to Tory Cottage by the short cut over the hill, in the sunny beauty of an April morning. Up to the present the weather had kept me in a more or less apologetic condition; anyone who has entertained a guest in the country knows the unjust weight of responsibility that rests on the shoulders of the host in the matter of climate, and Leigh Kelway, after two drenchings, had become sarcastically resigned to what I felt he regarded as my mismanagement.

Flurry took us into the house for a drink and a biscuit, to keep us going, as he said, till "we lifted some luncheon out of the Castle Knox people at the races", and it was while we were thus engaged that the first disaster of the day occurred. The dining-room door was open, so also was the window of the little staircase just outside it, and through the window travelled sounds that told of the close proximity of the stable-yard; the clattering of hoofs on cobble-stones, and voices uplifted in loud conversation.

Suddenly from this region there arose a screech of the laughter peculiar to kitchen flirtation, followed by the clank of a bucket, the plunging of a horse, and then an uproar of wheels and galloping hoofs. An instant afterwards Flurry's chestnut cob, in a dogcart, dashed at full gallop into view, with the reins streaming behind him, and two men in hot pursuit. Almost before I had time to realize what had happened, Flurry jumped through the half-opened window of the dining-room like a clown at a pantomime, and joined in the chase; but the cob was resolved to make the most of his chance, and went away down the drive and out of sight at a pace that distanced everyone save the kennel terrier, who sped in shrieking ecstasy beside him.

"Oh merciful hour!" exclaimed a female voice behind me. Leigh Kelway and I were by this time watching the progress of events from the gravel, in company with the remainder of Flurry's household. "The horse is desthroyed! Wasn't that the quare start he took! And all in the world I done was to slap a bucket of wather at Michael out the windy, and 'twas himself got it in place of Michael!"

"Ye'll never ate another bit, Bridgie Dunnigan," replied the cook, with the exulting pessimism of her kind. "The Master'll have your life!"

Both speakers shouted at the top of their voices, probably because in spirit they still followed afar the flight of the cob.

Leigh Kelway looked serious as we walked on down the drive. I almost dared to hope that a note on the degrading oppression of Irish retainers was shaping itself. Before we reached the bend of the drive the rescue party was returning with the fugitive, all, with the exception of the kennel terrier, looking extremely gloomy. The cob had been confronted by a wooden gate, which he had unhesitatingly taken in his stride, landing on his head on the farther side with the gate and the cart on top of him, and had arisen with a lame foreleg, a cut on his nose, and several other minor wounds.

"You'd think the brute had been fighting the cats, with all the scratches and scrapes he has on him!" said Flurry, casting a vengeful eye at Michael, "and one shaft's broken and so is the dashboard. I haven't another horse in the place; they're all out at grass, and so there's an end of the races!"

We all three stood blankly on the hall-door steps and watched the wreck of the trap being trundled up the avenue.

"I'm very sorry you're done out of your sport," said Flurry to Leigh Kelway, in tones of deplorable sincerity; "perhaps, as there's nothing else to do, you'd like to see the hounds—?"

I felt for Flurry, but of the two I felt more for Leigh Kelway as he accepted this alleviation. He disliked dogs, and held the newest views on sanitation, and I knew what Flurry's kennels could smell like. I was lighting a precautionary cigarette, when we caught sight of an old man riding up the drive. Flurry stopped short.

"Hold on a minute," he said; "here's an old chap that often brings me horses for the kennels; I must see what he wants."

The man dismounted and approached Mr. Knox, hat in hand, towing after him a gaunt and ancient black mare with a big knee.

"Well, Barrett," began Flurry, surveying the mare with his hands in his pockets, "I'm not giving the hounds meat this month, or only very little."

"Ah, Master Flurry," answered Barrett, "it's you that's pleasant! Is it give the like o' this one for the dogs to ate! She's a vallyble strong young mare, no more than shixteen years of age, and ye'd sooner be lookin' at her goin' under a side-car than eatin' your dinner."

"There isn't as much meat on her as 'd fatten a jackdaw," said Flurry, clinking the silver in his pockets as he searched for a matchbox. "What are you asking for her?"

The old man drew cautiously up to him.

"Master Flurry," he said solemnly, "I'll sell her to *your* honour for five pounds, and she'll be worth ten after you give her a month's grass."

Flurry lit his cigarette; then he said imperturbably, "I'll give you seven shillings for her."

Old Barrett put on his hat in silence, and in silence buttoned his coat and took hold of the stirrup leather. Flurry remained immovable.

"Master Flurry," said old Barrett suddenly, with tears in his voice, "you must make it eight, sir!"

"Michael!" called out Flurry with apparent irrelevance, "run up to your father's and ask him would he lend me a loan of his side-car."

Half an hour later we were, improbable as it may seem, on our way to Lisheen races. We were seated upon an outside-car of immemorial age, whose joints seemed to open and close again as it swung in and out of the ruts, whose tattered cushions stank of rats and mildew, whose wheels staggered and rocked like the legs of a drunken man. Between the shafts jogged the latest addition to the kennel larder, the eight-shilling mare. Flurry sat on one side, and kept her going at a rate of not less than four miles an hour; Leigh Kelway and I held on to the other.

"She'll get us as far as Lynch's anyway," said Flurry, abandoning his first contention that she could do the whole distance, as he pulled her on to her legs after her fifteenth stumble, "and he'll lend us some sort of a horse, if it was only a mule."

"Do you notice that these cushions are very damp?" said Leigh Kelway to me, in a hollow undertone.

"Small blame to them if they are!" replied Flurry. "I've no doubt but they were out under the rain all day yesterday at Mrs. Hurly's funeral."

Leigh Kelway made no reply, but he took his notebook out of his pocket and sat on it.

We arrived at Lynch's at a little past three, and were there confronted by the next disappointment of this disastrous day. The door of Lynch's farmhouse was locked, and nothing replied to our knocking except a puppy, who barked hystérically from within.

"All gone to the races," said Flurry philosophically, picking his way round the manure heap. "No matter, here's the filly in the shed here. I know he's had her under a car."

An agitating ten minutes ensued, during which Leigh Kelway and I got the eight-shilling mare out of the shafts and the harness, and Flurry, with our inefficient help, crammed the young mare into them.

As Flurry had stated that she had been driven before, I was bound to believe him, but the difficulty of getting the bit into her mouth was remarkable, and so also was the crab-like manner in which she sidled out of the yard, with Flurry and myself at her head, and Leigh Kelway hanging on to the back of the car to keep it from jamming in the gateway.

"Sit up on the car now," said Flurry when we got out on to the road; "I'll lead her on a bit. She's been ploughed anyway; one side of her mouth's as tough as a gad!"

Leigh Kelway threw away the wisp of grass with which he had been cleaning his hands, and mopped his intellectual forehead; he was very silent. We both mounted the car, and Flurry, with the reins in his hand, walked beside the filly, who, with her tail clasped in, moved onward in a succession of short jerks.

"Oh, she's all right!" said Flurry, beginning to run, and dragging the filly into a trot; "once she gets started—" Here the filly spied a pig in a neighbouring field, and despite the fact that she had probably eaten out of the same trough with it, she gave a violent side spring, and broke into a gallop.

"Now we're off!" shouted Flurry, making a jump at the car and clambering on; "if the traces hold we'll do!"

The English language is powerless to suggest the view-halloo with which Mr. Knox ended his speech, or to do more than indicate the rigid anxiety of Leigh Kelway's face as he regained his balance after the preliminary jerk, and clutched the back rail. It must be said for Lynch's filly that she did not kick; she merely fled, like a dog with a kettle tied to its tail, from the pursuing rattle and jingle behind her, with the shafts buffeting her dusty sides as the car swung to and fro. Whenever she showed any signs of slackening, Flurry loosed another yell at her that renewed her panic, and thus we precariously covered another two or three miles of our journey.

Had it not been for a large stone lying on the road, and had the filly not chosen to swerve so as to bring the wheel on top of it, I dare say we might have got to the races; but by an unfortunate coincidence both these things occurred, and when we recovered from the consequent shock, the tyre of one of the wheels had come off, and was trundling with cumbrous gaiety into the ditch.

Flurry stopped the filly and began to laugh; Leigh Kelway said something startlingly unparliamentary under his breath.

"Well, it might be worse," Flurry said consolingly as he lifted the tyre on to the car; "we're not half a mile from a forge."

We walked that half-mile in funereal procession behind the car; the glory had departed from the weather, and an ugly wall of cloud was rising up out of the west to meet the sun; the hills had darkened and lost colour, and the white bog cotton shivered in a cold wind that smelt of rain.

By a miracle the smith was not at the races, owing, as he explained, to his having 'the tooth-aches', the two facts combined producing in him a morosity only equalled by that of Leigh Kelway. The smith's sole comment on the situation was to unharness the filly, and drag her into the forge, where he tied her up. He then proceeded to whistle viciously on his fingers in the direction of a cottage, and to command, in tones of thunder, some unseen creature to bring over a couple of baskets of turf.

The turf arrived in process of time, on a woman's back, and was arranged in a circle in a yard at the back of the forge. The tyre was bedded in it, and the turf was with difficulty kindled at different points.

"Ye'll not get to the races this day," said the smith, yielding to a sardonic satisfaction; "the turf's wet, and I haven't one to do a hand's turn for me." He laid the wheel on the ground and lit his pipe.

Leigh Kelway looked pallidly about him over the spacious empty landscape of brown mountain slopes patched with golden furze and seamed with grey walls; I wondered if he were as hungry as I. We sat on stones opposite the smouldering ring of turf and smoked, and Flurry beguiled the smith into grim and calumnious confidences about every horse in the country. After about an hour, during which the turf went out three times, and the weather became more and more threatening, a girl with a red petticoat over her head appeared at the gate of the yard, and said to the smith:

"The horse is gone away from ye."

"Where?" exclaimed Flurry, springing to his feet.

"I met him walking wesht the road there below, and when I thought to turn him he commenced to gallop."

"Pulled her head out of the headstall," said Flurry, after a rapid survey of the forge. "She's near home by now."

It was at this moment that the rain began; the situation could scarcely have been better stage-managed. After reviewing the position, Flurry and I decided that the only thing to do was to walk to a public-house a couple of miles farther on, feed there if possible, hire a car, and go home.

It was an uphill walk, with mild generous raindrops striking thicker and thicker on our faces; no one talked, and the grey clouds crowded up from behind the hills like billows of steam. Leigh Kelway bore it all with egregious resignation.

I cannot pretend that I was at heart sympathetic, but by virtue of being his host I felt responsible for the breakdown, for his light suit, for everything, and divined his sentiment of horror at the first sight of the public-house.

It was a long, low cottage, with a line of dripping elm-trees overshadowing it; empty cars and carts round its door, and a babel from within made it evident that the racegoers were pursuing a gradual homeward route. The shop was crammed with steaming countrymen, whose loud brawling voices, all talking together, roused my English friend to his first remark since we had left the forge.

"Surely, Yeates, we are not going into that place?" he said severely; "those men are all drunk."

"Ah, nothing to signify!" said Flurry, plunging in and driving his way through the throng like a plough. "Here, Mary Kate!" he called to the girl behind the counter, "tell your mother we want some tea and bread and butter in the room inside."

The smell of bad tobacco and spilt porter was choking; we worked our way through it after him towards the end of the shop, intersecting at every hand discussions about the races.

"Tom was very nice. He spared his horse all along, and then he put into him—" "Well, at Goggin's corner the third horse was before the second, but he was goin' wake in himself." "I tell ye the mare had the hind leg fasht in the fore." "Clancy was dipping in the saddle." "'Twas a dam nice race whatever—"

We gained the inner room at last, a cheerless apartment, adorned with sacred pictures, a sewing-machine, and an array of supplementary tumblers and wine-glasses; but, at all events, we had it so far to ourselves.

At intervals during the next half-hour Mary Kate burst in with cups and plates, cast them on the table and disappeared, but of food there was no sign. After a further period of starvation and of listening to the noise in the shop, Flurry made a sortie, and, after lengthy and unknown adventures, reappeared carrying a huge brown teapot, and driving before him Mary Kate with the remainder of the repast. The bread tasted of mice, the butter of turf-smoke, the tea of brown paper, but we had got past the critical stage. I had entered upon my third round of bread and butter when the door was flung open, and my valued acquaintance, Slipper, slightly advanced in liquor, presented himself to our gaze. His bandy legs sprawled consequentially, his nose was redder than a coal of fire, his prominent eyes rolled crookedly upon us, and his left hand swept behind him the attempt of Mary Kate to frustrate his entrance.

"Good-evening to my vinerable friend, Mr. Flurry Knox!" he began, in the voice of a town crier, "and to the Honourable Major Yeates, and the English gintleman!"

This impressive opening immediately attracted an audience from the shop, and the doorway filled with grinning faces as Slipper advanced farther into the room.

"Why weren't ye at the races, Mr. Flurry?" he went on, his roving eye taking a grip of us all at the same time; "sure the Miss Bennetts and all the ladies was asking where were ye."

"It'd take some time to tell them that," said Flurry, with his mouth full; "but what about the races, Slipper? Had you good sport?"

"Sport is it? Divil so pleasant an afternoon ever you seen," replied Slipper. He leaned against a side table, and all the glasses on it jingled. "Does your honour know O'Driscoll?" he went on irrelevantly. "Sure you do. He was in your honour's stable. It's what we were all sayin'; it was a great pity your honour was not there, for the likin' you had to Driscoll."

"That's thrue," said a voice at the door.

"There wasn't one in the Barony but was gethered in it, through and fro," continued Slipper, with a quelling glance at the interrupter; "and there was tints for sellin' porther, and whisky as pliable as new milk, and boys goin' round the tints outside, feeling for heads with the big ends of their blackthorns, and all kinds of recreations, and the Sons of Liberty's piffler and dhrum band from Skebawn; though faith! there was more of thim runnin' to look at the races than what was playin' in it; not to mintion different occasions that the bandmasther was atin' his lunch within in the whisky tint."

"But what about Driscoll?" said Flurry.

"Sure it's him I'm tellin' ye," replied Slipper, with the practised orator's watchful eye on his growing audience. "'Twas within in the same whisky tint meself was, with the bandmasther and a few of the lads, an' we buyin' a ha'porth o' crackers, when I seen me brave Driscoll landin' into the tint, and a pair o' thim long boots on him; him that hadn't a shoe nor a stocking to his foot when your honour had him picking grass out o' the stones behind in your yard. 'Well,' says I to meself, 'we'll knock some sport out of Driscoll!'

"'Come here to me, acushla!' says I to him, 'I suppose it's some way wake in the legs y'are,' says I, 'an' the docthor put them on ye the way the people wouldn't thrample ye!'

"'May the divil choke ye!' says he, pleasant enough, but I knew by the blush he had he was vexed.

"'Then I suppose 'tis a left-tenant colonel y'are,' says I; 'yer mother must be proud out o' ye!' says I, 'an' maybe ye'll lend her a loan o' thim waders when she's rinsin' yer bauneen in the river!' says I.

"'There'll be work out o' this!' says he, lookin' at me both sour and bitther.

"'Well indeed, I was thinkin' you were blue moulded for want of a batin',' says I. He was for fightin' us then, but afther we had him pacificated with about a quarther of a naggin o' sperrits, he told us he was goin' ridin' in a race.

"'An' what'll ye ride?' says I.

"'Owld Bocock's mare,' says he.

"'Knipes!' says I, sayin' a great curse; 'is it that little staggeen from the mountains; sure she's somethin' about the one age with meself,' says I. 'Many's the time Jamesy Geoghegan and meself used to be dhrivin' her to Macroom with pigs an' all soorts,' says I; 'an' is it leppin' stone walls ye want her to go now?'

"'Faith, there's walls and every vari'ty of obstackle in it,' says he.

"'It'll be the best o' your play, so,' says I, 'to leg it away home out o' this.'

"'An' who'll ride her, so?' says he.

"'Let the divil ride her,' says I."

Leigh Kelway, who had been leaning back seemingly half asleep, obeyed the hypnotism of Slipper's gaze, and opened his eyes.

"That was now all the conversation that passed between himself and meself," resumed Slipper, "and there was no great delay afther that till they said there was a race startin' and the dickens a one at all was goin' to ride only two, Driscoll, and one Clancy. With that then I seen Mr. Kinahane, the Petty Sessions clerk, goin' round clearin' the coorse, an' I gethered a few o' the neighbours, an' we walked the fields hither and over till we seen the most of th' obstackles.

"'Stand aisy now by the plantation,' says I; 'if they get to come as far as this, believe me ye'll see spoort,' says I, 'an' 'twill be a convanient spot to encourage the mare if she's anyway wake in herself,' says I, cuttin' somethin' about five foot of an ash sapling out o' the plantation.

"'That's yer sort!' says owld Bocock, that was thravellin' the race-coorse, peggin' a bit o' paper down with a thorn in front of every lep, the way Driscoll'd know the handiest place to face her at it.

"Well, I hadn't barely thrimmed the ash plant—"

"Have you any jam, Mary Kate?" interrupted Flurry, whose meal had been in no way interfered with by either the story or the highly-scented crowd who had come to listen to it.

"We have no jam, only thraycle, sir," replied the invisible Mary Kate.

"I hadn't the switch barely thrimmed," repeated Slipper firmly, "when I heard the people screechin', an' I seen Driscoll an' Clancy comin' on, leppin' all before them, an' owld Bocock's mare bellusin' an' powdherin' along, an' bedad! whatever obstackle wouldn't throw *her* down, faith, she'd throw *it* down, an' there's the thraffic they had in it.

"'I declare to me sowl,' says I, 'if they continue on this way there's a great chance some one o' thim 'll win,' says I.

"'Ye lie!' says the bandmasther, bein' a thrifle fulsome after his luncheon.

"'I do not,' says I, 'in regard of seein' how soople them two boys is. Ye might observe,' says I, 'that if they have no convanient way to sit on the saddle, they'll ride the neck o' the horse till such time as they gets an occasion to lave it,' says I.

"'Arrah, shut yer mouth!' says the bandmasther; 'they're puckin' out this way now, an' may the divil admire me!' says he, 'but Clancy has the other bet out, and the divil such leatherin' and beltin' of owld Bocock's mare ever you seen as what's in it!' says he.

"Well, when I seen them comin' to me, and Driscoll about the length of the plantation behind Clancy, I let a couple of bawls.

" 'Skelp her, ye big brute!' says I. 'What good's in ye that ye aren't able to skelp her?' "

The yell and the histrionic flourish of his stick with which Slipper delivered this incident brought down the house. Leigh Kelway was sufficiently moved to ask me in an undertone if 'skelp' was a local term.

"Well, Mr. Flurry, and gintlemen," recommenced Slipper, "I declare to ye when owld Bocock's mare heard thim roars she sthretched out her neck like a gandher, and when she passed me out she give a couple of grunts, and looked at me as ugly as a Christian.

" 'Hah!' says I, givin' her a couple o' dhraws o' th' ash plant across the butt o' the tail, the way I wouldn't blind her; 'I'll make ye grunt!' says I, 'I'll nourish ye!'

"I knew well she was very frightful of th' ash plant since the winter Tommeen Sullivan had her under a side-car. But now, in place of havin' any obligations to me, ye'd be surprised if ye heard the blaspheemious expressions of that young boy that was ridin' her; and whether it was over-anxious he was, turnin' around the way I'd hear him cursin', or whether it was some slither or slide came to owld Bocock's mare, I dunno, but she was bet up agin the last obstackle but two, and before ye could say 'Schnipes', she was standin' on her two ears beyond in th' other field! I declare to ye, on the vartue of me oath, she stood that way till she reconnoithered what side would Driscoll fall, an' she turned about then and rolled on him as cosy as if he was meadow grass!"

Slipper stopped short; the people in the doorway groaned appreciatively; Mary Kate murmured, "The Lord save us!"

"The blood was dhruv out through his nose and ears," continued Slipper, with a voice that indicated the cream of the narration, "and you'd hear his bones crackin' on the ground! You'd have pitied the poor boy."

"Good heavens!" said Leigh Kelway, sitting up very straight in his chair.

"Was he hurt, Slipper?" asked Flurry casually.

"Hurt is it?" echoed Slipper in high scorn; "killed on the spot!" He paused to relish the effect of the denouement on Leigh Kelway. "Oh, divil so pleasant an afthernoon ever you seen; and indeed, Mr. Flurry, it's what we were all sayin', it was a great pity your honour was not there for the likin' you had for Driscoll."

As he spoke the last word there was an outburst of singing and cheering from a car-load of people who had just pulled up at the door. Flurry listened, leaned back in his chair, and began to laugh.

"It scarcely strikes one as a comic incident," said Leigh Kelway, very coldly to me; "in fact, it seems to me that the police ought—"

"Show me Slipper!" bawled a voice in the shop; "show me that dirty little undherlooper till I have his blood! Hadn't I the race won only for he souring the mare on me! What's that you say? I tell ye he did! He left seven slaps on her with the handle of a hayrake—"

There was in the room in which we were sitting a second door, leading to the back yard, a door consecrated to the unobtrusive visits of so-called 'Sunday travellers'. Through it Slipper faded away like a dream, and, simultaneously, a tall young man, with a face like a red-hot potato tied up in a bandage, squeezed his way from the shop into the room.

"Well, Driscoll," said Flurry, "since it wasn't the teeth of the rake he left on the mare, you needn't be talking!"

Leigh Kelway looked from one to the other with a wilder expression in his eye than I had thought it capable of. I read in it a resolve to abandon Ireland to her fate.

At eight o'clock we were still waiting for the car that we had been assured should be ours directly it arrived with Leigh Kelway's chief, returning from his fishing excursion.

Meanwhile Slipper, in the ditch, did not cease to announce that "Divil so pleasant an afthernoon ever ye seen as what was in it!"

MURIEL SPARK

b. 1918

She is a very private person. Facts about her are hard to come by: she was born and educated in Edinburgh, lived in Africa, returned during the war to work in the Political Information Department of the Foreign Office, became a poetry editor and historical biographer. She is best-known for her wryly humorous fiction.

Miss Pinkerton's Apocalypse

ONE EVENING, a damp one in February, something flew in at the window. Miss Laura Pinkerton, who was doing something innocent to the fire, heard a faint throbbing noise overhead. On looking up, "George! come here! come quickly!"

George Lake came in at once, though sullenly because of their quarrel, eating a sandwich from the kitchen. He looked up at the noise then sat down immediately.

From this point onward their story comes in two versions, his and hers. But they agree as to the main facts; they agree that it was a small round flattish object, and that it flew.

"It's a flying object of some sort," whispered George eventually.

"It's a saucer," said Miss Pinkerton, keen and loud, "an antique piece. You can tell by the shape."

"It can't be an antique, that's absolutely certain," George said.

He ought to have been more tactful, and would have been, but for the stress of the moment. Of course it set Miss Pinkerton off, she being in the right.

"I know my facts," she stated as usual, "I should hope I know my facts. I've been in antique china for twenty-three years in the autumn," which was true, and George knew it.

The little saucer was cavorting round the lamp.

"It seems to be attracted by the light," George remarked, as one might distinguish a moth.

Promptly, it made as if to dive dangerously at George's head. He ducked, and Miss Pinkerton backed against the wall. As the dish tilted on its side, skimming George's shoulder, Miss Pinkerton could see inside it.

"The thing might be radio-active. It might be dangerous." George was breathless. The saucer had climbed, was circling high above his head, and now made for him again, but missed.

"It is not radio-active," said Miss Pinkerton, "it is Spode."

"Don't be so damn silly," George replied, under the stress of the occasion.

"All right, very well," said Miss Pinkerton, "it is not Spode. I suppose you are the expert, George, I suppose you know best. I was only judging by the pattern. After the best part of a lifetime in china—"

"It must be a forgery," George said unfortunately. For, unfortunately, something familiar and abrasive in Miss Pinkerton's speech began to grind within him. Also, he was afraid of the saucer.

It had taken a stately turn, following the picture rail in a steady career round the room.

"Forgery, ha!" said Miss Pinkerton. She was out of the room like a shot, and in again carrying a pair of steps.

"I will examine the mark," said she, pointing intensely at the saucer. "Where are my glasses?"

Obligingly, the saucer settled in a corner; it hung like a spider a few inches from the ceiling. Miss Pinkerton adjusted the steps. With her glasses on she was almost her sunny self again, she was ceremonious and expert.

"Don't touch it, don't go near it!" George pushed her aside and grabbed the steps, knocking over a blue glass bowl, a Dresden figure, a vase of flowers and a decanter of sherry; like a bull in a china shop, as Miss Pinkerton exclaimed. But she was determined, and struggled to reclaim the steps.

"Laura!" he said desperately. "I believe it is Spode. I take your word."

The saucer then flew out of the window.

They acted quickly. They telephoned to the local paper. A reporter would come right away. Meanwhile, Miss Pinkerton telephoned to her two scientific friends—at least, one was interested in psychic research and the other was an electrician. But she got no reply from either. George had leaned out of the window, scanning the rooftops and the night sky. He had leaned out of the back windows, had tried all the lights and the wireless. These things were as usual.

The news man arrived, accompanied by a photographer.

"There's nothing to photograph," said Miss Pinkerton excitably. "It went away."

"We could take a few shots of the actual spot," the man explained.

Miss Pinkerton looked anxiously at the result of George and the steps.

"The place is a wreck."

Sherry from the decanter was still dripping from the sideboard.

"I'd better clear the place up. George, help me!" She fluttered nervously, and started to pack the fire with small coals.

"No, leave everything as it is," the reporter advised her. "Did the apparition make this mess?"

George and Miss Pinkerton spoke together.

"Well, indirectly," said George.

"It wasn't an apparition," said Miss Pinkerton.

The reporter settled on the nearest chair, poising his pencil and asking, "Do you mind if I take notes?"

"Would you mind sitting over here?" said Miss Pinkerton. "I don't use the Queen Annes normally. They are very frail pieces."

The reporter rose as if stung, then perched on a table which Miss Pinkerton looked at uneasily.

"You see, I'm in antiques," she rattled on, for the affair was beginning to tell on her, as George told himself. In fact he sized up that she was done for; his irritation abated, his confidence came flooding back.

"Now, Laura, sit down and take it easy." Solicitously he pushed her into an easy chair.

"She's overwrought," he informed the pressmen in an audible undertone.

"You say this object actually flew in this window?" suggested the reporter.

"That is correct," said George.

The camera-man trained his apparatus on the window.

"And you were both here at the time?"

"No," Miss Pinkerton said. "Mr. Lake was in the kitchen and I called out, of course. But he didn't see inside the bowl, only the outside, underneath where the manufacturer's mark is. I saw the pattern so I got the steps to make sure. That's how Mr. Lake knocked my things over. I saw inside."

"I am going to say something," said George.

The men looked hopefully towards him. After a pause, George continued, "Let us begin at the beginning."

"Right," said the reporter, breezing up.

"It was like this," George said. "I came straight in when Miss Pinkerton screamed, and there was a white convex disc, you realise, floating around up there."

The reporter contemplated the spot indicated by George.

"It was making a hell of a racket like a cat purring," George told him.

"Any idea what it really was?" the reporter inquired.

George took his time to answer. "Well, yes," he said, "and no."

"Spode ware," said Miss Pinkerton.

George continued, "I'm not up in these things. I'm extremely sceptical as a rule. This was a new experience to me."

"That's just it," said Miss Pinkerton. "Personally, I've been in china for twenty-three years. I recognized the thing immediately."

The reporter scribbled and inquired, "These flying discs appear frequently in China?"

"It was a saucer. I've never seen one flying before," Miss Pinkerton explained.

"I am going to ask a question," George said.

Miss Pinkerton continued, "Mr. Lake is an art framer. He handles old canvases but next to no antiques."

"I am going to ask. Are you telling the story or am I?" George said.

"Perhaps Mr. Lake's account first and then the lady's," the reporter ventured.

Miss Pinkerton subsided crossly while he turned to George.

"Was the object attached to anything? No wires or anything? I mean, someone couldn't have been having a joke or something?"

George gave a decent moment to the possibility.

"No," he then said. "It struck me, in fact, that there was some sort of Mind behind it, operating from outer space. It tried to attack me, in fact."

"Really, how was that?"

"Mr. Lake was not attacked," Miss Pinkerton stated. "There was no danger at all. I saw the expression on the pilot's face. He was having a game with Mr. Lake, grinning all over his face."

"Pilot?" said George. "What are you talking about—pilot!"

Miss Pinkerton sighed. "A tiny man half the size of my finger," she declared. "He sat on a tiny stool. He held the little tiny steering-wheel with one hand and waved with the other. Because, there was something like a sewing-machine fixed near the rim, and he worked the tiny treadle with his foot. Mr. Lake was not attacked."

"Don't be so damn silly," said George.

"You don't mean this?" the reporter asked her with scrutiny.

"Of course I do."

"I would like to know something," George demanded.

"You only saw the under-side of the saucer, George."

"You said nothing about any pilot at the time," said George. "I saw no pilot."

"Mr. Lake got a fright when the saucer came at him. If he hadn't been dodging he would have seen for himself."

"You mentioned no pilot," said George. "Be reasonable."

"I had no chance," said she. She appealed to the camera-man. "You see, I know what I'm talking about. Mr. Lake thought he knew better, however. Mr. Lake said, 'It's a forgery.' If there's one thing I do know, it's china."

"It would be most unlikely," said George to the reporter. "A steering-wheel and a treadle machine these days, can you credit it?"

"The man would have fallen out," the camera-man reflected.

"I must say," said the reporter, "that I favour Mr. Lake's long-range theory. The lady may have been subject to some hallucination, after the shock of the saucer."

"Quite," said George. He whispered something to the photographer. "Women!" Miss Pinkerton heard him breathe.

The reporter heard him also. He gave a friendly laugh. "Shall we continue with Mr. Lake's account, and then see what we can make of both stories?"

But Miss Pinkerton had come to a rapid decision. She began to display a mood hitherto unknown to George. Leaning back, she gave way to a weak and artless giggling. Her hand fluttered prettily as she spoke between gurgles of mirth. "Oh, what a mess! What an evening! We aren't accustomed to drink, you see, and now oh dear, oh dear!"

"Are you all right, Laura?" George inquired severely.

"Yes, yes, yes," said Miss Pinkerton, drowsy and amiable. "We really oughtn't have done this, George. Bringing these gentlemen out. But I can't keep it up, George. Oh dear, it's been fun though."

She was away into her giggles again. George looked bewildered. Then he looked suspicious.

"It's definitely the effect of this extraordinary phenomenon," George said firmly to the Press.

"It was my fault, all my fault," spluttered Miss Pinkerton.

The reporter looked at his watch. "I can quite definitely say you saw a flying object?" he asked. "And that you were both put out by it?"

"Put down that it was a small, round, flattish object. We both agree to that," George said.

A spurt of delight arose from Miss Pinkerton again.

"Women, you know! It always comes down to women in the finish," she told them. "We had a couple of drinks."

"Mr. Lake had rather more than I did," she added triumphantly.

"I assure you," said George to the reporter.

"We might be fined for bringing the Press along, George. It might be an offence," she put in.

"I assure you," George insisted to the photographer, "that we had a flying saucer less than an hour ago in this room."

Miss Pinkerton giggled.

The reporter looked round the room with new eyes; and with the air of one to whom to understand all is to forgive all, he folded his notebook. The camera-man stared at the pool of sherry, the overturned flowers, the broken glass and china. He packed up his camera, and they went away.

George gave out the tale to his regular customers. He gave both versions, appealing to their reason to choose. Farther up the road at her corner shop, Miss Pinkerton smiled tolerantly when questioned. "Flying saucer? George is very artistic," she would say, "and allowances must be made for imaginative folk." Sometimes she added that the evening had been a memorable one, "Quite a party."

It caused a certain amount of tittering in the neighbourhood. George felt this; but otherwise, the affair made no difference between them. Personally, I believe the story, with a preference for Miss Pinkerton's original version. She is a neighbour of mine. I have reason to believe this version because, not long afterwards, I too received a flying visitation from a saucer. The little pilot, in my case, was shy and inquisitive. He pedalled with all his might. My saucer was Royal Worcester, fake or not I can't say.

ROBERT LOUIS STEVENSON

1850–1894

Long before his premature death in Samoa, where he was living because of ill health, he had established a reputation both as an accomplished stylist and master storyteller. His works included not only adventures for children such as *Treasure Island* but also gripping stories for adults such as *Dr. Jekyll and Mr. Hyde*.

The Sire de Malétroit's Door

DENIS DE BEAULIEU was not yet two-and-twenty, but he counted himself a grown man, and a very accomplished cavalier into the bargain. Lads were early formed in that rough, warfaring epoch; and when one has been in a pitched battle and a dozen raids, has killed one's man in an honourable fashion, and knows a thing or two of strategy and mankind, a certain swagger in the gait is surely to be pardoned. He had put up his horse with due care, and supped with due deliberation; and then, in a very agreeable frame of mind, went out to pay a visit in the grey of the evening. It was not a very wise proceeding on the young man's part. He would have done better to remain beside the fire or go decently to bed. For the town was full of the troops of Burgundy and England under a mixed command; and though Denis was there on safe-conduct, his safe-conduct was like to serve him little on a chance encounter.

It was September 1429; the weather had fallen sharp; a flighty piping wind, laden with showers, beat about the township; and the dead leaves ran riot along the streets. Here and there a window was already lighted up; and the noise of men-at-arms making merry over supper within came forth in fits and was swallowed up and carried away by the wind. The night fell swiftly; the flag of England, fluttering on the spire-top, grew ever fainter and fainter against the flying clouds—a black speck like a swallow in the tumultuous, leaden chaos of the sky. As the night fell the wind rose, and began to hoot under archways and roar amid the tree-tops in the valley below the town.

Denis de Beaulieu walked fast and was soon knocking at his friend's door; but though he promised himself to stay only a little while and make an early return, his welcome was so pleasant, and he found so much to delay him, that it was already long past midnight before he said good-bye upon the threshold. The wind had fallen again in the meanwhile; the night was as black as the grave; not a star, nor a glimmer of moonshine, slipped through the canopy of cloud. Denis was ill-acquainted with the intricate lanes of Château Landon; even by daylight he had found some trouble in picking his way; and in this absolute darkness he soon lost it altogether. He was certain of one thing only—to keep mounting the hill; for his friend's house lay at the lower end, or tail, of Château Landon, while the inn was up at the head, under the great church spire.

With this clue to go upon he stumbled and groped forward, now breathing more freely in open places where there was a good slice of sky overhead, now feeling along the wall in stifling closes. It is an eerie and mysterious position to be thus submerged in opaque blackness in an almost unknown town. The silence is terrifying in its possibilities. The touch of cold window bars to the exploring hand startles the man like the touch of a toad; the inequalities of the pavement shake his heart into his mouth; a piece of denser darkness threatens an ambuscade or a chasm in the pathway; and where the air is brighter, the houses put on strange and bewildering appearances, as if to lead him farther from his way. For Denis, who had to regain his inn without attracting notice, there was real danger as well as mere discomfort in the walk; and he went warily and boldly at once, and at every corner paused to make an observation.

He had been for some time threading a lane so narrow that he could touch a wall with either hand, when it began to open out and go sharply downward. Plainly this lay no longer in the direction of his inn; but the hope of a little more light tempted him forward to reconnoitre. The lane ended in a terrace with a bartizan wall, which gave an outlook between high houses, as out of an embrasure, into the valley lying dark and formless several hundred feet below. Denis looked down, and could discern a few tree-tops waving and a single speck of brightness where the river ran across a weir. The weather was clearing up, and the sky had lightened, so as to show the outline of the heavier clouds and the dark margin of the hills. By the uncertain glimmer, the house on his left hand should be a place of some pretensions; it was surmounted by several pinnacles and turret-tops; the round stern of a chapel, with a fringe of flying buttresses, projected boldly from the main block; and the door was sheltered under a deep porch carved with figures and overhung by two long gargoyles. The windows of the chapel gleamed through their intricate tracery with a light as of many tapers, and threw out the buttresses and the peaked roof in a more intense blackness against the sky. It was plainly the hôtel of some great family of the neighbourhood; and as it reminded Denis of a town house of his own at Bourges, he stood for some time gazing up at it and mentally gauging the skill of the architects and the consideration of the two families.

There seemed to be no issue to the terrace but the lane by which he had reached it; he could only retrace his steps, but he had gained some notion of his whereabouts, and hoped by this means to hit the main thoroughfare and speedily regain the inn. He was reckoning without that chapter of accidents which was to make this night memorable above all others in his career; for he had not gone back above a hundred yards before he saw a light coming to meet him, and heard loud voices speaking together in the echoing narrows of the lane. It was a party of men-at-arms going the night round with torches. Denis assured himself that they had all been making free with the wine-bowl, and were in no mood to be particular about safe-conducts or the niceties of chivalrous war. It was as like as not that they would kill him like a dog and leave him where he fell. The situation was inspiriting but nervous. Their own torches would conceal him from sight, he reflected; and he hoped that they would drown the noise of his footsteps with their own empty voices. If he were but fleet and silent, he might evade their notice altogether.

Unfortunately, as he turned to beat a retreat, his foot rolled upon a pebble; he fell against the wall with an ejaculation, and his sword rang loudly on the stones. Two or three voices demanded who went there—some in French, some in English; but Denis made no reply, and ran the faster down the lane. Once upon the terrace, he paused to look back. They still kept calling after him, and just then began to double the pace in pursuit, with a considerable clank of armour, and great tossing of the torchlight to and fro in the narrow jaws of the passage.

Denis cast a look around and darted into the porch. There he might escape observation, or—if that were too much to expect—was in a capital posture whether for parley or defence. So thinking, he drew his sword and tried to set his back against the door. To his surprise, it yielded behind his weight; and though he turned in a moment, continued to swing back on oiled and noiseless hinges, until it stood wide open on a black interior. When things fall out opportunely for the person concerned, he is not apt to be critical about the how or why, his own immediate personal convenience seeming a sufficient reason for the strangest oddities and revolutions in our sublunary things; and so Denis, without a moment's hesitation, stepped within and partly closed the door behind him to conceal his place of refuge. Nothing was further from his thoughts than to close it altogether; but for some inexplicable reason—perhaps by a spring or a weight—the ponderous mass of oak whipped itself out of his fingers and clanked to, with a formidable rumble and a noise like the falling of an automatic bar.

The round, at that very moment, debouched upon the terrace and proceeded to summon him with shouts and curses. He heard them ferreting in the dark corners; and the stock of a lance even rattled along the outer surface of the door behind which he stood; but these gentlemen were in too high a humour to be long delayed, and soon made off down a corkscrew pathway which had escaped Denis's observation, and passed out of sight and hearing along the battlements of the town.

Denis breathed again. He gave them a few minutes' grace for fear of accidents, and then groped about for some means of opening the door and slipping forth again. The inner surface was quite smooth, not a handle, not a moulding, not a projection of any sort. He got his finger-nails round the edges and pulled, but the mass was immovable. He shook it, it was as firm as a rock. Denis de Beaulieu frowned and gave vent to a little noiseless whistle. What ailed the door? he wondered. Why was it open? How came it to shut so easily and so effectually after him? There was something obscure and underhand about all this that was little to the young man's fancy. It looked like a snare; and yet who could suppose a snare in such a quiet by-street and in a house of so prosperous and even noble an exterior? And yet—snare or no snare, intentionally or unintentionally—here he was, prettily trapped; and for the life of him he could see no way out of it again. The darkness began to weigh upon him. He gave ear; all was silent without, but within and close by he seemed to catch a faint sighing, a faint sobbing rustle, a little stealthy creak—as though many persons were at his side, holding themselves quite still, and governing even their respiration with the extreme of slyness.

The idea went to his vitals with a shock, and he faced about suddenly as if to defend his life. Then, for the first time, he became aware of a light about the level of his eyes and at some distance in the interior of the house—a vertical thread of light, widening towards the bottom, such as might escape between two wings of arras over a doorway. To see anything was a relief to Denis; it was like a piece of solid ground to a man labouring in a morass; his mind seized upon it with avidity; and he stood staring at it and trying to piece together some logical conception of his surroundings. Plainly there was a flight of steps ascending from his own level to that of this illuminated doorway; and indeed he thought he could make out another thread of light, as fine as a needle and as faint as phosphorescence, which might very well be reflected along the polished wood of a handrail. Since he had begun to suspect that he was not alone, his heart had continued to beat with smothering violence, and an intolerable desire for action of any sort had possessed itself of his spirit.

He was in deadly peril, he believed. What could be more natural than to mount the staircase, lift the curtain, and confront his difficulty at once? At least he would be dealing with something tangible; at least he would be no longer in the dark. He stepped slowly forward with outstretched hands, until his foot struck the bottom step; then he rapidly scaled the stairs, stood for a moment to compose his expression, lifted the arras and went in.

He found himself in a large apartment of polished stone. There were three doors; one in each of three sides; all similarly curtained with tapestry. The fourth side was occupied by two large windows and a great stone chimney-piece, carved with the arms of the Malétroits. Denis recognized the bearings, and was gratified to find himself in such good hands. The room was strongly illuminated; but it contained little furniture except a heavy table and a chair or two, the hearth was innocent of fire, and the pavement was but sparsely strewn with rushes clearly many days old.

On a high chair beside the chimney, and directly facing Denis as he entered, sat a little old gentleman in a fur tippet. He sat with his legs crossed and his hands folded, and a cup of spiced wine stood by his elbow on a bracket on the wall. His countenance had a strongly masculine cast; not properly human, but such as we see in the bull, the goat, or the domestic boar; something equivocal and wheedling, something greedy, brutal, and dangerous. The upper lip was inordinately full, as though swollen by a blow or a toothache; and the smile, the peaked eyebrows, and the small, strong eyes were quaintly and almost comically evil in expression. Beautiful white hair hung straight all round his head, like a saint's, and fell in a single curl upon the tippet. His beard and moustache were the pink of venerable sweetness. Age, probably in consequence of inordinate precautions, had left no mark upon his hands; and the Malétroit hand was famous. It would be difficult to imagine anything at once so fleshy and so delicate in design; the taper, sensual fingers were like those of one of Leonardo's women; the fork of the thumb made a dimpled protuberance when closed; the nails were perfectly shaped, and of a dead, surprising whiteness. It rendered his aspect tenfold more redoubtable, that a man with hands like these should keep them devoutly folded in his lap like a virgin martyr—that a man with so intense and startling an expression of face should sit patiently on his seat and contemplate people with an unwinking stare, like a god, or a god's statue. His quiescence seemed ironical and treacherous, it fitted so poorly with his looks.

Such was Alain, Sire de Malétroit.

Denis and he looked silently at each other for a second or two.

"Pray step in," said the Sire de Malétroit. "I have been expecting you all the evening."

He had not risen, but he accompanied his words with a smile, and a slight but courteous inclination of the head. Partly from the smile, partly from the strange musical murmur with which the Sire prefaced his observation, Denis felt a strong shudder of disgust go through his marrow. And what with disgust and honest confusion of mind, he could scarcely get words together in reply.

"I fear," he said, "that this is a double accident. I am not the person you suppose me. It seems you were looking for a visit; but for my part, nothing was further from my thoughts—nothing could be more contrary to my wishes—than this intrusion."

"Well, well," replied the old gentleman indulgently, "here you are, which is the main point. Seat yourself, my friend, and put yourself entirely at your ease. We shall arrange our little affairs presently."

Denis perceived that the matter was still complicated with some misconception, and he hastened to continue his explanations.

"Your door . . ." he began.

"About my door?" asked the other, raising his peaked eyebrows. "A little piece of ingenuity." And he shrugged his shoulders. "A hospitable fancy! By your own account, you were not desirous of making my acquaintance. We old people look for such reluctance now and then; and when it touches our honour, we cast about until we find some way of overcoming it. You arrive uninvited, but believe me, very welcome."

"You persist in error, sir," said Denis. "There can be no question between you and me. I am a stranger in this country-side. My name is Denis, damoiseau de Beaulieu. If you see me in your house, it is only——"

"My young friend," interrupted the other, "you will permit me to have my own ideas on that subject. They probably differ from yours at the present moment," he added with a leer, "but time will show which of us is in the right."

Denis was convinced he had to do with a lunatic. He seated himself with a shrug, content to wait the upshot; and a pause ensued, during which he thought he could distinguish a hurried gabbling as of prayer from behind the arras immediately opposite him. Sometimes there seemed to be but one person engaged, sometimes two; and the vehemence of the voice, low as it was, seemed to indicate either great haste or an agony of spirit. It occurred to him that this piece of tapestry covered the entrance to the chapel he had noticed from without.

The old gentleman meanwhile surveyed Denis from head to foot with a smile, and from time to time emitted little noises like a bird or a mouse, which seemed to indicate a high degree of satisfaction. This state of matters became rapidly insupportable; and Denis, to put an end to it, remarked politely that the wind had gone down.

The old gentleman fell into a fit of silent laughter, so prolonged and violent that he became quite red in the face. Denis got upon his feet at once, and put on his hat with a flourish.

"Sir," he said, "if you are in your wits, you have affronted me grossly. If you are out of them, I flatter myself I can find better employment for my brains than to talk with lunatics. My conscience is clear; you have made a fool of me from the first moment; you have refused to hear my explanations; and now there is no power under God will make me stay here any longer; and if I cannot make my way out in a more decent fashion, I will hack your door in pieces with my sword."

The Sire de Malétroit raised his right hand and wagged it at Denis with the fore and little fingers extended.

"My dear nephew," he said, "sit down."

"Nephew!" retorted Denis, "you lie in your throat"; and he snapped his fingers in his face.

"Sit down, you rogue!" cried the old gentleman, in a sudden, harsh voice, like the barking of a dog. "Do you fancy," he went on, "that when I had made my little contrivance for the door I had stopped short with that? If you prefer to be bound hand and foot till your bones ache, rise and try to go away. If you choose to remain a free young buck, agreeably conversing with an old gentleman—why, sit where you are in peace, and God be with you."

"Do you mean I am a prisoner?" demanded Denis.

"I state the facts," replied the other. "I would rather leave the conclusion to yourself."

Denis sat down again. Externally he managed to keep pretty calm; but within, he was now boiling with anger, now chilled with apprehension. He no longer felt convinced that he was dealing with a madman. And if the old gentleman was sane, what, in God's name, had he to look for? What absurd or tragical adventure had befallen him? What countenance was he to assume?

While he was thus unpleasantly reflecting, the arras that overhung the chapel door was raised, and a tall priest in his robes came forth and, giving a long, keen stare at Denis, said something in an undertone to Sire de Malétroit.

"She is in a better frame of spirit?" asked the latter.

"She is more resigned, messire," replied the priest.

"Now the Lord help her, she is hard to please!" sneered the old gentleman. "A likely stripling—not ill-born—and of her own choosing, too? Why, what more would the jade have?"

"The situation is not usual for a young damsel," said the other, "and somewhat trying to her blushes."

"She should have thought of that before she began the dance? It was none of my choosing, God knows that: but since she is in it, by our Lady, she shall carry it to the end." And then addressing Denis, "Monsieur de Beaulieu," he asked, "may I present you to my niece? She has been waiting your arrival, I may say, with even greater impatience than myself."

Denis had resigned himself with a good grace—all he desired was to know the worst of it as speedily as possible; so he rose at once, and bowed in acquiescence. The Sire de Malétroit followed his example and limped, with the assistance of the chaplain's arm, towards the chapel door. The priest pulled aside the arras, and all three entered. The building had considerable architectural pretensions. A light groining sprang from six stout columns, and hung down in two rich pendants from the centre of the vault. The place terminated behind the altar in a round end, embossed and honeycombed with a superfluity of ornament in relief, and pierced by many little windows shaped like stars, trefoils, or wheels. These windows were imperfectly glazed, so that the night air circulated freely in the chapel. The tapers, of which there must have been half a hundred burning on the altar, were unmercifully blown about; and the light went through many different phases of brilliancy and semi-eclipse. On the steps in front of the altar knelt a young girl richly attired as a bride. A chill settled over Denis as he observed her costume; he fought with desperate energy against the conclusion that was being thrust upon his mind; it could not—it should not—be as he feared.

"Blanche," said the Sire, in his most flute-like tones, "I have brought a friend to see you, my little girl; turn round and give him your pretty hand. It is good to be devout; but it is necessary to be polite, my niece."

The girl rose to her feet and turned towards the newcomers. She moved all of a piece; and shame and exhaustion were expressed in every line of her fresh young body; and she held her head down and kept her eyes upon the pavement, as she came slowly forward. In the course of her advance, her eyes fell upon Denis de Beaulieu's feet—feet of which he was justly vain, be it remarked, and wore in the most elegant accoutrement even while travelling. She paused—started, as if his yellow boots had conveyed some shocking meaning—and glanced suddenly up into the wearer's countenance. Their eyes met; shame gave place to horror and terror in her looks; the blood left her lips; with a piercing scream she covered her face with her hands and sank upon the chapel floor.

"That is not the man!" she cried. "My uncle; that is not the man!"

The Sire de Malétroit chirped agreeably. "Of course not," he said, "I expected as much. It was so unfortunate you could not remember his name."

"Indeed," she cried, "indeed, I have never seen this person till this moment—I have never so much as set eyes upon him—I never wish to see him again. Sir," she said, turning to Denis, "if you are a gentleman, you will bear me out. Have I ever seen you—have you ever seen me—before this accursed hour?"

"To speak for myself, I have never had that pleasure," answered the young man. "This is the first time, messire, that I have met with your engaging niece."

The old gentleman shrugged his shoulders.

"I am distressed to hear it," he said. "But it is never too late to begin. I had little more acquaintance with my own late lady ere I married her; which proves," he added with a grimace, "that these impromptu marriages may often produce an excellent understanding in the long-run. As the bridegroom is to have a voice in the matter, I will give him two hours to make up for lost time before we proceed with the ceremony." And he turned towards the door, followed by the clergyman.

The girl was on her feet in a moment. "My uncle, you cannot be in earnest," she said. "I declare before God I will stab myself rather than be forced on that young man. The heart rises at it; God forbids such marriages; you dishonour your white hair. Oh, my uncle, pity me! There is not a woman in all the world but would prefer death to such a nuptial. Is it possible," she added, faltering—"is it possible that you do not believe me—that you still think this"—and she pointed at Denis with a tremor of anger and contempt—"that you still think *this* to be the man?"

"Frankly," said the old gentleman, pausing on the threshold, "I do. But let me explain to you once for all, Blanche de Malétroit, my way of thinking about this affair. When you took it into your head to dishonour my family and the name that I have borne, in peace and war, for more than threescore years, you forfeited, not only the right to question my designs, but that of looking me in the face. If your father had been alive, he would have spat on you and turned you out of doors. His was the hand of iron. You may bless your God you have only to deal with the hand of velvet, mademoiselle. It was my duty to get you married without delay. Out of pure goodwill, I have tried to find your own gallant for you. And I believe I have succeeded. But before God and all the holy angels, Blanche de Malétroit, if I have not, I care not one jack-straw.

So let me recommend you to be polite to our young friend; for upon my word, your next groom may be less appetizing."

And with that he went out, with the chaplain at his heels; and the arras fell behind the pair.

The girl turned upon Denis with flashing eyes.

"And what, sir," she demanded, "may be the meaning of all this?"

"God knows," returned Denis gloomily. "I am a prisoner in this house, which seems full of mad people. More I know not; and nothing do I understand."

"And pray how came you here?" she asked.

He told her as briefly as he could. "For the rest," he added, "perhaps you will follow my example, and tell me the answer to all these riddles, and what, in God's name, is like to be the end of it."

She stood silent for a little, and he could see her lips tremble and her tearless eyes burn with a feverish lustre. Then she pressed her forehead in both hands.

"Alas, how my head aches!" she said wearily—"to say nothing of my poor heart! But it is due to you to know my story, unmaidenly as it must seem. I am called Blanche de Malétroit: I have been without father or mother for—oh! for as long as I can recollect, and indeed I have been most unhappy all my life. Three months ago a young captain began to stand near me every day in church. I could see that I pleased him; I am much to blame, but I was so glad that any one should love me; and when he passed me a letter, I took it home with me and read it with great pleasure. Since that time he has written many. He was so anxious to speak with me, poor fellow! and kept asking me to leave the door open some evening that we might have two words upon the stair. For he knew how much my uncle trusted me." She gave something like a sob at that, and it was a moment before she could go on. "My uncle is a hard man, but he is very shrewd," she said at last. "He has performed many feats in war, and was a great person at court, and much trusted by Queen Isabeau in old days. How he came to suspect me I cannot tell; but it is hard to keep anything from his knowledge; and this morning, as we came from mass, he took my hand in his, forced it open, and read my little billet, walking by my side all the while. When he had finished, he gave it back to me with great politeness. It contained another request to have the door left open; and this has been the ruin of us all. My uncle kept me strictly in my room until evening, and then ordered me to dress myself as you see me—a hard mockery for a young girl; do you not think so? I suppose, when he could not prevail with me to tell him the young captain's name, he must have laid a trap for him: into which, alas! you have fallen in the anger of God. I looked for much confusion; for how could I tell whether he was willing to take me for his wife on these sharp terms? He might have been trifling with me from the first; or I might have made myself too cheap in his eyes. But truly I had not looked for such a shameful punishment as this! I could not think that God would let a girl be so disgraced before a young man. And now I have told you all; and I can scarcely hope that you will not despise me."

Denis made her a respectful inclination.

"Madam," he said, "you have honoured me by your confidence. It remains for me to prove that I am not unworthy of the honour. Is Messire de Malétroit at hand?"

"I believe he is writing in the salle without," she answered.

"May I lead you thither, madam?" asked Denis, offering his hand with his most courtly bearing.

She accepted it; and the pair passed out of the chapel, Blanche in a very drooping and shamefast condition, but Denis strutting and ruffling in the consciousness of a mission, and the boyish certainty of accomplishing it with honour.

The Sire de Malétroit rose to meet them with an ironical obeisance.

"Sir," said Denis, with the grandest possible air, "I believe I am to have some say in the matter of this marriage; and let me tell you at once, I will be no party to forcing the inclination of this young lady. Had it been freely offered to me, I should have been proud to accept her hand, for I perceive she is as good as she is beautiful; but as things are, I have now the honour, messire, of refusing."

Blanche looked at him with gratitude in her eyes; but the old gentleman only smiled and smiled, until his smile grew positively sickening to Denis.

"I am afraid," he said, "Monsieur de Beaulieu, that you do not perfectly understand the choice I have to offer you. Follow me, I beseech you, to this window." And he led the way to one of the large windows which stood open on the night. "You observe," he went on, "there is an iron ring in the upper masonry, and reeved through that a very efficacious rope. Now, mark my words; if you should find your disinclination to my niece's person insurmountable, I shall have you hanged out of this window before sunrise. I shall only proceed to such an extremity with the greatest regret, you may believe me. For it is not at all your death that I desire, but my niece's establishment in life. At the same time, it must come to that if you prove obstinate. Your family, Monsieur de Beaulieu, is very well in its way; but if you sprang from Charlemagne, you should not refuse the hand of a Malétroit with impunity—not if she had been as common as the Paris road—not if she were as hideous as the gargoyle over my door. Neither my niece nor you, nor my own private feelings, move me at all in this matter. The honour of my house has been compromised; I believe you to be the guilty person; at least you are now in the secret; and you can hardly wonder if I request you to wipe out the stain. If you will not, your blood be on your own head! It will be no great satisfaction to me to have your interesting relics kicking their heels in the breeze below my windows; but half a loaf is better than no bread, and if I cannot cure the dishonour, I shall at least stop the scandal."

There was a pause.

"I believe there are other ways of settling such imbroglios among gentlemen," said Denis. "You wear a sword, and I hear you have used it with distinction."

The Sire de Malétroit made a signal to the chaplain, who crossed the room with long silent strides and raised the arras over the third of the three doors. It was only a moment before he let it fall again; but Denis had time to see a dusky passage full of armed men.

"When I was a little younger, I should have been delighted to honour you, Monsieur de Beaulieu," said Sire Alain; "but I am now too old. Faithful retainers are the sinews of age, and I must employ the strength I have. This is one of the hardest things to swallow as a man grows up in years; but with a little patience, even this becomes habitual. You and the lady seem to prefer the salle for what remains of your two hours; and as I have no desire to cross your preference, I shall resign it to your use with all the pleasure in the world. No haste!" he added, holding up his hand, as he saw a dangerous look come into Denis de Beaulieu's face. "If your mind revolts against hanging, it will be time enough two hours hence to throw yourself out of the window or upon the pikes of my retainers. Two hours of life are always two hours. A great many things may turn up in even as little a while as that. And, besides, if I understand her appearance, my niece has still something to say to you. You will not disfigure your last hours by a want of politeness to a lady?"

Denis looked at Blanche, and she made him an imploring gesture.

It is likely that the old gentleman was hugely pleased at this symptom of an understanding; for he smiled on both, and added sweetly: "If you will give me your word of honour, Monsieur de Beaulieu, to await my return at the end of the two hours before attempting anything desperate, I shall withdraw my retainers, and let you speak in greater privacy with mademoiselle."

Denis again glanced at the girl, who seemed to beseech him to agree.

"I give you my word of honour," he said.

Messire de Malétroit bowed, and proceeded to limp about the apartment, clearing his throat the while with that odd musical chirp which had already grown so irritating in the ears of Denis de Beaulieu. He first possessed himself of some papers which lay upon the table; then he went to the mouth of the passage and appeared to give an order to the men behind the arras; and lastly, he hobbled out through the door by which Denis had come in, turning upon the threshold to address a last smiling bow to the young couple, and followed by the chaplain with a hand-lamp.

No sooner were they alone than Blanche advanced towards Denis with her hands extended. Her face was flushed and excited, and her eyes shone with tears.

"You shall not die!" she cried, "you shall marry me after all."

"You seem to think, madam," replied Denis, "that I stand much in fear of death."

"Oh no, no," she said, "I see you are no poltroon. It is for my own sake—I could not bear to have you slain for such a scruple."

"I am afraid," returned Denis, "that you underrate the difficulty, madam. What you may be too generous to refuse, I may be too proud to accept. In a moment of noble feeling towards me, you forgot what you perhaps owe to others."

He had the decency to keep his eyes upon the floor as he said this, and after he had finished, so as not to spy upon her confusion. She stood silent for a moment, then walked suddenly away, and falling on her uncle's chair, fairly burst out sobbing. Denis was in the acme of embarrassment. He looked round, as if to seek for inspiration, and seeing a stool, plumped down upon it for something to do. There he sat, playing with the guard of his rapier, and wishing himself dead a thousand times over, and buried in the nastiest kitchen-heap in France. His eyes wandered round the apartment, but found nothing to arrest them. There were such wide spaces between the furniture, the light fell so baldly and cheerlessly over all, the dark outside air looked in so coldly through the windows, that he thought he had never seen a church so vast, nor a tomb so melancholy. The regular sobs of Blanche de Malétroit measured out the time like the ticking of a clock. He read the device upon the shield over and over again, until his eyes became obscured; he stared into shadowy corners until he imagined they were swarming with horrible animals; and every now and again he awoke with a start, to remember that his last two hours were running, and death was on the march.

Oftener and oftener, as the time went on, did his glance settle on the girl herself. Her face was bowed forward and covered with her hands, and she was shaken at intervals by the convulsive hiccup of grief. Even thus she was not an unpleasant object to dwell upon, so plump and yet so fine, with a warm brown skin, and the most beautiful hair, Denis thought, in the whole world of womankind. Her hands were like her uncle's; but they were more in place at the end of her young arms, and looked infinitely soft and caressing. He remembered how her blue eyes had shone upon him, full of anger, pity, and innocence. And the more he dwelt on her perfections, the uglier death looked, and the more deeply was he smitten with penitence at her continued tears. Now he felt that no man could have the courage to leave a world which contained so beautiful a creature; and now he would have given forty minutes of his last hour to unsay his cruel speech.

Suddenly a hoarse and ragged peal of cockcrow rose to their ears from the dark valley below the windows. And this shattering noise in the silence of all around was like a light in a dark place, and shook them both out of their reflections.

"Alas, can I do nothing to help you?" she said, looking up.

"Madam," replied Denis, with a fine irrelevancy, "if I have said anything to wound you, believe me, it was for your own sake and not for mine."

She thanked him with a tearful look.

"I feel your position cruelly," he went on. "The world has been bitter hard on you. Your uncle is a disgrace to mankind. Believe me, madam, there is no young gentleman in all France but would be glad of my opportunity, to die in doing you a momentary service."

"I know already that you can be very brave and generous," she answered. "What I *want* to know is whether I can serve you—now or afterwards," she added, with a quaver.

"Most certainly," he answered with a smile. "Let me sit beside you as if I were a friend, instead of a foolish intruder; try to forget how awkwardly we are placed to one another; make my last moments go pleasantly; and you will do me the chief service possible."

"You are very gallant," she added, with a yet deeper sadness . . . "very gallant . . . and it somehow pains me. But draw nearer, if you please; and if you find anything to say to me, you will at least make certain of a very friendly listener. Ah! Monsieur de Beaulieu," she broke forth—"ah! Monsieur de Beaulieu, how can I look you in the face?" And she fell to weeping again with a renewed effusion.

"Madam," said Denis, taking her hand in both of his, "reflect on the little time I have before me, and the great bitterness into which I am cast by the sight of your distress. Spare me, in my last moments, the spectacle of what I cannot cure even with the sacrifice of my life."

"I am very selfish," answered Blanche. "I will be braver, Monsieur de Beaulieu, for your sake. But think if I can do you no kindness in the future—if you have no friends to whom I could carry your adieux. Charge me as heavily as you can; every burden will lighten, by so little, the invaluable gratitude I owe you. Put it in my power to do something more for you than weep."

"My mother is married again, and has a young family to care for. My brother Guichard will inherit my fiefs; and if I am not in error, that will content him amply for my death. Life is a little vapour that passeth away, as we are told by those in holy orders. When a man is in a fair way and sees all life open in front of him, he seems to himself to make a very important figure in the world. His horse whinnies to him; the trumpets blow and the girls look out of window as he rides into town before his company; he receives many assurances of trust and regard—sometimes by express in a letter—sometimes face to face, with persons of great consequence falling on his neck. It is not wonderful if his head is turned for a time. But once he is dead, were he as brave as Hercules or as wise as Solomon, he is soon forgotten. It is not ten years since my father fell, with many other knights around him, in a very fierce encounter, and I do not think that any one of them, nor so much as the name of the fight, is now remembered. No, no, madam, the nearer you come to it, you see that death is a dark and dusty corner, where a man gets into his tomb and has the door shut after him till the Judgement Day. I have few friends just now, and once I am dead I shall have none."

"Ah, Monsieur de Beaulieu!" she exclaimed, "you forget Blanche de Malétroit."

"You have a sweet nature, madam, and you are pleased to estimate a little service far beyond its worth."

"It is not that," she answered. "You mistake me if you think I am so easily touched by my own concerns. I say so, because you are the noblest man I have ever met; because I recognize in you a spirit that would have made even a common person famous in the land."

"And yet here I die in a mousetrap—with no more noise about it than my own squeaking," answered he.

A look of pain crossed her face, and she was silent for a little while. Then a light came into her eyes, and with a smile she spoke again.

"I cannot have my champion think meanly of himself. Any one who gives his life for another will be met in Paradise by all the heralds and angels of the Lord God. And you have no such cause to hang your head. For . . . Pray, do you think me beautiful?" she asked, with a deep flush.

"Indeed, madam, I do," he said.

"I am glad of that," she answered heartily. "Do you think there are many men in France who have been asked in marriage by a beautiful maiden—with her own lips—and who have refused her to her face? I know you men would half despise such a triumph; but believe me, we women know more of what is precious in love. There is nothing that should set a person higher in his own esteem; and we women would prize nothing more dearly."

"You are very good," he said; "but you cannot make me forget that I was asked in pity and not for love."

"I am not so sure of that," she replied, holding down her head. "Hear me to an end, Monsieur de Beaulieu. I know how you must despise me; I feel you are right to do so; I am too poor a creature to occupy one thought of your mind, although, alas! you must die for me this morning. But when I asked you to marry me, indeed, and indeed, it was because I respected and admired you, and loved you with my whole soul, from the very moment that you took my part against my uncle. If you had seen yourself, and how noble you looked, you would pity rather than despise me. And now," she went on, hurriedly checking him with her hand, "although I have laid aside all reserve and told you so much, remember that I know your sentiments towards me already. I would not, believe me, being nobly born, weary you with importunities into consent. I too have a pride of my own: and I declare before the holy mother of God, if you should now go back from your word already given, I would no more marry you than I would marry my uncle's groom."

Denis smiled a little bitterly.

"It is a small love," he said, "that shies at a little pride."

She made no answer, although she probably had her own thoughts.

"Come hither to the window," he said, with a sigh. "Here is the dawn."

And indeed the dawn was already beginning. The hollow of the sky was full of essential daylight, colourless and clean; and the valley underneath was flooded with a grey reflection. A few thin vapours clung in the coves of the forest or lay along the winding course of the river. The scene disengaged a surprising effect of stillness, which was hardly interrupted when the cocks began once more to crow among the steadings. Perhaps the same fellow who had made so horrid a clangour in the darkness not half an hour before, now sent up the merriest cheer to greet the coming day. A little wind went bustling and eddying among the treetops underneath the windows. And still the daylight kept flooding insensibly out of the east, which was soon to grow incandescent and cast up that red-hot cannon-ball, the rising sun.

Denis looked out over all this with a bit of a shiver. He had taken her hand and retained it in his almost unconsciously.

"Has the day begun already?" she said; and then, illogically enough: "the night has been so long! Alas! what shall we say to my uncle when he returns?"

"What you will," said Denis, and he pressed her fingers in his.

She was silent.

"Blanche," he said, with a swift, uncertain, passionate utterance, "you have seen whether I fear death. You must know well enough that I would as gladly leap out of that window into the empty air as lay a finger on you without your free and full consent. But if you care for me at all, do not let me lose my life in a misapprehension; for I love you better than the whole world; and though I will die for you blithely, it would be like all the joys of Paradise to live on and spend my life in your service."

As he stopped speaking, a bell began to ring loudly in the interior of the house; and a clatter of armour in the corridor showed that the retainers were returning to their post, and the two hours were at an end.

"After all that you have heard?" she whispered, leaning towards him with her lips and eyes.

"I have heard nothing," he replied.

"The captain's name was Florimond de Champdivers," she said in his ear.

"I did not hear it," he answered, taking her supple body in his arms, and covered her wet face with kisses.

A melodious chirping was audible behind, followed by a beautiful chuckle, and the voice of Messire de Malétroit wished his new nephew a good morning.

ELIZABETH TAYLOR

1912–1975

Her work is renowned for its acute perception, coupled with an unusual blend of warmth and astringency. She began writing at school, but was thirty before anything was published. A tutor and librarian before her marriage, she is at her very best when writing about children.

In and Out the Houses

KITTY MILLER, wearing a new red hair-ribbon, bounced along the Vicarage drive, skipping across ruts and jumping over puddles.

Visiting took up all of her mornings in the school holidays. From kitchen to kitchen; round the village, she made her progress, and, this morning, felt drawn towards the Vicarage. Quite sure of her welcome, she tapped on the back door.

"Why, Kitty Miller!" said the Vicar, opening it. He looked quite different from in church Kitty thought. He was wearing an open-necked shirt and an old, darned cardigan. He held a tea-towel to the door-handle, because his fingers were sticky. He and his wife were cutting up Seville oranges for marmalade and there was a delicious, tangy smell about the kitchen.

Kitty took off her coat, and hung it on the usual peg, and fetched a knife from the dresser drawer.

"You are on your rounds again," Mr. Edwards said. "Spreading light and succour about the parish."

Kitty glanced at him rather warily. She preferred him not to be there, disliking men about her kitchens. She reached for an orange, and watching Mrs. Edwards for a moment out of the corners of her eyes, began to slice it up.

"What's new?" asked the Vicar.

"Mrs. Saddler's bad," she said accusingly. He should be at that bedside, she meant to imply, instead of making marmalade. "They were saying at The Horse and Groom that she won't last the day."

"So we are not your first call of the morning?"

She had, on her way here, slipped round the back of the pub and into the still-room, where Miss Betty Benford, eight months pregnant, was washing the floor, puffing and blowing as she splashed grey soapy water over the flags with a gritty rag. When this job was done—to Miss Betty's mind, not Kitty's—they drank a cup of tea together and chatted about the baby, woman to woman. The village was short of babies, and Kitty visualised pushing this one out in its pram, taking it round with her on her visits.

In his office, the landlord had been typing the luncheon menus. The keys went down heavily, his finger hovered, and stabbed. He often made mistakes, and this morning had typed 'Jam Fart and Custard'. Kitty considered—and then decided against—telling the Vicar this.

"They have steak-and-kidney pie on the set menu today," she said instead.

"My favourite!" groaned the Vicar. "I *never* get it."

"You had it less than a fortnight ago," his wife reminded him.

"And what pudding? If it's treacle tart I shall cry bitterly."

"Jam tart," Kitty said gravely. "And custard."

"I quite like custard, too," he said simply.

"Or choice of cheese and biscuits."

"I should have cheese and biscuits," Mrs. Edwards said.

It was just the kind of conversation Kitty loved.

"Eight-and-sixpence," she said. "Coffee extra."

"To be rich! To be rich!" the Vicar said. "And what are *we* having my dear? Kitty has caused the juices to run."

"Cold, of course, as it's Monday."

He shuddered theatrically, and picked up another orange. "My day off, too!"

Kitty pressed her lips together primly, thinking it wrong for clergymen to have days off, especially with Mrs. Saddler lying there, dying.

The three of them kept glancing at one another's work as they cut the oranges. Who was doing it finely enough? Only Mrs. Edwards, they all knew.

"I like it fairly chunky," the Vicar said.

When it was all done, Kitty rinsed her hands at the sink, and then put on her coat. She had given the Vicarage what time she could spare, and the morning was getting on, and all the rest of the village waiting. She was very orderly in her habits and never visited in the afternoons, for then she had her novel to write. The novel was known about in the village, and some people felt concerned, wondering if she might be another little Daisy Ashford.

With the Vicar's phrases of gratitude giving her momentum, Kitty tacked down the drive between the shabby laurels, and out into the lane.

"THE VICAR'S having cold," she told Mrs. De Vries, who was preparing tajine of chicken in a curious earthenware pot she had brought back from Morocco.

"Poor old Vicar," Mrs. De Vries said absent-mindedly, as she cut almonds into slivers. She had a glass of something on the draining-board and often took a sip from it. "Do run and find a drink for yourself, dear child," she said. She was one of the people who wondered about Daisy Ashford.

"I'll have a bitter lemon, if I may," Kitty said.

"Well, do, my dear. You know where to find it."

As Kitty knew everything about nearly every house in the village, she did not reply; but went with assurance to the bar in the hall. She stuck a plastic straw in her drink, and returned to the kitchen sucking peacefully.

"Is there anything I can do?" she enquired.

"No, just tell me the news. What's going on?"

"Mr. Mumford typed 'Jam Fart and Custard' on the menu card."

"Oh, he didn't! You've made me do the nose-trick with my gin. The *pain* of it!" Mrs. De Vries snatched a handkerchief from her apron pocket and held it to her face. When she had recovered, she said, "I simply can't wait for Tom to come home, to tell him that."

Kitty looked modestly gratified. "I called at the Vicarage, too, on my way."

"And what were *they* up to?"

"They are up to making marmalade."

"Poor darlings! They *do* have to scrimp and scratch. Church mice, indeed!"

"But isn't home-made marmalade nicer than shop?"

"Not all *that* much."

After a pause, Kitty said, "Mrs. Saddler's on her way out."

"Who the hell's Mrs. Saddler?"

"At the alms-house. She's dying."

"Poor old thing."

Kitty sat down on a stool and swung her fat legs.

"Betty Benford is eight months gone," she said shrugging her shoulders.

"I wish you'd tell me something about people I *know*," Mrs. De Vries complained, taking another sip of gin.

"Her mother plans to look after the baby while Betty goes on going out to work. Mrs. Benford, you know."

"Not next door's daily?"

"She won't be after this month."

"Does Mrs. Glazier know?" Mrs. De Vries asked, inclining her head towards next door.

"Not yet," Kitty said, glancing at the clock.

"My God, she'll go up the wall," Mrs. De Vries said with relish. "She's had that old Benford for years and years."

"What do you call that you're cooking?"

"It's a tajine of chicken."

"MRS. DE VRIES is having tajine of chicken," Kitty said next door five minutes later.

"And what might that be when it's at home?"

Kitty described it as best she could, and Mrs. Glazier looked huffy. "Derek wouldn't touch it," she said. "He likes good, plain, English food, and no messing about."

She was rolling out pastry for that evening's steak-and-kidney pie.

"They're having that at The Horse and Groom," Kitty said.

"*And* we'll have sprouts. *And* braised celery," Mrs. Glazier added, not letting Mrs. De Vries get away with her airs and graces.

"Shall I make a pastry rose to go on the top of the pie?" Kitty offered. "Mrs. Prout showed me how to."

"No, I think we'll leave well alone."

"Do you like cooking?" Kitty asked in a conversational tone.

"I don't mind it. Why?"

"I was only thinking that then it wouldn't be so hard on you when Mrs. Benford leaves."

Mrs. Benford was upstairs. There was a bumping, droning noise of a vacuum cleaner above, in what Kitty knew to be Mrs. Glazier's bedroom.

Mrs. Glazier, with an awful fear in her heart, stared, frowning, at Kitty, who went on, "I was just telling Mrs. De Vries that after Mrs. Benford's grandchild's born she's going to stay at home to mind it."

The fact that next door had heard this stunning news first made the blow worse, and Mrs. Glazier put a flour-covered hand to her forehead. She closed her eyes for a moment. "But why can't the girl look after the little— baby herself?"

Kitty took the lid off a jar marked 'Cloves' and looked inside, sniffing. "Her daughter earns more money at The Horse and Groom than her mother earns here," she explained.

"I suppose you told Mrs. De Vries that too."

Kitty went to the door with dignity. "Oh, no! I never talk from house to house. My mother says I'll have to stop my visiting, if I do. Oh, by the way," she called back, "you'd better keep your dog in. The De Vries's bitch is on heat."

She went home and sat down to lamb and bubble-and-squeak.

"The Vicar's having cold, too," she said.

"And that's *his* business," her mother said warningly.

A FEW DAYS later, Kitty called on Mrs. Prout.

Mrs. Prout's cottage was one of Kitty's favourite visits. Many years ago, before she was married, Mrs. Prout had been a school-teacher, and she enjoyed using her old skills to deal with Kitty. Keeping her patience pliant, she taught her visitor new card games (and they were all educational), and got on to collecting and pressing wild-flowers. She would give her pastry-trimmings to cut into shapes, and showed her how to pop corn and make fudge. She was extremely kind, though firm, and Kitty respected the rules—about taking off her Wellingtons and washing her hands and never calling on Mondays or Thursdays, because these were turning-out days when Mrs. Prout was far too busy to have company.

They were very serious together. Mrs. Prout enjoyed being authoritative to a child again, and Kitty had a sense of orderliness which obliged her to comply.

"They sent this from the Vicarage," she said, coming into the kitchen with a small pot of marmalade.

"How jolly nice!" Mrs. Prout said. She took the marmalade, and tilted it slightly, and it moved. Rather sloppy. But she thought no worse of the Vicar's wife for that. "That's really *jolly* nice of them," she said, going into the larder. "And they shall have some of my apple jelly, in fair return. *Quid pro quo,* eh? and one good turn deserves another."

She came out of the larder with a different little pot and held it to the light; but the clear and golden content did not move when she tipped it sideways.

"What's the news?" she asked.

"Mrs. Saddler still lingers on," Kitty said. She had called at the alms-houses to enquire, but the district nurse had told her to run off and mind her own business. "I looked in at the Wilson's on my way here. Mrs. Wilson was making a cheese and onion pie. Of course, they're vegetarians; but I have known him to sneak a little chicken into his mouth. I was helping to hand round at the De Vries's cocktail-party, and he put out his hand towards a patty. 'It's chicken,' I said to him in a low voice. 'Nary a word,' he said, and he winked at me and ate it."

"And now you *have* said a word," Mrs. Prout said briskly.

"Why, so I have," Kitty agreed, looking astonished.

Mrs. Prout cleared the kitchen table in the same brisk way, and said, "If you like, now, I'll show you how to make ravioli. We shall have it for our television supper."

"Make ravioli," cried Kitty. "You can't *make* ravioli. Mrs. Glazier buys it in a tin."

"So Mrs. Glazier may. But I find time to make my own."

"I shall be fascinated," Kitty said, taking off her coat.

"Then wash your hands, and don't forget to dry them properly. Isn't it about time you cut your nails?" Mrs. Prout asked, in her schoolmistressy voice, and Kitty, who would take anything from her, agreed. ("We all know Mrs. Prout is God," her mother sometimes said resentfully).

"Roll up those sleeves, now. And we'll go through your tables while we work."

Mrs. Prout set out the flour bin and a dredger and a pastry-cutter and the mincer. Going back and forth to the cupboard, she thought how petty she was to be pleased at knowing that by this time tomorrow, most of the village would be aware that she made her own ravioli. But perhaps it was only human, she decided. "Now this is what chefs call the *mise en place*," she explained to Kitty, when she had finished arranging the table. "Can you remember that? *Mise en place*."

"*Mise en place*," Kitty repeated obediently.

"SHALL I HELP you prepare the *mise en place*?" Kitty enquired of Mrs. Glazier.

"Mr. Glazier wouldn't touch it. I've told you he will only eat English food."

"But you have ravioli. That's Italian."

"I just keep it as a stand by," Mrs. Glazier said scornfully. She was very huffy and put out these days, especially with Mrs. De Vries next door and her getting the better of her every time. Annette de Vries was French, and didn't they all know it. Mrs. Glazier, as a result, had become violently insular.

"I can make ravioli," Kitty said, letting the *mise en place* go, for she was not absolutely certain about it. "Mrs. Prout has just been teaching me. She and Mr. Prout have television trays by the fire, and then they sit and crack walnuts and play cards, and then they have hot milk and whisky and go to bed. I think it is very nice and cosy, don't you?"

"Mr. Glazier likes a proper sit-down meal when *he* gets back. Did you happen to see Tiger anywhere down the lane?"

"No, but I expect he's next door. I told you their bitch is on heat. You ought to shut him up."

"It's their affair to shut *theirs* up."

"Well, I'm just calling there, so I'll shoo him off."

She had decided to cut short this visit. Mrs. Glazier was so bad-tempered these days, and hardly put herself out at all to give a welcome, and every interesting thing Kitty told her served merely to annoy.

"And I must get on with my jugged hare," Mrs. Glazier said, making no attempt to delay the departure. "It should be marinating in the port wine by now," she added grandly. "And I must make the soup and the croutons."

"Well, then, I'll be going," Kitty said, edging towards the door.

"And apricot mousse," Mrs. Glazier called out after her, as if she were in a frenzy.

"SHALL I PREPARE your *mise en place*?" Kitty enquired of Mrs. De Vries, trying her luck again.

"My! we *are* getting professional," said Mrs. De Vries, but her mind was really on what Kitty had just been telling her. Soup and jugged hare! She was thinking. What a dreadful meal!

She was glazing a terrine of chicken livers and wished that all the village might see her work of art, but having Kitty there was the next best thing.

"What's that?" she asked, as Kitty put the jar of apple jelly on the table.

"I have to take it to the Vicarage on my way home. It's some of Mrs. Prout's apple jelly."

Mrs. De Vries gave it a keen look, and notched up one point to Mrs. Prout.

She notched up another when she heard about the ravioli, and wondered if she had under-estimated the woman.

"I shooed that Tiger away," Kitty said.

"The wretched cur. He is driving Topaze insane."

Kitty mooched round the kitchen, peeking and prying. Mrs. De Vries was the only one in the village to possess a *mandoline* for cutting vegetables. There was a giant pestle and mortar, a wicker bread-basket, ropes of Spanish onions, and a marble cheese-tray.

"You can pound the fish for me, if you have the energy," said Mrs. De Vries.

As this was not a house where she was made to wash her hands first, Kitty immediately set to work.

"I was just going to have pears," Mrs. De Vries said, in a half-humorous voice. "But if the Glaziers are going in for apricot mousse I had better pull my socks up. That remark, of course, is strictly *entre nous*."

"THEN MRS. DE VRIES pulled her socks up, and made a big apple tart," Kitty told her mother.

"I have warned you before, Kitty. What you see going on in people's houses, you keep to yourself. Or you stay out of them. Is that finally and completely understood?"

"Yes, Mother," Kitty said meekly.

"MY DEAR GIRL, I couldn't eat it. I couldn't eat another thing," said Mr. Glazier, confronted by the apricot mousse. "A three-course meal. Why, I shouldn't sleep all night if I had any more. The hare alone was ample."

"I think Mr. De Vries would do better justice to his dinner," said Mrs. Glazier bitterly. She had spent all day cooking and was exhausted. "It's not much fun slaving away and not being appreciated. And what on earth can I do with all the left-overs?"

"Finish them up tomorrow and save yourself a lot of trouble."

Glumly, Mrs. Glazier washed the dishes, and suddenly thought of the Prouts sitting peacefully beside their fire, cracking walnuts, playing cards. She felt ill done by, as she stacked the remains of dinner in the fridge, but was perfectly certain that lie as she might have to to Kitty in the morning, the whole village should not know that for the second day running the Glaziers were having soup, and jugged hare, and apricot mousse.

NEXT DAY, eating a slice of apple tart, Kitty saw Mrs. De Vries test the soup and then put the ladle back into the saucepan.

"What the eye doesn't see, the heart cannot grieve over," Mrs. De Vries said cheerfully.

She added salt, and a turn or two of pepper. Then she took more than a sip from the glass on the draining-board, seeming to find it more to her liking than the soup.

"The Vicarage can't afford drinks," Kitty said.

"They *do* confide in you."

"I said to the Vicar, Mrs. De Vries drinks gin while she is cooking, and he said, 'Lucky old her'."

"There will be a lot of red faces about this village if you go on like this," said Mrs. De Vries, making her part of the prophesy come true at once. Kitty looked at her in surprise. Then she said—Mrs. De Vries's flushed face reminding her—"I think next door must be having the change of life. She is awfully grumpy these days. Nothing pleases her."

"You are too knowing for your years," Mrs. De Vries said, and she suddenly wished she had not been so unhygienic about the soup. Too late now. "How is your novel coming along?" she enquired.

"Oh, very nicely, thank you. I expect I shall finish it before I go back to school, and then it can be published for Christmas."

"We shall all look forward to that," said Mrs. De Vries, in what Kitty considered an unusual tone of voice.

"MRS. DE VRIES cuts up her vegetables with a *mandoline*," Kitty told Mrs. Glazier some days later.

"I always knew she must be nuts," said Mrs. Glazier, thinking of the musical instrument.

Seeing Kitty dancing up the drive, she had quickly hidden the remains of a shepherd's pie at the back of a cupboard. She was more than ever ruffled this morning, because Mrs. Benford had not arrived or sent a message. She had also been getting into a frenzy with her ravioli and, in the end, had thrown the whole lot into the dust-bin. She hated waste, especially now that her house-keeping allowance always seemed to have disappeared by Wednesday, and her husband was, in his dyspeptic way, continually accusing her of extravagance.

Kitty had been hanging about outside the alms-houses for a great part of the morning, and had watched Mrs. Saddler's coffin being carried across the road to the church. "Only one wreath and two relations," she now told Mrs. Glazier. "That's what comes of being poor. What are you having for dinner tonight? I could give you a hand?"

"Mr. Glazier will probably be taking me to The Horse and Groom for a change," Mrs. Glazier lied.

"They are all at sixes and sevens there. Betty Benford started her pains in the night. A fortnight early. Though Mr. Mumford thinks she may have made a mistake with her dates."

Then Mrs. Benford would never come again, Mrs. Glazier thought despondently. She had given a month's notice the week before, and Mrs. Glazier had received it coldly, saying—"I think I should have been informed of this before it became common gossip in the village." Mrs. Benford had seemed quite taken aback at that.

"Well, I mustn't hang around talking," Mrs. Glazier told Kitty. "There's a lot to do this morning, and will be from now on. When do you go back to school?"

"On Thursday."

Mrs. Glazier nodded, and Kitty felt herself dismissed. She sometimes wondered why she bothered to pay this call, when everyone else made her so welcome; but coming away from the funeral she had seen Mrs. De Vries driving into town, and it was one of Mrs. Prout's turning-out days. She had hardly liked to call at the Vicarage under the circumstances of the funeral, and The Horse and Groom being at sixes and sevens had made everyone there very boring and busy.

"I hope you will enjoy your dinner," she said politely to Mrs. Glazier. "They have roast Surrey fowl and all the trimmings."

When she had gone, Mrs. Glazier took the shepherd's pie from its hiding place, and began to scrape some shabby old carrots.

"KITTY WILL you stop chattering and get on with your pudding," her mother said in an exasperated voice.

Kitty had been describing how skilfully the undertaker's men had lowered Mrs. Saddler's coffin into the grave, Kitty herself peering from behind the tombstone of Maria Britannia Marlowe—her favourite dead person on account of her name.

It was painful to stop talking. A pain came in her chest, severe enough to slow her breathing, and gobbling the rice pudding made it worse. As soon as her plate was cleared she began again. "Mrs. Glazier has the change of life," she said.

"How on earth do you know about such things?" her mother asked in a faint note.

"As *you* didn't tell me, I had to find out the hard way," Kitty said sternly.

Her mother pursed her lips together to stop laughing, and began to stack up the dishes.

"How Mrs. De Vries will miss me!" Kitty said dreamily, rising to help her mother. "I shall be stuck there at school doing boring things, and she'll be having a nice time drinking gin."

"Now *that* is enough. You are to go to your room immediately," her mother said sharply, and Kitty looked at her red face reflectively, comparing it with Mrs. Glazier's. "You will have to find some friends of your own age. You are becoming a little menace to everyone with your visiting and we have got to live in this village. Now upstairs you go, and think over what I have said."

"Very well, mother," Kitty said meekly. If she did not have to help mother with the washing-up, she could get on with her novel all the sooner.

She went upstairs to her bedroom and spread her writing things out on the table and soon, having at once forgotten her mother's words, was lost in the joy of authorship.

Her book was all about little furry animals, and their small adventures, and there was not a human-being in it, except the girl, Katherine, who befriended them all.

SHE MANAGED a few more visits that holiday; but on Thursday she went back to school again, and then no one in the village knew what was happening any more.

GILLIAN TINDALL

b. 1938

"It is not the extra-ordinary possibility of life
after death which interests me . . . but the ordinariness of death,
the awkward mystery, within the context of daily life."
It was thus that Gillian Tindall, then a young graduate of
Oxford—and already an important novelist—introduced the
anthology from which this short story is taken.

The Loss

WHEN TOM HATCHER'S wife Susan died it was pretty bad for him, and yet not—he realised in queer, grey moments of lucidity—quite as bad as he had thought it might be. He had expected the pain and loneliness to be unbearable—or, rather, bearable only in the sense that he would bear it because he had to. Instead, the very fact that he had had the time and the knowledge to envisage beforehand just what it would be like, seemed, when the time came, to make the experience subtly different. The pain was already familiar. He had begun to get used to it even before it happened.

It was pretty bad at times, all the same. Not just at first, when all he felt was the sheer relief that it was at last *over*, that she was no longer suffering and that there would be no more visits to that side-ward which had become as familiar to him as the lounge at home. Also, people were very kind. They had all been expecting it too, of course, he and Susan had let their closest friends know pretty much how things stood, everyone had therefore been poised ready on the side-lines, so to speak, with cautious words of comfort and tumblers of whisky. People offered to help him pack up her things, invited him to 'drop in any time' for the good hot meals they felt he wouldn't be bothering to cook himself: some of them almost overdid it, he felt. After all, by the time the end came he had been to all intents living alone for the best part of two months already, and for most of the year he had been the one doing the cooking, the shopping, the cleaning even, because of course Susan hadn't felt up to it. He was used to the routine. As a schoolmaster, his working day outside his home ended at four, he had time to do after that what another man might not have been able to. And then, later, when he'd had a bite to eat while watching that news round-up programme, at the moment when the blank evening ahead might have menaced him with despair, there were always books to correct and tomorrow's lessons to think about. He was, he greyly reckoned, more fortunate than many men in that his life fell naturally into this particular healing shape. He was under no illusions about the need just to keep going, the way in which 'keeping busy' did actually help even though it seemed a bit mechanical, a bolt-hole from pain rather than any real solution . . . 'Solution'? There were ultimately no solutions to intractable facts. He knew that, he was a grown-up. There would be no solution to Susan's dying or to his missing her, any more than there had been a solution to the fact of their childlessness, which had cost them so many fruitless tests and hopes, and Susan, at one time, so many tears. But she—they—had got over it. The last five years, before the wretched kidney business started, had been really happy for both of them. And he told himself he was adult enough to believe—dourly, for the moment, on trust, as an act of faith—that it was quite possible that one day he himself would be happy again too.

Later, when their friends had realised that he could after all manage, that loss had not transformed him into some haggard and incompetent travesty of his former self, the pressing invitations did fall off a bit. Actually, that time, about four months after, was the worst time—not because of anything his friends did or didn't do, but simply because it was. He began to sleep an alarming amount, as if sleep itself were a drug, and even feared, for a week or two, that he wasn't going to be able to hold his own at work—that he was going to have to give in, ask for time off, get tranquillisers or pep pills or something from his doctor—play the role, in fact, after all, of the grief-stricken widower. But he managed to get through this time without anybody realising, chiefly, he thought, thanks to Jess.

Jess had been Susan's dog, bought only the year before she died, when they still clung to the idea that she was just run down and needed the fresh air and exercise which a young dog would inevitably provide. After the first few months, however, it had been Tom who had taken the bouncing, girlish creature out, early morning and evening, for runs on Parliament Hill. But Jess still loved Susan best because Susan had fed her, right up to when she went into hospital for the last time, and anyway Tom had always referred to her as 'Susan's dog'—or, jokingly—'that silly bitch of yours' because he had never particularly liked dogs, as a matter of fact, and was very down on what he had always called 'sentimentality' about animals. When he got fond of Jess it was in spite of himself, he thought, a matter of propinquity, like an unmaternal woman coming to love a child simply through the necessity of looking after it.

Jess was a golden cocker spaniel with a long plumey tail which picked up dead leaves on every outing and huge pink-padded paws on which she liked to race through mud. She was enchantingly affectionate and maddeningly indiscriminate. She would fawn on anyone; Tom growled that she was hopeless as a watchdog. Susan had replied laughingly that they hadn't *got* her as a watchdog and that Jess's friendliness ought to be an example to both of them. She had said that they had both been getting too selfish and set in their ways: it was good for them to have a young thing like Jess tearing around, savaging slippers, stealing chops, making shamefaced puddles, or worse, in the middle of the night when they hadn't heard her scratching and whining. After this had happened several times they left their bedroom door open to hear better, and then of course Jess took to creeping up from her basket in the hall once they were both asleep. Once she tried to get into bed with them, as if she believed herself the size of a kitten who might easily escape detection—she was always trying to get on people's laps, it seemed a long time before she realised that she had become quite a large dog. Tom had taken her sternly downstairs and told her to stay there, but the next night she had been up again. Finally they compromised: Jess might creep in and sleep on the rug by the dressing table—they were prepared to pretend they didn't know she was there—but if, said Tom firmly, there were whinings or tail thumpings or other attempts to join them in bed out she must go. He was not going to share his married life with a dog. Evidently Jess must have understood the situation because the compromise worked, and she never leapt joyously onto the eiderdown till Tom was up at 7.30 and putting his dressing gown on.

When Susan was no longer there she did not at once insinuate herself into the bed in her place—no, not at once. For a week, she was clearly puzzled. But Susan had been away before and come back—Jess was fairly confident this time, looking for her mistress on the side nearest the wall each morning. But because he hated to see her look, and to see the disappointment in her foolish, toffee-brown eyes, Tom took to calling her briskly the moment he got out of bed and urging her downstairs ahead of him. Gradually she got into the new routine and seemed to forget the old. By and by she even ceased looking round, faintly puzzled, for another person when Tom gave her her plate of food. She was, thought Tom, with the painful realism of which he made a perverse solace, beginning to forget.

It was not till one night about a fortnight after Susan had died that she—Jess—first came while he was lying awake and wretched, and pushed her nose into his hand outstretched on the pillow. He thought afterwards that she must have heard him tossing about and surmised, with some canine cunning beyond organised reason, that this was an opportunity not to be missed. But perhaps, too, she had understood at some level that he was miserable and was, simply, trying to comfort him, as people were always telling one dogs did . . . In any case at that moment he neither knew nor cared what her true motives and understanding were, but simply gathered her large, exuberant body onto the bed with a groan and buried his face in the clean, feathery undergrowth round her neck.

After that, of course, she slept on his bed every night, there was no stopping her. He still went through the ritual of making her sit down on the rug and telling her to stay there. But it was perfectly well understood between them that she climbed onto the bed after he was asleep and often before . . . After a while he began to wait to hear the soft rustle and pad, to feel the slight lurch of the bed as she sprung delicately over his legs and settled herself comfortably within touching distance. Then, reassured by her presence, he would drift off.

On those mornings in the Bad Patch when it seemed as if he could not face shaving and breakfasting and going to school that day, or indeed life at all, it was for Jess that he heaved himself out of bed, since she had to be let out. It was for Jess that he went into the kitchen and while he fed her he automatically fed himself. Then, since Jess had to have her early morning run he got dressed anyway, and so one thing led to another and he got to school after all. One day, he had the idea of taking her with him, and that helped enormously. Why, he wondered, had he not thought of it before? She had undoubtedly been lonely in the house all day, she had begun to make messes before he could get home to her, and to whine, the neighbour said. Now she came with him to school, sat behind the blackboard and was much happier. So was he. His classes made much of her. She made much of them in return. The Head didn't object, merely warning Tom to keep on the right side of the school-keeper and not to let an inspector see her. For the first time in nearly twenty-five years of variegated teaching he found himself becoming A Character. Lovable Old Mr. Hatcher with his dog. Well, well. It wasn't perhaps the image he would have wanted to present—had ever thought he would present, for that matter, in the days when he was young and unscarred by things and known for energy and tough discipline—a bit of a bastard, in fact. But it helped for the moment to find himself Lovable Old Mr. Thatcher and his dog. Oh yes, it helped.

In the playground she would bound around retrieving a tennis ball again and again for a knot of admirers, while he himself kept an eye open from a safe vantage point to make sure no one mistreated her. There were one or two boys—just one or two, mind, and not in any of his sets—whom he didn't entirely trust. Other boys used to gather round him telling him about *their* dogs, real, imaginary or longed for, the Alsatians their brothers were going to give them when they were sixteen or the champion greyhounds their uncles were breeding. He found he had joined, unawares, a new club which transcended age, intelligence or status. At midday Jess used to skedaddle down to the kitchens, where the dinner-ladies soon learnt to have something tasty for her. Tom used to go down too, apparently casually, to thank them, but in fact to check that they weren't giving her pastry or cake or God knows what. Women always overfed dogs, even Susan had tended to, worrying because Jess's scatty, pubescent form was so thin . . . She had filled out now and was beautiful. She had already been in season, twice, with the maximum of mess, inconvenience and noisily optimistic barking. Later, he must think about getting her mated to someone worthy of her, try to plan it so that the puppies would come near the end of the summer term . . . But not yet. He did not want to share her with puppies yet.

One fine March day, when it was nearly six months since Susan died, he drove out to spend a Saturday in the Hertfordshire countryside where they had often picnicked. He looked at a couple of churches, took Jess for a good long walk and sat in a cleared copse to eat his sandwiches while she chased imaginary rabbits enthusiastically through the stumps. Here, as everywhere, he was reminded of former occasions when Susan had been with him, but he had become quite used to this perpetual undercurrent of memory, it no longer ruined his day for him. He took pleasure in Jess's almost hysterical appreciation of the outing, and had considerable difficulty in luring her back into the car again when it was time to turn for home.

Two days later, she went.

He had taken her out onto Parliament Hill after school and had got into casual conversation with a neighbour, owner of a badly behaved poodle. When they called and whistled for their respective dogs, the poodle reappeared readily enough but there was no sign of Jess.

For ten minutes or so he did not worry seriously. She had done this several times before, it was her way of teasing, and he kept expecting that she would, from one moment to the next, be there, flying across the darkening grass from a great distance, ears and tail streaming, tongue flapping, mouth agape as if she was laughing. Not till almost half an hour had gone by, and he could no longer see beyond the nearer clumps of trees, did real dread suddenly strike home to him. She had never been gone nearly as long as this before.

Wretched, he made his way back home. It was not far, she would no doubt follow him in her own good time; she was hardly likely to get lost in her familiar streets, and if she did she had her collar on, someone would bring her back . . . But he could swallow no supper and soon he was out again, tramping the Hill and then the whole Heath in case she had wandered further there and lost herself among unfamiliar scrub, calling and calling in the darkness. At one point a keeper with a flash-light joined him, stood by him a few minutes while he called, feeling a fool. The man listened to a description of Jess and promised to look out for her. Dogs, he said, sounding kind and experienced, often lost themselves on the Heath: they went after something that smelt interesting, see, and then wandered in circles, but they nearly always turned up next morning looking pretty ashamed and sorry for themselves. Tom wasn't to worry too much. For a few minutes, after the man had gone on his way, Tom did feel fatuously cheered by the keeper's calm. Only gradually, as loneliness and fear settled on him once more, did he realise that of course the man was calm because he didn't care—why should he care? It wasn't his dog.

In the end he went home because what else could he do? He left the gate open and the side door wedged ajar. Lying alone in bed he felt cold and tried his hardest to fix on an image of Jess, cold too of course, but basically *safe*, huddled under some bush, waiting for the morning light to trot home, tail between legs. For a long time he couldn't sleep, but at last got off by telling himself that if he did so he would be wakened by the soft pad of Jess's feet on the stairs, the thump and lurch as she sprang onto the bed, and the night past would seem like a bad dream . . .

He woke. There was no Jess. Cold seemed to have settled in his stomach and his feet. He huddled on some warm clothes and went out into the piercing early morning. Almost no one was about on the Hill. He met another keeper and gave him Jess's description too, and this one took out his notebook and wrote it down. The gesture should have reassured Tom, but instead he felt worse. Now Jess was officially Missing. He called and called all round their usual haunts, still expecting to hear her flying feet on the turf, her excited bark, yet knowing at the same time that he was not likely to, that wherever Jess was it was unlikely now to be here. As he walked slowly home again to swallow a cup of coffee before leaving for work, he had a very complete image of her, in last night's darkness, not huddled beneath a bush as in his earlier fancy, but looking for her way home, running head down with a ghastly precision right into the path of a lorry.

The police would know. Run-over dogs were supposed to be reported to them, weren't they? He gulped his coffee and rushed to call at the police station on his way to school. The young policeman was quite kind, said no accident of any kind had been reported in the area last night and that dogs often turned up again as right as rain—he shouldn't worry too much. They would call him at once if any lost dog answering to Jess's description were brought in. Once again he was illogically comforted, and once again the comfort evaporated ten minutes later.

He came home again in the dinner hour, possessed by an image of Jess returning wet and draggled in his absence and wandering dejectedly off again because he was not there. There was no sign of her. He made sure the side door was open, put down meat, dog-biscuits . . . He had told no one at school that she was missing. His B-stream maths thought that he hadn't brought her today because they had played up a bit last week when she was there.

That evening, realising that he had had nothing but coffee for twenty-four hours, he forced himself to swallow a tin of soup before setting out again for the Hill. It was twenty-four hours since she had disappeared. Illogically, he convinced himself that this was therefore the moment when she would reappear, racing down the wind toward him just as if today were yesterday, the last twenty-four hours wiped out . . . She didn't.

When at last darkness drove him home again he rang the vet, who said had she been coming into heat by any chance?

"I didn't see any sign of it. But it's possible, isn't it? Particularly at this time of year." It wasn't actually, likely. Her last heat had been just before Christmas. But he seized on the hope, elaborating it in his mind. Of course, Jess would be ranging north London in a ferment of desire looking for a mate. Had found one, no doubt, if not several. But when her desire was satiated she would turn for home.

"She had her collar on of course—?" said the vet. "Well then. Let's just hope for the best. You've tried Battersea Dogs' Home, I expect? . . . Yes, they'll let you know. But in another day or two she may very well come trotting in as cool as you please."

He saw her doing it. He saw her constantly, whenever he closed his eyes. Only it just did not happen.

On Friday, at dinner-time, he packed up his books and left for home on the pretext of a sick headache. He had indeed slept so little the last three nights that 'a headache' was as good a phrase as any for the sense of shivering unreality which possessed him. That afternoon on the Heath as he walked and called and called again—people who passed were beginning to look at him oddly, he thought, but that didn't matter, nothing mattered—he met the black poodle owner and told her what had happened. She expressed shocked concern and wondered if perhaps Jess had gone off on her own looking for those rabbit-haunted woods where she had so enjoyed herself the weekend before.

It was a long shot, but what else could he do? At least to drive out there passed the time, provided the illusion of doing something. But there once again in the empty copse he felt, this time, terribly alone, and his visit of the preceding week-end might have been an idyllic memory from years before, long gone beyond recall. He could hardly believe now, that he had not then been perfectly happy. The time when Jess had been his constant companion was already, in the space of a few days, beginning to acquire for him the fabulous quality of a lost golden era, such as youth or liberty.

On Sunday he busied himself by typing out a score of neat notices on cardboard, covering them with polythene, and going round the neighbourhood fixing them to posts and trees. He was not sure if one was allowed to do this but did not care. He also had cards posted in half a dozen local newsagents. 'Missing since Tuesday 7 March, cocker spaniel bitch, 18 months, light brown colour . . .' He thought humbly of the times when, glancing over boards in the past, he himself had seen such notices and had not registered any particular emotion, had not been arrested in pity and sympathy . . . He had not understood what pain such a notice represented.

The woman in one newsagent was particularly kind, creasing her face and clinking her tongue. She'd lost her doggie, she said—getting on for four years ago, now, that would be. She still thought she saw him in the street sometimes and called out his name, but of course it was never him. Those people must be really wicked, mustn't they, to do such a thing and cause such unhappiness?

He murmured some vague assent and promised to let her know if he had any luck. Only when he got outside the shop did he realize that she had been referring to the possibility of Jess having been stolen, for one of several purposes.

The thought had already occurred to him. But he pushed it from his mind again. He spent the afternoon ranging systematically over the Heath, taking it in sections, searching every patch of trees. Tomorrow he would ring Battersea Dogs' Home again, see if any new spaniel had been brought in.

The first person to mention the word 'laboratory' to him was Wrighty, the fat old science master at school. Wrighty had a dog himself, a wheezing dachshund of great antiquity: in another, happier life Tom had seen it waddling round last Open Day and had faintly despised it. It transpired that Wrighty had a morbid dread of his dog being stolen and subjected to nameless experiments and had had it tattooed with a special number on the inside leg—"so that any lab. would see it, and know this is someone's pet and all they have to do is return it to a certain address and there'll be no questions asked." Wrighty represented the business of stealing pets and selling them to laboratories for vivisection as a vast, highly organised and satanic conspiracy. Tom's heart quailed within him though his reason tried to resist Wrighty's pessimism.

"But good heavens surely any lab. would know that a dog like Jess isn't likely to be an unwanted stray?"

Wrighty shook his head dubiously. These people were pretty unscrupulous. Heartless—they'd have to be, wouldn't they? If they thought they could get away with it . . .

"In that case," snapped Tom, "why should a tattooed number help?" But he was cursing himself that he'd never thought of it himself, never realised that any such system existed. In his mind Jess's smooth inner flank was extended before him, *there*, safe and receptive, and the vet was there too with an inky punch in his hand saying: "Just hold her firmly, would you? It'll just be a bit of a prick for her, over in a moment . . ." And then there, on the milk-caramel skin, were the identifying, saving numbers.

When he got home that evening, after his usual painful session on the Hill—the ritual of calling and whistling her each night he dreaded yet felt compelled to perform—he sat down and concocted a short, careful but (he hoped) pungent letter for circulation to laboratories. It was a long shot, perhaps, but Tom was not the man to leave undone anything that possibly could be done. In the letter he wrote, after describing Jess, that he was not interested in legal proceedings, that he simply wanted her back—"and so does my little boy, who is crying for her". He was normally a truthful man, almost pedantically so, but this lie seemed to flow naturally from him without making the smallest dent in his conscience. The truth: "*I* am crying for her, every night" would have been impossible to write. But children were allowed to cry, and surely even a vivisectionist's heart would be softened by this? Vivisectionists always justified their unpleasant trade, he understood, by saying that they placed ultimate human welfare above that of animals. That had been his own viewpoint too. In the past, before he had understood anything.

Normally, when he had any duplicating to be done—test papers and so forth—he asked the school secretary to do it for him. But, with the exception of Wrighty who kept himself to himself, Tom had told no one at school yet that Jess was lost, and quailed so far from doing so: every time he mentioned the fact to anyone the admission of it seemed to make it more real and potentially permanent. So he waited after four till the secretary had gone home and then worked the machine himself. He ran off four hundred copies. Surely that would be enough? Then he went down to central London to an anti-vivisectionist league whom he had rung earlier in the day, and picked up from them a list of licensed laboratories. There were well over four hundred places listed. He would have to do another batch of copies.

For the next week all his spare time was spent addressing envelopes. At least this was something to do. It even felt constructive. When he carted yet another basketful to the post box he almost felt as if all those letters despatched represented something achieved, something solid. Surely, he felt illogically, such endeavour should eventually produce some result? He had grown up in a world of study, of exams and scholarships, a world in which efforts made with sufficient application and intensity of purpose normally produced results. It was hard to shed the habit of rational optimism.

Sooner than he expected, the replies began to come, thudding through his letter boxes in batches each morning, gaily littering the mat when he got home in the afternoons. After the first few he no longer opened them with much hope, but he still opened them. Some of them were mere formal notes, regretting to inform him. Others seemed to have a slightly indignant note "would wish to assure you that this laboratory never purchases animals from dealers . . ." Others wrote with what seemed both kindness and real concern. Sometimes the letter would be from the top man himself, in his own writing "—wanted to let you know without delay that we are, alas, unable to help you in your search . . . Do hope most sincerely that it may prove fruitful . . . quite understand what you and your family must be going through". One lab. even sent a multi-colour ball pen stamped with their name "as a small gift for your little boy. I know how hard such an experience must hit a child . . ." He used the pen for marking. As it could write both red and blue according to how you twisted it, it was most useful. Not that he did any more marking than he could help that week, and his lessons went unprepared. There was always old stuff to fall back on, and he was not capable of more . . .

The letters were, oddly, for all their lack of concrete help, some sort of solace. They also reminded him of something. After a while he realised that it was a little like it had been receiving letters after Susan had died: "*So very sorry to hear your sad news . . . if there is anything we can do . . . our thoughts are with you.*" Letters of condolence, the formal recognition that a loss demands. He did not throw them away, but kept them altogether in an old box file. A record of his endeavours, thence of the strength of his feeling. A testament of love.

He ate little, moved abstractedly through the days working the minimum, vague and testy when anyone spoke to him. He felt as if his body were made of some strange substance, heavier than usual. He experienced pains in his stomach and supposed that these must be due to his continual tension. For he was constantly on the alert, even at school, constantly listening. In counterbalance to his lethargic, vague body his hearing seemed to have become abnormally acute. He heard, even from up in the bathroom, the soft chink and flap of a letter arriving, or the creak of the gate outside, or the tiny vibration the phone makes before it even begins to ring. He heard boards shift and furniture expand and curtains move in the breeze. He could almost hear the bulbs pushing their way through the soil outside. And every time a dog barked anywhere within half a mile outside he started to his feet, listening intently.

All this awareness made him very tired. At night, his loneliness was soon blotted out in an exhausted sleep. In sleep, she was waiting for him. Not—oh not—in the dreadful mangled shapes of his rational daytime fears, brown eyes glazed with death, soft fur mangled and bloodied by the wheels of cars, but in her own shape, whole and real. She leapt onto the bed and licked his face so that he started up crying "Jess—at last—" And then he awoke. She came running up the small garden to him and he knew beyond any doubt that all the last two weeks had been a bad dream, nothing more. And then he awoke. He caressed her smooth head, played with her collar, told a friend at his side how he had had this frightful, damn stupid dream about losing her . . . And then he awoke.

When term ended he knew that he could, in any case, have held out for only a very few more days. The world of narrowed intensity in which he was living was almost incompatible with ordinary existence. In any case he had just inserted advertisements in several papers, both local and national—cursing himself for not having thought of this before. He needed all his time for driving out to inaccessible points on the perimeter of London, various places where a trickle of telephone callers were all sure that they had seen Jess. In response to one particularly emphatic and encouraging woman he even went to see a dog in Gloucestershire. But it turned out to be brown and white, and not a bitch anyway.

He didn't, in fact, find these fruitless journeys, after the first one, so desperately disappointing. He had begun to arm himself against disappointment, he did not undertake each one really expecting that Jess would be at the end of it. It was almost as if the journeys were some sort of end in themselves. Something to do—a further testament of his love.

By and by there were no more phone calls. But he still continued every day, driving round London, its suburbs and the country beyond, always looking, searching, peering forward, skidding to sudden stops a few times when an arching back, a plumey tail bobbing by the kerb had convinced him for a half a second that it was her, truly her.

It was at the fourth or fifth of these sudden stops that a heavy lorry ran into the back of him. It had been entirely his fault: he recognized that blearily and immediately, even through the pain that lacerated his back and took his breath away. A crowd gathered and the clamorously competing sirens of police and ambulance vehicles seemed to fill the air surprisingly quickly. People were pretty efficient, really; he felt vaguely grateful to them. The steering wheel was pressed into his chest, the door had buckled in on him and they had to cut the metal away to get him out. Quite soon he was in hospital and likely to be there, he realised with a dawning sense of relief and relaxation, for a good long while. Really, what with the way he had been feeling, it seemed the best place for him at the moment. He even wondered, between the waves of morphia and the intermittent stabs of pain, if he had gone and had the accident on purpose to get himself here.

OVER THE NEXT six weeks his body gradually repaired itself, and people endlessly told him what a lucky man he was that he was not, after all it seemed, going to be left with a crippled back, paralysed legs or a neck he couldn't turn. He came to believe them, and learnt to smile at them. It was, after all, rather nice being lucky. He didn't seem to have played that role for a long time.

After the hospital, they sent him to a convalescent home for a month, near Brighton, and he played chess and chatted and was gently bored and went for rather careful walks along the shore. He felt luckier than ever here, among so many people who would never be entirely whole again, and at times was tempted to show off, rather.

By the time he was passed fit for work again the summer term was the best part over. The Head, who had visited him in Brighton, said "Don't think of getting back into harness till September, old man—I'll make it OK with the Office. Why don't you pop off abroad or somewhere on a really nice long holiday? Make the most of it?"

As a matter of fact that was just what he intended. He'd made a good friend in the convalescent home—chap called Jo, in a wheel-chair now, he'd never be able to get back into harness himself, but he was getting a pension from his firm and had just had a good fat sum in compensation from the firm of the stupid bugger who'd done for him . . . Anyway Jo was an old hand at foreign travel, knew half a dozen languages, and was just looking for someone to team up with this summer on a trip to Italy —someone to push the wheelchair and lend a bit of a hand in the bathroom and so on . . . Tom agreed with alacrity to Jo's proposal. Not that Jo was the most exciting person in the world, but Tom was tired of excitement—tired to death of it, as a matter of fact, and Jo was a really good sort. It would be grand, anyway, to have a really long trip abroad without worrying too much about the expense and to feel at the same time that he was doing someone else a good turn.

He went back home for a few days first just to make sure everything was alright and to arrange about having letters forwarded and so on.

The house, with all the windows and doors carefully locked by a neighbour in his absence, felt oddly unfamiliar. He wasn't entirely sure, as a matter of fact, if he wanted to keep it. Mightn't it be better for him to get some smaller place, a flat perhaps? He might even think of teaming up with someone . . . With Jo, perhaps, if this summer's trip went well.

There was a good film on locally he wanted to see. He was on his way out when the phone rang. He almost didn't answer it. When he did so he nearly put the receiver down again because the fool on the end was using a pay box and didn't know how to get through, then—

"'Allo-*oo*?" said a woman's voice at last, loud and aggrieved.

"Hall*o*. This is 094-9269."

"It's about your dog. See, we've just seen the bit in the paper—In an old bit of paper that was round the shopping—"

With the greatest reluctance he asked, after a pause:

"Where do you live?"

"'Ounslow. Well we found her by the edge of the M4, see, and we did put a notice in the pet shop at the time, but no one claimed her—"

"When was this?"

"March. She's a brown cocker spaniel see—just like it says."

With a sinking heart he heard himself say:

"I'll be over first thing tomorrow morning. No—not first thing, because I'll have to come by public transport, I've just remembered. But I'll be there by eleven. If you'd just give me your address—"

A tudor villa in a run-down residential district. Too near the motorway now, probably, for comfort: he could hear the stationary, continuous sound of the unseen traffic as he stood by the gate. A bald lawn with a broken bicycle. A heavy motor-bike parked by the front door. Milk bottles on the step and a banging window. When he rang the bell barking began, and he turned his head sharply, but it was only two collies who rounded the corner from the back of the house and bore down on him, all noisy self-advertisement. Behind them came a boy of about ten in shrunk jeans and heavy boots. He stopped short on seeing Tom and retreated shouting "Mum. *Mu-um*." Tom waited resignedly. Long experience of boys had made him familiar with homes like this, with everything anyhow and the basic parental good nature too sloppy and unfocused to be worthy of the name. If that boy got into trouble ever and was asked by some well-meaning social worker how he got on with his family he would hunch his shoulders and say vaguely, as if he did not understand the question "Awright . . ."

He had known before she in turn appeared that Mum would be a blowsy woman with slippers and bare legs, and he was right. For a moment she seemed to have forgotten all about his coming. Then she remembered and became friendly.

"Oh come in do. Just step over—yes, that's right. Do excuse the mess won't you, we're a bit upside down. Trev—my husband, that is, and my eldest boy—they're doing a bit of decorating, see."

The littered hall smelt strongly of dog, and contained a large number of things which could have had nothing to do with decorating. Through the open door of the kitchen ahead he caught sight of mounds of dirty crockery and plates on the floor. As if following his eye she said, laughing defensively:

"If I don't put our dishes on the floor see, they just jump up and lick them on the tables. Proper devils they are—fair wearing me out. I tell you, I shan't be sorry to see the back of yours—if she *is* yours. That's five of 'em I've had on my hands for the last two months; the two collies, my husband's prize greyhound what's out in the shed, another puppy this fellow here brought in—" aiming a vaguely affectionate blow at her younger son—"and yours. Driving me mad, they are."

He murmured what was intended to be both thanks in advance and disclaimers in case 'his' should prove after all not to be . . . How much real hope had he? He did not know. He felt confused. He was straining his ears for a known bark, a known scutter of feet on the smeary lino-tiles—and yet this was not like it had been before. The intensity, the sense of personal effort and involvement, were lacking. He felt disorientated, as if he were playing a part. Playing himself, perhaps, of months ago. Was it really so long? Yes. Time had passed, in hospital, at Brighton. Nothing it seemed had remained exactly the same. He was cured. But there was still that slight stiffness in his back, now and probably forever, which would prevent him from taking games at school any more. And perhaps a new kind of stiffness . . . weakness . . . elsewhere too . . .

They went through the kitchen, past the reek of cooking horsemeat and lights, out into a squalid back yard. "There," said the woman, pointing unnecessarily, "there tied up by the fence."

She had been whining and snuffling as they emerged from the kitchen, but for some reason he had not registered the fact. Now, at the sight of them, she let forth a spate of high-pitched barking that did not stop.

"There," said the woman fatuously, "seems to know you, doesn't she?"

"She barks at everyone like that," said a man who had just joined them from nowhere, adding dourly to Tom, "On heat, she is. Goes on like that at everyone just now. That's why she's tied up. Kev, don't you let those collies out here again, or I'll give you what-for."

Brown. Indubitably the same breed as Jess. Much heavier, and in need of a bath. Fat, foolish, barking hysterically. Limping a bit, he noticed. A hind leg.

"Yeah, she was like that when we found her," said the man, "Lame, I mean. Was she before?"

"No. Mine isn't. Wasn't . . . I mean . . ." Trying to collect his slithering thoughts, he said: "Did she have a collar on?"

"No. Reckon someone pinched it maybe. Pinched her, perhaps, and then couldn't keep her. Wouldn't wonder—right nuisance, she is, even when she isn't in season. Meaning no offence to you, of course," the man added hastily.

Swallowing, he stepped forward, caressed her head. She fawned on him, trying to rub herself against him. Then she turned her attention with equal enthusiasm to the boy.

For something to say, he said:

"It's funny that the police never connected her with my description . . . You did say you'd reported her to them, didn't you?"

"That's right," said the woman. "The kid went down there to tell 'em . . . Didn't you Kev?"

They all looked at him. He looked away. Abruptly his mother cried: "Kev—*did you*?"

"I meant to," he said sullenly after a silence.

His mother hit out at him with hasty and perfunctory aim. He dodged and began to whine: "I did mean to Mum, honest, I jus' forgot . . ."

"Forgot. I'll see you don't forget another time," said his father grimly, as if it were no surprise to him and the whole family were simply going through some sort of charade for the visitor's benefit.

"I'm ever so sorry," said the woman turning to Tom with fulsome insincerity. "I did think he 'ad. I *told* him to but you know what boys are, and this one's potty on dogs, I think he's mental or something, I really do . . ."

He didn't listen to them. He went on staring at the dog as she squirmed before them in an ecstasy of undirected anticipation. And he simply didn't know.

It *could* be Jess. She was the right colour and size, and the changes *could* be accounted for by the lapse of time, by idiotic over-feeding, by several things . . . He simply did not know. He who had thought once he would know Jess out of millions, simply could not now be sure if this were her or not. He had carried an image of her in his heart every moment day and night for weeks: every time he had closed his eyes for a second she had been there, gambolling behind his aching lids, flying, ears flapping, down the wind on the Hill . . . But perhaps that was the trouble. He had carried this image with him for so long that the picture had begun to wear itself out like a film incessantly being run. And he had become confused. The Jess he was now trying desperately to recall was not perhaps even the real, original Jess but Jess at second-hand, the quintessential, ideal, golden Jess who had lived behind his eyelids, the shadow he had pursued so obsessionally, with such desire and pain. That shadow had gone, suddenly and completely, at the moment when the lorry had rammed into the back of his car. She had not accompanied him in the ambulance to hospital, had never visited him there. It was as if the accident that had miraculously spared him for a further extension of life had killed her, for good.

The noisy, indiscriminate, flesh and blood spaniel before him now seemed to have nothing to do with the golden shadow, or with the dead past at all. It might well be Jess, he told himself again; he didn't think so but that was just prejudice, it was perfectly possible . . . He simply did not know.

What's more, he felt that he would never know. He was under no illusions any more. If this brown bitch were not Jess then this was the end, he would never find her anywhere else. This was his chance. If he took it—?

If he took it he *might* be taking a completely strange dog, a dog who might, even with proper food and discipline, remain fat and stupid and almost certainly lame, a dog who would only come to represent to him, as time went by, a cruel disappointment and a daily regret and resentment. He knew in that moment that he wanted Jess and he wanted absolute certainty, no second best would do.

Perhaps, even if this dog were not Jess, sufficient love and effort could transform her into a living image of the original . . . Perhaps. But so much of his love and effort had been expended in the search for her that he felt he had not that much to offer any more. An intensity within himself was worn out too.

And, in any case, with Jess or any other dog on his hands, he would not be able to go abroad with Jo. He was particularly unwilling to let Jo down, he thought . . .

Turning to the boy, he said:

"So you're fond of dogs? You fond of this one now? Is that why you didn't want to report her to the police?"

The child nodded wordlessly, one eye on his mother. Perhaps he was afraid of her. It wasn't a very convincing nod. But Tom decided to take it for what it was. He faced the parents squarely.

"It's not my dog," he said.

Their faces fell. But they looked resigned. Perhaps they had really expected this.

"Oh. Not yours then?"

"No. Not mine." And he added, not just politely but as if apologizing for himself:

"I'm sorry . . . But there it is."

JOHN WAIN

1925–1994

An English critic and novelist, Wain studied at Oxford and was elected fellow of St John's College. As a professor of poetry, he helped many embryo poets while producing his often highly sophisticated novels, some of which linked him, during the fifties, with the "angry young men" of the day. His short stories, like this one, can be starkly elemental.

While the Sun Shines

"YOU WERE HIRED as a tractor driver and that's what you'll do on this farm, or get out," he said.

"I was hired by your father, not you," I said.

"Same thing," he said. "I'm running the place while he's away."

That was the whole trouble. If Mr. Cartwright hadn't wrenched his back and gone off to hospital, the say-so would have been his and then there'd have been no question of mowing that field. Not after what happened to Daniel.

But of course the son, Robert, he'd got his knife into me. He wanted me out of there, and it was all the same to him whether I refused an order and gave him the chance to sack me or whether I went ahead and the tractor rolled on me and put me in hospital or in the graveyard. He wouldn't sleep or eat any worse. He was one of the hard sort: red-faced, thick-legged, with that cold stare. Even then, he might have turned out all right if it hadn't been for her. What she put him through, it made me feel sorry even for him, at times he must have felt he couldn't trust another man within twenty miles of her. Those eyes! And good-looking with it. "My husband doesn't let me even *look* at another man," she said to me, that time we were alone in the kitchen. And considering the *way* she looked at them, I didn't blame him.

Not that I wanted any. I'm a married man and I get on all right with my wife. And if you're all right at home, why go about looking for it? Nothing messes things up faster than that. And with two kids to feed and young Jimmy starting to school, I didn't want to give up this job, right in the middle of the summer. Of course a good tractor driver can always get work, but by early July the farms are all staffed up, and it would have been building-site work. I don't like that.

So there we were. I wanted to stay on, Mr. Cartwright was quite satisfied with my work, but young Mr. Robert wanted me out because he thought his wife was looking at me. That's a laugh. She'd have looked at any man who wasn't a hundred years old. They'd have had to hire a ghost to drive the tractor if they wanted to be sure of keeping her on the straight and narrow. And she was quite safe with me anyway, if he'd only known it. It was on the tip of my tongue, once or twice, to tell him so, but of course I couldn't. It wasn't possible to touch on the matter at all, it was such a sore spot with him. Had she given him trouble with other men before? Or was it just that he was jealous and knew she was that way inclined, you might say, and went mad every time he saw her rest her eyes on another bloke? I didn't know and I didn't care. I just wanted to drive the tractor and take a fair week's wage home. But it wasn't part of my job to kill myself.

"Look," I said, "I can drive a tractor as well as anybody. I've driven every type and done every kind of work. But not across that field. It's too steep for a tractor, and that's the end of it."

"If that's the end of it, you can pick up your cards and go today," he said, giving me that hard stare out of his light-blue eyes. "There's fifteen quids' worth of hay on that slope alone." And he walked off, into the house, before I could answer. All very well for him. But I'd seen Daniel since the accident and I knew that Daniel would never drive a tractor again.

He'd been ploughing on this very steep slope, the one you can see from the main road. It's a big field and most of it isn't so bad, but about halfway along it goes very steep and then, right in the middle of the steepest bit, there's a big bulge. The ground just seems to come out, suddenly, and then go back again. I suppose it was all right for horses. And since tractors came in, I don't believe they used that field for anything but grazing. But they must have had a change of policy, one way or another. I wasn't in these parts then and I don't know. What I do know is that they sent Daniel out to plough it with the big old tractor they had then, and he never complained or hesitated, just drove it straight along the slope, and when it got to the bulge, it rolled over on him and crushed his pelvis. He'll never drive a tractor again. And he's fifty; too late to learn another job.

I walked over to the tractor and stood looking at it in the sunshine. It was a new one, bright yellow. Even the tyres hadn't got muddy yet, and the paint was in showroom condition. Mr. Cartwright had made a great point of how they were getting a new one that would be more stable than the one that rolled on Daniel. As if there was all that difference between one tractor and another. A tractor's a tractor, and when it starts to roll, it rolls, and if you're driving, you just go over with it. Some of the caterpillar-track jobs are safer, I admit, but this was an ordinary farm type.

I just couldn't make up my mind. Nobody wants to get killed or badly injured just for a bit of hay. On the other hand, I knew he'd be glad of the chance to sack me. And as if to chime in with that thought, out of the farmhouse comes the girl who's the cause of the blasted mess I'm in.

She gave me that come-on look as she went past. Of course, her face was turned the opposite way from the house. He was probably watching her with a shotgun in his big meaty hands. Yvonne, her name was. I'd Yvonne her. Causing nothing but a lot of trouble.

"Robert tells me you're going mowing this morning," she said, all innocent.

"Expect so," I said, and I turned to bend over the tractor's oil tank. It was quite full, I knew that, but I didn't want her sending me any more of those signals. I'm as human as anybody, but I had serious thoughts on my mind.

She clicked past me—she was wearing some kind of foreign wooden shoes and a simple print dress. Together they added up to something far from simple, if you follow me. I kept my eyes well down on the dipstick until she went back into the house.

Then I thought, well, I might make a start, at any rate. There was all the rest of the field to do. If I decided not to do the bulge, when I got to it, that would mean the sack, but at least I'd mow the rest of the hay, for Mr. Cartwright's sake. He was a decent old bloke, and he couldn't do anything on the farm himself, now that his back was bad, so the work would get behind anyway. So I got into the seat and started the engine. I'd been working with this tractor since I came to the farm, a matter of three or four weeks, and it handled pretty well, I must say.

The cutter was already fixed on behind. I'd seen to that the night before. It was the type of cutter that has no wheels of its own, just fastens on to the back of the tractor and has one lever to stop and start it and another to move it up and down. You keep it raised till you get to the grass you're going to cut and then you lower it as you go along each row and raise it again when you get to the end. It takes a lot of patience, because you have to keep your eye on it all the time, as well as steer the tractor, and if the ground is uneven, you have to keep reversing and going back over bits you've missed through not bringing the cutter down low enough. If you bring it down too far, it digs into the ground. It's fiddling work, going back five and six times on every row; you're lucky if you get finished with one medium-sized field in half a day, and then you're dead tired with concentrating so hard and twisting round all the time on your seat. And on your own, of course, all the time, never anybody to pass the time of day with or have a joke like you would with your mates in building-site work. Then they say tractor drivers get paid a lot. And on top of that to get rolled on like Daniel.

So I went down to the field. Mary had given me some sandwiches and a flask of tea. I decided to mow the rest of the field, leaving out the bit where Daniel had bought it, and then go down to the pub and have a beer with my sandwiches and leave the tea till later. The afternoon would be very heavy, I could tell that. I kept my mind off the question of what exactly I'd be doing in the afternoon. I might be in an ambulance going to hospital, or I might be picking up my cards and going home to tell Mary I was sacked.

I mowed all morning. After about an hour, my back started aching with all the twisting back and forth. The cutter was always going too low or too high. Once it dug itself into the ground and began to drag, so that I had to slam the brakes on. It had earth and grass wedged in the cutting blades. Took me half an hour to clear it properly. Then off again, with the thing clacking behind me. What with the drumming of the tractor, the smell of hot oil covering up the smell of the hay, and the *clack-clack* of the blades, I began to think very kindly towards a quiet corner seat in the pub and a cool dark pint of beer. But I had to get a fair morning's work in first.

I did it all except the dangerous bit and then I drove the tractor down to the pub and parked it right outside. It was half a mile at least, and I wasn't going to waste time walking. I went in, got my pint, opened my box of sandwiches and was just settling down, passing the time of day with old Ken, the landlord, and one or two others, when I heard a noise I thought was familiar. I looked out of the window. Mr. Robert's car. He drove a Jag. Probably Yvonne wouldn't ride in anything else, but in any case, he was the smarty-pants Young Farmers' Club type who would have to have a fast car like he'd have to breathe.

I saw him looking at the tractor and then he took his wife into the saloon bar, very smart for summer visitors and very pricey. He stayed long enough to settle her with a drink and then he came in to the public bar, looking for me.

"There you are," he says, coming straight to the point. "Using the tractor for personal transport, I see."

"It's either that or take a much longer lunch break," I told him.

"Any reason why you shouldn't eat your lunch in the field?" he asked. Oh, he was out to get me, the red-faced pup.

"I'm in the habit of having a pint with my lunch, Mr. Cartwright," I said, very clearly. "I'm entitled to forty minutes, the union'll back me on that, and it's my own affair where I spend them."

"But the tractor's my affair," he said: "I pay for the fuel it costs for you to run the thing round like a taxi."

"Please go outside if you want a quarrel," said old Ken, getting ready to show us the door.

"Have you finished that field?" said Robert, ignoring Ken completely.

"All but the bit that's too steep," I said. I could feel myself beginning to shake, he was annoying me so much.

"Well, remember that's what the tractor's for," he said, giving me a really mean look. He turned to go back to the saloon bar, and at that moment I happened to look past Ken's head and right through the serving hatch into the saloon. You could see anyone who was standing there, though you couldn't see the rest of the room. And Yvonne had the upper half of herself well and truly framed in the hatch, looking across, taking it all in. Her eyes were very bright. I suppose she liked to see men quarrel. I hated her worse than him.

We got a bit of peace then, in the public bar, but it was all spoiled for me by knowing that the two of them were in the saloon. So I just finished up my sandwiches and had another half of beer, to wash them down, and went out to the tractor again. I hadn't told Ken or any of the others about what was on my mind. Sometimes a man's best alone. Their advice couldn't help me and I didn't want to spoil my lunch break talking about it.

I drove the tractor back to the field. The grass I'd cut during the morning was already drying. It was very good mowing weather. To my eye it already looked a different green from the part that was still uncut. There were a lot of flowers in it, mostly buttercups and clover. There were a few poppies, but not many, because it was good soil.

I got the tractor in position as if I was going on, but I still hadn't made up my mind. The engine was going, so I didn't hear the Jaguar drive up, but suddenly it was there on the road, at the bottom of the slope. I looked down at it and saw Robert and Yvonne get out. She stayed by the car and he came into the field and walked up towards me. I stopped the engine to hear what he had to say.

"You've made a pretty good job of this," he said, looking round at the field. "Finish this bit and you can knock off."

"If I do this bit I'll knock off for keeps, as like as not," I said. But I didn't press it too much. He must have wanted to smooth things out a bit, after the way he'd insulted me down at the pub. He'd cooled down and realised he'd gone too far. If he sacked me on the same day as he'd quarrelled with me like that, in front of witnesses, it would be all over the district that he was a farmer who treated his hands badly.

He blinked up at me. "You can do what you think best," he said. "If you don't want to mow that slope, don't." Then he turned round, before I could say anything, and went back down to the Jaguar and Yvonne.

That left me in the clear. All I had to do was turn the tractor round, take it back to the farm and call it a day. He wouldn't sack me. He'd given in to my judgment. He must have known damn well that he wouldn't drive a tractor along that slope himself, not for fifty thousand pounds, and he knew how it would look if he made me do it, under threat of the sack, and then I got killed. That was how his mind was working. He didn't like me any better than before, and he still wanted to get me out of eyeshot of his wife, I knew that.

I started the engine. And now comes the bit that's hard to explain. All of a sudden I didn't want to leave the field without mowing that slope. I was frightened, but now that Robert had backed down, it was a matter between me and my fear. He was out of it and so was his silly bitch of a wife. And now, for the first time, I really felt I couldn't turn my back on the job. Am I making it clear? I don't suppose so. It's just that—well, I was a tractor driver and the field was waiting. I felt that if I did it and got away with it, I'd feel better every time I climbed up on a tractor, for the rest of my working life.

So now I was trapped, and in the strongest trap of all: one of my own making. If the boss tells you to do something foolhardy or else he'll sack you, and you tell him to go to hell, that's all right—you've shown your independence. But if he tells you to do it if you feel able to, and leaves it up to your own judgment, what then? You can turn away from it and still live with yourself, right enough. But for the rest of your life you'll wonder what would have happened. Whether you were right to put your own safety first. Whether you would have made it after all.

So there was the slope, with its uncut grass, waiting.

For a moment I just sat there, looking at it. I kept the engine turning over, and the tractor was shaking under me as if it was already getting ready to buck me off and roll on me. I took my cap off and there was a rim of sweat where it lay against my forehead. Jesus, I was frightened.

I knew Robert's eyes were fixed on me and I knew what he must be thinking, but I hadn't any energy to spare for him now. Yvonne would be watching me, too, and thinking her own little thoughts, but the same applied. No time for that now. Although I knew they were close by, I felt as if they were millions of miles away, on another planet. There were no other people in the world: there was only me, and the tractor, and the tall green grass with the flowers in it. And the field, lying so still in the afternoon sunlight, with that horrible hump sticking out in it. Sort of bulging out, as if it wanted to mock me. *Come on*, it seemed to be saying, *and I'll treat you like I treated Daniel.*

The cutter was rattling behind me, in time to the shaking of the tractor. It seemed to be impatient to get going. I couldn't tell whether it was on my side or the tractor's.

Did I really have to do this? I put my cap back on and leaned for a second on the mudguard at the top of the nearside rear wheel. It was vibrating with that same metallic *drum, drum, drum* that ran all through the tractor and up through the seat into my spine. It seemed to me, at the moment, like the drumming of the soldiers of death coming for me.

I shifted right over on the seat and leaned my weight on the offside wheel, the one on my right. I'd decided already to tackle the slope in that direction, right side high and left side low. When I got to the end of each row—that is, if I *did* get to the end and didn't tip over right away on the first run—I wasn't going to turn round and come back. I was going to go down to the bottom of the field, where it was level and come back to this side again. My reason was that to keep an eye on the cutter, I had to twist round to the left and look back. This meant I would naturally lean my weight to the right, up the slope. Not that it would make much difference. I'm not a very heavy man.

I looked again at the slope ahead of me. Well, I was ready to go. Suddenly I felt, in my belly, the terrible lurching feeling the tractor would make as it went over. As Daniel must have felt it. My insides churned round and round and my bones felt chalky, as if they'd snap straight away. Daniel must have seen the world turn over and the green slope come rushing up at him. Then the sickening weight of the tractor rolling on him and the *drum, drum, drum* in his ears. Forty-five minutes before they could drag it off him. Where did they find a fool to try to work over the same stretch again? A fool like me?

But it was too late to turn back now, really too late. For fifteen pounds' worth of hay, I was going to invite a big yellow tractor to roll on me. And not even my own fifteen pounds. I let in the clutch, moved as far as I could over to the right, and we went forward.

Almost at once the right-hand wheel started shifting up and down, as if it had too little weight to hold it steady. I pressed down on the mudguard with my whole strength, and at the same time moved the lever to bring the cutter down to mowing level. *Let's cut some grass before we go over*, I thought. Then I swivelled my head to look where I was going. The small wheels in front were running softly through the long stalks. They were trying to turn to the left, of course, and run down the slope. Trying to save my life. I held them straight.

I was doing four things at once now. Holding firmly on to the steering wheel to keep the whole outfit on course. Working the lever that raised and lowered the cutter. Looking ahead and looking back, twisting my head and shoulders back and forth without stopping. And keeping the weight of my body clenched against that right-hand mudguard. Oh, yes, and there was one more thing I was doing, a fifth thing. I was giving out the cold sweat of fear through every pore in my skin. "Jesus," I heard my voice saying quietly, "Jesus. This is it. Jesus. This is it, Jesus. This is it." I wasn't swearing. I was *praying*.

I smelt the sweet grass. Behind me it would be bleeding as the blades cut it. But the scent of its green blood would be drowned in diesel smoke, like the scent of my fear. On we went. Here came the hump: I drove straight on to it at the steepest point. Suddenly, I couldn't bear the thought of working up to the worst point, sweating with fear all the time, and then getting it. If we were going over, I wanted to go over on the first run.

The tractor shook heavily under me, I threw my weight hard to the right, stiffened my right arm on the steering wheel, and turned to look back at the cutter. It was working well, taking off the grass only an inch or two above ground level.

Up went the right-hand wheel. *Jump off*, something seemed to scream in my ear. But I couldn't. There was nowhere to jump to. I couldn't climb up over the huge bumping wheel on my right. So I just kept looking back at the cutter, and steering absolutely steady.

The whole right-hand side came up. It came up farther than I had allowed for even in my worst thoughts. It came up, it came up. And suddenly it went down and we were still driving straight on and still cutting hay.

I opened up and went fast. We bounced along to the end of the row with the cutter jumping up and down, clacking away like mad and missing several patches of that fifteen pound grass. I didn't care. I had come through, I had won, I was the king of the world. If I felt like a burst of speed, I could have one, because I was the king and could have anything.

I swung the tractor round and drove down to the bottom of the field. Not to parade myself in front of Robert and Yvonne, because I had truly forgotten that they were on this earth. Simply because that was the way to position the outfit to cut another row. I drove fast, singing, and the tractor rolled and bounced. The seat underneath me was jumping like a goat. Round with the wheel again and I was charging along beside the bottom hedge. And suddenly I was beside the parked Jaguar and Robert's face was staring, for an instant, right into mine. It looked sick. Sick with fear and sick with rage. I saw it all. He'd been as frightened as I was, watching me. But now that it was over, his spirits didn't lift up like mine. They sank right down, because I'd beat him all ends up.

There was nothing I could do to make him feel better. I couldn't get off the crest of my wave just then, not for anybody. I just kept my foot down and roared along to the end of the field, then up again to begin another row.

This time, it was easy. I kept my weight well over to the right, just in case, but my mind was careless. The worst part was done; we had it licked. I just held the tractor steady and this time the cutter was at just the right height. I could have won a mowing competition with that row.

Round again, singing "I'm the king, I'm the king," to no tune at all, and this time the Jaguar had gone. I fancied there was a scorched place on the road where it had been standing. I kept on with the mowing until the last blade of grass was cut. That was it. I'd have to come back, in a day or two, to turn it over, but that held no terrors now. I could stay on this farm for the rest of my life, if I wanted to, and work over that slope whenever it was needed. Ploughing, mowing, harvesting, spraying, anything. Me and the tractor, we'd beaten it.

I drove back to the farm. There was no sign of the Jaguar. I got out a spanner and unfastened the cutter and cleaned it with an oily rag and put it away. The sun was still shining warmly, and it beat on my back and dried the sweat under my shirt, and there was plenty to dry.

I was just coming out of the shed after putting the cutter away when Yvonne came out of the house and stood looking at me.

"Finished for the day?" she asked me.

"I thought you'd gone out," I said.

"Bob had to go into Banbury," she said. "There's a man he's got to talk to about seeds or something."

"Oh," I said.

"He wanted me to go along. He was quite cross when I wouldn't. But I told him I had a headache. It's so *close* today." And she shook her head as if to clear it. Or to make the light quiver in her yellow hair. "I'm better now, though," she said.

"Well, I'm off," I said. But I still stood there.

"I should think you need a drink," she said. "What with everything."

"They're not open," I said.

"There's plenty in the house," she said. "Plenty of everything."

What could I do? Another time, I'd have gone straight back to Mary and the kids. But today I was the king, I'd won and it was a case of winner take all.

So she went into the house and I went in after her.

SIR HUGH WALPOLE

1884–1941

He was a genial man of attractive appearance: a bibliophile,
patron of art and benefactor of authors less successful than himself.
He greatly admired Trollope (of whom he wrote a biography)
and he resembled him in that, as Trollope said of himself,
he was "impregnated with his own creations".
Walpole was a lifelong bachelor . . .

Bachelors

IN ANY CATHEDRAL town there must of necessity be certain characters who are bound and tied to the cobble-stones of the place from whose heart they have sprung. One can picture them in no other town or country—they are that place's property as surely as are the Town Hall, the Baths, the Market Place, and the Cathedral. Their very peculiarities, their little idiosyncrasies, are proudly suggested in that column of the local newspaper headed, "Are You Aware That——?" and, always, their names are to be found after "Amongst those present were——" when any kind of festivity, civic or personal, has occurred.

The cathedral town of S—— in Glebeshire boasted Henry and Robert Chandler, Esqs., amongst their most distinguished 'features'. 'Features' they were, and no visitor could spend a week in that pleasant city without having them pointed out to him, just as he had already been directed towards the great west-end window of the cathedral or the magnificent golden tomb of the Dryden St. Pomfrets.

Harry and Robin Chandler had spent all their days enclosed by the pleasant shelter of S——. They had indeed gone first to Rugby and afterwards to Trinity, Cambridge, but from these places they had always returned to S—— with such precipitation and eagerness that it was evident that even whilst their bodies were being harassed and driven in wilder places their souls were resting in S——.

Robin Chandler was, at the time of this crisis in his history, fifty-five years of age, Harry ten years younger, and they lived at the corner of the Close in a house shaped like a teapot, and had a motherly and rotund widow as their housekeeper. Of the two, Robin was most certainly the 'character'. He *looked* a 'character'. He was precisely the kind of old gentleman whom you would expect to find in the close of an English cathedral. You would say, on seeing Robin Chandler, "Ah! *there* he is!" and you would connect him with the other old gentlemen and the other old maids whom you had, in your time, met in cathedral cities. Robin looked more than his age because his hair was white and his figure rotund. His face was round and amiable and a little foolish, and this foolishness was to be attributed to the fact that he was never sure what he would do with his mouth. He would be amused and would laugh heartily, but even in the climax of the laugh his mouth would wander a little and tremble uncertainly at the corners. He had a dimple in each cheek, and a fine high forehead from which his hair was brushed straight back into a kind of white waterfall that tumbled down the back of his head. He was short and fat and very neat, being dressed generally in pepper-and-salt trousers, a brown velvet waistcoat with brass buttons, a black coat and a black tie. When out of doors he wore a soft black hat cocked jauntily over one ear, and he always trotted along, moving his feet very slightly one in front of the other. He stopped a thousand times during his walk down the High Street, greeting his friends (he had no enemies in the world), and he always had a number of gentle queer things to say—things that no one else would have thought of saying. His interests were natural history, stamps, bowls, and, of course, his brother—and this last swallowed up the others even as the serpent in the Bible swallowed up all the other serpents.

Harry Chandler was of quite another kind: of middle height, red-faced, short brown moustache, brown hair cut close to his head, his eyes confident and unintelligent, his attitude that of a man who knows his world, takes many baths, and has no doubts about anything. He stood at the head of the sporting interests of S——, being president of the golf club and the cricket club; his interests were also apparently political, for he was a most important member of the Conservative Club that had its palatial apartments half-way down the High Street. He might be seen any morning of the week striding along in a tweed jacket and large and balloon-like knickerbockers, his face very red, his eyes very wide and staring, his air that of a man who knows his power and values it. "Ha, Benson!" he would say, or, "Ha, Rawlings!" or even, "Good-day to you, Bumpus!" and sometimes, when a local infant threatened his progress, "Out of the way, little one, out of the way!" People said, with considerable truth, that it was strange that two brothers, who were so continually together, should be so different, but when one knew Robin Chandler intimately one discovered that he had been endeavouring, all his days, to acquire some of his brother's habits and characteristics. He would try at times to be domineering, hearty, and monosyllabic, and of course he always failed. He had the pleasantest of voices, but it was the voice of an amiable canary, and he never could express himself without using a great number of words. That Robin worshipped his brother was one of the items of natural history treasured by the city of S——.

He had worshipped from that day, so many years ago, when a lonely little boy of ten, he had been informed that he was henceforth to have a companion in life.

He had been, always, from the first a submissive character who depended very much on other people's affection for happiness. It had been, the ladies of S—— always said, a shamefully one-sided affair.

Harry Chandler's attitude to his brother was one of indulgent tolerance. "Dear old fellow," he would call him. "He's an odd kind of chap, my brother," he would confide to a listening friend. "You'd never think we were brothers, now, would you? You should just see him try to play golf. Stands there with his legs apart, his body stiff as a rod, biting his lips, don't you know—serious as anything—and then he clean misses it, you know. He's a dear old fellow, but, between you and me, a bit of an old woman."

Robin was quite aware of his brother's attitude, but, indeed, no other seemed possible. He had watched, with wide-eyed wonder, his brother's growth. The things Harry could do! Was there anyone who played games with such confidence, anyone who could hold his own in a gathering of men with such assurance and success, anyone so fascinating in a drawing-room, anyone in the world with such captivating *savoir-faire*? Robin, himself, was afraid of women, except very old and lonely ones. He had, long ago, been 'horribly' in love, and she might, one imagines, have loved him in return had he pursued the matter; but—what *would* Harry do without him? No, until Harry himself married, Robin must send the other sex to limbo. And through all these years what agitations there had been! For a long time it had seemed as certain that Harry would marry as that night must follow the day. That his brother was fascinating to women Robin held as surely as that he himself had no attraction for them whatever! Terrible hours! Terrible apparitions of beautiful young women to whom Harry would give their first golfing lesson! Terrible 'alarums and excursions'! "Oh! I hear, Mr. Chandler, that we are to congratulate your brother . . .!" Is not S—— a cathedral city?

And yet, always, Robin was delivered. Through all these years Harry had not been even engaged. Robin wondered at the women, but, from his heart, was grateful to them, and, with every year, the assurance of safety grew. Now, always, he put the terrible thought from him. Sometimes in the night it would leap out from the dark, with mouth a-grin and widespread claws. "What'll you do, my friend, if it *does* happen? It may, you know. Plenty of time yet . . . A nice kind of time you'll have alone——" Well, that was a bad half-hour, but at the end of it the grinning beast was beaten back to its lair.

There was nothing that Harry could do that did not interest Robin, and this, men at the club said, was bad for Harry.

"Really, Chandler's getting a bit of a bore. Thinks the least little thing he's done ought to be sent up to the *Times*. All that silly old brother of his."

But they liked 'the silly old brother'—liked him, were the truth known, better than Harry. Robin would have been immensely surprised at his popularity had he ever known it.

There came an afternoon. It was half-past four on a day of late October, and the cathedral bells were drowsily ringing for evensong. Robin was standing at the window of the little smoking-room, where they always had tea, waiting his brother's return from golf. It was dusk, and at the farther end of the Close, above an ivy-covered wall, low between two old Georgian houses, the blue evening sky, fading into palest saffron, showed. The cobbles had caught the evening light, and figures—two old ladies, a canon, an old gentleman in a bath-chair—were moving, like notes in a piece of music, across the grass square to the cathedral doors.

It was a sight that Robin had seen year after year from that same window, and it had always for him drama as intense as anything that Napoleon or Wellington can have felt from the top of some smoke-clad hill. "There's Miss Barton. I thought she was in London. I wonder whether her brother's left her anything in his will. There's Prendergast. It's his month, I suppose. How cross it will make him, having to come in from his golf!"

He was conscious, as he heard the bells, of the quiet, cosy little room behind him filled with dusty old things that belonged to every period of his experiences—old college photographs, old books, old caps that his brother had worn in different teams which his presence had honoured. There, too, the kettle was humming, the tea-cake was hot, the clock—the same old gold clock—ticked the minutes away. He ruffled his hair with his hand, until he looked more than ever like an amiable, well-fed bird. The bells had fallen to a slow monotone—"Hurry up—hurry up—hurry up . . ." There were steps on the cobbles, a key in the door, a pause in the hall, then his brother had come in.

"Fancy, Harry," said Robin, moving towards the tea-things, "Miss Brandon's back. I wonder whether——"

"I say, old man"—Harry's voice was, for perhaps the first time in his life, nervous and hesitating—"Robin, old boy—hem! You must congratulate me—hem—yes—ha!—I'm engaged to Miss Pinsent. She—hum—accepted me on the—hum—golf-course this afternoon."

II

THERE FOLLOWED then for Robin Chandler the most terrible weeks, weeks far more terrible than anything that he had ever imagined possible for human courage to support.

It was demanded of him, on every side, that he should be false. He must be false to his brother; he must pretend to him that he was glad and happy that this had occurred; he must be false to all the old women of S——, who crowded about him, eagerly watching for any sign of that wound which, they were assured amongst themselves, his brother's engagement must have dealt him; above all, he must be false to the girl, Iris Pinsent, who instantly demanded his affection and (such was always her attitude to the other sex) protection from the roughness of the world.

Iris Pinsent—golden, fragile, and appealing—was straight from the schoolroom. Her father had, six months before, arrived at S—— as governor of its prison, and, during those six months, Iris had put up her hair and 'come out'. She had seemed to Robin so entirely of the schoolroom that he had never, for the wildest instant, considered her as a possible wife for anybody.

Now every day she appeared, ran over their old teapot house as though it were her own, won the instant and undying hatred of Mrs. Rumbold, the housekeeper, sat upon Harry's knee, pulled Harry's hair, untied his tie and tied it up again, laughed and sang and danced about the two elderly men as though they were puppies quite new to a brilliant world.

No one—not Robin himself—had any conception of the depths of Robin's suffering. "Mr. Robert Chandler *must* be feeling his brother's engagement," said one old lady to another old lady, and *another* old lady to *another* old lady. "But really you wouldn't think so, to look at him. He'll feel it after the marriage though, when he's all alone"—and the old ladies either licked their lips or wiped their eyes, according to their characters.

To Robin it was exactly as though he were standing on the very edge of a slimy and bottomless pit. Towards this pit his feet were slipping, and soon, very soon, the inevitable moment of descent would come; but meanwhile, gripping with his feet, digging his hands into the slime, he would hold on as long as he could . . . the world should not know until it must.

He trotted about the town, went to tea parties, played bowls, was as neat and as careful, as interested in his neighbours' affairs, as kind and thoughtful as ever he had been. Harry Chandler, who was, of course, not a discerning man, was hurt at this indifference.

"Really, Robin," he said one evening, when they were alone, "I don't believe you'll mind it a bit when I'm gone."

Robin paused, then said—"Of course, Harry, I shall miss you—terribly," and that was all.

Robin, in fact, ran from his despair. There were horrible moments when it caught him up, and then there was a grinding cold at his heart; but these moments with all the force of his character he beat down. But what was he to do? What should he, could he, do? He had devoted his life, every moment and thought of it, to his brother's interests. He could not now, at his age, build up other gods, worship at other shrines. His bowls, his stamps, he laughed aloud when he thought of them. His life had been simply that he should watch his brother's triumphs, soften his brother's defeats, listen to his brother's ideas, anticipate his brother's wants. This may seem to many a humiliating rôle for a man: Robin Chandler did not feel it so; he was simply grateful that he had so splendid a person as his brother to play shadow to. He fancied that many people in the town thought him a lucky fellow.

No longer, even now, was there any need of him as audience, no longer was his opinion invited, no longer his praise demanded—and yet, even in these early weeks of the engagement, Robin fancied that Miss Pinsent was not proving quite so good a listener as she might. Indeed he began to wonder whether Miss Pinsent liked being a listener at all. She had so much to say, so many of her own achievements and triumphs to recount. Robin, as he watched the two of them together, wondered at first how any one *could* treat his brother with such casual equality; then, as the days passed and this became a common sight, he wondered whether there had not been something a little absurd about his own attitude.

Very reluctantly and only after a very considerable time Robin was compelled to confess to himself that Harry was not quite at his best as a lover. Harry, whilst Miss Pinsent sprang around him, laughed at him, mocked him, imitated him, burlesqued him, was often at a loss. He had found at once that his heavy, authoritative manner had no effect upon Miss Pinsent.

"Ha!—hum——" she would imitate him. "How d'y do, Rawlings."

Robin, listening in amazement, wondered whether there could be any love in Miss Pinsent's heart, but apparently love there really was, of a kittenish, puppyish kind. Another astonishing thing was that Miss Pinsent was, it seemed, more afraid of Robin than of Harry. She was only, on the rarest occasions, 'kittenish' with Robin, but would stand in front of him and ask him quite serious questions about Life and bowls and bird's eggs, and Robin would ruffle his hair and answer her to the best of his ability. Really, Robin was forced to confess to himself, poor Harry looked quite foolish and even silly on many occasions. "Why does he let her behave like that?" he thought. "I do hope that other people don't notice it."

He was pleasantly aware—if anything could be pleasant at this terrible time—that he was acquiring now an independent existence in people's eyes. This had begun, of course, with people being sorry for him, but that the proud little man would not allow for a moment. He had been, for many, many years, overshadowed by his brother; but now that his brother was allotted and disposed of, Robin Chandler stood out all by himself.

"Poor little Mr. Chandler!" the ladies said. "We must show him a little kindness just now." And Robin was obliged to confess that he liked it. Nevertheless, it must not be supposed that, during all this time, he was not an utterly miserable man.

Then, as the weeks passed, his discomfort grew. He wished, how fervently, that his brother would deal with the girl in some more dignified and satisfactory fashion. "Why, even I," Robin thought to himself, "have more influence over her than he has. She never plays about with me like that. Really, Harry——"

But the tragic side of it all was that Harry was not a happy lover. Why was he a lover at all, if not a happy one? All Harry's fine spirit had departed. His honest brow wore a puzzled look that never in all its five-and-forty years it had worn before. He began sentences, "I wonder whether——" "Do you think, Robin——" and then never finished them. He abandoned the Conservative Club, and although he played golf with Miss Pinsent on most afternoons of the week, that beloved game seemed to have lost most of its charm.

He no longer on his return would proclaim to his brother that he had done a bogey five in three, or beaten old Major Waggett (his special foe) by two up and three to play. No, he returned and drank his tea in silence. Robin's heart ached for him.

Once the two of them had, in Robin's presence, a most horrible quarrel. They were all having tea together in the little dusty smoking-room, and Miss Pinsent, striking unexpectedly her lover in the chest (one of her loving, playful tricks), upset his tea. He swore then with a frank volubility that spoke of many weeks' difficult restraint. She cried, rushed from the room and the house, vowing that she would never return . . .

But, of course, she did return, and that very shortly afterwards. There was a reconciliation—but Robin found, to his own exceeding surprise, that he was rather ashamed of both of them. "I wish—I wish," he thought, "that I didn't see Harry like this. Love affects people very strangely."

Then, on an afternoon of pouring rain, Robin Chandler was beating his way up the High Street, hastening home to warmth and tea. He was sheltered by an enormous umbrella, and this gave him precisely the appearance of a walking mushroom. His arm was touched, and, turning round, he saw Miss Pinsent, who was looking bedraggled and unhappy, without any umbrella at all.

"I didn't know it was going to rain. It looked so fine . . ." Her voice trembled and she betrayed the imminence of tears—she took his arm and they walked along together. Then, suddenly, he was aware that she was talking about Harry, and speaking as though she needed Robin's advice about him. Robin's heart began to beat fast. "Did he really think that Harry loved her? . . . Would Harry really be kind to her? . . . Of course she was very fond of him, but . . . Did he think that differences in ages *really* made much trouble afterwards? . . . Of course she was very fond . . ."

This may be definitely put down as the most critical moment in all Mr. Robin Chandler's long life. The Tempter, with that bewildering precipitance and complete disregard for the justice of a forewarning prelude that he invariably betrays, sprang, there and then, in the dripping High Street of S——, upon the poor little man.

Robin saw, with a horrible distinctness, that the power was given him to sway Miss Pinsent. A little hesitation on his part, an unexpressed but nevertheless definite agreement with her as to the danger of unequal ages in marriage, a hint or two as to possible harshnesses and brutalities in Harry's character—he saw with amazing and horrible clearness that these things would be quite enough. By to-morrow afternoon Mr. Henry Chandler would no longer be engaged to Miss Iris Pinsent . . .

They halted for an instant at the top of the High Street. The wind was rushing round the corner and the rain lashed the umbrella. Robin could see the wall of the cathedral, very grey and grim, and one corner of the Close with the rain running in little driven lines across the cobbles.

"You'll have your brother back again . . . You won't be a lonely, lonely old man . . ."

Then with a shake of his shoulders the thing was gone and, as they drove their way into the Close, he began eagerly, exhaustively, almost breathlessly, to prove to her that his brother was indeed a god among men.

III

IT WAS ARRANGED that Harry should go and stay with the Pinsents for a week in a house that they had in the country some miles from S——, and that during that time the date of the wedding should be settled. Robin saw with confused feelings his brother's departure; it was the first time for many years that they had been separated—this was melancholy enough—but also he was compelled to admit that it was a relief to him that, for a week at any rate, he would not be forced to watch his brother under such conditions. He found, indeed, that in a resigned, rather dejected kind of fashion, he was quite happy. Mrs. Rumbold, the housekeeper, could not make enough fuss of him. Harry had always been so emphatically the master in the house that she had never considered Mr. Robert. It had always been Harry who had arranged the hours of meals, and did he in the summer come in very late, well, then, Mr. Robert waited.

But now——! No, Mr. Harry had acted as a selfish and inconsiderate man, leaving poor Mr. Robert all alone 'without a thought'. What did an old thing of his age want to do with marriage—choosing so young a girl, too—almost indecent! Had Miss Pinsent treated Mrs. Rumbold with care and deference, then there might have been another opinion altogether. As it was—"She's a regular young Slap-in-the-face, if you ask me," said Mrs. Rumbold to her chosen friends. "Slap and come again, that's what *she* is. You mark my words."

Therefore Robin received an attention, a deference, that had never been his before. And not only from Mrs. Rumbold! The whole town offered it him. The town had always been fond of him, but so modest, and retiring had he been that the comment always was—"Mr. Robert Chandler? . . . Oh yes! . . . Such a nice little man. No one sees very much of him. No one *knows* him, you might say, but you couldn't help liking him!"

But, during this week, in what an amazing way did he expand, flourish, blossom! It was at first incredible to him that people should be interested in him for himself, and fifty-five years' convictions about life are difficult things to shake. But behold! Whereas before it had been, "Oh, Mr. Chandler, your brother has so kindly promised to dine with us on Thursday night, I wonder whether you could come too?" Now it was, "Do come and dine, Mr. Chandler, *any* night as long as you give us a day or two's notice." People found him indeed a great deal more amusing by himself than he had been before in his brother's company. Always there had been that anxious glance in his brother's direction to see whether everything were well, always that modest hesitation about giving any opinion at all whilst his brother was present.

Now he would sit perched on the edge of a sofa, his hands on his fat little knees, the dimples dancing in his cheeks, his hair on end, his chuckle (a chuckle entirely his own) over some joke that he saw ahead of him and would very shortly deliver to his audience. By the end of the week he had decided that:

(1) He liked women after all.

(2) He would be perfectly wretched alone, but that he would bear up as well as he could.

(3) He'd really no idea that he'd got so much to say.

(4) He felt younger than he had ever done before.

"Still," he said to himself, "dear old Harry's marriage will be too dreadful. I simply don't know what I shall do with myself."

The afternoon of Harry's return arrived. Robin stood at the window as he had done on that other horrible day when he had first heard of the engagement.

He was inevitably reminded of that day, for now again there, above the low wall, pale blue was fading into saffron, across the grass figures were stealing; already the bell was dropping into its "Hurry up—hurry up—hurry up."

Robin watched, and then suddenly, like a flame, like a fire, came the truth. He knew, yes, he knew, let him deny it as he might, that never in all his five-and-fifty years had he enjoyed a week as he had enjoyed this last one. He had tasted delights, known extravagances and excitements that had never before been his. He had been free!

He stared round bewildered. What treachery to Harry! What irony that so soon he should have changed from despair to what was not far from triumph! He remembered the bitter dismay that so short a time ago had, in this very room, wrapped him round.

But now he was a man of freedom! No one's shadow, depending upon no one in the world for his independent happiness! His eyes fell upon a picture above the fireplace, a water-colour painting of a grey fell and a blue lake at evening. It was a picture that he loved, but Harry had declared it "A dreary thing"—and it was only this week that it had been raised to that place of honour. After all, Harry would not care now, now when so soon he was to have a house of his own.

The door was flung open, and Harry was there, there with him in the room.

"I say!" he closed the door behind him and came forward. "Robin, she's chucked me!"

"Oh!"

"Yes—jolly well chucked me—last night when we were alone she told me. Been mistaken . . . misjudged her feelings—was too young . . . all the rest of it."

"Oh! Harry . . . Oh, I'm sorry!"

Harry strode twice or thrice up and down the room. "Yes, chucked, by Jove! At first, you know, you could have knocked me down with a feather. But now—damn it—I don't know, Robin, that I'm not glad. She said it was largely some talk she'd had with you about me—how you'd praised me no end, and then she'd seen that she didn't feel about me quite like that, and that she couldn't marry me unless she did. The contrast struck her, don't you know . . ."

He paused, then went on: "But I'm glad, dashed if I'm not. It's awful being engaged . . . I felt it all the time, really. She never said things about me as you've always done—never knew me a bit as you do. It's a relief to be free—it *is* really. I missed you like anything. You were always so sympathetic and understanding. It'll be jolly to have you to tell things to again . . . Yes—dash it—hum—ha—— Won't the fellows at the club laugh? . . . Well, I must go and clean. Tell old Ma Rumbold to hurry with the tea."

He went out.

Robin waited a little, then, with the very shadow of a sigh, walked to the window. He looked out for a moment at the gathering dusk, then got a chair, climbed on to it and carefully took down the water-colour from the wall.

H.G. WELLS

1886–1946

Anatole France styled him, "the greatest intellectual force in the English-speaking world." Trained as a scientist and blessed with a visionary's imagination, he became a brilliant and prolific exponent of science-fiction, writing novels such as *The Time Machine*. His non-S.F. work includes several delightfully ingenious short stories.

The Man Who Could Work Miracles

IT IS DOUBTFUL whether the gift was innate. For my own part, I think it came to him suddenly. Indeed, until he was thirty he was a sceptic, and did not believe in miraculous powers. And here, since it is the most convenient place, I must mention that he was a little man, and had eyes of a hot brown, very erect red hair, a moustache with ends that he twisted up, and freckles. His name was George McWhirter Fotheringay—not the sort of name by any means to lead to any expectation of miracles—and he was clerk at Gomshott's. He was greatly addicted to assertive argument. It was while he was asserting the impossibility of miracles that he had his first intimation of his extraordinary powers. This particular argument was being held in the bar of the Long Dragon, and Toddy Beamish was conducting the opposition by a monotonous but effective "So *you* say", that drove Mr. Fotheringay to the very limit of his patience.

There were present, besides these two, a very dusty cyclist, landlord Cox and Miss Maybridge, the perfectly respectable and rather portly barmaid of the Dragon. Miss Maybridge was standing with her back to Mr. Fotheringay, washing glasses; the others were watching him, more or less amused by the present ineffectiveness of the assertive method. Goaded by the Torres Vedras tactics of Mr. Beamish, Mr. Fotheringay determined to make an unusual rhetorical effort. "Looky here, Mr. Beamish," said Mr. Fotheringay. "Let us clearly understand what a miracle is. It's something contrariwise to the course of nature done by power of Will, something what couldn't happen without being specially willed."

"So *you* say," said Mr. Beamish, repulsing him.

Mr. Fotheringay appealed to the cyclist, who had hitherto been a silent auditor, and received his assent—given with a hesitating cough and a glance at Mr. Beamish. The landlord would express no opinion, and Mr. Fotheringay, returning to Mr. Beamish, received the unexpected concession of a qualified assent to his definition of a miracle.

"For instance," said Mr. Fotheringay, greatly encouraged. "Here would be a miracle. That lamp, in the natural course of nature, couldn't burn like that upsy-down, could it, Beamish?"

"*You* say it couldn't," said Beamish.

"And you?" said Fotheringay. "You don't mean to say—eh?"

"No," said Beamish reluctantly. "No, it couldn't."

"Very well," said Mr. Fotheringay. "Then here comes someone, as it might be me, along here, and stands as it might be here, and says to that lamp, as I might do, collecting all my will—'Turn upsy-down without breaking, and go on burning steady,' and—Hullo!"

It was enough to make anyone say "Hullo!" The impossible, the incredible, was visible to them all. The lamp hung inverted in the air, burning quietly with its flame pointing down. It was as solid, as indisputable as ever a lamp was, the prosaic common lamp of the Long Dragon bar. Mr. Fotheringay stood with an extended forefinger and the knitted brows of one anticipating a catastrophic smash. The cyclist, who was sitting next the lamp, ducked and jumped across the bar. Everybody jumped, more or less. Miss Maybridge turned and screamed. For nearly three seconds the lamp remained still. A faint cry of mental distress came from Mr. Fotheringay. "I can't keep it up," he said, "any longer." He staggered back, and the inverted lamp suddenly flared, fell against the corner of the bar, bounced aside, smashed upon the floor, and went out.

It was lucky it had a metal receiver, or the whole place would have been in a blaze. Mr. Cox was the first to speak, and his remark, shorn of needless excrescences, was to the effect that Fotheringay was a fool. Fotheringay was beyond disputing even so fundamental a proposition as that! He was astonished beyond measure at the thing that had occurred. The subsequent conversation threw absolutely no light on the matter so far as Fotheringay was concerned; the general opinion not only followed Mr. Cox very closely but very vehemently. Everyone accused Fotheringay of a silly trick, and presented him to himself as a foolish destroyer of comfort and security. His mind was in a tornado of perplexity, he was himself inclined to agree with them, and he made a remarkably ineffectual opposition to the proposal of his departure.

He went home flushed and heated, coat-collar crumpled, eyes smarting and ears red. He watched each of the ten street lamps nervously as he passed it. It was only when he found himself alone in his little bedroom in Church Row that he was able to grapple seriously with his memories of the occurrence, and ask, "What on earth happened?"

He had removed his coat and boots, and was sitting on the bed with his hands in his pockets repeating the text of his defence for the seventeenth time, "*I* didn't want the confounded thing to upset," when it occurred to him that at the precise moment he had said the commanding words he had inadvertently willed the thing he said, and that when he had seen the lamp in the air he had felt that it depended on him to maintain it there without being clear how this was to be done. He had not a particularly complex mind, or he might have stuck for a time at that 'inadvertently willed', embracing, as it does, the abstrusest problems of voluntary action; but as it was, the idea came to him with a quite acceptable haziness. And from that, following, as I must admit, no clear logical path, he came to the test of experiment.

He pointed resolutely to his candle and collected his mind, though he felt he did a foolish thing. "Be raised up," he said. But in a second that feeling vanished. The candle was raised, hung in the air one giddy moment, and as Mr. Fotheringay gasped, fell with a smash on his toilet-table, leaving him in darkness save for the expiring glow of its wick.

For a time Mr. Fotheringay sat in the darkness, perfectly still. "It did happen, after all," he said. "And 'ow I'm to explain it I *don't* know." He sighed heavily, and began feeling in his pockets for a match. He could find none, and he rose and groped about the toilet-table. "I wish I had a match," he said. He resorted to his coat, and there were none there, and then it dawned upon him that miracles were possible even with matches. He extended a hand and scowled at it in the dark. "Let there be a match in that hand," he said. He felt some light object fall across his palm, and his fingers closed upon a match.

After several ineffectual attempts to light this, he discovered it was a safety-match. He threw it down, and then it occurred to him that he might have willed it lit. He did, and perceived it burning in the midst of his toilet-table mat. He caught it up hastily, and it went out. His perception of possibilities enlarged, and he felt for and replaced the candle in its candlestick. "Here! *you* be lit," said Mr. Fotheringay, and forthwith the candle was flaring, and he saw a little black hole in the toilet-cover, with a wisp of smoke rising from it. For a time he stared from this to the little flame and back, and then looked up and met his own gaze in the looking glass. By this help he communed with himself in silence for a time. "How about miracles now?" said Mr. Fotheringay at last, addressing his reflection.

The subsequent meditations of Mr. Fotheringay were of a severe but confused description. So far as he could see, it was a case of pure willing with him. The nature of his first experiences disinclined him for any further experiments except of the most cautious type. But he lifted a sheet of paper, and turned a glass of water pink and then green, and he created a snail, which he miraculously annihilated, and got himself a miraculous new tooth-brush. Somewhen in the small hours he had reached the fact that his will-power must be of a particularly rare and pungent quality, a fact of which he had certainly had inklings before, but no certain assurance. The scare and perplexity of his first discovery was now qualified by pride in this evidence of singularity and by vague intimations of advantage. He became aware that the church clock was striking one, and as it did not occur to him that his daily duties at Gomshott's might be miraculously dispensed with, he resumed undressing, in order to get to bed without further delay. As he struggled to get his shirt over his head, he was struck with a brilliant idea. "Let me be in bed," he said, and found himself so. "Undressed," he stipulated; and, finding the sheets cold, added hastily, "and in my nightshirt—no, in a nice soft woollen nightshirt. Ah!" he said with immense enjoyment. "And now let me be comfortably asleep . . ."

He awoke at his usual hour and was pensive all through breakfast-time, wondering whether his overnight experience might not be a particularly vivid dream. At length his mind turned again to cautious experiments. For instance, he had three eggs for breakfast; two his landlady had supplied, good, but shoppy, and one was a delicious fresh goose-egg, laid, cooked, and served by his extraordinary will. He hurried off to Gomshott's in a state of profound but carefully concealed excitement, and only remembered the shell of the third egg when his landlady spoke of it that night. All day he could do no work because of this astonishingly new self-knowledge, but this caused him no inconvenience, because he made up for it miraculously in his last ten minutes.

As the day wore on his state of mind passed from wonder to elation, albeit the circumstances of his dismissal from the Long Dragon were still disagreeable to recall, and a garbled account of the matter that had reached his colleagues led to some badinage. It was evident he must be careful how he lifted frangible articles, but in other ways his gift promised more and more as he turned it over in his mind. He intended among other things to increase his personal property by unostentatious acts of creation. He called into existence a pair of very splendid diamond studs, and hastily annihilated them again as young Gomshott came across the counting-house to his desk. He was afraid young Gomshott might wonder how he had come by them. He saw quite clearly the gift required caution and watchfulness in its exercise, but so far as he could judge the difficulties attending its mastery would be no greater than those he had already faced in the study of cycling. It was that analogy, perhaps, quite as much as the feeling that he would be unwelcome in the Long Dragon, that drove him out after supper into the lane beyond the gasworks, to rehearse a few miracles in private.

There was possibly a certain want of originality in his attempts, for apart from his will-power Mr. Fotheringay was not a very exceptional man. The miracle of Moses' rod came to his mind, but the night was dark and unfavourable to the proper control of large miraculous snakes. Then he recollected the story of 'Tannhäuser' that he had read on the back of the Philharmonic programme. That seemed to him singularly attractive and harmless. He stuck his walking-stick—a very nice Poona-Penang lawyer—into the turf that edged the footpath, and commanded the dry wood to blossom. The air was immediately full of the scent of roses, and by means of a match he saw for himself that this beautiful miracle was indeed accomplished. His satisfaction was ended by advancing footsteps. Afraid of a premature discovery of his powers, he addressed the blossoming stick hastily: "Go back." What he meant was "Change back"; but of course he was confused. The stick receded at a considerable velocity, and incontinently came a cry of anger and a bad word from the approaching person. "Who are you throwing brambles at, you fool?" cried a voice. "That got me on the shin."

"I'm sorry, old chap," said Mr. Fotheringay, and then realized the awkward nature of the explanation, caught nervously at his moustache. He saw Winch, one of the three Immering constables, advancing.

"What d'yer mean by it?" asked the constable. "Hullo! It's you, is it? The gent that broke the lamp at the Long Dragon!"

"I don't mean anything by it," said Mr. Fotheringay. "Nothing at all."

"What d'yer do it for then?"

"Oh, bother!" said Mr. Fotheringay.

"Bother, indeed! D'yer know that stick hurt? What d'yer do it for, eh?"

For the moment Mr. Fotheringay could not think what he had done it for. His silence seemed to irritate Mr. Winch. "You've been assaulting the police, young man, this time. That's what *you* done."

"Look here, Mr. Winch," said Mr. Fotheringay, annoyed and confused, "I'm very sorry. The fact is——"

"Well?"

He could think of no way but the truth. "I was working a miracle." He tried to speak in an off-hand way, but try as he would he couldn't.

"Working a——! 'Ere, don't you talk rot. Working a miracle, indeed! Miracle! Well, that's downright funny! Why, you's the chap that don't believe in miracles . . . Fact is, this is another of your silly conjuring tricks—that's what this is. Now, I tell you——"

But Mr. Fotheringay never heard what Mr. Winch was going to tell him. He realized he had given himself away, flung his valuable secret to all the winds of heaven. A violent gust of irritation swept him to action. He turned on the constable swiftly and fiercely. "Here," he said, "I've had enough of this, I have! I'll show you a silly conjuring trick, I will! Go to Hades! Go, now!" He was alone.

Mr. Fotheringay performed no more miracles that night, nor did he trouble to see what had become of his flowering stick. He returned to the town, scared and very quiet, and went to his bedroom. "Lord!" he said, "it's a powerful gift—an extremely powerful gift. I didn't hardly mean as much as that. Not really . . . I wonder what Hades is like?"

He sat on the bed taking off his boots. Struck by a happy thought he transferred the constable to San Francisco, and without any more interference with normal causation went soberly to bed. In the night he dreamt of the anger of Winch.

The next day Mr. Fotheringay heard two interesting items of news. Someone had planted a most beautiful climbing rose against the elder Mr. Gomshott's private house in the Lullaborough Road, and the river as far as Rawling's Mill was to be dragged for Constable Winch.

Mr. Fotheringay was abstracted and thoughtful all that day, and performed no miracles except certain provisions for Winch, and the miracle of completing his day's work with punctual perfection in spite of all the bee-swarm of thoughts that hummed through his mind. And the extraordinary abstraction and meekness of his manner was remarked by several people, and made a matter for jesting. For the most part he was thinking of Winch.

On Sunday evening he went to chapel, and oddly enough, Mr. Maydig, who took a certain interest in occult matters, preached about 'things that are not lawful'. Mr. Fotheringay was not a regular chapel goer, but the system of assertive scepticism, to which I have already alluded, was now very much shaken. The tenor of the sermon threw an entirely new light on these novel gifts, and he suddenly decided to consult Mr. Maydig immediately after the service. So soon as that was determined, he found himself wondering why he had not done so before.

Mr. Maydig, a lean, excitable man with quite remarkably long wrists and neck, was gratified at a request for a private conversation from a young man whose carelessness in religious matters was a subject for general remark in the town. After a few necessary delays, he conducted him to the study of the Manse, which was contiguous to the chapel, seated him comfortably, and, standing in front of a cheerful fire—his legs threw a Rhodian arch of shadow on the opposite wall—requested Mr. Fotheringay to state his business.

At first Mr. Fotheringay was a little abashed, and found some difficulty in opening the matter. "You will scarcely believe me, Mr. Maydig, I am afraid"—and so forth for some time. He tried a question at last, and asked Mr. Maydig his opinion of miracles.

Mr. Maydig was still saying "Well" in an extremely judicial tone, when Mr. Fotheringay interrupted again: "You don't believe, I suppose, that some common sort of person—like myself, for instance—as it might be sitting here now, might have some sort of twist inside him that made him able to do things by his will."

"It's possible," said Mr. Maydig. "Something of the sort, perhaps, is possible."

"If I might make free with something here, I think I might show you by a sort of experiment," said Mr. Fotheringay. "Now, take that tobacco-jar on the table, for instance. What I want to know is whether what I am going to do with it is a miracle or not. Just half a minute, Mr. Maydig, please." He knitted his brows, pointed to the tobacco-jar and said: "Be a bowl of vi'lets." The tobacco-jar did as it was ordered.

Mr. Maydig started violently at the change, and stood looking from the thaumaturgist to the bowl of flowers. He said nothing. Presently he ventured to lean over the table and smell the violets; they were fresh-picked and very fine ones. Then he stared at Mr. Fotheringay again.

"How did you do that?" he asked.

Mr. Fotheringay pulled his moustache. "Just told it—and there you are. Is that a miracle, or is it black art, or what is it? And what do you think's the matter with me? That's what I want to ask."

"It's a most extraordinary occurrence."

"And this day last week I knew no more that I could do things like that than you did. It came quite sudden. It's something odd about my will, I suppose, and that's as far as I can see."

"Is *that*—the only thing. Could you do other things besides that?"

"Lord, yes!" said Mr. Fotheringay. "Just anything." He thought, and suddenly recalled a conjuring entertainment he had seen. "Here!" He pointed. "Change into a bowl of fish—no, not that—change into a glass bowl full of water with goldfish swimming in it. That's better! You see that, Mr. Maydig?"

"It's astonishing. It's incredible. You are either a most extraordinary . . . But no——"

"I could change it into anything," said Mr. Fotheringay. "Just anything. Here! be a pigeon, will you?"

In another moment a blue pigeon was fluttering round the room and making Mr. Maydig duck every time it came near him. "Stop there, will you," said Mr. Fotheringay; and the pigeon hung motionless in the air. "I could change it back to a bowl of flowers," he said, and after replacing the pigeon on the table worked that miracle. "I expect you will want your pipe in a bit," he said, and restored the tobacco-jar.

Mr. Maydig had followed all these later changes in a sort of ejaculatory silence. He stared at Mr. Fotheringay and, in a very gingerly manner, picked up the tobacco-jar, examined it, replaced it on the table. "*Well!*" was the only expression of his feelings.

"Now, after that it's easier to explain what I came about," said Mr. Fotheringay; and proceeded to a lengthy and involved narrative of his strange experiences, beginning with the affair of the lamp in the Long Dragon and complicated by persistent allusions to Winch. As he went on, the transient pride Mr. Maydig's consternation had caused passed away; he became the very ordinary Mr. Fotheringay of everyday intercourse again. Mr. Maydig listened intently, the tobacco-jar in his hand, and his bearing changed also with the course of the narrative. Presently, while Mr. Fotheringay was dealing with the miracle of the third egg, the minister interrupted with a fluttering extended hand——

"It is possible," he said. "It is credible. It is amazing, of course, but it reconciles a number of difficulties. The power to work miracles is a gift—a peculiar quality like genius or second sight—hitherto it has come very rarely and to exceptional people. But in this case . . . I have always wondered at the miracles of Mahomet, and at Yogi's miracles, and the miracles of Madame Blavatsky. But, of course! Yes, it is simply a gift! It carries out so beautifully the arguments of that great thinker"—Mr. Maydig's voice sank—"his Grace the Duke of Argyll. Here we plumb some profounder law—deeper than the ordinary laws of nature. Yes—yes. Go on. Go on!"

Mr. Fotheringay proceeded to tell of his misadventure with Winch, and Mr. Maydig, no longer overawed or scared, began to jerk his limbs about and interject astonishment. "It's this what troubled me most," proceeded Mr. Fotheringay; "it's this I'm most mijitly in want of advice for; of course he's at San Francisco—wherever San Francisco may be—but of course it's awkward for both of us, as you'll see, Mr. Maydig. I don't see how he can understand what has happened, and I dare say he's scared and exasperated something tremendous, and trying to get at me. I dare say he keeps on starting off to come here. I send him back, by a miracle, every few hours, when I think of it. And of course, that's a thing he won't be able to understand, and it's bound to annoy him; and, of course, if he takes a ticket every time it will cost him a lot of money. I done the best I could for him, but of course it's difficult for him to put himself in my place. I thought afterwards that his clothes might have got scorched, you know—if Hades is all it's supposed to be—before I shifted him. In that case I suppose they'd have locked him up in San Francisco. Of course I willed him a new suit of clothes on him directly I thought of it. But, you see, I'm already in a deuce of a tangle——"

Mr. Maydig looked serious. "I see you are in a tangle. Yes, it's a difficult position. How you are to end it . . ." He became diffuse and inconclusive.

"However, we'll leave Winch for a little and discuss the larger question. I don't think this is a case of the black art or anything of the sort. I don't think there is any taint of criminality about it at all, Mr. Fotheringay—none whatever, unless you are suppressing material facts. No, it's miracles—pure miracles—miracles, if I may say so, of the very highest class."

He began to pace the hearthrug and gesticulate, while Mr. Fotheringay sat with his arm on the table and his head on his arm, looking worried. "I don't see how I'm to manage about Winch," he said.

"A gift of working miracles—apparently a very powerful gift," said Mr. Maydig, "will find a way about Winch—never fear. My dear Sir, you are a most important man—a man of the most astonishing possibilities. As evidence, for example! And in other ways, the things you may do . . ."

"Yes, *I've* thought of a thing or two," said Mr. Fotheringay. "But—some of the things came a bit twisty. You saw that fish at first? Wrong sort of bowl and wrong sort of fish. And I thought I'd ask someone."

"A proper course," said Mr. Maydig, "a very proper course—altogether the proper course." He stopped and looked at Mr. Fotheringay. "It's practically an unlimited gift. Let us test your powers, for instance. If they really *are* . . . If they really are all they seem to be."

And so, incredible as it may seem, in the study of the little house behind the Congregational Chapel, on the evening of Sunday, Nov. 10, 1896, Mr. Fotheringay, egged on and inspired by Mr. Maydig, began to work miracles. The reader's attention is specially and definitely called to the date. He will object, probably has already objected, that certain points in this story are improbable, that if any things of the sort already described had indeed occurred, they would have been in all the papers a year ago. The details immediately following he will find particularly hard to accept, because among other things they involve the conclusion that he or she, the reader in question, must have been killed in a violent and unprecedented manner more than a year ago. Now a miracle is nothing if not improbable, and as a matter of fact the reader *was* killed in a violent and unprecedented manner a year ago. In the subsequent course of this story that will become perfectly clear and credible, as every right-minded and reasonable reader will admit. But this is not the place for the end of the story, being but little beyond the hither side of the middle. And at first the miracles worked by Mr. Fotheringay were timid little miracles—little things with the cups and parlour fitments, as feeble as the miracles of Theosophists, and, feeble as they were, they were received with awe by his collaborator. He would have preferred to settle the Winch business out of hand, but Mr. Maydig would not let him. But after they had worked a dozen of these domestic trivialities, their sense of power grew, their imagination began to show signs of stimulation, and their ambition enlarged. Their first larger enterprise was due to hunger and the negligence of Mrs. Minchin, Mr. Maydig's housekeeper. The meal to which the minister conducted Mr. Fotheringay was certainly ill-laid and uninviting as refreshment for two industrious miracle-workers; but they were seated, and Mr. Maydig was descanting in sorrow rather than in anger upon his housekeeper's shortcomings, before it occurred to Mr. Fotheringay that an opportunity lay before him. "Don't you think, Mr. Maydig," he said, "if it isn't a liberty, I——"

"My dear Mr. Fotheringay! Of course! No—I didn't think."

Mr. Fotheringay waved his hand. "What shall we have?" he said, in a large, inclusive spirit, and, at Mr. Maydig's order, revised the supper very thoroughly. "As for me," he said, eyeing Mr. Maydig's selection, "I am always particularly fond of a tankard of stout and a nice Welsh rarebit, and I'll order that. I ain't much given to Burgundy," and forthwith stout and Welsh rarebit promptly appeared at his command. They sat long at their supper, talking like equals, as Mr. Fotheringay presently perceived with a glow of surprise and gratification, of all the miracles they would presently do. "And, by the bye, Mr. Maydig," said Mr. Fotheringay, "I might perhaps be able to help you—in a domestic way."

"Don't quite follow," said Mr. Maydig, pouring out a glass of miraculous old Burgundy.

Mr. Fotheringay helped himself to a second Welsh rarebit out of vacancy, and took a mouthful. "I was thinking," he said, "I might be able (*chum*, *chum*) to work (*chum*, *chum*) a miracle with Mrs. Minchin (*chum*, *chum*)—make her a better woman."

Mr. Maydig put down the glass and looked doubtful. "She's—She strongly objects to interference, you know, Mr. Fotheringay. And—as a matter of fact—it's well past eleven and she's probably in bed and asleep. Do you think, on the whole——"

Mr. Fotheringay considered these objections. "I don't see that it shouldn't be done in her sleep."

For a time Mr. Maydig opposed the idea, and then he yielded. Mr. Fotheringay issued his orders, and a little less at their ease, perhaps, the two gentlemen proceeded with their repast. Mr. Maydig was enlarging on the changes he might expect in his housekeeper next day, with an optimism that seemed even to Mr. Fotheringay's supper senses a little forced and hectic, when a series of confused noises from upstairs began. Their eyes exchanged interrogations, and Mr. Maydig left the room hastily. Mr. Fotheringay heard him calling up to his housekeeper and then his footsteps going softly up to her.

In a minute or so the minister returned, his step light, his face radiant. "Wonderful!" he said, "and touching! Most touching!"

He began pacing the hearthrug. "A repentance—a most touching repentance—through the crack of the door. Poor woman! A most wonderful change! She had got up. She must have got up at once. She had got up out of her sleep to smash a private bottle of brandy in her box. And to confess it too! . . . But this gives us—it opens—a most amazing vista of possibilities. If we can work this miraculous change in *her* . . ."

"The thing's unlimited seemingly," said Mr. Fotheringay. "And about Mr. Winch——"

"Altogether unlimited." And from the hearthrug Mr. Maydig, waving the Winch difficulty aside, unfolded a series of wonderful proposals—proposals he invented as he went along.

Now what those proposals were does not concern the essentials of this story. Suffice it that they were designed in a spirit of infinite benevolence, the sort of benevolence that used to be called post-prandial. Suffice it, too, that the problem of Winch remained unsolved. Nor is it necessary to describe how far that series got to its fulfilment. There were astonishing changes. The small hours found Mr. Maydig and Mr. Fotheringay careering across the chilly market-square under the still moon, in a sort of ecstasy of thaumaturgy, Mr. Maydig all flap and gesture, Mr. Fotheringay short and bristling, and no longer abashed at his greatness. They had reformed every drunkard in the Parliamentary division, changed all the beer and alcohol to water (Mr. Maydig had over-ruled Mr. Fotheringay on this point), they had, further, greatly improved the railway communication of the place, drained Flinder's swamp, improved the soil of One Tree Hill, and cured the Vicar's wart. And they were going to see what could be done with the injured pier at South Bridge. "The place," gasped Mr. Maydig, "won't be the same place to-morrow. How surprised and thankful everyone will be!" And just at that moment the church clock struck three.

"I say," said Mr. Fotheringay, "that's three o'clock! I must be getting back. I've got to be at business by eight. And besides, Mrs. Wimms——"

"We're only beginning," said Mr. Maydig, full of the sweetness of unlimited power. "We're only beginning. Think of all the good we're doing. When people wake——"

"But——" said Mr. Fotheringay.

Mr. Maydig gripped his arm suddenly. His eyes were bright and wild. "My dear chap," he said, "there's no hurry. Look"—he pointed to the moon at the zenith—"Joshua!"

"Joshua?" said Mr. Fotheringay.

"Joshua," said Mr. Maydig. "Why not? Stop it."

Mr. Fotheringay looked at the moon.

"That's a bit tall," he said after a pause.

"Why not?" said Mr. Maydig. "Of course it doesn't stop. You stop the rotation of the earth, you know. Time stops. It isn't as if we were doing harm."

"H'm!" said Mr. Fotheringay. "Well." He sighed. "I'll try. Here——" He buttoned up his jacket and addressed himself to the habitable globe, with as good an assumption of confidence as lay in his power. "Jest stop rotating, will you," said Mr. Fotheringay.

Incontinently he was flying head over heels through the air at the rate of dozens of miles a minute. In spite of the innumerable circles he was describing per second, he thought; for thought is wonderful—sometimes as sluggish as flowing pitch, sometimes as instantaneous as light. He thought in a second, and willed. "Let me come down safe and sound. Whatever else happens, let me down safe and sound."

He willed it only just in time, for his clothes, heated by his rapid flight through the air, were already beginning to singe. He came down with a forcible, but by no means injurious bump in what appeared to be a mound of fresh-turned earth. A large mass of metal and masonry, extraordinarily like the clock-tower in the middle of the market square, hit the earth near him, ricochetted over him, and flew into stonework, bricks, and masonry, like a bursting bomb. A hurtling cow hit one of the larger blocks and smashed like an egg. There was a crash that made all the most violent crashes of his past life seem like the sound of falling dust and this was followed by a descending series of lesser crashes. A vast wind roared throughout earth and heaven, so that he could scarcely lift his head to look. For a while he was too breathless and astonished even to see where he was or what had happened. And his first movement was to feel his head and reassure himself that his streaming hair was still his own.

"Lord!" gasped Mr. Fotheringay, scarce able to speak for the gale, "I've had a squeak! What's gone wrong? Storms and thunder. And only a minute ago a fine night. It's Maydig set me on to this sort of thing. *What* a wind! If I go on fooling in this way I'm bound to have a thundering accident! . . . Where's Maydig? What a confounded mess everything's in!" He looked about him so far as his flapping jacket would permit. The appearance of things was really extremely strange. "The sky's all right anyhow," said Mr. Fotheringay. "And that's about all that is all right. And even there it looks like a terrific gale coming up. But there's the moon overhead. Just as it was just now. Bright as mid-day. But as for the rest—— Where's the village? Where's—where's anything? And what on earth set this wind ablowing? *I* didn't order no wind."

Mr. Fotheringay struggled to get to his feet in vain, and after one failure, remained on all fours, holding on. He surveyed the moonlit world to leeward, with the tails of his jacket streaming over his head. "There's something seriously wrong," said Mr. Fotheringay. "And what it is—goodness knows."

Far and wide nothing was visible in the white glare through the haze of dust that drove before a screaming gale but tumbled masses of earth and heaps of inchoate ruins, no trees, no houses, no familiar shapes, only a wilderness of disorder vanishing at last into the darkness beneath the whirling columns and streamers, the lightnings and thunderings of a swiftly rising storm. Near him in the livid glare was something that might once have been an elm-tree, a smashed mass of splinters, shivered from boughs to base, and further a twisted mass of iron girders—only too evidently the viaduct—rose out of the piled confusion.

You see, when Mr. Fotheringay had arrested the rotation of the solid globe, he had made no stipulation concerning the trifling movables upon its surface. And the earth spins so fast that the surface at its equator is travelling at rather more than a thousand miles an hour, and in these latitudes at more than half that pace. So that the village, and Mr. Maydig, and Mr. Fotheringay, and everybody and everything had been jerked violently forward at about nine miles per second—that is to say, much more violently than if they had been fired out of a cannon. And every human being, every living creature, every house, and every tree—all the world as we know it—had been so jerked and smashed and utterly destroyed. That was all.

These things Mr. Fotheringay did not, of course, fully appreciate. But he perceived that his miracle had miscarried, and with that a great disgust of miracles came upon him. He was in darkness now, for the clouds had swept together and blotted out his momentary glimpse of the moon, and the air was full of fitful struggling tortured wraiths of hail. A great roaring of wind and waters filled earth and sky, and, peering under his hand through the dust and sleet to windward, he saw by the play of the lightnings a vast wall of water pouring towards him.

"Maydig!" screamed Mr. Fotheringay's feeble voice amid the elemental uproar. "Here!—Maydig!"

"Stop!" cried Mr. Fotheringay to the advancing water. "Oh, for goodness' sake, stop!"

"Just a moment," said Mr. Fotheringay to the lightnings and thunder. "Stop just a moment while I collect my thoughts . . . And now what shall I do?" he said. "What *shall* I do? Lord! I wish Maydig was about."

"I know," said Mr. Fotheringay. "And for goodness' sake let's have it right *this* time." He remained on all fours, leaning against the wind, very intent to have everything right.

"Ah!" he said. "Let nothing what I'm going to order happen until I say 'Off!' . . . Lord! I wish I'd thought of that before!"

He lifted his little voice against the whirlwind, shouting louder and louder in the vain desire to hear himself speak. "Now then!—here goes! Mind about that what I said just now. In the first place, when all I've got to say is done, let me lose my miraculous power, let my will become just like anybody else's will, and all these dangerous miracles be stopped. I don't like them. I'd rather I didn't work 'em. Ever so much. That's the first thing. And the second is—let me be back just before the miracles begin; let everything be just as it was before that blessed lamp turned up. It's a big job, but it's the last. Have you got it? No more miracles, everything as it was—me back in the Long Dragon just before I drank my half-pint. That's it! Yes."

He dug his fingers into the mould, closed his eyes, and said "Off!"

Everything became perfectly still. He perceived that he was standing erect. "So *you* say," said a voice.

He opened his eyes. He was in the bar of the Long Dragon, arguing about miracles with Toddy Beamish. He had a vague sense of some great thing forgotten that instantaneously passed. You see, except for the loss of his miraculous powers, everything was back as it had been; his mind and memory therefore were now just as they had been at the time when this story began. So that he knew absolutely nothing of all that is told here, knows nothing of all that is told here to this day. And among other things, of course, he still did not believe in miracles.

"I tell you that miracles, properly speaking, can't possibly happen," he said, "whatever you like to hold. And I'm prepared to prove it up to the hilt."

"That's what *you* think," said Toddy Beamish, and "Prove it if you can."

"Looky here, Mr. Beamish," said Mr. Fotheringay. "Let us clearly understand what a miracle is. It's something contrariwise to the course of nature done by power of Will . . ."

OSCAR WILDE

1854–1900

"I have nothing to declare but my genius," he is reputed to have told a customs official. An Irishman, he delighted in being outrageous. Nevertheless he wrote such masterpieces as *The Picture of Dorian Gray* and *The Importance of Being Earnest* and, before the tragic scandal which destroyed him, some delightful tales for his children.

The Happy Prince

HIGH ABOVE the city, on a tall column, stood the statue of the Happy Prince. He was gilded all over with thin leaves of fine gold, for eyes he had two bright sapphires, and a large red ruby glowed on his sword-hilt.

He was very much admired indeed. "He is as beautiful as a weathercock," remarked one of the Town Councillors who wished to gain a reputation for having artistic tastes; "only not quite so useful," he added, fearing lest people should think him unpractical, which he really was not.

"Why can't you be like the Happy Prince?" asked a sensible mother of her little boy who was crying for the moon. "The Happy Prince never dreams of crying for anything."

"I am glad there is someone in the world who is quite happy," muttered a disappointed man as he gazed at the wonderful statue.

"He looks just like an angel," said the Charity Children as they came out of the cathedral in their bright scarlet cloaks and their clean white pinafores.

"How do you know?" said the Mathematical Master, "you have never seen one."

"Ah! but we have, in our dreams," answered the children; and the Mathematical Master frowned and looked very severe, for he did not approve of children dreaming.

One night there flew over the city a little Swallow. His friends had gone away to Egypt six weeks before, but he had stayed behind, for he was in love with the most beautiful Reed. He had met her early in the spring as he was flying down the river after a big yellow moth, and had been so attracted by her slender waist that he had stopped to talk to her.

"Shall I love you?" said the Swallow, who liked to come to the point at once, and the Reed made him a low bow. So he flew round and round her, touching the water with his wings, and making silver ripples. This was his courtship, and it lasted all through the summer.

"It is a ridiculous attachment," twittered the other Swallows; "she has no money, and far too many relations"; and indeed the river was quite full of Reeds. Then, when the autumn came they all flew away.

After they had gone he felt lonely, and began to tire of his lady-love. "She has no conversation," he said, "and I am afraid that she is a coquette, for she is always flirting with the wind." And certainly, whenever the wind blew, the Reed made the most graceful curtsies. "I admit that she is domestic," he continued, "but I love travelling, and my wife, consequently, should love travelling also."

"Will you come away with me?" he said finally to her, but the Reed shook her head, she was so attached to her home.

"You have been trifling with me," he cried. "I am off to the Pyramids. Good-bye!" and he flew away.

All day long he flew, and at night-time he arrived at the city. "Where shall I put up?" he said; "I hope the town has made preparations."

Then he saw the statue on the tall column.

"I will put up there," he cried; "it is a fine position, with plenty of fresh air." So he alighted just between the feet of the Happy Prince.

"I have a golden bedroom," he said softly to himself as he looked round, and he prepared to go to sleep; but just as he was putting his head under his wing a large drop of water fell on him. "What a curious thing!" he cried; "there is not a single cloud in the sky, the stars are quite clear and bright, and yet it is raining. The climate in the north of Europe is really dreadful. The Reed used to like the rain, but that was merely her selfishness." Then another drop fell.

"What is the use of a statue if it cannot keep the rain off?" he said; "I must look for a good chimney-pot," and he determined to fly away.

But before he had opened his wings, a third drop fell, and he looked up, and saw—Ah! what did he see?

The eyes of the Happy Prince were filled with tears, and tears were running down his golden cheeks. His face was so beautiful in the moonlight that the little Swallow was filled with pity.

"Who are you?" he said.

"I am the Happy Prince."

"Why are you weeping then?" asked the Swallow; "you have quite drenched me."

"When I was alive and had a human heart," answered the statue, "I did not know what tears were, for I lived in the Palace of Sans-Souci, where sorrow is not allowed to enter. In the daytime I played with my companions in the garden, and in the evening I led the dance in the Great Hall. Round the garden ran a very lofty wall, but I never cared to ask what lay beyond it, everything about me was so beautiful. My courtiers called me the Happy Prince, and happy indeed I was, if pleasure be happiness. So I lived, and so I died. And now that I am dead they have set me up here so high that I can see all the ugliness and all the misery of my city, and though my heart is made of lead yet I cannot choose but weep."

"What! is he not solid gold?" said the Swallow to himself. He was too polite to make any personal remarks out loud.

"Far away," continued the statue in a low musical voice, "far away in a little street there is a poor house. One of the windows is open, and through it I can see a woman seated at a table. Her face is thin and worn, and she has coarse, red hands, all pricked by the needle, for she is a seamstress. She is embroidering passion-flowers on a satin gown for the loveliest of the Queen's maids-of-honour to wear at the next Court ball. In a bed in the corner of the room her little boy is lying ill. He has a fever, and is asking for oranges. His mother has nothing to give him but river water, so he is crying. Swallow, Swallow, little Swallow, will you not bring her the ruby out of my sword-hilt? My feet are fastened to this pedestal and I cannot move."

"I am waited for in Egypt," said the Swallow. "My friends are flying up and down the Nile, and talking to the large lotus-flowers. Soon they will go to sleep in the tomb of the great King. The King is there himself in his painted coffin. He is wrapped in yellow linen, and embalmed with spices. Round his neck is a chain of pale green jade, and his hands are like withered leaves."

"Swallow, Swallow, little Swallow," said the Prince, "will you not stay with me for one night, and be my messenger? The boy is so thirsty, and the mother so sad."

"I don't think I like boys," answered the Swallow. "Last summer, when I was staying on the river, there were two rude boys, the miller's sons, who were always throwing stones at me. They never hit me, of course; we swallows fly far too well for that, and besides I come of a family famous for its agility; but still, it was a mark of disrespect."

But the Happy Prince looked so sad that the little Swallow was sorry. "It is very cold here," he said; "but I will stay with you for one night, and be your messenger."

"Thank you, little Swallow," said the Prince.

So the Swallow picked out the great ruby from the Prince's sword, and flew away with it in his beak over the roofs of the town.

He passed by the cathedral tower, where the white marble angels were sculptured. He passed by the palace and heard the sound of dancing. A beautiful girl came out on the balcony with her lover. "How wonderful the stars are," he said to her, "and how wonderful is the power of love!"

"I hope my dress will be ready in time for the State ball," she answered; "I have ordered passion-flowers to be embroidered on it: but the seamstresses are so lazy."

He passed over the river, and saw the lanterns hanging to the masts of the ships. He passed over the Ghetto, and saw the old Jews bargaining with each other, and weighing out money in copper scales. At last he came to the poor house and looked in. The boy was tossing feverishly on his bed, and the mother had fallen asleep, she was so tired. In he hopped, and laid the great ruby on the table beside the woman's thimble. Then he flew gently round the bed, fanning the boy's forehead with his wings. "How cool I feel!" said the boy, "I must be getting better"; and he sank into a delicious slumber.

Then the Swallow flew back to the Happy Prince, and told him what he had done. "It is curious," he remarked, "but I feel quite warm now, although it is so cold."

"That is because you have done a good action," said the Prince. And the little Swallow began to think, and then he fell asleep. Thinking always made him sleepy.

When day broke he flew down to the river and had a bath. "What a remarkable phenomenon!" said the Professor of Ornithology as he was passing over the bridge. "A swallow in winter!" And he wrote a long letter about it to the local newspaper. Everyone quoted it, it was full of so many words that they could not understand.

"Tonight I go to Egypt," said the Swallow, and he was in high spirits at the prospect. He visited all the public monuments, and sat a long time on top of the church steeple. Wherever he went the Sparrows chirruped, and said to each other, "What a distinguished stranger!" so he enjoyed himself very much.

When the moon rose he flew back to the Happy Prince. "Have you any commissions for Egypt?" he cried; "I am just starting."

"Swallow, Swallow, little Swallow," said the Prince, "will you not stay with me one night longer?"

"I am waited for in Egypt," answered the Swallow. "Tomorrow my friends will fly up to the Second Cataract. The river-horse crouches there among the bulrushes, and on a great granite throne sits the God Memnon. All night long he watches the stars, and when the morning star shines he utters one cry of joy, and then he is silent. At noon the yellow lions come down to the water's edge to drink. They have eyes like green beryls, and their roar is louder than the roar of the cataract."

"Swallow, Swallow, little Swallow," said the Prince, "far away across the city I see a young man in a garret. He is leaning over a desk covered with papers, and in a tumbler by his side there is a bunch of withered violets. His hair is brown and crisp, and his lips are red as a pomegranate, and he has large and dreamy eyes. He is trying to finish a play for the Director of the Theatre, but he is too cold to write any more. There is no fire in the grate, and hunger has made him faint."

"I will wait with you one night longer," said the Swallow, who really had a good heart. "Shall I take him another ruby?"

"Alas! I have no ruby now," said the Prince: "my eyes are all that I have left. They are made of rare sapphires, which were brought out of India a thousand years ago. Pluck out one of them and take it to him. He will sell it to the jeweller, and buy firewood, and finish his play."

"Dear Prince," said the Swallow, "I cannot do that"; and he began to weep.

"Swallow, Swallow, little Swallow," said the Prince, "do as I command you."

So the Swallow plucked out the Prince's eye, and flew away to the student's garret. It was easy enough to get in, as there was a hole in the roof. Through this he darted, and came into the room. The young man had his head buried in his hands, so he did not hear the flutter of the bird's wings, and when he looked up he found the beautiful sapphire lying on the withered violets.

"I am beginning to be appreciated," he cried; "this is from some great admirer. Now I can finish my play," and he looked quite happy.

The next day the Swallow flew down to the harbour. He sat on the mast of a large vessel and watched the sailors hauling big chests out of the hold with ropes. "Heave a-hoy!" they shouted as each chest came up. "I am going to Egypt!" cried the Swallow, but nobody minded, and when the moon rose he flew back to the Happy Prince.

"I am come to bid you good-bye," he cried.

"Swallow, Swallow, little Swallow," said the Prince, "will you not stay with me one night longer?"

"It is winter," answered the Swallow, "and the chill snow will soon be here. In Egypt the sun is warm on the green palm-trees, and the crocodiles lie in the mud and look lazily about them. My companions are building a nest in the Temple of Baalbek, and the pink and white doves are watching them, and cooing to each other. Dear Prince, I must leave you, but I will never forget you, and next spring I will bring you back two beautiful jewels in place of those you have given away. The ruby shall be redder than a red rose, and the sapphire shall be as blue as the great sea."

"In the square below," said the Happy Prince, "there stands a little match-girl. She has let her matches fall in the gutter, and they are all spoiled. Her father will beat her if she does not bring home some money, and she is crying. She has no shoes or stockings, and her little head is bare. Pluck out my other eye, and give it to her, and her father will not beat her."

"I will stay with you one night longer," said the Swallow, "but I cannot pluck out your eye. You would be quite blind then."

"Swallow, Swallow, little Swallow," said the Prince, "do as I command you."

So he plucked out the Prince's other eye, and darted down with it. He swooped past the match-girl, and slipped the jewel into the palm of her hand. "What a lovely bit of glass!" cried the little girl; and she ran home, laughing.

Then the Swallow came back to the Prince. "You are blind now," he said, "so I will stay with you always."

"No, little Swallow," said the poor Prince, "you must go away to Egypt."

"I will stay with you always," said the Swallow, and he slept at the Prince's feet.

All the next day he sat on the Prince's shoulder, and told him stories of what he had seen in strange lands. He told him of the red ibises, who stand in long rows on the banks of the Nile, and catch goldfish in their beaks; of the Sphinx, who is as old as the world itself, and lives in the desert, and knows everything; of the merchants, who walk slowly by the side of their camels and carry amber beads in their hands; of the King of the Mountains of the Moon, who is as black as ebony, and worships a large crystal; of the great green snake that sleeps in a palm-tree, and has twenty priests to feed it with honey-cakes; and of the pygmies who sail over a big lake on large flat leaves, and are always at war with the butterflies.

"Dear little Swallow," said the Prince, "you tell me of marvellous things, but more marvellous than anything is the suffering of men and of women. There is no Mystery so great as Misery. Fly over my city, little Swallow, and tell me what you see there."

So the Swallow flew over the great city, and saw the rich making merry in their beautiful houses, while the beggars were sitting at the gates. He flew into dark lanes, and saw the white faces of starving children looking out listlessly at the black streets. Under the archway of a bridge two little boys were lying in one another's arms to try and keep themselves warm. "How hungry we are!" they said. "You must not lie here," shouted the watchman, and they wandered out into the rain.

Then he flew back and told the Prince what he had seen.

"I am covered with fine gold," said the Prince, "you must take it off, leaf by leaf, and give it to my poor; the living always think that gold can make them happy."

Leaf after leaf of the fine gold the Swallow picked off, till the Happy Prince looked quite dull and grey. Leaf after leaf of the fine gold he brought to the poor, and the children's faces grew rosier, and they laughed and played games in the street. "We have bread now!" they cried.

Then the snow came, and after the snow came the frost. The streets looked as if they were made of silver, they were so bright and glistening; long icicles like crystal daggers hung down from the eaves of the houses, everybody went about in furs, and the little boys wore scarlet caps and skated on the ice.

The poor little Swallow grew colder and colder, but he would not leave the Prince, he loved him too well. He picked up crumbs outside the baker's door when the baker was not looking, and tried to keep himself warm by flapping his wings.

But at last he knew that he was going to die. He had just enough strength to fly up to the Prince's shoulder once more. "Good-bye, dear Prince!" he murmured, "will you let me kiss your hand?"

"I am glad that you are going to Egypt at last, little Swallow," said the Prince, "you have stayed too long here; but you must kiss me on the lips, for I love you."

"It is not to Egypt that I am going," said the Swallow. "I am going to the House of Death. Death is the brother of Sleep, is he not?"

And he kissed the Happy Prince on the lips, and fell down dead at his feet.

At that moment a curious crack sounded inside the statue, as if something had broken. The fact is that the leaden heart had snapped right in two. It certainly was a dreadfully hard frost.

Early the next morning the Mayor was walking in the square below in company with the Town Councillors. As they passed the column he looked up at the statue: "Dear me! how shabby the Happy Prince looks!" he said.

"How shabby, indeed!" cried the Town Councillors, who always agreed with the Mayor: and they went up to look at it.

"The ruby has fallen out of his sword, his eyes are gone, and he is golden no longer," said the Mayor; "in fact, he is little better than a beggar!"

"Little better than a beggar," said the Town Councillors.

"And here is actually a dead bird at his feet!" continued the Mayor.

"We must really issue a proclamation that birds are not to be allowed to die here." And the Town Clerk made a note of the suggestion.

So they pulled down the statue of the Happy Prince. "As he is no longer beautiful he is no longer useful," said the Art Professor at the University.

Then they melted the statue in a furnace, and the Mayor held a meeting of the Corporation to decide what was to be done with the metal. "We must have another statue, of course," he said, "and it shall be a statue of myself."

"Of myself," said each of the Town Councillors, and they quarrelled. When I last heard of them they were quarrelling still.

"What a strange thing!" said the overseer of the workmen at the foundry. "This broken lead heart will not melt in the furnace. We must throw it away." So they threw it on a dust-heap where the dead Swallow was also lying.

"Bring me the two most precious things in the city," said God to one of His Angels; and the Angel brought Him the leaden heart and the dead bird.

"You have rightly chosen," said God, "for in my garden of Paradise this little bird shall sing for evermore, and in my city of gold the Happy Prince shall praise me."

ANGUS WILSON

1913–1991

A wry distinction characterized Angus Wilson!
A prominent figure on the literary scene, a witty speaker,
an inspired lecturer, he came to writing only after a
successful career as a Civil Service administrator.
His most famous novels include *Anglo-Saxon Attitudes*
and *Old Men at the Zoo*.

Realpolitik

JOHN HOBDAY sat on the edge of his desk and swung his left leg with characteristic boyishness. He waited for the staff to get settled in their seats and then spoke with careful informality.

"I know how frightfully busy you are. As a matter of fact I am myself," he said, with the half-humorous urchin smile that he used for such jokes. Only his secretary, Veronica, gave the helpful laugh he expected. It was not going to be an easy meeting, he decided. "So I'm not going to waste your time with a lot of talk," he went on, "I just thought . . ."

He paused and beat with his pencil against the desk whilst Mrs. Scrutton moved her chair fussily out of the sunlight. "Ready?" he asked with an over-elaborate smile. "Right. Then we'll start again. As I was saying, we're all very busy, but all the same I thought it was time we had a little meeting. I've been here a week now and although I've had some very helpful chats with each of you in turn, we've never had a chance to get together and outline our plans." None of the three who formed his audience made any response. Veronica, who remembered him taking over new departments at the Ministry during the war, thought he hasn't got the right tone, he doesn't realize that he's coming up against deeper loyalties with these people, loyalties to scholarship and ideas. She almost felt like letting him fend for himself, but old habits were too strong.

"I'm sure it's what everybody's been wanting," she said in her deep voice. She had gauged rightly, his moment of uncertainty had gone, her faithful bark had guided him at the crucial moment. Mrs. Scrutton tried to discomfort him. She rustled the papers on her lap and whispered audibly to Major Sarson, "Our plans. *His* plans for us would be more honest." But it was too late, she had missed her chance. John merely frowned at the interruption and it was Mrs. Scrutton who was left with burning cheeks, hiding her embarrassment by lighting a fresh cigarette.

"As you know," John went on, and Veronica could tell by the loud trumpeting, rhetorical note of his voice that he was once more the confident salesman lost in the dream world of the grandiose schemes he was putting before them, "I've got some very big ideas for the Gallery. I'm not an expert in any way as you people are, but I think that's possibly why Sir Harold's executors chose me for the job. They felt the Gallery had already got its full weight of scholars and experts, what it needed was a man with administrative experience, whose training had led him to take an over-all view of things, to think, shall I say, widely rather than deeply. That's why they got me in. But I'm going to be absolutely frank with you," tossing a lock of brown, wavy hair from his forehead, he stared at his audience with a wide-eyed appeal, "I need *your* help, without my staff I can get nowhere."

Major Sarson winced slightly. All this theatricality and the loud pitch of John's voice got on his nerves, besides he could feel a draught round his legs. It's like some damned Methodist preacher fellow, he thought.

"You've been grand in this first week," John went on, "absolutely grand. I don't mind telling you now that when I arrived I was dead scared. You'd all been here for years, you knew the collections backwards, you had your own ways of running the place, and above all you'd had the inestimable advantage of knowing Sir Harold, of hearing exactly what was in his mind when he bought this picture or that object, of knowing what his ideals were in giving the public the benefit of his taste and experience. I felt sure you were bound to resent me as an outsider, and I knew I'd have done the same in your place."

The faces in front of him were quite unresponsive. He isn't going to get anywhere with sentimental appeals, thought Veronica, these people are idealists, there's nothing more hardboiled. The damned fools, thought John, they have the chance of turning this tin pot, cranky provincial gallery into a national institution and they won't play ball. Well if they can't see which way their own chances lie, they're not getting in the way of mine. They'll have to come to heel or go. His voice became a little sharper, a shade less ingenuous and friendly.

"You've all told me your views in our various little chats. Sometimes we've agreed, sometimes we haven't. You've inclined to the feeling that all is for the best in the best of all possible worlds; I've felt that some changes were needed, that the scope of the work here wanted broadening, that the organisation wanted, let's face it, bringing up to date a bit, and in all this the Board has agreed with me."

Tony Parnell's baby face had grown steadily more pouting and scowling as John had been speaking. To think of this mountebank in charge of the Gallery, a professional careerist, who understood nothing of Sir Harold's ideas and aims, who had even laughed when he'd spoken to him of the metaphysical aspects of technique in painting. He had banked so much on becoming Curator. Sir Harold had spoken so often of him as "my torchbearer, the youngest member of our staff," and now these awful business men who had got control of the estate had put this creature in. Major Sarson and Mrs. Scrutton were too old to fight these changes, he had promised before the meeting that *he* would make the challenge. Now was his opportunity. Red in the face, he opened his mouth, but in his nervousness his voice emerged a high falsetto. John smiled across at Veronica.

"The Board haven't had much opportunity of agreeing with us since they haven't heard our views," Tony squeaked.

"My dear Parnell," said John, and his tone was purposely patronizing and offensive. The old ones he regarded without rancour as dead wood to be cleared away, but Tony he disliked personally for his assumptions of scholarly disinterestedness and moral superiority. "Don't let that worry you. As soon as you've got your ideas clear come along and push them at the Board as much as you like. I shouldn't use too much of your favourite art jargon if I was you; the Board are anxious to help but they're only ordinary business men and they might not understand. If you follow my advice you'll come down to earth a bit, but of course that's entirely your affair."

Mrs. Scrutton fingered the buttons on her checked tweed coat nervously. "There's no need to bully Mr. Parnell," she said.

"Oh, come," said John jocosely, "if Parnell's going to have the ladies on his side I shall have to surrender." To his delight he saw that Tony was frowning with annoyance.

"Do let me deal with this in my own way," he said to Mrs. Scrutton, whose lip began to tremble.

So that severe grey bobbed hair and man's collar and tie could dissolve early into tears, thought John, so much the better.

"Mrs. Scrutton was only trying to help you, Parnell," said Major Sarson. "Don't let us forget our manners, please."

John yawned slightly. "When the little civil war's over," he said, "I'd just like to outline our main functions. As I see them they're these: Relations with the Public, that's you, Parnell; Display, Mrs. Scrutton; Research, Major Sarson. Miss Clay," he indicated Veronica, "is maid of all work. And I, well, I'm the Aunt Sally, ready to stop the bricks and pass on the bouquets."

Major Sarson looked at his watch impatiently. "I quite agree with you, Major," said John, "the sooner we get finished the better. No true gentlemen continue to hold meetings after opening time." The old man's face twitched violently, no one before had referred overtly to his notorious weakness.

"I'd like to take the public first," said John. "You've done a first-rate job, Parnell—within its limits. But you haven't gone far enough. You've got real enthusiasm and that's half the battle—but only half. You give the public first-rate value in lectures and catalogues when they get here, but you don't try to get them to come. I know what you're going to say, 'They'll come if they're interested'. But aren't you being a bit hard on the poor, tired, pushed-around public of today? They've got to be told about the place. You've got to compete with the cinema, the football team *and* the fireside radio. In short you've got to advertise and you can't do that unless you have figures." Here John paused and picked up a file of papers.

"You have all the figures there," said Tony sulkily.

"I know," said John, "but don't you think they're just a bit too general? 'So many people visited the Gallery on August 5th, so many on November 3rd.' But what sort of people? Who are we catering for? Were they Chinamen, shopgirls, farmers, or just plain deaf-mutes? To tell us anything these figures want breaking down into groups—so many foreigners, so many over-forties, so many under-twenties. That's the way to build up a picture. Now supposing you run over these figures in the way that I suggest and we'll talk again."

Tony was about to protest that this task was impossible, but John held up his hand. "No, no, time's very short and there's one more point I want to raise before we pass on to Display." Mrs. Scrutton drew her coat tightly round her. "It's about the lecture room. Sir Louis Crippen was saying something at the last Board meeting about its not being free for his archaeological society when he needed it. Do you know anything about that?"

Tony Parnell hesitated. "Well, actually," he said, "Mrs. Scrutton makes all the lecture hall arrangements."

"But isn't it the PRO's pigeon?" asked John.

"Yes," said Tony, "but . . . well . . . Mrs. Scrutton . . ."

"I see," said John coldly. "Perhaps you'd enlighten me, then, Mrs. Scrutton."

The grey bob shook as she answered, an involuntary shake that was to prove the prelude to age's palsy. "Sir Louis asked for Tuesday and Tuesdays are always booked by Miss Copley," she said.

"Miss Copley?"

Mrs. Scrutton guessed that he knew the answer and her reply attempted a rebuke. "Miss Copley is an old and true friend to the Gallery," she said. "She's been giving her lectures to Schools on Tuesdays for many years."

"No doubt," said John, "but I still think Sir Louis should have preference."

"I don't agree at all," said Major Sarson, "it would be most unfair."

"Yes, why should Sir Louis receive special treatment?" asked Mrs. Scrutton.

"Well, frankly," replied John, "because although Miss Copley may be a very old friend, Sir Louis is a very influential one and the Gallery needs influential friends."

Before Mrs. Scrutton there floated Sir Harold's features, like Erasmus she had thought him, the last of the humanists. Major Sarson too, remembered his old friend's handshake and his firm clear voice. "Sarson," he had said, "this money came to me through false standards, false distinctions. There shall be no distinctions in its use but those of scholarship." The eyes of both these old people filled with tears.

John turned to Veronica. "You've nothing to do, Miss Clay," he said "In future you will take on the lecture hall arrangements. Anything important you'll refer to me." Mrs. Scrutton made a gesture of protest. "No, no," said John. "I'm not going to let you wear yourself out on these minor details, you're far too valuable to the Gallery. Besides, you've got more than a full time job with Display if it's properly carried out."

Tony Parnell half rose from his chair "I thought the Lecture Hall arrangements came under Public Relations?"

"So did I," said John, "until you disillusioned me.

"Next we come to Display. I suppose no side of our work has been more revolutionized in recent years. The Philadelphia report, you know, and the Canadian Association series," he went on, smiling at Mrs. Scrutton. She suddenly felt very tired, she had seen these documents but had never been able to bring herself to read them. "But there's no need for me to mention these things to you," John continued. "Your arrangement of the miniature collection," and he sighed in wonder. "Well, I'm going to pay you a great compliment there. Your arrangement of the miniatures not only makes one want to look at them, it makes it impossible for one not to look at them. I'm sure, Mrs. Scrutton, you'll agree with my wish that some other sides of the collection had the same advantages as the miniatures—the jewellery, for instance, and the armour. But that's not your fault. There's just too much for one person, that's all there is to it. The same applies to the research. I'm not going to embarrass Major Sarson by talking about his position as a scholar," he waved his hand towards the old man who went red round the ears, "suffice to say what we all know, that the Gallery is honoured by the presence of the world's greatest authority on the Dutch school, and a great scholar of painting generally. Though I doubt, by the way, whether the Major's exactly fond of the moderns. I sometimes wish that the Gallery possessed only paintings, I'm sure Major Sarson does. Unfortunately that isn't the case. I fully sympathized with him when he spoke to me as he did of 'those wretched pots and pans'," here John laughed patronizingly, "but I doubt if a ceramics man would. Frankly," he said, turning to Major Sarson, "I consider it disgraceful that a scholar of your calibre should be taken off your real work in this way. Now how, you may ask, do I suppose to remedy the situation? Well the answer is that I propose to treble the staff. From next month new staff will begin to arrive—some students from the Universities, some more experienced men from other galleries and museums."

There was silence for a minute, then Mrs. Scrutton spoke. "Does the Board know of this?"

"Yes," said John, "they fully approve the scheme."

"Do they realize the expense involved?" asked Tony, the practical man.

"The Board are business men," said John, "they know that outlay must precede returns." He looked round at their faces. "Well, I think that's all," he said. "I know you will give the new members of the staff the same cooperation you have given me, whether it is a question of instructing and training them, or in some cases of working under them." His tone was openly sarcastic.

"Do I understand that people will be put over us?" asked Mrs. Scrutton.

"In cases where experts are brought in, it may be necessary to make revisions in seniority," said John.

"You realize, of course, that in such an eventuality we should resign," said Major Sarson.

"That would be a great loss to the Gallery, but we could not, of course, control your decisions," replied John, and opening the door, he bowed them out.

"Golly," said Veronica, "you do tell some lies, don't you? Or have the Board ratified your staff changes?"

"How many more times must I tell you, Veronica, that truth is relative," said John.

Veronica looked down for a minute. "I'll make you some coffee," she said.

"Yes," said John, "Victory always makes me thirsty. I cannot help being satisfied when I think of the well merited unpleasant few weeks those three are going to have. The punishment of incompetence is always satisfactory."

"Mmm," said Veronica doubtfully.

"What's that mean? You've not fallen for this sentimental stuff about Sir Harold, have you?"

"Good Lord, no," said Veronica. "It's not those misfits I'm worrying about, it's you."

"Me?" said John. "Why?"

"You're getting too fond of bullying," said Veronica, "it interferes with your charm, and charm's essential for your success." She went out to make the coffee.

What Veronica said was very true, thought John, and he made a note to be more detached in his attitude. All the same these criticisms were bad for his self-esteem. For all her loyalty Veronica knew him too well, got too near home. Charm was important to success, but self-esteem was more so. His imagination began to envisage further staff changes, perhaps a graduate secretary would really be more suitable now.

P.G. WODEHOUSE

1881–1975

Even in his irrepressible nineties, Pelham Grenville Wodehouse, the creator of Jeeves and Bertie Wooster, was still writing. "And if you ask me to tell you frankly if I like my names Pelham Grenville, I must confess that I do not. At the font I remember protesting vigorously to the clergyman, but he stuck to his point."

The Fiery Wooing of Mordred

THE PINT OF LAGER breathed heavily through his nose.

"Silly fathead!" he said. "Ash-trays in every nook and cranny of the room—ash-trays staring you in the eye wherever you look—and he has to go and do a fool thing like that."

He was alluding to a young gentleman with a vacant, fish-like face who, leaving the bar-parlour of the Anglers' Rest a few moments before, had thrown his cigarette into the waste-paper basket, causing it to burst into a cheerful blaze. Not one of the little company of amateur fire-fighters but was ruffled. A Small Bass with a high blood pressure had had to have his collar loosened, and the satin-clad bosom of Miss Postlethwaite, our emotional barmaid, was still heaving.

Only Mr. Mulliner seemed disposed to take a tolerant view of what had occurred.

"In fairness to the lad," he pointed out, sipping his hot Scotch and lemon, "we must remember that our bar-parlour contains no grand piano or priceless old walnut table, which to the younger generation are the normal and natural repositories for lighted cigarette-ends. Failing these, he, of course, selected the waste-paper basket. Like Mordred."

"Like who?" asked a Whisky and Splash.

"Whom," corrected Miss Postlethwaite.

The Whisky and Splash apologized.

"A nephew of mine. Mordred Mulliner, the poet."

"Mordred," murmured Miss Postlethwaite pensively. "A sweet name."

"And one," said Mr. Mulliner, "that fitted him admirably, for he was a comely lovable sensitive youth with large, fawn-like eyes, delicately chiselled features, and excellent teeth. I mention these teeth, because it was owing to them that the train of events started which I am about to describe."

"He bit somebody?" queried Miss Postlethwaite, groping.

"No. But if he had had no teeth he would not have gone to the dentist's that day, and if he had not gone to the dentist's he would not have met Annabelle."

"Annabelle whom?"

"Who," corrected Miss Postlethwaite.

"Oh, shoot," said the Whisky and Splash.

"Annabelle Sprockett-Sprockett, the only daughter of Sir Murgatroyd and Lady Sprockett-Sprockett of Smattering Hall, Worcestershire. Impractical in many ways," said Mr. Mulliner, "Mordred never failed to visit his dentist every six months, and on the morning on which my story opens he had just seated himself in the empty waiting-room and was turning the pages of a three-months-old copy of the *Tatler* when the door opened and there entered a girl at the sight of whom—or who, if our friend here prefers it—something seemed to explode on the left side of his chest like a bomb.

The *Tatler* swam before his eyes, and when it solidified again he realized that love had come to him at last.

Most of the Mulliners have fallen in love at first sight, but few with so good an excuse as Mordred. She was a singularly beautiful girl, and for a while it was this beauty of hers that enchained my nephew's attention to the exclusion of all else. It was only after he had sat gulping for some minutes like a dog with a chicken bone in its throat that he detected the sadness in her face. He could see now that her eyes, as she listlessly perused her four-months-old copy of *Punch*, were heavy with pain.

His heart ached for her, and as there is something about the atmosphere of a dentist's waiting-room which breaks down the barriers of conventional etiquette he was emboldened to speak.

"Courage!" he said. "It may not be so bad, after all. He may just fool about with that little mirror thing of his, and decide that there is nothing that needs to be done."

For the first time she smiled—faintly, but with sufficient breadth to give Mordred another powerful jolt. "I'm not worrying about the dentist," she explained. "My trouble is that I live miles away in the country and only get a chance of coming to London about twice a year for about a couple of hours. I was hoping that I should be able to put in a long spell of window-shopping in Bond Street, but now I've got to wait goodness knows how long I don't suppose I shall have time to do a thing. My train goes at one-fifteen."

All the chivalry in Mordred came to the surface like a leaping trout. "If you would care to take my place——"

"Oh, I couldn't."

"Please. I shall enjoy waiting. It will give me an opportunity of catching up with my reading."

"Well, if you really wouldn't mind——"

Considering that Mordred by this time was in the market to tackle dragons on her behalf or to climb the loftiest peak of the Alps to supply her with edelweiss, he was able to assure her that he did not mind. So in she went, flashing at him a shy glance of gratitude which nearly doubled him up, and he lit a cigarette and fell into a reverie. And presently she came out and he sprang to his feet, courteously throwing his cigarette into the waste-paper basket.

She uttered a cry. Mordred recovered the cigarette.

"Silly of me," he said, with a deprecating laugh. "I'm always doing that. Absent-minded. I've burned two flats already this year."

She caught her breath.

"Burned them to the ground?"

"Well, not to the ground. They were on the top floor."

"But you burned them?"

"Oh, yes. I burned them."

"Well, well!" She seemed to muse. "Well, good-bye, Mr.——"

"Mulliner. Mordred Mulliner."

"Good-bye, Mr. Mulliner, and thank you so much."

"Not at all, Miss——"

"Sprockett-Sprockett."

"Not at all, Miss Sprockett-Sprockett. A pleasure."

She passed from the room, and a few minutes later he was lying back in the dentist's chair, filled with an infinite sadness. This was not due to any activity on the part of the dentist, who had just said with a rueful sigh that there didn't seem to be anything to do this time, but to the fact that his life was now a blank. He loved this beautiful girl, and he would never see her more. It was just another case of ships that pass in the waiting-room.

Conceive his astonishment, therefore, when by the afternoon post next day he received a letter which ran as follows:

Smattering Hall,
Lower Smattering-on-the-Wissel,
Worcestershire.

Dear Mr. Mulliner,

My little girl has told me how very kind you were to her at the dentist's to-day. I cannot tell you how grateful she was. She does so love to walk down Bond Street and breathe on the jewellers' windows, and but for you she would have had to go another six months without her little treat.

I suppose you are a very busy man, like everybody in London, but if you can spare the time it would give my husband and myself so much pleasure if you could run down and stay with us for a few days—a long week-end, or even longer if you can manage it.

With best wishes,
Yours sincerely,
Aurelia Sprockett-Sprockett.

Mordred read this communication six times in a minute and a quarter and then seventeen times rather more slowly in order to savour any *nuance* of it that he might have overlooked. He took it that the girl must have got his address from the dentist's secretary on her way out, and he was doubly thrilled—first, by this evidence that one so lovely was as intelligent as she was beautiful, and secondly because the whole thing seemed to him so frightfully significant. A girl, he meant to say, does not get her mother to invite fellows to her country home for long week-ends (or even longer if they can manage it) unless such fellows have made a pretty substantial hit with her. This, he contended, stood to reason.

He hastened to the nearest post office, dispatched a telegram to Lady Sprockett-Sprockett assuring her that he would be with her on the morrow, and returned to his flat to pack his effects. His heart was singing within him. Apart from anything else, the invitation could not have come at a more fortunate moment, for what with musing on his great love while smoking cigarettes he had practically gutted his little nest on the previous evening, and while it was still habitable in a sense there was no gainsaying the fact that all those charred sofas and things struck a rather melancholy note and he would be glad to be away from it all for a few days.

IT SEEMED to Mordred, as he travelled down on the following afternoon, that the wheels of the train, clattering over the metals, were singing "Sprockett-Sprockett"—not "Annabelle," of course, for he did not yet know her name—and it was with a whispered "Sprockett-Sprockett" on his lips that he alighted at the little station of Smattering-cum-Blimpstead-in-the-Vale, which, as his hostess's note-paper had informed him, was where you got off for the Hall. And when he perceived that the girl herself had come to meet him in a two-seater car the whisper nearly became a shout.

For perhaps three minutes, as he sat beside her, Mordred remained in this condition of ecstatic bliss. Here he was, he reflected, and here she was—here, in fact, they both were—together, and he was just about to point out how jolly this was and—if he could work it without seeming to rush things too much—to drop a hint to the effect that he could wish this state of affairs to continue through all eternity, when the girl drew up outside a tobacconist's.

"I won't be a minute," she said. "I promised Biffy I would bring him back some cigarettes."

A cold hand seemed to lay itself on Mordred's heart.

"Biffy?"

"Captain Biffing, one of the men at the Hall. And Guffy wants some pipe-cleaners."

"Guffy?"

"Jack Guffington. I expect you know his name, if you are interested in racing. He was third in last year's Grand National."

"Is he staying at the Hall, too?"

"Yes."

"You have a large house-party?"

"Oh, not so very. Let me see. There's Billy Biffing, Jack Guffington, Ted Prosser, Freddie Boot—he's the tennis champion of the county—Tommy Mainprice, and—oh, yes, Algy Fripp—the big-game hunter, you know."

The hand on Mordred's heart, now definitely iced, tightened its grip. With a lover's sanguine optimism, he had supposed that this visit of his was going to be just three days of jolly sylvan solitude with Annabelle Sprockett-Sprockett. And now it appeared that the place was unwholesomely crowded with his fellow men. And what fellow men! Big-game hunters . . . Tennis champions . . . Chaps who rode in Grand Nationals . . . He could see them in his mind's eye—lean, wiry, riding-breeched and flannel-trousered young Apollos, any one of them capable of cutting out his weight in Clark Gables.

A faint hope stirred within him.

"You have also, of course, with you Mrs. Biffing, Mrs. Guffington, Mrs. Prosser, Mrs. Boot, Mrs. Mainprice, and Mrs. Algernon Fripp?"

"Oh, no, they aren't married."

"None of them?"

"No."

The faint hope coughed quietly and died.

"Ah," said Mordred.

While the girl was in the shop, he remained brooding. The fact that not one of these blisters should be married filled him with an austere disapproval. If they had had the least spark of civic sense, he felt, they would have taken on the duties and responsibilities of matrimony years ago. But no. Intent upon their selfish pleasures, they had callously remained bachelors. It was this spirit of *laissez-faire*, Mordred considered, that was eating like a canker into the soul of England.

He was aware of Annabelle standing beside him.

"Eh?" he said, starting.

"I was saying: 'Have you plenty of cigarettes?' "

"Plenty, thank you."

"Good. And of course there will be a box in your room. Men always like to smoke in their bedrooms, don't they? As a matter of fact, two boxes—Turkish and Virginian. Father put them there specially."

"Very kind of him," said Mordred mechanically.

He relapsed into a moody silence, and they drove off.

IT WOULD BE agreeable (said Mr. Mulliner) if, having shown you my nephew so gloomy, so apprehensive, so tortured with dark forebodings at this juncture, I were able now to state that the hearty English welcome of Sir Murgatroyd and Lady Sprockett-Sprockett on his arrival at the Hall cheered him up and put new life into him. Nothing, too, would give me greater pleasure than to say that he found, on encountering the dreaded Biffies and Guffies, that they were negligible little runts with faces incapable of inspiring affection in any good woman.

But I must adhere rigidly to the facts. Genial, even effusive, though his host and hostess showed themselves, their cordiality left him cold. And, so far from his rivals being weeds, they were one and all models of manly beauty, and the spectacle of their obvious worship of Annabelle cut my nephew like a knife.

And on top of all this there was Smattering Hall itself.

Smattering Hall destroyed Mordred's last hope. It was one of those vast edifices, so common throughout the countryside of England, whose original founders seem to have budgeted for families of twenty-five or so and a domestic staff of not less than a hundred. "Home isn't home," one can picture them saying to themselves, "unless you have plenty of elbow room." And so this huge, majestic pile had come into being. Romantic persons, confronted with it, thought of knights in armour riding forth to the Crusades. More earthy individuals felt that it must cost a packet to keep up. Mordred's reaction on passing through the front door was a sort of sick sensation, a kind of settled despair.

How, he asked himself, even assuming that by some miracle he succeeded in fighting his way to her heart through all these Biffies and Guffies, could he ever dare to take Annabelle from a home like this? He had quite satisfactory private means, of course, and would be able, when married, to give up the bachelor flat and spread himself to something on a bigger scale—possibly, if sufficiently *bijou*, even a desirable residence in the Mayfair district. But after Smattering Hall would not Annabelle feel like a sardine in the largest of London houses?

Such were the dark thoughts that raced through Mordred's brain before, during and after dinner. At eleven o'clock he pleaded fatigue after his journey, and Sir Murgatroyd accompanied him to his room, anxious, like a good host, to see that everything was comfortable.

"Very sensible of you to turn in early," he said, in his bluff, genial way. "So many young men ruin their health with late hours. Now you, I imagine, will just get into a dressing-gown and smoke a cigarette or two and have the light out by twelve. You have plenty of cigarettes? I told them to see that you were well supplied. I always think the bedroom smoke is the best one of the day. Nobody to disturb you, and all that. If you want to write letters or anything, there is lots of paper, and here is the waste-paper basket, which is always so necessary. Well, good night, my boy, good night."

The door closed, and Mordred, as foreshadowed, got into a dressing-gown and lit a cigarette. But though, having done this, he made his way to the writing-table, it was not with any idea of getting abreast of his correspondence.

It was his purpose to compose a poem to Annabelle Sprockett-Sprockett. He had felt it seething within him all the evening, and sleep would be impossible until it was out of his system.

Hitherto, I should mention, my nephew's poetry, for he belonged to the modern fearless school, had always been stark and rhymeless and had dealt principally with corpses and the smell of cooking cabbage. But now, with the moonlight silvering the balcony outside, he found that his mind had become full of words like 'love' and 'dove' and 'eyes' and 'summer skies'.

> *Blue eyes*, wrote Mordred . . .
> *Sweet lips*, wrote Mordred . . .
> *Oh, eyes like skies of summer blue* . . .
> *Oh, love* . . .
> *Oh, dove* . . .
> *Oh, lips* . . .

With a muttered ejaculation of chagrin he tore the sheet across and threw it into the waste-paper basket.

Blue eyes that burn into my soul,
  Sweet lips that smile my heart away,
Pom-pom, pom-pom, pom something whole (Goal?)
  And tiddly-iddly-umpty-ay (Gay? Say? Happy day?)

Blue eyes into my soul that burn,
  Sweet lips that smile away my heart,
Oh, something something turn or yearn
  And something something something part.

You burn into my soul, blue eyes,
  You smile my heart away, sweet lips,
Short long short long of summer skies
  And something something something trips. (Hips?
    Ships? Pips?)

He threw the sheet into the waste-paper basket and rose with a stifled oath. The waste-paper basket was nearly full now, and still his poet's sense told him that he had not achieved perfection. He thought he saw the reason for this. You can't just sit in a chair and expect inspiration to flow—you want to walk about and clutch your hair and snap your fingers. It had been his intention to pace the room, but the moonlight pouring in through the open window called to him. He went out on to the balcony. It was but a short distance to the dim, mysterious lawn. Impulsively he dropped from the stone balustrade.

The effect was magical. Stimulated by the improved conditions, his Muse gave quick service, and this time he saw at once that she had rung the bell and delivered the goods. One turn up and down the lawn, and he was reciting as follows:

TO ANNABELLE

Oh, lips that smile! Oh, eyes that shine
  Like summer skies, or stars above!
Your beauty maddens me like wine,
  Oh, umpty-pumpty-tumty love!

And he was just wondering, for he was a severe critic of his own work, whether that last line couldn't be polished up a bit, when his eye was attracted by something that shone like summer skies or stars above and, looking more closely, he perceived that his bedroom curtains were on fire.

Now, I will not pretend that my nephew Mordred was in every respect the cool-headed man of action, but this happened to be a situation with which use had familiarized him. He knew the procedure.

"Fire!" he shouted. A head appeared in an upstairs window. He recognized it as that of Captain Biffing.

"Eh?" said Captain Biffing.

"Fire!"

"What?"

"Fire!" vociferated Mordred. "F for Francis, I for Isabel . . ."

"Oh, fire?" said Captain Biffing. "Right ho."

And presently the house began to discharge its occupants.

In the proceedings which followed, Mordred, I fear, did not appear to the greatest advantage. This is an age of specialization, and if you take the specialist off his own particular ground he is at a loss. Mordred's genius, as we have seen, lay in the direction of starting fires. Putting them out called for quite different qualities, and these he did not possess. On the various occasions of holocausts at his series of flats, he had never attempted to play an active part, contenting himself with going downstairs and asking the janitor to step up and see what he could do about it. So now, though under the bright eyes of Annabelle Sprockett-Sprockett he would have given much to be able to dominate the scene, the truth is that the Biffies and Guffies simply played him off the stage.

His heart sank as he noted the hideous efficiency of these young men. They called for buckets. They formed a line. Freddie Boot leaped lissomely on to the balcony, and Algy Fripp, mounted on a wheel-barrow, handed up to him the necessary supplies. And after Mordred, trying to do his bit, had tripped up Jack Guffington and upset two buckets over Ted Prosser, he was advised in set terms to withdraw into the background and stay there.

It was a black ten minutes for the unfortunate young man. One glance at Sir Murgatroyd's twisted face as he watched the operations was enough to tell him how desperately anxious the fine old man was for the safety of his ancestral home and how bitter would be his resentment against the person who had endangered it. And the same applied to Lady Sprockett-Sprockett and Annabelle. Mordred could see the anxiety in their eyes, and the thought that ere long those eyes must be turned accusingly on him chilled him to the marrow.

Presently Freddie Boot emerged from the bedroom to announce that all was well.

"It's out," he said, jumping lightly down. "Anybody know whose room it was?"

Mordred felt a sickening qualm, but the splendid Mulliner courage sustained him. He stepped forward, white and tense. "Mine," he said.

He became the instant centre of attention. The six young men looked at him.

"Yours?"

"Oh, yours, was it?"

"What happened?"

"How did it start?"

"Yes, how did it start?"

"Must have started somehow, I mean," said Captain Biffing, who was a clear thinker. "I mean to say, must have, don't you know, what?"

Mordred mastered his voice.

"I was smoking, and I suppose I threw my cigarette into the waste-paper basket, and as it was full of paper . . ."

"Full of paper? Why was it full of paper?"

"I had been writing a poem."

There was a stir of bewilderment.

"A what?" said Ted Prosser.

"Writing a what?" said Jack Guffington.

"Writing a *poem*?" asked Captain Biffing of Tommy Mainprice.

"That's how I got the story," said Tommy Mainprice, plainly shaken.

"Chap was writing a poem," Freddie Boot informed Algy Fripp.

"You mean the chap writes poems?"

"That's right. Poems."

"Well, I'm dashed!"

"Well, I'm blowed!"

Their now unconcealed scorn was hard to bear. Mordred chafed beneath it. The word 'poem' was flitting from lip to lip, and it was only too evident that, had there been an 's' in the word, those present would have hissed it. Reason told him that these men were mere clods, Philistines, fatheads who would not recognize the rare and the beautiful if you handed it to them on a skewer, but that did not seem to make it any better. He knew that he should be scorning them, but it is not easy to go about scorning people in a dressing-gown, especially if you have no socks on and the night breeze is cool around the ankles. So, as I say, he chafed. And finally, when he saw the butler bend down with pursed lips to the ear of the cook, who was a little hard of hearing, and after a contemptuous glance in his direction speak into it, spacing his syllables carefully, something within him seemed to snap.

"I regret, Sir Murgatroyd," he said, "that urgent family business compels me to return to London immediately. I shall be obliged to take the first train in the morning."

Without another word he went into the house.

IN THE MATTER of camping out in devastated areas my nephew had, of course, become by this time an old hand. It was rarely nowadays that a few ashes and cinders about the place disturbed him. But when he had returned to his bedroom one look was enough to assure him that nothing practical in the way of sleep was to be achieved here. Apart from the unpleasant, acrid smell of burned poetry, the apartment, thanks to the efforts of Freddie Boot, had been converted into a kind of inland sea. The carpet was awash, and on the bed only a duck could have made itself at home.

And so it came about that some ten minutes later Mordred Mulliner lay stretched upon a high-backed couch in the library, endeavouring by means of counting sheep jumping through a gap in a hedge to lull himself into unconsciousness.

But sleep refused to come. Nor in his heart had he really thought that it would. When the human soul is on the rack, it cannot just curl up and close its eyes and expect to get its eight hours as if nothing had happened. It was all very well for Mordred to count sheep, but what did this profit him when each sheep in turn assumed the features and lineaments of Annabelle Sprockett-Sprockett and, what was more, gave him a reproachful glance as it drew itself together for the spring?

Remorse gnawed him. He was tortured by a wild regret for what might have been. He was not saying that with all these Biffies and Guffies in the field he had ever had more than a hundred to eight chance of winning that lovely girl, but at least his hat had been in the ring. Now it was definitely out. Dreamy Mordred may have been—romantic—impractical—but he had enough sense to see that the very worst thing you can do when you are trying to make a favourable impression on the adored object is to set fire to her childhood home, every stick and stone of which she has no doubt worshipped since they put her into rompers.

He had reached this point in his meditations, and was about to send his two hundred and thirty-second sheep at the gap, when with a suddenness which affected him much as an explosion of gelignite would have done, the lights flashed on. For an instant, he lay quivering, then, cautiously poking his head round the corner of the couch, he looked to see who his visitors were.

It was a little party of three that had entered the room. First came Sir Murgatroyd, carrying a tray of sandwiches. He was followed by Lady Sprockett-Sprockett with a siphon and glasses. The rear was brought up by Annabelle, who was bearing a bottle of whisky and two dry ginger ales.

So evident was it that they were assembling here for purposes of a family council that, but for one circumstance, Mordred, to whom anything in the nature of eavesdropping was as repugnant as it has always been to all the Mulliners, would have sprung up with a polite "Excuse me" and taken his blanket elsewhere. This circumstance was the fact that on lying down he had kicked his slippers under the couch, well out of reach. The soul of modesty, he could not affront Annabelle with the spectacle of his bare toes.

So he lay there in silence, and silence, broken only by the swishing of soda-water and the *whoosh* of opened ginger-ale bottles, reigned in the room beyond.

Then Sir Murgatroyd spoke.

"Well, that's that," he said, bleakly.

There was a gurgle as Lady Sprockett-Sprockett drank ginger ale. Then her quiet, well-bred voice broke the pause.

"Yes," she said, "it is the end."

"The end," agreed Sir Murgatroyd heavily. "No good trying to struggle on against luck like ours. Here we are and here we have got to stay, mouldering on in this blasted barrack of a place which eats up every penny of my income when, but for the fussy interference of that gang of officious, ugly nitwits, there would have been nothing left of it but a pile of ashes, with a man from the Insurance Company standing on it with his fountain-pen, writing cheques. Curse those imbeciles! Did you see that young Fripp with those buckets?"

"I did, indeed," sighed Lady Sprockett-Sprockett.

"Annabelle," said Sir Murgatroyd sharply.

"Yes, father?"

"It has seemed to me lately, watching you with a father's eye, that you have shown signs of being attracted by Algernon Fripp. Let me tell you that if ever you allow yourself to be ensnared by his insidious wiles, or by those of William Biffing, John Guffington, Edward Prosser, Thomas Mainprice, or Frederick Boot, you will do so over my dead body. After what occurred to-night, those young men shall never darken my door again. They and their buckets! To think that we could have gone and lived in London."

"In a nice little flat . . ." said Lady Sprockett-Sprockett.

"Handy for my club . . ."

"Convenient for the shops . . ."

"Within a stone's throw of the theatres . . ."

"Seeing all our friends . . ."

"Had it not been," said Sir Murgatroyd, summing up, "for the pestilential activities of these Guffingtons, these Biffings, these insufferable Fripps, men who ought never to be trusted near a bucket of water when a mortgaged country-house has got nicely alight. I did think," proceeded the stricken old man, helping himself to a sandwich, "that when Annabelle, with a ready intelligence which I cannot over-praise, realized this young Mulliner's splendid gifts and made us ask him down here, the happy ending was in sight. What Smattering Hall has needed for generations has been a man who throws his cigarette-ends into waste-paper baskets. I was convinced that here at last was the angel of mercy we required."

"He did his best, father."

"No man could have done more," agreed Sir Murgatroyd cordially. "The way he upset those buckets and kept getting entangled in people's legs. Very shrewd. It thrilled me to see him. I don't know when I've met a young fellow I liked and respected more. And what if he is a poet? Poets are all right. Why, dash it, I'm a poet myself. At the last dinner of the Loyal Sons of Worcestershire I composed a poem which, let me tell you, was pretty generally admired. I read it out to the boys over the port, and they cheered me to the echo. It was about a young lady of Bewdley, who sometimes behaved rather rudely . . ."

"Not before mother, father."

"Perhaps you're right. Well, I'm off to bed. Come along, Aurelia. You coming Annabelle?"

"Not yet, father. I want to stay and think."

"Do what?"

"Think."

"Oh, think? Well, all right."

"But, Murgatroyd," said Lady Sprockett-Sprockett, "is there no hope? After all, there are plenty of cigarettes in the house, and we could always give Mr. Mulliner another waste-paper basket . . ."

"No good. You heard him say he was leaving by the first train to-morrow. When I think that we shall never see that splendid young man again . . . Why, hullo, hullo, hullo, what's this? Crying, Annabelle?"

"Oh! mother!"

"My darling, what is it?" A choking sob escaped the girl.

"Mother, I love him! Directly I saw him in the dentist's waiting-room, something seemed to go all over me, and I knew that there could be no other man for me. And now . . ."

"Hi!" cried Mordred, popping up over the side of the couch like a jack-in-the-box.

He had listened with growing understanding to the conversation which I have related, but had shrunk from revealing his presence because, as I say, his toes were bare. But this was too much. Toes or no toes, he felt that he must be in this.

"You love me, Annabelle?" he cried.

His sudden advent had occasioned, I need scarcely say, a certain reaction in those present. Sir Murgatroyd had leaped like a jumping bean. Lady Sprockett-Sprockett had quivered like a jelly. As for Annabelle, her lovely mouth was open to the extent of perhaps three inches, and she was staring like one who sees a vision.

"You really love me, Annabelle?"

"Yes, Mordred."

"Sir Murgatroyd," said Mordred formally, "I have the honour to ask for your daughter's hand. I am only a poor poet . . ."

"How poor?" asked the other, keenly.

"I was referring to my art," explained Mordred. "Financially, I am nicely fixed. I could support Annabelle in modest comfort."

"Then take her, my boy, take her. You will live, of course"—the old man winced—"in London?"

"Yes. And so shall you."

Sir Murgatroyd shook his head.

"No, no, that dream is ended. It is true that in certain circumstances I had hoped to do so, for the insurance, I may mention, amounts to as much as a hundred thousand pounds, but I am resigned now to spending the rest of my life in this infernal family vault. I see no reprieve."

"I understand," said Mordred, nodding. "You mean you have no paraffin in the house?"

Sir Murgatroyd started.

"Paraffin?"

"If," said Mordred, and his voice was very gentle and winning, "there had been paraffin on the premises, I think it possible that to-night's conflagration, doubtless imperfectly quenched, might have broken out again, this time with more serious results. It is often this way with fires. You pour buckets of water on them and think they are extinguished, but all the time they have been smouldering unnoticed, to break out once more in—well, in here, for example."

"Or the billiard-room," said Lady Sprockett-Sprockett.

"*And* the billiard-room," corrected Sir Murgatroyd.

"And the billiard-room," said Mordred. "And possibly—who knows?—in the drawing-room, dining-room, kitchen, servants' hall, butler's pantry and the usual domestic offices, as well. Still, as you say you have no paraffin . . ."

"My boy," said Sir Murgatroyd, in a shaking voice, "what gave you the idea that we have no paraffin? How did you fall into this odd error? We have gallons of paraffin. The cellar is full of it."

"And Annabelle will show you the way to the cellar—in case you thought of going there," said Lady Sprockett-Sprockett. "Won't you, dear?"

"Of course, mother. You will like the cellar, Mordred, darling. Most picturesque. Possibly, if you are interested in paraffin, you might also care to take a look at our little store of paper and shavings, too."

"My angel," said Mordred, tenderly, "you think of everything."

He found his slippers, and hand in hand they passed down the stairs. Above them, they could see the head of Sir Murgatroyd, as he leaned over the banisters. A box of matches fell at their feet like a father's benediction.

Acknowledgments

HOW SOON CAN I LEAVE?, © Susan Hill 1971, was first published in *Penguin Modern Stories 7.*

THE GHOST by Richard Hughes, copyright 1926 from *A Moment of Time*, is reprinted by permission of the author and Chatto & Windus Ltd.

YOUNG ARCHIMEDES by Aldous Huxley, © Mrs. Laura Huxley 1924, is reprinted by permission of Mrs. Laura Huxley and Chatto & Windus Ltd.

THE LOVE GAME, © Francis King 1971, is reprinted by permission of Francis King.

THE OLD CHIEF MSHLANGA, © Doris Lessing 1951, is reprinted by permission of Jonathan Clowes Ltd., London, on behalf of Doris Lessing.

THE CRUSADER'S KEY, first published November 1935, is from *God Likes Them Plain* by Eric Linklater. Reprinted by permission of Jonathan Cape Ltd.

THE OUTSTATION by W. Somerset Maugham is reprinted by permission of the Literary Executor of W. Somerset Maugham and William Heinemann Ltd.

THREE LAMBS, copyright Liam O'Flaherty, is reprinted by permission of the Peters Fraser & Dunlop Group Ltd.

SAD ABOUT MISS BRENT, © Glen Petrie 1970, was first published in Macmillan's *Winters Tales 16.*

THE REGULATOR, © John Prebble 1958, is from *Spanish Stirrup* by John Prebble. Reproduced by permission of Curtis Brown Ltd., London, on behalf of the copyright owner.

ELEVEN O'CLOCK, © V. S. Pritchett, is reprinted by permission of the Peters Fraser & Dunlop Group Ltd.

THE WALL, © William Sansom 1963, is from *The Stories of William Sansom* published by the Hogarth Press.

SUSPICION, © Dorothy L. Sayers 1945, is from *In the Teeth of the Evidence and Other Stories* by Dorothy L. Sayers. Reprinted by permission of David Higham Associates Ltd.

THE SERENADE, copyright Bernard Shaw, is from *The Black Girl in Search of God* by Bernard Shaw. Reprinted by permission of The Society of Authors on behalf of the Bernard Shaw Estate.

WELL I'M —!, copyright G. E. M. Skues, *Sidelights, Sidelines and Reflections*, is reprinted by permission of Leo Cooper Ltd.

LISHEEN RACES, SECONDHAND by E. Œ. Somerville and Martin Ross is from *Some Experiences of an Irish R.M.* Reprinted by permission of John Farquharson Ltd.

MISS PINKERTON'S APOCALYPSE, copyright © Muriel Spark 1958, is from *The Go-Away Bird and Other Stories* by Muriel Spark, published by Macmillan. Reprinted by permission of the author and David Higham Associates.

IN AND OUT THE HOUSES, © Elizabeth Taylor 1970, is from *The Devastating Boys* by Elizabeth Taylor. Reprinted by permission of the author and Chatto & Windus Ltd.

THE LOSS, © Gillian Tindall 1973, is from *Dances of Death* by Gillian Tindall. Reprinted by permission of Curtis Brown Ltd. on behalf of Gillian Tindall.

WHILE THE SUN SHINES is from *The Life Guard* by John Wain. Reprinted by permission of Curtis Brown Ltd., London, on behalf of the Estate of John Wain. © Copyright © John Wain 1967.

THE ILLUSTRATIONS were by

JANET ARCHER, page 174

BARBARA BROWN, pages 40, 50, 135, 210, 215, 285

FAITH JACQUES, pages 117, 227

ANNE KNIGHT, pages 60, 93, 220, 240, 262, 345

ROBERT MICKLEWRIGHT, pages 144, 195, 247, 320, 331

JIM RUSSELL, pages 9, 12, 66, 78, 223, 268, 295, 311, 353

VIRGINIA SMITH, pages 106, 250, 360

ELISABETH TRIMBY, page 170